CAPTURED

The door slammed shut, shrouding Regan in darkness. A firm hand clamped across her mouth, choking her scream into a muffled squeal.

A man's powneath her breasts. Her br... her off the floor, kicki... against his hand. A tab... crystal lamp. A glass j... loded in a choking cloud...

Regan pounded her fists into her captor's hips. She tried to scratch his face, then went down onto the soft bed beneath his weight. The air expelled from her lungs. Pressed against the intruder's chest, his threatening size came to mind. The smell of salt spray assailed her senses.

A ragged whisper ruffled her hair and she felt the scratch of a jaw that hadn't seen the sharp side of a razor in at least a week.

"I haven't come all this way to be unmanned by a slip of a girl," he said.

The rich baritone voice and hardened body belonged to no local fop. He flipped her easily onto her back. Pressing a muscled thigh between hers, he subdued her struggles. His shirt was damp, his body warm. She felt the hilt of his cutlass, heavy against her hips . . .

My Lord Pirate

Laura Renken

JOVE BOOKS, NEW YORK

This is a work of fiction. Names, characters, places, and incidents are either the product of the author's imagination or are used fictitiously, and any resemblance to actual persons, living or dead, business establishments, events, or locales is entirely coincidental.

MY LORD PIRATE

A Jove Book / published by arrangement with the author

PRINTING HISTORY
Jove edition / January 2001

All rights reserved.
Copyright © 2001 by Laura Renken.
This book, or parts thereof, may not be reproduced in any form without permission.
For information address: The Berkley Publishing Group, a division of Penguin Putnam Inc., 375 Hudson Street, New York, New York 10014.

The Penguin Putnam Inc. World Wide Web site address is http://www.penguinputnam.com

ISBN: 0-515-12984-4

A JOVE BOOK®
Jove Books are published by The Berkley Publishing Group, a division of Penguin Putnam Inc., 375 Hudson Street, New York, New York 10014.
JOVE and the "J" design are trademarks belonging to Penguin Putnam Inc.

PRINTED IN THE UNITED STATES OF AMERICA

10 9 8 7 6 5 4 3 2 1

*I'd like to extend my heartfelt gratitude to
Anita Baker, Barbara Cary, Elysa Hendricks,
Jan Hunsicker, Linda Kamschroeder, Janet Kendall,
Jean Newlin and my wonderful Windy City RWA chap-
ter. This book wouldn't have been possible without you.
Thank you for your never-ending support.*

*And finally, to my wonderful parents,
John and Joann Herring,
just because I love you.*

Chapter One

September 1690
Jamaica

"Draw no blood, men. Remember, this is to be a wedding party."

"Aye, Cap'n. It be some kind of party by the sound of it."

Over the crash of waves breaking against the rocks, strains of a minuet drifted through the darkness. The pale moon lit a desolate landscape barely visible in the heavy salt mist. Tormented vegetation clung to the lifeless hillside, which rose from a boulder-strewn inlet where only a suicidal fool would take refuge.

His enemies called him Pirate. Dark Lord of the seas. No nation controlled him. Vengeance drove him. It ruled him now, colder and harder than the iron that had once shackled his limbs.

Talon Drake stood with his feet apart, the scuffed soles of his jackboots half buried in the debris littering the shore. Hands braced on his hips, his eyes fastened on the pillared residence stark white against the pall of a blackened sky. Its extravagance was a sickening mockery to the impoverished village it overlooked.

"Will the house be heavily guarded, milord?"

"You can wager the crown jewels it is, Sulley. You know

how His Excellency, the governor, values his worthless neck."

A burst of wind caught in the silken folds of Talon's black shirt made damp by sea spray. More than the hint of bad weather clawed at his control. Ribbed with sharp rocks, the cliff shaped itself into a stone escarpment. No visible trail would guide him. He was about to make a raid. All to snatch the governor's precious betrothed from beneath the popinjay's very nose.

"I hear she's a rare beauty, milord."

A knot of loathing tightened his chest. "She's a Welles."

"She's barely more than a child. Innocent of her family's crimes, milord."

Talon dropped his arms to his side, his cutlass scraping the rocks as he faced the needle-thin man beside him. Silver eyes narrowed on the crop of white hair. "Sulley, I told you to cover that grizzled head of yours. You'll get the lot of us hanged for your carelessness."

"Aye, sir!" Sulley's jaw worked nervously as he fumbled with the black sash tied at his waist. "I'm not as rememberin' as I used to be, milord. I don't know why ye brought me along."

Talon felt himself grin. "You've a fatherly look about you. An English lass facing the devil's own might be more co-operative with you watching over her."

"If you say so, sir. It's good to see you so considerate of the lady."

Talon snorted at Sulley's absurd tenderness. Being good to the lady wasn't what he had in mind. "This is a raiding party, Sulley." Talon's gaze raked the six battle-hardened men standing at arms behind his dead father's loyal steward. "Consideration only works if it doesn't get us killed. Remember that, old man. Or you'll cost us all our lives."

Regan Welles stepped from the elegantly decorated ballroom into the fresh air. Lifting her face into the plumeria-scented breeze, she gazed at the stars scattered across a black sky. Sirius was visible. And the Orion belt. Their beauty was like a benediction after the past few hours of cloying chatter. The pomp and splendor of her half brother's life left her winded.

At her approach, four stout seamen in formal dress snapped to attention. Each held lanterns that contributed to the glow surrounding the gardens below the verandah. Regan walked past them, her limp more noticeable with her exhaustion.

"Is this not the most beautiful night?"

The musical voice summoned Regan's attention. She turned back to the ballroom, smiling at her cousin running with unladylike grace toward her. Arabella's tabby petticoat flowered beneath a rich buff silk gown. Her blond ringlets bounced prettily around a face flushed with excitement.

Their fathers were brothers, but she and Arabella were more like sisters than cousins. "Leaving your engagement party?" Regan chastened. "Won't Harrison be looking for you?"

"His Excellency is a busy man."

Arm in arm, she walked with Arabella into the garden. Moisture in the grass dampened Regan's slippers. "As the governor's wife, I expect you'll be just as busy once you've married."

Arabella whirled with childlike abandon. "Isn't he the most handsome man you've ever seen?"

Ten years Regan's senior, her half brother would forever possess that distinction in her heart. Harrison Kendrick had been nine when their newly widowed mother married William Welles. Regan was born a year later. Since her first steps, she'd adored the man her father had accepted as his own son. The stepson who would one day become the youngest governor of Jamaica.

"You're happy then?" Regan needed to know.

"Oh, yes." Arabella faced her, blue eyes reflecting like sapphires in the warm glow of lantern light. "I'm living a dream. A wonderful glorious dream."

She was like a doll with her porcelain-blond curls and delicate heart-shaped face flushed with excitement. Regan oft wondered what life would have been like had she possessed such fine coloring and features. With dark brown hair and eyes the odd color of island cinnamon, she felt decadent compared to Arabella's aristocratic beauty. At eighteen, Arabella was only two years younger than Regan. Yet, Regan felt like an old maid in the wake of her cousin's impending marriage.

Suddenly, she wanted to hug her cousin, tell her how much she loved and missed her over the years. How glad she was to be back among the family, if only temporarily.

"Harrison will make you a fine husband despite what your father thinks."

"Mother was right to honor the marriage contract." Arabella lifted her dainty nose in disdain. "I don't know what has gotten into Papa. I shall never forgive him for not attending tonight. His actions have put a blight on the Welles name and insulted Harrison terribly."

"Your handsome prince seems unaffected by the slight."

"You're always so calm about these things."

"Only because you're so dramatic."

"And nervous. I can't breathe." She gripped her waist and laughed. "How can you breathe?"

"Because I refuse to be trussed in this sweltering heat for the sake of fashion." Besides, Regan reasoned, she could be a shriveled corpse and still never have a stylish seventeen-inch waist.

"Mother would have the vapors."

Which was normal. Regan's aunt had a permanent case of the vapors. "You should suggest she loosen her stays."

Arabella stifled a fit of giggles. "You're as naughty as you always were. How have you survived convent life all these years?"

Regan fingered a pale pink hibiscus bloom. "It hasn't been so bad, really." She plucked the flower and slid it behind Arabella's ear. Their eyes met. Regan felt the burn of tears. Next to her half brother, Arabella was the only family left alive that she truly loved. They'd shared a trunk load of correspondence over the years.

"I can't believe you'll be taking your vows with the church soon." Arabella's voice softened. "Why, I remember you were always getting into trouble when we were children. I think your father wanted a boy." She laughed. "You used to climb everything. Little Monkey. That's what your mama called you."

Fidgeting with the lace on her sleeve, Regan's mood dampened. Very few people knew her by that name.

"Maybe, if I'd had the courage to follow you just once—"

"Please, Arabella. I'm not that person anymore."

Arabella flung her arms around Regan, mussing her stubbornly coifed hair. The curly mass tumbled down her back.

"Thank you for allowing me to steal you away from Martinique. I know it's been hard on you, returning to Jamaica . . ." She shivered. "Making the trip from London frightened me after what happened to your parents. With the piracy and the terrible threats against our family, I didn't know what to expect."

The past few years almost every ship in the family's once profitable fleet had met disaster at the hands of the infamous Talon Drake. Arriving unscathed in Jamaica had been something of a miracle. Regan chose to think it was because the notorious pirate met his deserved fate at the bottom of an unforgiving sea; the very same grave where her parents lay buried. Or better yet, dangling at the end of a rope from the King's gibbet.

"Arabella!"

Arabella leaped back. "Mother's calling!" Her mortified gaze dropped in a panicked inspection of her gown. "They must be getting ready to make the announcement. I look a dreadful mess."

"You look beautiful."

"My lace fan!" Arabella lifted stricken eyes. "I must have my fan. A lady doesn't appear in front of an audience without her fan."

Indeed, to make such a fashion *faux pas* could prove an unfortunate blunder for the governor's debutante bride. Regan's pale blue fan would not substitute for the elegant pearl encrusted one Harrison had presented to Arabella earlier that evening.

"Where did you leave it? I'll fetch it," Regan offered, leading her cousin out of the exotic garden back onto the marble verandah.

"I must have left it in my bedroom when I went up with Mother earlier. Please hurry."

"Breathe, Arabella—" Regan squeezed her cousin's hand. "—or you'll pass out."

Making an attempt at composure, Arabella nodded. "My

room is well lit. You'll see it on the dresser—"

"Look at you, child." Arabella's mother swooped down on her despondent daughter with the cranky disposition of a nasty owl. "How many times have I told you not to come out in this horrid night air? And what nonsense is this?" Tearing the flower from Arabella's hair, she pierced Regan in accusation. "Hurry, child," she clucked as if Arabella were a two-year-old. "His Excellency is waiting."

Forgotten on the huge verandah, Regan watched them go. A familiar pang of loneliness knocked against her ribs. The old feeling annoyed her. Years ago, she'd ceased questioning the reasons her aunt disliked her so. Jealousy definitely wasn't the issue. Arabella possessed incomparable beauty and grace. She'd attended the best schools offered young ladies of good standing. Perhaps it was because Regan was an oddity. A cripple. An embarrassment.

Ignoring the subtle ache in her hip, Regan entered the stately residence through another set of French doors. Her slippered feet carried her swiftly over the polished marbled hallway of her brother's palace, as she referred to his residence. His extravagance these days bordered on the eccentric.

She followed the wide mahogany staircase past beautiful paintings worthy of a king's fortune. At the top of the stairs, she slowed beside one particularly priceless piece. It looked strangely familiar. She'd seen its like presented to a visiting French emissary by her father while he was Chief Justice of Jamaica.

"Milady."

Regan's heart gave a start. She knew that voice, and felt her face warm. "Captain Roth." She smiled.

He stepped from the governor's private library. "You've wandered far from the festivities."

Flashy gold ribband ornamented his green doublet. Wearing a full bottomed periwig to which burnt alabaster had been added to give it body, he was almost unrecognizable as the captain of the *Viper*, who brought her here from Martinique. With considerable flourish, he swept his ostrich-plumed hat from his head.

"Do I sense your approval, Lady Regan?"

"Captain Roth, you look like a true gentleman."

Black currant eyes flashed over the pale curves of her breasts, sending nervous tendrils over her skin. "Milady—" He closed the short distance between them. "—I've been remiss."

"Have you?"

"I've not asked you to dance as I promised."

Surely, he knew her limp made it impossible to dance. It was unseemly, as her aunt would say, for someone who couldn't walk gracefully to take up the minuet. "I can't. Arabella needs—"

He casually placed his hand on the wall, almost touching her face. "And I insist you take time for yourself, milady."

While sailing from Martinique on board the *Viper*, she'd accepted his flirting as a matter of course because Arabella's presence always inspired such foppish behavior from men. Now, with her cousin nowhere to be found, Regan's usual wit mutinied. A need to tactfully change the subject was at hand.

She looked around him into the library shadowed in darkness. "If His Excellency catches you in there, he'll have your handsome periwig for breakfast, Captain Roth."

"Rest assured, I've no need of state secrets." He stepped away and closed the door. "My men and I are checking the grounds."

"Is anything wrong?"

"False alarm, I'm sure. The governor's guard watches over the front. And the back . . . well, the back overlooks the cliff." He grinned. "Perhaps you would care to view the scenery?"

"If it's the landscape you really wish to view, Captain Roth," she replied in her most dulcet tone, " 'tis better seen in daylight."

Roth stepped back and bowed in acquiescence. "Touché, milady."

Regan recognized that she'd just successfully flirted. "Are you always so bold with the ladies, Captain?"

"Only with those who don't bite."

Suddenly very pleased, she laughed. "I'll remember that."

"I shall await your pleasure downstairs, Lady Regan."

She watched him descend the stairs, listening until his steps faded on the marble floor. A fierce need to forget logic just once and indulge in her own femininity overtook her. Perhaps 'twas the music in the air that stirred the air around her. This was a happy celebration, after all. There should be nothing wrong with enjoying herself for once.

Heady with a sense of purpose, Regan whirled on her heel and hurried down the hallway. Reaching her cousin's room, she started to open the heavy door. Her hand stilled on the brass latch. A draft curled around her feet and slithered up her stockings. The smell of smoking flax tasted acrid in her mouth.

Regan eyed the dim hall behind her. Some of the wall sconces were out as if a burst of wind had extinguished the flame.

Refusing to heed her childish fear of the dark, she opened the door and hurried inside. Her heart grounded to a stop. Arabella had reassured her the room was lit. Light from the hallway pooled around her feet, framing her protectively within its faded golden circumference.

Regan felt utterly alone in a world bereft of human life. Then sensed she wasn't. The door slammed shut, shrouding her in darkness.

A hand clamped across her mouth, choking her scream into a muffled squeal. She bit down.

"Bloody hell!" The oath split the darkness.

A man's powerful arm encircled her rib cage beneath her breasts. Her breath exhaled in a rush as he lifted her off the floor, kicking wildly, her cries muted and weak against his hand. A table crashed to the floor shattering the crystal lamp. A glass jar of lavender-scented powder exploded in a choking cloud of dust.

Regan pounded her fists into her captor's hips. She tried to scratch his face, then went down onto the soft bed beneath his weight. The air expelled from her lungs. Pressed against the intruder's chest, his threatening size came to mind. The smell of salt spray assailed her senses.

This man had climbed over Arabella's balcony from the cliff! Only a madman scaled a rock, better suited for the winged creatures that nested within its shadowed crevices?

That he dared the impossible—a raid on the governor's residence—made him extremely dangerous.

A ragged whisper ruffled the hair on her cheek, and she felt the scratch of a jaw that hadn't seen the sharp side of a razor for at least a week. "I haven't come all this way to be unmanned by a slip of a girl." The rich baritone voice and hardened body belonged to no local fop. He flipped her easily on her back. Pressing a muscled thigh between hers, he subdued her struggles. His shirt was damp. His body warm. She felt the hilt of his cutlass heavy against her hips.

Pinning her wrists above her head with one hand, he gripped her chin with the other. "Especially when I have much to offer to our future, Lady Welles."

Dear Lord! Regan couldn't believe this was happening. "How . . . do you know my name?"

"The cut of your gown tells me you're no servant." His hand boldly made his point. "Who else would venture into her own room, but the lady herself?"

Regan started to scream.

"You open your mouth any wider, you won't like what I stuff into it." His breath was hot against her face and smelled oddly of mint. "Rags are nasty things, especially when you don't know where they've been."

"What do you want? Who are you?"

"I assure you, this isn't a social call."

"How foolish of me to think otherwise."

"Ahh—" A hint of white flashed against a face shadowed by darkness. "—a woman with spirit. How refreshing. Sulley! Strike the flint. I have a hankering to see just what I've bargained the devil for this night."

"You'll not get away with this." The threat lacked the force she intended. Her heart thundered in her ears. Regan heard the snap of movement somewhere behind her.

The dull light of a candle filled the tight space over the bed. Her captor's face, so close to her own, came to life. Silver eyes probed hers with fatalistic indifference. And to her horror, her heart leapt with more than the heady rush of panic. A black scarf covered his head, accentuating the lethally handsome features of his face. With the exception of Captain Roth, she'd never seen anyone so unfashionably tanned. His gaze invaded her senses, hesitating a fraction on her mouth before moving to the swell of her breasts. All she could hear was the pounding of her own wild heart. Against her will, heat settled in the nervous pit of her belly.

"You're not what I expected." His slight English accent was aristocratic, sculpted like the man, and to Regan's ears not without a hint of disappointment.

"Really!" She'd yield nothing to this miscreant. Least of all her pride. "And does slinking about a lady's bedchamber qualify you to form such an opinion?"

With one hand clamped to her wrist, he wrenched her to her feet. Her knees felt rubbery, and she stumbled against the firm wall of his chest. A dark shirt with billowing sleeves, opened to his waist, baring his chest. Vibrant heat licked her.

Sakes alive! She was nearly a nun. What was she doing reacting with lascivious thoughts to a dangerous prowler? A lice-ridden knave, no doubt, intent on thievery and mayhem. Mayhaps, even murder!

"A child, you said." The disgruntled snort seemed aimed at someone behind her. "Of docile temperament and beauty?"

"That's what he said, sir," the unseen man replied.

"When a man doesn't know his own daughter, I question his wit, Sulley."

Daughter? What did he mean? Her father was dead.

It took a frayed minute to realize he spoke to yet another man on the balcony. Dizziness fell over her. Regan wanted to scream, needed to scream if she were to warn her brother. But it was her captor's presence that commanded her silence. He loomed like a shroud over her will.

Standing eye-level to the expanse of bronzed flesh, she caught the flash of metal, a necklace, hanging around his neck. Her gaze dropped to the black sash knotted at his waist. It held the heavy hilt of a cutlass, the size a sure testament to this man's formidable strength. But as her eyes narrowed on the fingers that still restrained her hand, her stomach knotted.

She could do nothing but stare at the harrowing scars that banded his wrist. This man bore the cruel mark of bondage. Compassion assailed her. Nay, terrified her. Only the most tortured victims or slaves endured manacles long enough to viciously scar a man's flesh.

Her attention shifted abruptly to his face. Silver eyes were fastened on her, and froze the chaotic beat of her heart.

"Are you satisfied with what you see, milady?" He seemed amused by her gaping perusal.

Her flush deepened. "Who . . . are you?"

He bowed over her hand. His fingers were warm against hers, intensifying her own confusing reaction to his touch. Her skin tingled and shivered.

"Talon Drake at your service, milady."

"Drake!"

His atrocities against her parents joined his name with the devil! She snatched back her hand and as if that alone would cast away the fiery remnant of his loathsome touch.

"And I have the pleasure of informing you that you're coming with me."

"Never." She struck out at him and found her hand snatched from its purpose. The air between them sparked with the violence of a hurricane and churned her belly.

His eyes glittered when they again plundered hers. "Never is a long time, milady."

"I'll be no prisoner of yours, Talon Drake," she whispered, fighting to keep hold of her courage.

Her nails cut his flesh. Dark drops of blood beaded his skin. His grip on her wrist never tightened. Yet, his power over her was as complete as the darkness beyond the swirling light of the candle.

"Sulley," Drake called without taking his eyes from hers. "I need to check our way."

Her chin lifted slightly. "Do you intend to kill me?"

"The idea certainly has merit, milady. But fortunately for you, I need you alive." His mouth lifted in a grin. "For now."

The rogue mocked her fear. "I've not the money to pay a ransom if that's what you're after."

"Rest assured, you're more valuable to me than any ransom."

An awful lump rose in her throat. "Tell me what you want then?"

Flashing her a white smile, Talon Drake released her and stepped back into the scant light. In a showcase of masculine gallantry, he raised his cutlass in a mockery of a salute and damned her with eyes as silver as the finest sterling.

"Why nothing less than to marry you, Lady Arabella."

Chapter Two

Talon Drake wanted Arabella! Good Lord!

Regan's mind tumbled in confusion. What would he do if he discovered that he'd captured the wrong Welles? Her life would surely be forfeit. Then what would happen to poor Arabella? "You're . . . why you're completely mad!"

The blackguard offered her a slow smile and the sound of soft laughter. "More than you could possibly know, milady."

The sheer reputation of this man made her knees go weak. His daring exploits against the Spanish had earned him fame of legendary proportions. The man was immortal on the seas. Rumor abounded that even the king regaled him a hero, but only behind closed doors.

Beneath the swashbuckling veneer, Drake was naught but a notorious pirate, a criminal of England, infamous for his despicable deeds against her family. And his vendetta toward her brother was common lore.

She had to escape! To warn Harrison that Arabella was in danger!

"Soldiers, *Capitaine*," a bass whisper resonated from the balcony.

Drake watched her gaze swing to the voice. He must have seen hope flash in her eyes. "Gag her." He dragged the scarf from his head. Dark hair, torn from a queue, fell around his shoulders. Backing a step to the gold velvet drapes that framed the double glass doors, he ripped a tassel from its mooring and tossed it to Sulley. "And tie her. We're getting out of here."

"Sit, milady." An elfin man stepped forward.

Taken aback by the contrasting gentleness reflected in his watery blue eyes, she allowed him to guide her to a chair.

"The cap'n took great risk comin' for you tonight, milady," Sulley whispered as if such daunting courage could sway her opinion of the blackguard. "He'll not harm ye."

Hardly aware as the older man fumbled to tie her hands, her gaze followed Drake as he strode to the bedroom door. She sought a weakness in this man. She had to find something. Shamelessly, Regan stared. It was an effort not to. His masculine presence was a palpable thing as warm as the air she breathed. He frightened her beyond compare. Worse, even, than the darkness. With the heavy cutlass gripped easily in one hand, he braced the other hand on the latch. She heard the ominous click of the bolt slide in place.

"We are ready, *Capitaine*." A corsair appeared from the balcony, nearly dwarfing his captain. Raised cicatrices, ritual tattoos, whirled around his cheeks. Leather baldrics crisscrossed over a short crimson waistcoat. A brace of pistols and a stiletto rattled in the sash around his waist. Swarthy and barrel-chested, he presented a fearsome picture. "We will fight this Kendrick, *oui*?"

"You just try!" Regan rasped. "He'll kill the scurvy lot—"

The corsair shifted his full regard upon her, and she fairly swallowed her tongue. His shocking assessment drummed against her ribs. Suddenly frightened he somehow knew her identity, she abruptly dropped her gaze.

"The girl is under my protection, Piers."

"And who watches over you, *Capitaine*?"

A chuckle answered her ears, and snapped up her head. The cur was laughing at her. "I'll handle her, Piers. Get over the balcony and take the men back to the ship. Sulley knows the other way out," Drake said.

"I must gag you now, milady," Sulley said in apology.

"You know this house?" she accused.

"Aye, milady. Before you came, I worked with the staff."

"But you're with him . . . a pirate."

"Aye, that I am," he agreed with total lack of recompense.

Wind gusted through the opened balcony door, tangling her hair. She could hear the distance crash of waves on the beach. And voices. Faint, but stirring on the wind. Her brother's guard. They were near . . . Then she felt the black sash wrap around her mouth. The masculine scent of it emerged to surround her. Salt and sea spray.

Regan blinked to find Drake standing before her. A wedge of moonlight fractured the shadows on his face. He'd extinguished the light. "You've been wise to keep your tongue, milady." He leaned a booted foot on the chair next to her thigh. "I intend to take you down the cliff another way, less dangerous to you. But if you tempt me . . ." The darkness didn't dim the predatory flash of white when he smiled down at her. "I'll throw you over the ledge, and hope someone catches you before you hit bottom."

Regan's eyes widened. A tepid burst of wind teased his hair. He held her gaze. Could he sense her mounting hysteria?

Then something flashed in his eyes—a flicker of humanity that even his stern expression denied. "Curse your eyes, girl." He stepped away. "You only have to do as you're told, and we'll all make it out alive. Do you understand?"

Snuffed behind the gag, Regan's breath wedged in her throat. An absurd stirring of gratitude weakened her resolve, but she got hold of herself. He was making her forget that she would soon be dragged to some sordid pirate's lair.

Regan lunged. Her bound fists connected with the trusting Sulley's chest. Unbalanced, he fell against his captain. Drake swore. She leapt past him out the door onto the balcony. Two powerful hands gripped her waist. The gag stifled her screams. Amid a writhing mass of petticoats, Drake flung her over his shoulder. Terror eclipsed her control. His threat to throw her off the cliff lent strength to her fight. Clawing at her gag, she ripped it from her mouth just as he dropped her back on her feet. The wind took the black scarf over the rail. She slammed against the wall. Drake covered her body with his, pressing her face into the unyielding mass of his hair-roughened chest.

"I warned you what I would do, you little fool!"

The heat of him poured over her like scalding liquid. "I'll not go with you! I'll not!"

His leg wedged between her thighs, pressing her back against the exterior of the stone wall. She could feel the steady thump of his heart, a contradiction to the frenzied tattoo in her own chest.

"Sulley," he rasped. "What's going on with our friends?"

"I . . . I hear them, sir." Sulley's panicked reply came back in a rushed whisper. "In the garden, over there, milord."

Talon cursed.

Far below, the bay rippled with whitecaps in the moonlight.

His ship, always his first concern, lay anchored a hundred yards around the lee side of the ridge, invisible in the darkness. It might as well be a thousand miles the other side of the world for all the good it would do him now. Talon shifted. The humidity pressed around him. With the girl subdued against his chest, he tried to listen for sound. Orange blossoms scented the air, distracting him from his purpose. Against his will, his lips tested the fragrance of the girl's hair.

"I'm sorry, sir," Sulley whispered. "I let her get away. Do ye . . . do ye think they know we're up here?"

Talon could count on it. An air of expectancy charged the night. Cicadas and frogs. Even the crickets waxed silent.

"Thanks to our docile captive, I think our celebrated goose has just been cooked, Sulley."

"I hope they hang you," the girl hissed.

"I'd rather they not. If it's all the same to you."

Her velvet gaze snapped with fierce emotion. "It's not the same to me, Captain Drake. If that's what you're called among your gentler peers."

"Milord, to you," he snorted.

"Milord?" she scoffed. "Milord pirate of the great seas. Murderer and thief, you are."

A brow lifted. The regal tilt of her chin as she stared up at him, the rebellious set of her full mouth spoke eloquently of her struggle to face him without flinching. Yet, she'd boldly shredded his character to rags. No man would dare such a feat to his face. She was exquisite, he thought, and foolishly brave to fight him.

Shouts from Talon's men, scattered over the grounds and brought him up. "Christ, that's Piers."

"They'll not leave ye now, milord." The urgency in Sulley's voice put his own dire position in perspective.

Clamping a hand over the girl's mouth, Talon muffled her response and hauled her thrashing with him to his knees. Her breathing shallow, she collapsed against his chest.

Talon touched his mouth to the delicate whorl on the girl's ear. Her shiver sent heat racing to his loins. "One breath too loud and you'll force me to carry you out of here. Unconscious."

A dangerous measure of defiance flashed in her eyes that provoked him to grip her chin in warning. "Do not tempt me, sweet."

She jerked her away. "Don't touch me . . . you, you beast!"

"A beast?" He smiled thinly. The sentiment hardly did him justice.

"Whoreson. Knave."

"Aye." He tied her wrists to the balcony slats. "You're half right."

He could feel her panicked heartbeat. A dark surge of admiration needled him. It occurred to him that she'd displayed more mettle than he'd expected to find in a Welles. His young bride-to-be possessed an unexpected fire in her blood. And warmed his a degree or two.

Awareness assaulted him. The stark emotion was unexpected as her spirit touched something inside long since dead: a reckless hunger not spurred by hate or vengeance, but by a passion far more dangerous. She became real to him. A heartbeat in his palm, making him forget what he was.

The feeling repelled him. She was a bloody Welles for Christ sakes. He dared not give in to softness and tamped it down, crushing it beneath his will: one that had been tested often against the lethal end of a whip.

"Your men will suffer for their loyalty to you, milord pirate."

"Being a Welles, you're obviously a stranger to loyalty," he said flatly.

"You're wrong. There are people I too would die for."

"Are there?" Annoyed, he stood. Her obvious passion made him again question her father's knowledge of his only child. "You've got me curious. You'll have to tell me who they are one day, sweet."

"What are ye doing, milord?" Sulley followed him to the rope.

"You won't survive Kendrick's butchers, my friend. The plan's changed. I'll find my own way out through the servants' passageway." Talon yanked on the thick hemp curled in a mess at Sulley's feet. Still attached to the wooden brace that supported the floor of the balcony, the rope lead to a pathway that skirted the top of the inlet where their dinghy was anchored. "You're going down. The same way we came up." He wrapped the end length around the man's reed-thin waist. "Find your way to the ship anyway you can. If I'm not there within a quarter hour of you, tell Marcus to sail without me."

"But milord—"

Shots broke the night. The sound of voices moved away.

"Do it, Sulley! And tell Piers, if he's alive when this is over, I'll have him keel-hauled for disobeying my order."

Talon crouched and lowered the old man over the edge into a chasm of darkness. The rope slipped and burned his palms. Clenching his teeth, he braced the soles of his boots against the wooden slats.

"They'll catch you," the girl promised with vigor.

She again claimed his gaze. "Ah, but the night is still young, sweet. And I still have you."

Moonlight flashed in her brown eyes. Her mane of hair swirled in disarray to her waist. He caught the quick rise and fall of her breasts, noting with masculine interest the white curve of her skin. Her small waist, the flair of her hips, so evident beneath her skirts received more than a passing glance. His interest, purely mercenary, flickered back to her face. A worthy prize indeed, he decided.

But could he trust Arabella's father not to betray him once he delivered his side of the bargain? Not likely. Talon had already set in motion his plan. A wedding vow, even one made in hell, would see his bargain with Robert Welles sealed.

Her small nose tilted at his perusal. "Perhaps you think to woo your future bride with flowers after you've tied and gagged her into submission? An acceptable deed for a pirate, no doubt."

"I need no rope or gag to woo a woman. Pirate or nay."

She rewarded him with an indignant gasp. "You're a vicious sea cur, Captain Drake. A woman would be mad to submit willingly to you or your ilk."

"Perhaps," he conceded with a wicked grin, "but I've never had one submit unwillingly. Yet."

The rope jerked. Sulley was free.

Talon edged over to his defiant captive. Her eyes widened as he pulled a knife from his boot. "Time to go, sweet." He silently chuckled at her reticence. She needed to be afraid. With his thoughts now bent on escape, he cut her bonds. "The night awaits."

And if he got out of this alive, it would be a bloody miracle.

The pirate was surely insane!

Regan watched him open Arabella's bedroom door. He no longer had the gag so he put a hand over her mouth. Moving her within the embrace of his arms, he measured the direction of voices before slipping into the hallway. He intended to take her out through the servants' entrance. Strands of a minuet floated over the rush of blood in her ears. Panic tightened her throat. Of all the half-crazed schemes. What kind of kidnapper put his victim's safety over his own life? She didn't want to consider that this fearless knave could actually care for her welfare.

Her limp, more pronounced now after her struggles, slowed his pace. She stumbled. "Please," she whispered over his hand.

His eyes raked her curiously. Without a word, he lifted her. Whatever protests Regan had been about to lodge remained unsaid. Her hands braced his chest. His skin felt obscenely warm beneath her touch. "I—"

"You've hurt your leg? Or is this a ruse to put you in my arms?"

"I'd as soon lie with a snake."

He stopped. Suddenly lowering her to the floor, he muffled her mouth. Voices downstairs alerted her. "Keep that orchestra playing." It was Harrison's voice. Firm. In command. "Find Arabella. I want her guarded."

Waiting for his order to protect her as well, Regan froze. Did Drake know there was another Lady Welles in residence?

"And search every damn room in this house. I want Drake!"

Her captor swiftly pulled her inside the nearest room and quietly closed the door behind them. She squeezed her eyes shut. Harrison hadn't even missed her presence. Her courage battled with the darkness that swallowed her.

Outside the wind began sheeting against the window. Somewhere downstairs a clock chimed, barely audible over the strains of the minuet still happily playing amidst the chaos surrounding the rest of the house. Cloaked by Drake's powerful body, Regan gripped the pirate's shirt, clinging to his human presence as if he were candlelight. He held himself braced with his hands against the wall. It took her a frantic moment to realize he was staring at her.

Her chin shot up. His eyes wandered over her face, captured her breath, and made quick work of her will. Time ceased to function. Heat flushed her skin. His mouth poised a hot whisper's breath from hers and combed her nerves in a caress.

"A snake?" he queried with amusement, shattering the spell.

She ducked beneath his arm and whirled in a flurry of skirts to face her tormentor. Her awareness of him scared her senseless. "You will never get out of this place alive. Harrison will find me."

He stalked her across the room. They were in Harrison's library. "Kendrick is a peacock who couldn't find his ass in a fog bank."

What was happening to her? That this man would send

her courage scurrying when she needed it so desperately to fight? She wanted to scream, but couldn't seem to draw breath into her lungs.

A dark copper Persian carpet covered the hardwood floor. Her brother's library was an antithesis to the rest of his house. Mahogany furniture darkened a room already suffocating from a lack of light and fresh air. Heavy baroque-style bookshelves lined the walls.

Regan's skirts swished. She brushed against the huge desk that dominated the south corner of the room. In the shadows, she could barely make out its cluttered contents. But Drake did. His expression suddenly changed. Regan spun to seek what new demons she faced.

Father's old navigational maps were spread across an innocent beam of moonlight on the desk. Drake stepped around her and uncurled the first chart. He flattened his palms against the aged edges.

Regan recognized the celestial depiction of Orion in the top right corner of the parchment. A shield clutched within the outstretched claws of an eagle marked the chart's bottom corner. A white Spanish mission with an empty bell gable the size of her palm colored the opposite corner.

With a quiet oath that sounded ridiculously like a prayer of thanks, Drake folded the chart and shoved it inside his shirt. Regan met his stare with disbelief. "Why, you're nothing but a thief."

"This map is worth more to me than gold." His shimmering gaze stroked her face then dipped lower. "Almost as much as you, milady bride."

The beat of her heart was a treacherous thing in her chest. Heat flushed her face. She could fight him in all things, but this strange power between them was beyond her ken. Fear suddenly seized her in suffocating waves. She whirled to flee and landed in his arms.

"Oh, no you don't." Drake smothered her screams. He carried her like so much fluff toward the darkness at the opposite end of the room and tossed her unceremoniously onto the settee. Before she guessed what he was about, he flipped up her skirts.

"Your affection for me is well proved, sweet."

"No!" She fought his grip on her mouth. "What are you doing?"

He boldly shredded the top tier of her petticoat. In one swift movement, he rolled her onto the floor, bound and gagged like a lamb to slaughter. "I've no desire to knock you senseless, Arabella."

The door suddenly flung open and Harrison's angry voice filled the confines of the room. Regan's breath caught. Drake pressed his body over hers. One warm hand snatched her bound wrists, subduing her completely. His hard-muscled thigh lay across her exposed knees.

"Keep your men on the cliffs. I want Drake found. Then I want that bastard's ship!"

"You forget who he is, Excellency." The unmistakable drawl belonged to Captain Roth.

"He is not a phantom in the night, Roth. The man's only human."

Regan's heart beat frantically. Her head turned sideways on the floor. From beneath the settee, she glimpsed Harrison standing in a ribbon of light spilling through the doorway. She squeezed her eyes shut. The silver buckles adorning his black shoes chimed as he walked ahead of Captain Roth to the desk.

A flint sparked. Candlelight pushed away part of the darkness. Light wedged between two pieces of furniture onto the carpet at Regan's feet. She thrust her gaze to the sculpted cornices on the ceiling and listened intently as items were shuffled around the desk. Drake's breath fanned over her temple. If she could slide her leg . . . Drake's single grip on her hands tightened. His lips slid over her cheek past the tangle of her hair to her ear.

"This is not the courtship I envisioned between us," he breathed into her ear, "but don't fret." Her furious gaze shot to his. The very devil danced in his silver eyes as he held her glare. "I promise to make amends before the night is through."

She heard a rush in her ears, felt the life pulse in his body.

"Bloody Hell!" The furious roar made her jump. Crystal

chinked. Papers hit the floor in Harrison's frenzied search. "Impossible. The map is gone."

"Is this what you're about, Kendrick? Some bloody treasure map?"

"The man's a criminal. And so are his men. Interrogate them by any means. I want that map back!"

Regan felt rather than heard Drake's quiet oath. His grip on her hands loosened. He was no longer watching her. She followed his gaze.

Harrison braced himself on the desk. "The rest of his men will be halfway to Tortuga by tomorrow if we don't find them first."

"If you think they'll leave their captain to die, you don't know his men."

"And you do? Or maybe you're still one of them? Is that it?"

"Don't push me, Kendrick."

"Or what? You'll leave and forfeit your Letter of Marque? If I'm not mistaken that would make you a pirate, Roth."

Only the sound of tree branches hitting the roof could be heard in the silence that followed. Regan held her breath.

"But then I wouldn't be the first to fall outside the auspices of the law. Would I, *Excellency*?" Roth's bootsteps were muffled as he walked with purpose to the door.

Talon drew back, and quieter than the salt-scented breeze, rolled away. The air took on a strange chill. Regan pushed down her skirts and, rotating on her elbow, struggled to stand.

"Jeesus, Roth. Just find Drake. Is that too much to ask?"

"I'll save him the trouble, Excellency." The menacing scrape of a cutlass against scabbard spun both men around and froze Regan's warning in her throat. Sword raised, Talon Drake stepped into the candlelight surrounding the desk. A figure in black, he loomed larger than life in Regan's eyes. A threat to everything she held dear. She clawed at the bonds on her ankles. They unraveled in her frenzy to escape.

"Drake. By God—"

The sword point stopped inches from Harrison's chest. "Where are my men, Kendrick?"

Still tearing at her gag, Regan struggled to her feet. Her brother's wild-eyed gaze pinned her in disbelief. He swung on Drake.

"Bastard." Harrison kicked the chair into Drake. "Guard!"

Drake elbowed him across the jaw. Regan cried out. Ripping off her gag, she ran toward her brother crumpled on the floor. Drake leapt over one corner of the desk to intercept her.

Struggling to get past, she pounded his chest with her bound hands. "You've killed him!"

"I'm not that lucky, sweet." The pirate wrapped her against him.

"Milady . . ." Roth's gaze narrowed on Regan.

"I'm all right, Captain."

She didn't miss the flare of possessive concern spark his eyes, and knew that Talon had seen it, too. His arm tightened around her.

Roth's eyes gripped Talon's. "You haven't changed, Drake."

"Unlike you, *old friend*," he said with exaggerated civility. "Is torturing my men now your forté?"

"Count your blessings His Excellency wants you alive." With his cutlass drawn, Roth opened the door. An order brought a half-dozen soldiers spilling through the door. Regan wheeled in Drake's arms. His gaze fell on her. She couldn't catch her breath.

"It's not common that we have the honor of entertaining such a worthy guest," Roth said. A flick of one gloved hand, and the soldiers followed his command to spread out. "Last I heard your head was worth five thousand Doubloons to the Spanish crown."

"You do me an injustice." Drake lifted his head and met Roth's gaze with indifference. "Ten thousand is the figure more exact."

"A gentleman knows when the fight is over, Drake," Roth quietly said. "Isn't that what you once were?"

Heart pounding, Regan looked up into Drake's eyes. They roamed her face. "Aye, and what I shall be again, Roth."

"Move away from the girl."

His fingers were warm against her cheek. "A kiss, milady bride . . . for luck."

The shock of his words opened her mouth and his lips sealed her startled gasp. Her bound hands protested the intimacy, the stark intrusion of his tongue, his relentless grip on her spine as he bent her backward. The world dimmed. She forgot to breathe. Good Lord. The man mocked them all!

"Seize him!" someone finally yelled.

Talon flung Regan behind him out of the fight. A knife flew from his grip into the first soldier who moved. Talon kicked out, landing a solid blow to a redcoat's stomach. The gun in the man's hand dropped as he reeled backward into the armed detail. The whole lot went down in a tangle of arms and legs. Without pause, Talon swung his cutlass and met Roth's charge.

"You're a fool, Drake," Roth gritted out. Standing nose to nose, their swords crossed over their heads, slid and met again. Talon's hair gleamed blue-black in the candlelight. "For all the good this will do your father after the crows pick your bones clean. I would have let you live."

"Long enough to hang." Talon slashed up and lunged out the door.

"He's mine!" Roth yelled.

An anxious glance at Harrison told Regan he remained unconscious. Her hands shook. She touched her throbbing mouth. The clang of steel spun her around. Snatching up a fallen pistol, she stumbled to the doorway. Redcoats blocked her view.

Regan shoved through her brother's guard. Talon and Roth were on the stairs. She shuddered with each thrust and parry, the crash of steel vibrating through every bone. Captain Roth was an expert swordsman, but Regan had never seen anyone fight like Talon. Every blow smashed with relentless fury as he parried and countered.

Servants screamed. Inside the ballroom, people began to turn as the commotion and sounds of combat rang louder than the music. Heart banging against her ribs, Regan gripped the mahogany banister and scurried down the curving stairs. Pushing past a bay of watchers, she followed Talon out the opened glass doors onto the marble verandah.

Roth pursued Talon down the steps into the lush gardens.

Blade met blade, glinting silver in the moonlight, then amber as the light of a torch danced with demonic ease against the swords. Talon slammed backward against a marble statue and ducked. Roth's blade struck stone. Sparks flashed. Roth renewed his attack. Sidestepping a fatal blow, Drake caught Roth's blade and sent it flying.

The tip of his cutlass nudged Roth's throat. "Where are my men?"

"Stables . . . you won't make it—"

Drake swung his left fist and cracked Roth in the jaw.

Regan's heart slammed against her chest. "Don't kill him!"

Breathing hard, Drake stumbled back. She ran to Roth's side and dropped to the damp grass beside him. Her skirts flared around her. Testing the captain's jaw, his cheek, his forehead, with her still bound hands, she checked for damage.

Cold steel against her chin captured her attention. Her gaze slowly lifted and she looked up into Drake's silver eyes. Regan searched his face with warring emotions she didn't nearly understand. His black shirt was dampened with sweat and clung to his shoulders. He was a despicable rogue. The man flouted justice. He'd murdered her parents. Harrison had told her so himself.

Soldiers were running from the direction of the cliffs. "Another day, milady bride," he promised, then whirled into the wretched shadows that would swallow him up forever.

She pressed a fist to her mouth in a futile effort to stay the memory of his touch. Thunder rumbled over the mountains that overlooked the bay. Wind gusts lifted her hair. The pirate was swift enough to outrun them all. To escape.

She blinked. The cowards behind her were doing nothing.

"No!" Regan dragged up the pistol. She'd once shot a bull's-eye at thirty yards. Farther with a musket. She used to hunt with Father, back when she wore breeches, and ran barefoot in the sand on these very shores. Before an accident broke her leg and left her scarred. Before Talon Drake murdered her parents and forever changed the course of her life. He would pay. By God, as the barracuda preys on flesh, he would pay!

"Stop!" Lifting her skirts, she ran after him. She lost a slipper. "I'll shoot you, Captain! I swear it!"

Talon swung around.

Raking his gaze past his Excellency's fainthearted guard, he found the wrathful beauty, pistol in hand, braced before them all. The porcelain swell of her breasts strained against the scalloped edge of her bodice. Her mass of hair lifted in the breeze. She looked more the fabled sea witch than any aristocrat's pampered daughter.

"Please. Lay down your sword." A chalky wedge of moonlight illuminated her shiny eyes. "Or you'll force me to shoot."

Men filtered out of the ballroom, spilling onto the verandah. Talon glanced at the cliffs, listened to the shouts, and brought his gaze back to hers. He looked into the black cycloptic eye of a pistol wavering in her hands. Five years of fighting her family and he had to choose this moment to come across one member with more courage than the whole cowardly lot.

Defying her threat, he stepped backward into the night.

And the darkness exploded in a burst of gunpowder.

Hot lead tore into Talon's upper arm throwing him backward against a tree branch. Wood cracked with the impact. A ribbon of blood snaked around his fingers, down the hilt of the cutlass. Talon lifted his head in disbelief. She'd shot him!

"I couldn't let you escape," she whispered. "I couldn't!"

The world reeled. He went to his knees.

Rabid-faced soldiers jumped him at once. A boot heel viciously struck him on the back, crushing him facedown into the dirt. It was the girl who cried out as they dragged him to his feet. Her tawny eyes stared at him in oblique horror. His sea witch.

Curse her soul.

He'd bested the devil himself, only to face the horned one again in the form of one lethal woman. A bloody Welles. Now he'd pay for his carelessness with the lives of his men.

Then a fist smashed his jaw, dropping him into the darkness.

Chapter Three

"Regan! I'm so glad to finally see you at breakfast." Arabella breezed into the dining room on a rainbow of dazzling color. Her ruffled lavender skirts made a vivid contrast with the yellow ribbons flowing in her hair.

Regan swallowed the slice of orange she'd been chewing. Arabella's cheer made her groan. She eased behind the freesia centerpiece that dominated the dining room in an eruption of twisted branches and tortured flowers wilting from thirst.

"I've been dreadfully worried about you. You've been hiding in your room for days." Arabella wiggled onto the chair across from Regan. Primly adjusting the flounces of her voluminous skirt, she looked around as if to check their privacy. "Everyone is still talking about how you captured the pirate. It's been terribly exciting."

"You're being dramatic, Arabella."

Undeterred by Regan's lack of enthusiasm, Arabella leaned her elbows on the table and slid the crystal vase aside. Long blond curls fell over her shoulders, framing her ample cleavage. "Captain Roth inquired about you before he left."

Regan thought of the dashing captain with a bittersweet sense of regret, wishing she'd never gone to Arabella's room that night. He'd departed three days ago to search for Drake's ship.

"Anyway," Arabella ignored Regan's exasperation, "I'm glad to see you're finally making an appearance. It's not like you to be so squeamish. Why, I remember years ago when you dueled that . . . that, what was his name?"

"Stanley Spendlove."

Arabella laughed. She lifted her hand, beckoning to a servant standing against the far wall. He was a slave. One of thousands brought to the island yearly by unscrupulous slavers plying the flesh trade. Regan would never adjust to Harrison's use of slaves. Mama had adamantly opposed the horrid practice.

"Yes. Stanley." Arabella plucked a sugary confection from the tray the white-clad servant bowed over her. "He thought it all very amusing that a mere girl threatened him. And then you shot his hat off his head. He fainted."

"The man was a pompous oaf," Regan said, declining the offer of sweets the servant offered. "Besides, he deserved what he got."

"Imagine calling William Welles, the Chief High Justice of Jamaica, a thieving pirate. And now, you actually caught one yourself. Talon Drake, no less!" She lowered her voice again in her most conspiratorial tone. "Why, the man has plundered a hundred ships on the Spanish Main. Mostly slavers. He's ever tweaking the nose of the Spanish. Do you know there's a substantial reward out for him? And to think you shot him. After he kissed you, too!"

A kiss meant for Arabella. Irrationally, she felt betrayed by that knowledge. And life with Father Henri at the convent left her ill prepared to understand the baser pleasure shared by men and women. Drake branded more than that kiss into her soul.

"Why would Talon Drake want to kidnap you, Arabella?" The question startled her cousin. "Has anyone cared to find out?"

"He probably came to do his worst," she managed in her usual melodramatic flair.

"Oh truly, Arabella, the man didn't seem that desperate."

Huge turquoise eyes regarded her pointedly.

"I only meant he doesn't seem to be a man who lacks for feminine attention."

"Surely you're not attracted to the rogue?"

"Of course not." Regan shoveled sugar into her tea.

"But you're still thinking about him? Even after five days."

Vigorously stirring the tea, she asked, "What compels a man to break into the governor's private residence? On the very night of his wedding announcement? To steal his betrothed?"

Arabella gazed up at Regan from beneath delicately shaped brows. Contrary to her character, her face was serious. "Everyone knows of his vengeance against our family," she said with quiet logic. "He sank your parents' ship."

Regan swallowed. How could one man possess such a dichotomy of character? Two very different selves: one that discriminately killed, and one that would give up his life for his men?

"But why the vendetta?" she asked. "No one has ever explained."

"What difference does it make? He murdered your parents. You should be proud that you're the one responsible for his demise."

"Please, Arabella." Regan sipped her tea, grimacing. She despised Harrison's tea. A healthy dose of sugar did nothing to alleviate the strange taste. "I do wish everyone would stop thinking I did something heroic." She set down the cup. "I didn't."

"You're too modest, sister," an autocratic voice responded.

Regan's gaze jumped nervously. Harrison leaned in the doorway with his arms crossed. Perfectly fitted from the full width of his shoulders to the tops of his shiny buckled shoes, he looked resplendent in a plum satin doublet embroidered five inches deep with silver lace. A fashionable periwig, the color of his own sun-bronzed hair, covered his head. Face powder concealed the bruise on his jaw.

He straightened and approached the table. Though not much taller than Regan's gawky height, his commanding presence filled the room. Regan discovered she still possessed a childlike awe of her half brother. There was no softness about his middle that bespoke a life of ease. At twenty, the king had knighted him for his heroic efforts in battling piracy. Two years ago at twenty-seven, he'd become the youngest man appointed the high office of governor. Regan's pride in her half brother tempered the disappointment she harbored over their failing relationship.

"Excellency," Arabella murmured, "good morning."

Eyes the same cinnamon color as Regan's turned to Arabella. "You look lovely, my dear." Harrison bent over his giddy betrothed. Tilting her chin, he kissed her full on the mouth.

Regan averted her eyes. The act seemed a cruel taunt in the face of Talon Drake's public claim on Arabella.

"True love is a fine thing, sister mine." Harrison's brash gaze made Regan feel unseemly. "No pirate will steal what belongs to me."

A blush subdued Arabella's cheerfulness. Harrison rested his hands on the back of her chair. Ruby and sapphire rings glittered in the hot sunlight slanting through the windows. "You've recovered from your ordeal?"

"I wasn't hurt," she quietly murmured, suddenly wanting to go back to her room.

"I'm proud of you, Regan."

The compliment stole her guard and she yielded slightly to his approval. To the need to please him. Her posture became less rigid. She'd come to Jamaica to be with him. To reclaim that special part of his life that she'd lost over the years. She didn't want to argue. But his calm was completely at odds with her distress.

He sat at the head of the long mahogany table. A servant appeared with a silver platter of fruit. "You'll be glad to know the brigand you shot has been condemned to the gallows."

"How can you have tried him so quickly? Without telling me?"

"I'm the governor, Regan. I do what I want. Don't look so shocked," he said popping a mango slice in his mouth. "You've been in no condition to leave the house. Admit it."

In truth, she hadn't been well since arriving in Jamaica, a month past. She kneaded her temples with fingertips that trembled. "I don't know what's been wrong with me."

"Ah, Regan." He sighed. "Perhaps you have doubts as to the pirate's guilt. After all, it's because of you that he'll hang.

But don't let your emotions interfere with your duty to me or to our parents' memory."

She snapped her head up. "I would never do such a thing."

"The pirate will hang tomorrow. You'll be there to witness it."

Regan fingered the lace bordering the fancy Dutch linen tablecloth. She hadn't considered the possibility of attending a public execution; it would be expected of her. Hadn't she lost the most at Talon Drake's hands? But she'd seen what happened to men hanged for piracy. His body would be dipped in tar, bound with metal straps and hung from a gibbet overlooking the cay. They'd hanged a pirate only last year on Martinique. His body was left to dry in the sun like a grape, until he was naught but a shriveled corpse.

"Regan." Harrison drew her watery gaze. "I'm not a cruel person. I know you've suffered these past years. I only want what's best so you can put your demons to rest. You'll let this go."

He read her traitorous thoughts instantly. "Good God, Regan, are you completely mad? You're lucky to be alive."

She came to her feet.

"Sit down."

"I can't!"

"The devil, you say."

Regan wheeled away from the ugly flash of disappointment in his eyes. A breeze billowed the curtains behind her. She stopped at the window and listened to the distant crash of the surf. The smell of sea brine, intimately familiar, twisted around her.

What had gotten into her?

Father would have called it a silly female affliction and promptly banished her to bed.

Mama would have wrapped her in arms of velvet.

"I'm sorry," she whispered. "But there are unanswered questions."

Harrison shoved his chair from the table. Pulling a parchment from his coat, he dropped it on the table. A moment later his palms cupped her shoulders. "Ah, Little Monkey," he said quietly, calling her by her childhood nickname for the first time in years. Her eyes opened onto his face. "You have a soft heart. That's always been your weakness. Read what I just brought you. Then tell me you won't be there tomorrow to see the rogue hang."

He walked out of the room, leaving servants scurrying in his wake. Regan's breath caught on a sob. Would she forever be a disappointment to him as she had been to her father?

Since she was a child, she'd clung to her half brother, treasuring every morsel of his affection. Though it had hurt her that Harrison had been the beloved one in her father's eyes, her relationship with Harrison remained strong. Until her parents' deaths left him in charge of their massive estate. Then Harrison sold their sugar plantation and sent her to their Uncle Henri in Martinique. In that month, she'd lost everything.

During the years that followed, she'd lived and worked with Father Henri at the orphanage, wishing the time to pass, waiting for Harrison to summon her. She understood now that he'd set his sights on a more elevated position in society. He went alone to London to achieve his goals at court. If Regan had learned anything over the years, it was that Harrison Kendrick always achieved his goal.

And he wanted Talon Drake dead.

She looked out across the bay. On a long sandspit that separated Kingston Harbor from the Caribbean, the godless city of Port Royal baked in the sunshine. The sea was a mirror, its glistening surface broken occasionally by the ripple of feeding sharks.

"Regan . . ."

She turned. Arabella was reading the parchment Harrison cast on the table. "This was written by the Chief High Justice of Jamaica. Your father." She picked up the single sheaf. "Look. His signature."

In the years since her parents were killed, Regan had never read anything written by either of them. Not their will and testament. Not even old letters. The pain of her parents' death was too great. She stared at the paper now, her sense of loss overwhelming. Then a word slowly focused. Scrawled across the parchment in bold letters she read the name: *Brendan Drake, Earl of Sunderland.*

"It's a writ of execution." Regan swallowed.

"Carried out ten years ago at Gallows Point." Arabella read the inscription. "This is Talon Drake's father . . ." She looked up. "Regan, the man was aristocracy. Why wasn't he tried in England?" Turning the parchment over, she presented Regan with the rest. "Talon Drake was convicted by the Vice-Admiralty court in Jamaica of murder and piracy. Along with his brother, Marcus. He also had a younger sister. I don't see any record of what happened to her. His whole family was imprisoned, including all their servants. Oh Regan," Arabella rasped. "They must have been awful people."

Regan took the parchment. Her throat ached. When she spoke, her voice sounded strange. "Father destroyed his life."

"Your father was Chief Justice, Regan. That's why his name is on the writ. I'm sure it wasn't personal."

She remembered the scars on Drake's wrists. What he must have endured in prison. Her eyes closed.

Everything fell into place like missing pieces of a puzzle.

Until a few years ago when Drake attacked and sank her parents' ship, she'd been blissfully ignorant of his existence. The parchment crackled in her fist. She never understood his vendetta against her family. Now, she knew he'd rooted himself in a lifetime of vengeance against her family. Her brother. Against her.

Arabella fluffed her skirts. "What do you suppose one wears for a hanging?"

Regan's gaze swept over her cousin. "If you'll excuse me. I have a headache." The excuse was no lie. She suffered a continuous ache in her temples.

Seeking some semblance of peace, Regan returned to the sanctuary of her room. Lying on the plush eyelet lace of her bed, she stared at the gauzy cloth draped from the canopy bedstead. She kept reliving every moment of that night with Talon Drake. It would not leave her.

She turned on her stomach. The bed ropes groaned with her movement. Lifting on her elbow, she reached beneath her pillow and withdrew a length of braided silver. The day after Drake's capture, Regan found his necklace. The hint of silver gleaming from the balcony slats had caught her attention. She'd kept the discovery of the trinket to herself. She didn't know why.

The silver amulet, embossed with a strange coat of arms, was the size of a guinea. The color resembled Talon Drake's eyes. She ran her thumb over the metal: a shield clutched within the outstretched claws of an eagle. Its familiarity kept drawing her eyes back to its shiny surface. And a fear she just began to perceive slithered over her.

Regan reached beneath her mattress and slid out the map she'd hidden there. It had fallen from the pirate's shirt that night in the garden. Harrison had torn up the grounds searching for the chart.

As she'd done everyday since she found it, Regan spread out the map on the bed. Blood stained the ragged edges that blurred as tears filled her eyes. She smoothed the corners. Her heart raced with dread. The same eagle crest marked the bottom.

What did it mean?

This map was more than a navigational chart. Since her youth, Regan had always loved studying the stars. During the weeks she spent traveling between Jamaica and the convent on Martinique, navigation had become a hobby. And she recognized the landmarks.

Harrison was hunting the fabled treasure of Puerto Bello. Father's obsession.

Regan shut her eyes. She knew the legend. Though Henry Morgan's sack on Puerto Bello took place before her birth, she'd often listened to her father and Uncle Robert's account of the famous battle. The loot from the attack had been reputed to be in the millions. Many alleged the treasure had been split and spirited away from the ruined city. No one ever saw it. Henry Morgan denied its existence. But anybody who could read a map chased the dream.

Every instinct warned Regan that this map was evil. It created monsters from normal, loving human beings. Lord in Heaven. Had Father murdered Drake's father for it?

The answer terrified her.

She stood. Dizziness assailed her as she snatched up the flint from the mahogany stand beside her bed, and stepped out onto the verandah. Sunlight hit her face.

Regan knelt and burned the map, ending forever Father's sordid legacy. Ashes floated away on the breeze. No one would ever connect Father to that map. No one! Talon Drake would go to the gallows for her parents' murder, and Regan would return to Martinique in a week and take her vows before God.

Once back inside her room, Regan laid down. Her tongue tasted thick. As she drifted to sleep, she decided Cook's awful-tasting tea had an advantage after all. It numbed her emotions.

A sordid hanging drew everyone from the bowels of the community. Clouds churned in the sky over Port Royal. Wind chopped the water of the inlet and lifted Regan's skirts. She stood behind the governor's staff on the special scaffolding constructed just for the occasion. Her stomach rolled. Seeking oblivion, she studied the stiff maroon scallops on her sleeves, but the noise of the crowd lifted her gaze. Townsfolk lining the cobbled maze of Wharfside Street roared as the two-wheeled cart carrying the cortege of prisoners lumbered toward the gallows. Their place of execution marked the end of the one-lane dirt road.

Behind Regan, a huge stone fortress that housed Jamaica's red-coated militia served as a gruesome backdrop to the macabre affair. No one manned the embrasures. Reveling soldiers, content to watch the executions, lined the walls of the battlement.

Four men and a youth faced the gallows this day.

Regan recognized Piers's huge frame among the condemned, his hands bound behind him. His imminent death seemed unjust in the face of the sacrifice he'd made trying to save his captain.

Braced against the rocky jolt of the dead cart, Talon Drake faced his execution with cold arrogance. The shadow of a beard darkened his chiseled features. His hair, tied with a thong behind his head, glistened wet in the heat. He still wore the same black shirt, now torn and caked with blood down to the sash tied around his hips. The rigid set of his wide shoulders betrayed no sign of injury.

With his hands lashed behind him, he was encumbered enough to appear helpless. But Regan knew better. She'd felt his strength wrap around her. She knew the power in those muscles, barely restrained now in his captivity. What kind of past forged the strength to withstand so much pain? And still show contempt in the face of death? Shaken by his courage, Regan felt the intensity of his presence. His pull was her weakness, her downfall.

Look away, she bid, but the horror compelled her to stare.

The crowd jeered as the guards prodded the condemned out of the wagon with pikes the length of a man's leg. Regan's stomach heaved sickeningly. The youth was just a child. She could see his bright orange hair. Tattered clothes barely covered his skinny body.

"Harrison said the boy was convicted of stealing," Arabella whispered in a small tight voice. "He has no kin to speak for him."

"This is madness."

A guard with the paunch of a melon shoved the youth face first to the ground. Talon Drake's booted foot connected with the rotund assailant, sending a cheer up from the crowd. A pike smashed across Drake's head and drove him to his knees. As he slumped over in the dirt, a thin trail of blood flowed from a gash above his temple.

Regan whirled away. She gripped the back rail of the platform. Soon Harrison would read the charges.

Talon Drake deserves his fate!

She opened her eyes to the churning sky. The humidity suffocated her. Sweat trickled down her spine. She'd been a fool to come here today. Compared to the icy reality of justice, any rage she once felt dimmed. No one deserved to die this way—not even Talon Drake, and certainly not that boy.

Behind her, an uneasy silence rippled over the crowd.

Then a strange sound carried over the wind—the rattle of piping from a ship's rigging. Regan looked toward the copse of palms on the far end of the cay. Skimming the treetops, the tip of a masthead became visible through the wind-tossed fronds.

Unable to mouth a single utterance, she watched with a mixture of fascination and horror as a sleek three-masted vessel sailed into full view of the assembly. Wind to port beam, with every inch of black canvas spread, the square-rigger was lying over steeply as it rounded the bend. The infamous Jolly Roger flapped on the mizzen. She recognized the scarlet banner—the skull and crossbones embraced by two crossed swords—as Talon Drake's own flag.

"My God," a feminine voice shrieked. Hysterical murmurs rippled over the crowd. "It's the *Dark Fury!*"

Panic erupted among the militia lining the walls behind the scaffold. A cheer went up somewhere in the crowd. Regan felt an irrational surge of joy. So, Harrison had underestimated the *Fury*'s crew and loyalty to their pirate captain. Drake's ship had never left Jamaica. They would not allow him to die.

The *Dark Fury* squared away. Regan knew enough about ships to realize this one was coming in to do battle.

Flame exploded from the gun deck.

The *Fury* released a thundering volley of fire into the fortified embankment of the fortress. Horses reared in terror. Mortar and dust rained down on Regan. Screams filled the air. People pushed over one another to escape the platform situated too close to the fortress walls.

Someone bumped Regan, tearing off her hat. She stumbled backward to the wooden floor, her skirts trampled in the chaos. Pulling her knees to her chest, she held the rail for dear life, lest she see the day ended beneath the heels of this maddened crowd.

The ground trembled beneath the violent assault on the fortress. Finally, the platform cleared of screaming people as they swarmed toward the fleeing carriages. Dazed, Regan lifted her head and caught a glimpse of the ship, barely visible through the swirling pall of gunsmoke. Her powerful cannons boomed repeatedly, thrashing the beachhead where His Majesty's Royal sloops lay anchored. Single-masted schooners and a British man-of-war choked Port Royal's inlet, easy prey for the *Fury*'s wrath.

Torn between grudging admiration for the daring feat and the horror of the attack, Regan struggled awkwardly to her feet.

Then Arabella was shaking her arm. "Regan!"

She blinked at the strange apparition of Arabella, dirty-faced and mussed as if she'd taken a fall. She could barely hear her cousin's frantic words over the noise of the guns.

"We must get out of here!"

The air smelled of kelp and gunpowder. Pushed by the wind, a cloud of gritty dust began to creep across the bay toward the blue line of mountains beyond Kingston. Townsfolk dressed in short canvas trousers and straw hats lined the wharves that stretched out into the bay. Regan's gaze stopped cold.

At the foot of the mangled walls of the fortress, the scaffold lay in ruins. The prisoners were gone.

Her panicked gaze moved to the narrow ridge of boulders behind her, past the rock-littered road. Fancy carriages were stranded single file. The road paralleled the beach and people were running in all their finery toward town.

Regan pulled Arabella off the platform. "What happened to your mother?"

"I don't know. She was beside me. Then I lost her in the crowd. Harrison took a detail of men to the fortress batteries. Oh, Regan. I've never seen him so livid."

"He can hardly fire now without destroying his own ships." Regan stopped.

Crushed beneath the pile of broken stones that had once been part of the fortress wall, a man lay buried. Regan glimpsed the gray cuff of a uniform. The wicked pike of his profession was still gripped in the grisly remains of his hand.

Horrified, she backed away and felt her petticoat rip. She turned to Arabella.

"Do you see her, Regan? She's in the harbor, beneath the very nose of Harrison's navy. Her captain must be mad."

Regan couldn't believe her eyes. In a cloud of black canvas, the *Fury* was heeling round. The massive figurehead of a bloodred eagle flying beneath the bowsprit glared at the enemy. She bore down on a British man-of-war that was trying unsuccessfully to tack into a position of defense. In a series of explosions, the *Fury*'s cannons delivered a devastating broadside to the governor's prized warship. Shrouds parted dramatically, then crumbled. Like a lady in the throes of a sickening faint, the masts splintered to the deck in a billowing heap of canvas.

⸱ Her profile in view again, the *Dark Fury* thrashed through the water with defiant relish. In her wake the sea smoldered with listing ships, the governor's proud fleet in shambles.

What next? The people? Regan swung around, seeking escape. Alone and in the open, she felt vulnerable. Rubble blocked the road. Every horse had run off. Not a single individual of the governor's entourage remained. With her leg, it would be a treacherous walk through the debris. Her slippers pinched from hours of standing.

Regan pulled Arabella down the rocky path to the dirty beach littered with coconut husks. A sense of urgency drove her. Even when Arabella protested the pace, her breathing shallow beneath tightly laced stays, Regan pushed on. She couldn't put aside the dreadful sensation that her life was in danger.

And in that moment, she saw him.

Supported between the giant, Piers, and a gray-jacketed guard, Talon Drake lifted his head. Silver eyes locked with hers, radiating through her heart like hot pitch.

Even the *Fury*'s cannons faded to obscurity.

Without realizing it, she'd stopped. Arabella, who'd been following at a clipped pace, collided with her. Regan's foot caught the edge of an abandoned wheel. She tumbled headlong into the surf. A wave drenched her with humiliating ease, drowning her scream in a mouthful of disgusting water.

From behind a waterfall of tangled hair, Regan glared at the rounded tip of a black boot that appeared a scant inch from her nose. The wash of tiny silver bubbles sucked at the silt beneath its sole, providing her with the fleeting hope that this man would sink into oblivion.

Spitting sand from her mouth, she tilted her head back. No longer supported by his fellow sea rats, Talon Drake stood with his feet apart. Dark leggings clung to well-muscled thighs and tucked into jackboots. Tipping her head, her gaze abruptly halted. His face, no longer tamed by dim candlelight in Arabella's room, left her almost breathless.

His gaze glittered over her prostrated form. "Your devotion is late in coming, sweet."

Regan slapped the sash hanging at his waist out of her face. "You mean you're not a God, Captain Drake? How disappointing."

"Only to you, I'm sure." His mild voice belied the murder in his eyes and did much to silence her retort.

Two brawny hands rudely gripped her arms and dragged her to her feet. A half dozen men, bristling with pistols and an armament of cutlery that would put a royal chef to shame, fanned out in a predatory stance around their captain. A more gaudily mismatched group of brigands she'd never met!

"Bloody hell, Cap'n," one of her captors guffawed, a grizzled tar dressed in the remnants of a British naval uniform. "Sink me but fate's delivered the conniving wench back into your hands."

In the blue smoke that clouded the beach, Drake's eyes pierced her with the savage intensity of tempered steel. "Aye, if one trusts fate."

She jerked herself free from the brutes who held her. One of them laughed. Piers. And to think she'd felt sorry for him.

Regan's chin lifted in a haughty attempt to wrest control of her nerves. She marshaled her attention on the man who held the power over her life. "If you leave us, I'll not scream and bring the soldiers down on your head."

"Madam." Drake sloshed forward in the water and caught her arm in a steely grip. "My patience has just ended. We've an appointment to keep. Time is running out." He started walking. The sand sucked her slippers off her feet.

Standing like a waif where she'd been left behind, Arabella's pitiful sob gripped Regan. The realization hit her.

Drake still thought she was Arabella!

She tried to pry his fingers off her arm. Her wet skirts tangled her legs and she tripped. "You can't do this—"

"Many a man's dying words, don't let it be yours."

Arabella threw herself against Regan, digging her feet into the sand. "Let her go!"

Regan tore herself from Drake and shielded Arabella behind her. Never mind that she was outnumbered or that her sodden dress probably weighed at least two hundred pounds; Drake would have a fight on his hands.

"Cap'n, I vote we take 'em both." The suggestion belonged to a boy barely old enough to grow whiskers. He scratched his crotch and leered at Arabella. "That one would do much to ease our needs."

A hearty response followed, reducing Arabella to whimpers.

Regan threaded her fingers through knotted hair. It curled over her breasts nearly to her hips. Lord, she had to find a way to get out of this. Where was Harrison's militia? She darted a glimpse up the fortress walls. The chaos of panic and the smoke of burning ships had obscured her predicament.

"Madam?" Drake's voice was no louder than a rasp. But Regan's gaze whipped around as if he'd lashed her.

Drunk with fever, his eyes caught the fire of ships burning in the bay. A moment of terror rendered Regan helpless. "Unless your maid chooses to share your fate, I suggest she leave while I've a mind to be generous with her life." Talon nodded toward Piers. "We've no more time to waste. Drag her, carry her, I don't care," he snapped. "Kendrick's guard will soon realize we're free."

Regan whirled and met her cousin's terrified gaze. Arabella balled a fist in her mouth as if to keep from bursting into tears.

With a choking sob, she suddenly turned and fled.

Disbelief paralyzed Regan and jolted her to action at once. "No!" She twisted on her weak leg and fell into the sand, hitting her head. Then Piers was standing over her, pulling her back to her feet. Regan swung her fists, pounding hysterically on his chest and shoulders, screaming as he caught her hands in his.

"Do not fear, little monkey," he said for her ears alone.

Too distraught to do anything but stare stupidly at the macabre tattoos snaking around his huge arms, her gaze darted to his. The only things he lacked to complete the menacing caricature were big pointy teeth. The fragile grip she held on reality vanished.

The world tilted. Amid the surrounding chaos, Regan felt the strength of familiar arms before she hit the ground.

And for a moment, she was home.

Chapter Four

Talon watched the girl crumble at Piers's feet. For a mere instant, he regretted the fear in her dark eyes.

The sensation didn't last. His sea witch had nearly killed him. That she still possessed the power to stir his emotions insulted him.

A resurgence of bitterness tested his temper. Survival over the past ten years had cost him his soul. Driven by a voracious hunger for vengeance against the corrupt magistrate who destroyed him, and the Spanish crown who'd ruthlessly enslaved him, his appetite for justice forbid him compassion, especially for the pampered daughter of a Welles. An enemy who'd made him what he was—a man whose ill-famed reputation even among the Brethren of Tortuga was deserved.

His mouth twisted. Arabella was nothing but the means to end an injustice forged in the blood of his family. He would not be so remiss as to forget that again. Through her, he would regain his freedom and his family's honor. The girl's father, who'd been in hiding from Kendrick for months, had promised to deliver Talon back his life if he got her away from Kendrick's blackmailing hands. Clearly, the man doted on the little harridan to want her back at all.

Someone touched his shoulder. Instinct jolted his arm. He went for the hilt of a sword that wasn't there. Behind a blur of pain, his gaze narrowed on the boyish features of his boatswain. Dressed in the ill-fitting uniform of a prison guard, his lanky arms protruded from the sleeves. Jaime had been one of the fortunate few to escape the governor's mansion with Sulley.

"Yer bleedin' somethin' awful, Cap'n."

Talon followed his gaze to the ground. Bright red droplets dripped from a sticky trail of blood down his hand. The sand around his boot was soaked crimson.

"Ye need a binding for that wound."

"I agree. But not now." Talon motioned his men past and walked at a slower pace behind them. "They'll not try and hang the lot of us a second time."

"We worried they'd succeed the first time. Captain Marcus always did fancy a dramatic entrance. Yer brother will be remembered in the governor's prayers tonight."

Talon wasn't amused. When the *Dark Fury* bore down on them like a great bird of prey, he'd almost been impressed enough to forgive his brother's tardy arrival. "If I live through this bloody week, I'll be thanking Marcus for being so considerate of his timing. How did you and the men get back here?"

Jaime slowed to Talon's awkward gait. "We sailed across the bay last night. Marcus will be waitin' fer us at Smuggler's Cove. The *Viper's* been breathing down our neck. Couldn't take a chance on a fight. Not with you facing the noose."

Roth. Talon's former cellmate turned nemesis. "The *Viper* will have the pleasure of our company soon, Jaime. You can count on it."

"Aye, we figured as much."

Talon found Piers through the haze of smoke. With the girl cradled against his broad shoulder, he trotted toward the end of the cay. Piers seemed too protective of the chit, he realized, irritated with the big man's sentimentality when it came to stray animals and women.

"She's a lot of trouble, Cap'n. That one is. It'll not go well for the wench when the men learn that she's the one what shot ye."

Talon dragged his gaze from the girl. "She's not to be harmed."

Above the beach, on the fortress wall, the sentry cannons bellowed to life. The shattering explosions nearly dropped

Talon to his knees. Smoke broiled out of the embrasures, blanketing the steep walls in a choking cloud of gunpowder.

Kendrick had finally pulled his derelict militia together to make a stand. Talon turned into the water, his gaze narrowing on the dark canvas fast fading from the inlet. Spray flew in sheets over the *Fury*'s bow. With her masts canted over sharply, she made an easy target. Talon cursed.

"Them's thirty-two pounders, Cap'n. They'll tear 'er to shreds," one of his men said. Water sloshed. Others fell in behind him. "Her 'ole underbelly is up for the takin'."

Nothing set the spark to Talon's temper quite as fiercely as seeing his ship in danger. The feel of it now lent new strength to his weakened limbs. "We have a rendezvous to make, men." He started walking. His boots kicked up a fine spray of water as he dredged his way up the beach. "And not much time to spare."

Many of the townsfolk gathered along the beach were no longer watching the unfurling drama at sea. Their eyes shifted with cautious interest to Talon. Faces betrayed recognition. But even as their uneasy glances slid to the limp girl draped in the arms of the wickedest looking pirate they'd ever seen, no one gave him away.

Piers always did have a certain theatrical flair with the public. But as Talon had learned over the years, terror was simple to instill and easy to manage. Terrified people didn't get themselves killed with heroics.

Talon reached the cutter shortly after his men. Its naked mainmast jutted toward an angry sky. The wind stirred up sand and whirled it in an eddy at his feet. He glanced behind him at the fortress overlooking the harbor. Red-coated figures ran about the ramparts, their frenzied actions directed toward the top mizzen shroud of his ship. Talon knew he had little time before the sentry spotted the small boat in the harbor.

Movement near the palm trees arrested his attention.

"Capitaine?" Piers called.

Talon could hear the boat being pushed into the surf. Nothing stirred on the eddy but clumps of long sea grass bristling in the wind. Yet, he sensed he was being watched. Turning abruptly, he waded into chest high water. He grabbed the thick edge of the boat with both hands, but lacked the strength to heave over its side. Someone gripped the wrist of his good arm.

Piers pulled him into the boat.

"If you have a yearning for the scenery, *Capitaine*, I suggest sitting at the front of the craft."

Palms pressed against his knees to catch his breath, Talon followed the broad swing of Piers's arm. His gaze stopped abruptly on the unconscious girl sprawled in a wet foam of petticoats against the planking near the jib. Dark wavy hair spread around her like seaweed in the surf. Her face tilted slightly away from him. Thick lashes dark as coal dust spiked against porcelain smooth skin. The sodden burgundy gown bled a despairing brown into her lace collar, intensifying her pale features. And something feral flickered within him. Savage and protective at once.

Even buried in the black bowels of Port Royal's finest dungeon, he'd thought of her constantly.

Talon stepped between the shoulders of his men. He dropped onto the bench beside the girl and started to work the knots securing the sail. "Put your backs into the oars men! And watch your heads." The jib swung around. "Let's get off this sand spit."

Jaime took the rudder at the back of the boat. Talon glanced again at the shore where he'd seen movement a few minutes earlier.

Footprints led to the water. Talon cursed. Watching him from beneath a mop of bright orange hair, a lone boy stood on a barren stretch of sand. Talon hadn't seen the kid after *Dark Fury* made kindling of the scaffold. Canvas dungarees reached over his knobby knees. The once white, sleeveless shirt swallowed his skinny shoulders. A stick, clutched like a broadsword in his hand, dragged at his feet as he watched the lumbering boat bob further away.

"Looks like you have a straggler, *Capitaine*," Piers said.

The rest of the men turned. Talon sensed an unexpected change in their mood.

God's blood! The whole scurvy lot of heathen buccaneers suddenly embodied a wealth of fatherly concern. Yet, Talon was no less affected. The boy had faced the gallows with more courage than most men. A short future aboard a pirate ship was preferable to no future here in Port Royal.

"We have room for one more, *mon ami*," Piers said quietly.

Talon rubbed his temples with the heel of his palms. The acrid veil of smoke clinging to the air stung his eyes. "Then I suggest you do the honors, Piers."

Steadying himself on the thin masthead, Piers rose to his great height and cupped his hands around his mouth. "Must we row back and fetch you, *garçon*?"

The boy tossed away his stick and dove into the surf.

Awareness hit Regan like a bolt of lightning. Then she realized it was thunder. A resounding explosion cracked the sky. She came up sputtering, her scream muffled by the gag stuffed in her mouth. Her wrists were bound with—she glared aghast at her hands—someone had tied her with her own stockings! Her gaze shot up.

Silver eyes plumbed hers with an intensity that sent her heart racing. The vague feeling that Talon Drake had been watching her for some time shimmered over her.

"Good afternoon, milady."

He'd shed his shirt. 'Twas her finest petticoat he'd shredded to bind his wounds. The dainty lace-edged affair contrasted with the darkly corded muscle in his arms and chest.

"Are you not pleased with the cut of the bandage, milady?" he chided. "I took the liberty of appropriating my medical supplies."

A red kerchief covered his head and knotted at the base of his neck. Dark stubble heightened his handsome features, flushed now with fever. Heart pounding, Regan found it difficult to disdain the manly look of him. He lowered her gag. She noted it pained him to move.

The captain of the *Dark Fury* was her foe. "That you suffer now is small penance to pay for your crimes, milord pirate."

Drake tilted her chin with his forefinger. "Men have died for lesser deeds than those you've committed against me." He paused, allowing for the full measure of his threat. One dark brow slanted. "My patience is not limitless, sweet."

She wrenched her chin free from his touch, before outrage

gave way to numbness, drowning her with the frightening
reality that she was truly Talon Drake's prisoner. A bruising
uncertainty clouded her future. She felt herself pale. Surely,
some compassionate deed tempered the man's nefarious reputation. Yet, no redeeming attribute surfaced to ply her mind
with ease. The Dutch and Spanish alike had tasted the bite
of his sword. He served beneath no flag but his own, granted
no quarter to his prey.

But obviously, he considered Arabella of great importance
or he wouldn't have risked so much to capture her. As long
as he thought she was his intended victim, he'd not hurt her.
Would he?

"I'll untie you if you promise to behave," he said. "No
more guns. Or knives. No running away—"

"I vow to see you hang, pirate! I swear it."

"Beware, milady," he drawled, and the deep rich voice
lowered. "You're fortunate that you carry some value to me.
And I indulge in your comeliness. But I'll not pay for the
pleasure of bedding you with the lives of my men."

Seized by a darker force Regan couldn't name, her heart
slammed against her chest. The memory of his kiss raced to
the very nether regions of her sex. His gaze leisurely raked
her face. It was a look of easy sensuality, born of the boast
that he could read her thoughts. And that the blush on her
face was due to more than fear.

"Capitaine—"

Another huge clap of thunder shuddered through the boat.
Regan's gaze snapped to Piers who stood behind the captain,
half-listening as Drake spoke to one of the crew. His golden
earring glistened in the light. The swirls of snakelike cicatrices on his face gave him a fearsome presence that contra-
dicted the warmth in his eyes as he studied her. A vague
familiarity nudged her. The memory of the nickname he'd
called her on shore worried and confused her at once.

In the interest of her life, Regan dismissed them both.
She'd fight her battles on land where she wasn't at risk of
being thrown to the sharks. Twisting on her side, she startled
to find herself staring directly into a boy's freckled face. The
soft contour of his chin, his pert nose, made him pretty. Unblinking, she met his lively blue eyes; he was the boy from

the gallows. Had Drake kidnaped him also? As soon as the question came to mind, she dismissed it. Unlike her, the boy was neither bound nor gagged. Indeed, he looked quite unafraid for his life.

The boy's lips lifted tentatively, confirming her observation. Regan could not imagine the black plague of the seas taking an orphan into his care. She frowned. The generous image his actions conjured did not fit the truth of his character.

"In half an hour that sloop will overtake us." The pirate's somber words interrupted her thoughts.

Regan's interest turned abruptly from the boy.

"I'm putting you and the men on shore, Piers. He'll not go after you with me in his sights."

" 'Tis murder, leavin' ye, Cap'n," a crewman spoke up. "Ye bein' injured the way y'are and not able to use yer cutlass."

"My orders are not up for committee vote, Jaime."

"The boy is right, *Capitaine*," Piers replied. "We go where you go. Besides," he commiserated, "your brother, he will slice our gizzards into little pieces if we leave you a second time."

"I don't recall that you left me the first time, Piers. In fact you should all be slapped in chains for your disobedience."

Piers nodded ruefully. "*Oui*, we should," he agreed for the unrepentant lot.

Shocked by the strange camaraderie these men shared, Regan watched the curious exchange. Such insolence in her brother's ranks would have earned them a flogging.

Taking advantage of the captain's inattention, she raised herself slightly and dared a peek over the side of the boat. Etched against the turbulent sky, a sloop was bearing down on them from the direction of Port Royal, which was barely visible now. Distant fingers of lightning spiked across the pewter sky. She caught her breath. The sloop was flying the colors of the governor himself.

Harrison was coming for her!

The hollow sound of the cutter slapping over the water filled the heavy silence. Drake drew in the sails. "We'll make a break for it in these shoals. It's too shallow for that sloop to come within two hundred yards of the shore."

Unlike Port Royal's golden beaches, this landing faced a wall of vegetation.

"Do you know this place, then?" Piers asked.

Drake wiped the sweat off his brow with his forearm. "I know it well. So does Kendrick. You men wanted a fight. You'll likely find one. And you, sweet bride—" He nudged Regan with his boot. "—remove that dress."

Regan choked back a pitiful cry. What depravity did he have in mind? Freeing her hands and feet, he tried to turn her.

"No!" Regan kicked out, her fight neutralized by the weight of her skirts. "Please. Don't do this."

"Get out of the dress, Arabella." He finally sliced the tiny fastenings at her back. "I don't have time for this."

Her sleeves slipped off her shoulders. After he'd finished, she dared to lift her chin and found his hooded glare fastened on her face. Black rings encircled the silver in his eyes. They were dilated and bright with fever or anger, she couldn't tell.

"You have my permission to shoot me again—" He slashed through bindings on her skirt. "—if I lay a hand on you with anything akin to lust. You're too much trouble to appeal to anyone but the most desperate." Another crack of thunder and the first heavy drops of rain splattered on her nose. "Now, remove the damn dress."

Biting back tears, Regan slid her arms out of her sleeves. Then the rain let loose in warm drenching sheets, blinding her.

"We are blessed, *Capitaine*," Piers boomed, amid the sudden rousing cheers. "They'll not see our landing."

"Get over the side men," Drake yelled, "and Piers. Hide this boat. We might get away yet."

Movement erupted. The men grabbed canvas-wrapped supplies and weapons. One by one they slid over the sides into the bay and swam toward shore. With a reassuring nod from Drake, the boy followed.

Lightning sluiced against the low sky. Regan desperately searched through the downpour for any sign of the sloop.

Braced against the pitching boat, Drake pulled her up. Regan looked directly at the middle of his chest and dimly registered his height. Before she had the foresight to stop its descent, her dress slithered along with her dignity into a brown puddle at her feet. Gaping down at her hardened nipples that teased the soaked batiste of her chemise, she failed to dispel her own shocked reaction before his arm came around her back, and she suddenly found herself straddling Talon's thigh for balance. Her eyes shot to his.

There was nothing soft about this man from the texture of his skin to the darkness looming in his gaze. Something dangerous and hot arced between them like tiny threads of flame.

"Can you swim?" Talon yelled over the slashing rain.

"Take care of yourself, pirate. I can swim without your help." Shoving away from him, she dove over the side of the boat. Near the shoals, she knew it was a risky jump, but chanced it. Anything to get away from this appalling feeling between them.

She'd been an accomplished swimmer as a child before a badly broken leg had left her nearly crippled. Kicking against her petticoat, Regan rode the swell. She fought the fabric entangling her ankles. Her dress would have anchored her like a rock.

The surge towed her backward. Struggling to stay afloat, she swam harder. Her knee scraped rocks. A massive wave dumped her in the rolling surf. "You crazy fool!" A well-muscled arm clamped around her waist. Drake dragged her sputtering out of the water and dropped her on the dirt. His chest heaved. "You could have broken your neck."

"It's mine to break!" Salt and rain stung her eyes.

"Think again, Arabella. You won't get off that easy."

He staggered away and dropped on a rock beneath a wind-thrashed pimento tree. The rain plastered the red scarf to his head. His black hair hung in disarray to his shoulders. Grimacing, he pried off his boots and water sloshed out. Regan stared at him. She wanted to cry. And she never cried.

He'd done this to her. Weariness weighed heavily against her pressing her deeper into her own grave.

For God's sake, don't think!

She couldn't allow herself to think. Not about Arabella, nor Talon Drake. Like footsteps in the sand, her existence was about to vanish forever.

No. Harrison would find her. He would!

Talon's men started cutting a path through the thick vegetation. She looked beyond the wall of rain and trees but could see no indication of where this place was. She only knew they'd made it from Port Royal to the main island across the bay.

Something touched her hand. Distracted by the activity and her own thoughts of escape, Regan glanced down. Her heart jolted. A black, furry spider with white dots attached itself firmly to her wrist. Its long disjointed legs moved up her arm. Screaming, she slapped it off and watched it rebound like a spring. She clawed at the ground trying to untangle herself from her petticoats.

A black boot planted itself on top of the poisonous beast.

Regan stared at the mangled body squishing out from beneath the boot. With nerves already frayed, she no longer trusted herself to speak. A huge uncontrollable sob ripped her lungs. Her disheveled hair shielded her face. She'd never be able to untangle the mess, she thought irrationally, wiping at her face with muddied fists. The spider had reduced her to a blithering idiot.

Talon gently took her arm and pulled her to her feet. She tried to stop the flow of tears, but couldn't. He caught her chin, and for all his strength, his grip was tender as she met his searching gaze. "The beast is dead, Arabella. You're safe."

"Safe!" It galled her that he possessed the power to make her cry. That he dared torment her with kindness when she knew the true nature of his character. "The beast is still very much alive, Captain Drake," she railed, hating her own weakness more than she hated him.

"Only in your imagination, Arabella."

"Is it my imagination that has kidnaped me? That has sought to humiliate and compromise me? You are the only beast here." She flung the words in his face.

The lightning around them became one in his eyes. But she wasn't finished. Oh, no! She'd make him regret everything he'd ever done to her and her family. "But not for long. Harrison or Captain Roth will find me. Men of honor, they are. You'll not get away with this. They'll hunt you down, and kill you."

Talon Drake laughed. "Are you worth so much to them?"

"Yes." She stumbled over the word. "Harrison . . . loves me."

"Love?" His gaze, little impaired by the wet state of her attire, made quick work of her modesty. "I doubt love is what he has in mind, sweet."

His boldness made her gasp. Behind her, she heard Piers splash out of the water. He'd hidden the boat, sealing her fate.

With his arrival, Talon turned the full force of his attention away from her. "Keep her from my sight, Piers. Or I swear to heaven, I'll not be responsible for what I do." Spinning on his heel, he followed his men.

The boy, who was standing behind him, furiously held Regan's gaze as if to denounce her words against his precious benefactor as blasphemy. Then he too spun away on bare feet darting off after the pirate captain.

To her astonishment, before she could run away, the French barbarian scooped her up. He was taking her out of sight of the bay. "Let me go!" Her fists pounded his chest. "Do you know what you've done to my life?"

White teeth flashed. "I imagine I just improved it, *chéri*."

"Improved it!" Regan slapped her dripping hair out of her face.

Talon Drake would surely kill her if he discovered the truth of her deception. She shut her eyes, willing herself from this nightmare to awaken on Martinique as if Arabella had never asked her to come to Jamaica, never asked her to leave Father Henri.

"You know who I am? How?"

He laughed. A rich timbre she'd heard someplace before. "Aye, little monkey." The golden earring bobbed with his movement. "You are the girl who learned to walk again when no one but your gentle mother believed you could."

Chapter Five

Talon had not been home in over ten years.

The once magnificent plantation house stood alone within the cumbersome embrace of ancient trees. Its pillared roof and balcony were on the verge of collapse, and a once manicured garden now defeated by the encroaching jungle, were all that remained of the opulent splendor that was the home where Talon spent his youth. Where elegant balls were once held and life was celebrated to its richest capacity.

Death reeked within these aged walls. The death of his mother and sister, his whole way of life. Too weary to feel anything, he felt nothing at all. Time had destroyed more than this place. It had destroyed him.

His weight balanced between two men, Talon moved forward into the vine-encrusted courtyard. He twisted to find Piers carrying the girl. Her eyes widened as he caught her gaze. Her long dark hair, damp from the rain, tumbled in disarray over her shoulders, covering her shift. He followed the slight tremble of her hand as she pushed the hair from her face. Fatigue shadowed her skin.

Something stirred within him. Lust? Or guilt?

Dammit to hell.

The conflicting emotions savaged what remained of his patience and dulled his momentary sense of triumph. Such double-edged sentiment made him reckless. No matter how helpless she looked, he knew better.

Talon shifted his attention to Piers. "See that she and the boy are fed," he said tersely. "Then bring her to me."

A measure of revenge would be his tonight.

Yet, even as his mind filled with retribution, the same thought hours later yielded only a strange sense of regret that he must claim her by force if he had to. Talon suffered no illusions about his character. By the time they reached her father, Arabella would belong to him. He would never give her father a chance to back away from his agreement.

The moon broke from behind the clouds only to be chased again into the darkness. Exasperated by his muddled thoughts, Talon swigged from the flask of rum he'd nursed to near emptiness. Leaning against one of the rotting pillars holding the roof of the house, he listened to the night sounds of cicadas and frogs. Restlessness stirred him.

He heard a door click shut. "The boy is finally asleep," Piers said. "It is probably the first night's rest he has had in years."

"And the girl?"

"She is still awake."

"Did she eat anything?"

"She has refused to eat and drink in the company of pirates."

Talon gripped the flask's thin neck. "A more disagreeable woman I've never met. Better to tame a dragon than that fire-breathing wench."

Piers folded his large hands behind his back. "Aye," he agreed, visibly struggling to affect a somber visage. "That one has declared war on you."

Talon gave Piers a sharp look. "And this amuses you?"

"She is a good match for you. I will be curious to see which one of you wins. Though, by the look of you, she has a head start by far. You have not been this beaten since I pulled you from the hold of that Spanish Galleon."

Talon dismissed his quartermaster's silly musings with a frown. "Did you find anything for her to wear?"

"Nothing that rats had not nested in."

In a group of men accustomed to taking what they wanted, she was trouble enough without inciting their lust. Her white shift and petticoat accentuated her feminine curves. The thrust of her breasts against a cloth too sheer for his imagination, her nicely rounded bottom tapering into long legs, bode ill for men whose hunger couldn't be appeased with mere food. The girl was ripe for more than just a sound thrashing, and he hadn't gotten her out of his mind since he first laid his eyes on her.

"You should forget this plan of yours," Piers said quietly. "It will only find you dead. And the fabled treasure of Puerto Bello has already killed many men in the keeping of its secret."

"The treasure is no fable, Piers. And I saw the second map. I had it in my hands."

"That chart Robert Welles has is worthless without it," he argued. "He is using you against Kendrick to get the gold."

"Welles has proof that will clear my name. And he wants his precious Arabella away from Kendrick before we make our move."

"Then this is about more than treasure?"

"Aye. It is about my life."

Piers looked away, his face suddenly grim. "You should have been more precise with your plans."

"If the treasure exists, I'll find it, Piers. Robert Welles will never see a bloody doubloon of it until I've a King's pardon in my hands. I'll have my life and that of my brother's given back if I have to kill for it."

"You have already killed for it, *mon ami*."

"Is this to be another lecture, Piers?"

"Vengeance is eating you up. It is a very bad thing."

"Aye, it's eating me. Like a pestilence gnawing me from the inside out. I ache with the filth of it. But it's kept me alive these past years when nothing else could. Have I not a right to claim the truth and all that goes with it? Have I not a right to see Kendrick ruined in the eyes of that pasty-faced king he worships?"

"So you wish to become respectable. You, the finest pirate on the Main."

Talon threw the bottle into the darkness where it shattered in the courtyard below. Only Piers or Marcus ever told him what to do with his life. And it irritated the hell out of him. "I'll see my bargain with Arabella's father finished," Talon finally said. "There's a man in Tortuga. A mapmaker who sailed with my father after the sack on Puerto Bello. We'll take Robert's map to him."

"You will not make it to the ship in your condition," Piers said after a few moments. "You can hardly stand as it is."

"That's why I'm sending you. With Captain Roth prowling these waters, Marcus will not be able to keep the *Dark Fury* hidden."

"Your brother will not leave you."

"He's not to engage the *Viper*. If you don't see us in a week, he's to go to Tortuga. Marcus knows how important this is."

"And the girl?"

"She stays. I'm not of a mind to kill her," Talon said, cursing the need to explain himself, even to Piers who knew him better than most.

"It is not for her that I worry."

"Am I a babe who needs constant coddling?" he snapped. "You're as irritating as Sulley."

Piers merely lowered his bushy brows. "Then I leave you to ponder your fate, *Capitaine*. Let us hope when this is over, we will be the wiser for the choices that we have both made."

Talon watched him leave. Damn the man and his philosophical wit. His arm throbbed. He should be resting. But he rarely slept. He couldn't bring himself to do it now. His thoughts returned to the map and the riches it foretold.

The treasure, the privateer Henry Morgan's plunder from his infamous raid on Puerto Bello over twenty years ago. Talon had been twelve at the time. His father had been one of Morgan's trusted captains, transporting his own share of the gold after the attack. But his father never took the gold to Jamaica. Two maps were made of that venture, each worthless without the other. Only his father knew the secret.

And Brendan Drake had died because of it.

So, Talon spent years casting his line into the waters to catch the sharks that murdered his father and imprisoned him and Marcus. When Arabella's father found him in Tortuga last year with the opportunity to clear the Drake name, Talon rekindled his plan to see justice rendered in a decade-old crime that had stripped him of his humanity and his life.

An ironic smile tightened his mouth. It was refreshing to know that Kendrick and Arabella's father, two of the men involved in the conspiracy against his family, were now at each other's throats. The third, the *Honorable* Chief Justice, William Welles, the blackguard who'd signed his father's death warrant, lay dead at the bottom of the ocean. Fate lent William Welles a taste of his own justice.

Talon's gaze narrowed on the glass doors that opened into his bedroom. Light creeping through the dirt-encrusted panes bathed him in muted gold. Unbidden memories rose. Stark images tamed by his gentle mother's laughter. She'd loved this grand house, her husband and her children.

A tarnished candelabrum cast a dim glow over the huge four-poster bed that dominated his old room. Two faded yellow damask chairs turned in toward each other, a small round table and lamp between them. A grand wardrobe with lopsided doors sat against water-stained walls where mud daubers, their empty nests layering the wall like a volcanic eruption, had ruined the green and gold-laced wallpaper. An effort had been made to clean the vicinity.

At last, his gaze found Arabella. His mood sobered. She struggled with her ropes. Reluctantly, he admired her tireless passion to beat him. Her courage to fight against the odds.

The light illumined her body beneath her petticoat. A welcoming hunger replaced the softness inside. He needed the strength. What he had in store for her was more merciful than anything shown his mother and sister. With a brutal shove, Talon slammed the door against the wall in a thunderous bang.

The girl spun, her huge brown eyes luminous in the shadows slanting across her face. Braced against the door frame, Talon surveyed his prize. Amused, he watched her retreat stopped by the roped tethered from the bed to her wrists. He hurt too much to laugh at her unusual show of cowardice.

Thoughtfully, he ran his hand over his bristly face as he stepped across the threshold into the room. Her wary gaze tracked his advance. He expected some snide comment about his ragged appearance and found himself strangely disappointed that she didn't oblige him with a verbal joust.

Without giving her his back, Talon eased onto the bed and removed his boots, tossing them aside. They landed with a thunk against the wooden floor. He noticed fresh linens on the bed and knew that Jaime had returned from the nearby settlement with the supplies.

"I need you to look at my arm," he said bluntly. She didn't move. His eyes narrowed on the tilt of her chin. "You're a lot of trouble, Arabella. Since you find it tiresome to serve me, perhaps I should let you serve my men instead. It doesn't much matter to me what kind of shape you're in when this is over, as long as you're still alive." He was pleased to see the glitch of doubt in her eyes. He didn't intend to share the she-dragon with another man. But she didn't have to know that.

"You're a cruel bastard, Talon Drake."

The bed groaned beneath his weight as he eased back. "My character was never in doubt."

"You should be dead. How you've managed to survive the past week, I'll never know."

"Are you sorry that your shot missed my head?"

She gripped the bedstead at his feet. "I was not aiming for your head, pirate. I was aiming for your heart."

His gaze traveled appreciatively over her shapely form. "Then I should be grateful for your bad aim."

"That you should. I rarely miss."

"Are you so skilled with firearms that you've killed many men?"

"It's because I'm so skilled that I have yet to kill anyone," she said imperiously. Lifting her bound wrists for his examination, she advanced to his side. "Do you expect me to wear these ropes while I attend you, milord pirate?" Her eyes seemed to smile at him. "Or are you afraid I'll murder you, yet?"

His hand closed around her throat. "That thought has crossed my mind," he agreed, bringing her down onto the soft mattress. Their eyes clashed. The feel of her body, soft and warm against his, battled savagely with his restraint. "But be warned, I'm not so easy to kill, milady," he said slowly. "You should know that by now."

He waited for her to lose her nerve, to batter him across the head. She did none of these things. "Are you daring me to try again, milord pirate?"

He would dare her to open her mouth and let him in. His lips brushed her temple. "No doubt your will is stronger than that lovely neck of yours. It's not my desire to test either to the point of breaking."

He loosened his hold and she shot off the bed. Emotions warred in her expression. As if to defy his power over her, she straightened. With a toss of her long hair, she sat down, stiff-backed beside him on the bed. "I will tend your wound, pirate," she offered. "But not because you've cowered me into doing so." Her bravado was a front. Her hands were shaking as she plied the frayed edge of the bandage. "You're bleeding."

"A common state these days."

"And drunk, by the smell of the rum on your breath."

"Not drunk enough," he murmured.

Her fingers felt cool against his hot skin as she struggled against her bonds to unwrap the bandage from around his shoulder. He didn't trust her enough to untie her. Tangled hair spilled over his chest. Absently, he touched it, fingering its silken strands. The faint scent of orange blossoms assailed his senses. His gaze followed the line of her profile, bent close to his face. Thick sooty lashes framed dark eyes. She wasn't beautiful in the traditional sense. Indeed, she was like the thorn in a bed of roses.

Suddenly, he realized a desire to ply open the blossom without violence. To taste the nectar of her submission. He would have her.

But not tonight.

Unable to bear Talon's scrutiny a moment longer, Regan lifted her eyes and glared at him. "Do you mind? I cannot concentrate with you staring at me."

"Perhaps you would like for me to go someplace else."

"Yes," Regan snapped back, distraught to find herself again on the verge of tears. "I would like for you to go to the devil."

"A sentiment shared by many, I assure you."

"And I suppose being injured is commonplace for you? A

professional hazard one might say." Even as she made the flippant remark, her gaze strayed over his powerful chest and arms. He didn't have to answer. His body bore the scars of his past and present. He'd been whipped while at Port Royal. She blinked, appalled by the wounds crisscrossing his ribs. She closed her eyes. Blast it all, if she wasn't going to faint again.

She instantly became aware that he was staring.

"You look pale," he observed. "You should have eaten something."

"I'd just as soon starve."

"If you think that will save you from your fate, you're wrong."

"And what is my fate, pirate? A cold and watery grave? Like your other victims?"

His knuckles grazed her cheek. "Your fate is with me, Arabella."

Regan swiftly bent her attention back to the underside of his arm. "The ball passed through." She hated the tremble in her voice. "There could be wadding inside. I'll need to make sure."

"Have a care, my sweet," he rasped the words. "If I die no one will protect you from my men. They're not nearly so forgiving of your faults as I."

"What?" She blinked, confronting his silver gaze.

"It doesn't much matter if you are a woman. You're a Welles. And they hate your family every bit as much as I do."

She jerked away from him. He didn't deserve her help. It was on the tip of her tongue to vent her sentiment but one look at his wound silenced her. "If you didn't want my help, why did you ask?"

"Do you have the stomach for it?"

"I know a little of medicine." At his skeptical look, she added, "I spent a few years with the sisters of St. Mary's on Martinique."

Talon made no sound as she peeled the bandage from his arm. Dried blood tore at the ragged edges of the wound. His eyes remained riveted on her face, making mincemeat of her nerves. Her teeth gripped her bottom lip. She was determined not to cry out. How could he endure the pain when she was dying of it herself? Fresh blood oozed over her fingers and dripped to the floor. He deserved her hate, but she didn't have it in her to enjoy his pain.

"Piers is from Martinique." His whisper startled her.

"He is?" That would account for his familiarity. Her gaze suddenly focused on Talon watching her. Hastily, she reapplied herself to the gruesome task at hand. "Then he probably told you the sisters are famous for their knowledge of the healing arts."

"St. Mary's is a convent."

"It's more of an orphanage. A hospital. People from all over the West Indies travel there."

"Why were you there?" he asked suddenly.

She pressed the bandage against his arm to staunch the flow of blood. Then met his feverish gaze. "When I was ten . . . I broke my leg," she told him. "It took nearly three years for me to walk again. While I was with the sisters, I learned much about the ways of healing."

His flint-like gaze flickered with disbelief. "Your father sent you to a convent?"

"The doctors here said it was for the best."

"And you believed that?"

Her eyes flashed. "What would someone like you know of the choices he had to make?"

"Someone like me wouldn't have sent you away."

She looked at him. There was none of the mockery she expected to see in his eyes. Her lashes fell as she abruptly dropped her gaze from his. "Mama's family is French," she tried to explain, unable to stomach his silent accusation against her family. "In truth, he was hardly abandoning me to strangers."

"I thought your mother was high society English."

Lord, she'd forgotten who she was supposed to be. High society indeed. Arabella's mother was a blue-blooded phony if ever there was one. Regan's mother was not pressed from the same mold. She'd been kind and gentle. Now she was dead.

Regan's heart twisted and any momentary softness she'd felt for the dreaded pirate vanished. Drake knew not the kind of woman he'd sent to her grave. She dared no response, for as surely as the night was dark, she'd betray herself.

Talon's gaze sharpened on hers. "You're not at all what I expected, Arabella."

"And what did you expect?" she demanded, peeved by his comment. "Someone beautiful of a sweet and docile temperament, perhaps?" she mocked his very words from that night in Arabella's bedroom. Why she should goad him, she didn't know. But he made her reckless. "Did you not consider that the kind of treatment you've shown me would have wilted such a frail flower?"

A dark brow lifted. "And have you been treated poorly?"

"You and your men are . . . beasts."

She saw that he was laughing at her. "I'm beginning to think your island education has limited your vocabulary. You have a fondness for that word."

The insult was too much. She started to stand. In a motion that belied his weakness, Drake grabbed her wrists. "Stay, milady."

He looked barely conscious. Regan felt the first spark of hope that escape might be within her grasp. The knife he produced from the sash around his waist silenced her thoughts. His gaze lifted past her into the darkness by the door.

"Jaime, bring the lady some hot water. Has Andy returned from the settlement?"

"Aye, sir. A half hour ago."

Regan startled. She hadn't heard Jaime come into the room.

"Did he bring back everything?"

Jaime's eyes shot to hers, and to her decimated imagination she had the horrible suspicion some great torture was being planned for her benefit. "Aye, that they did, sir."

Drake severed her bonds. "The lady will need a needle and some thread. And Jaime," Talon's gaze fixed on her face. "If she tries to escape, you have my permission to shoot her."

Chapter Six

Morning light filtered in thin streams through the dirt encrusted glass. Heat spilled over Regan. She continued gnawing on the rope that tethered her bound hands to the bedstead. Sweat beaded on her upper lip. Straining to hear any hint of approaching steps, she lifted her head to listen for sounds outside the room. Her gaze abruptly stopped on Talon. After a restless night, he finally slept.

Angered by the curious trip of her heart, Regan glared at his profile. Dark with stubble, his chiseled features seemed more pronounced in the fractured light slanting across the bed. Unbound by a scarf, damp black hair fell around bronzed shoulders. Sleep did little to tame his strength.

He moaned softly, tossing his head.

Regan held her breath, waiting for his eyes to flutter open. She'd endured his unblinking stare all night, as she tried desperately to make it through the long hours without fainting. The process of cleaning the wounds on his back and arm had taken its toll on them both. He'd finally lost consciousness after she finished stitching his arm. But not before he had the audacity to tie her again. Even half-unconscious, the pirate tied a knot strong enough to anchor a ship to the bottom of the ocean.

Regan waited. He didn't move.

Letting out a rush of pent-up air, she lowered her head again to chew on the rope. She should be happy that he was ill, jumping with joy at his possible demise. Talon deserved no less than God's full wrath for his deeds.

A mosquito buzzed around her head, driving her to distraction. Her scanty clothes had dried to the comfort of stiff vellum and provided no security. Her teeth ached. She imagined her mouth was chafed red from rubbing against the rough hemp.

Bloody rope!

Urgency drove her. Regan intended to escape. With Talon weakened from his wounds, it was now or never. She was confident in her ability to outwit his men, who seemed more concerned about their captain than keeping a stern eye on her.

If only she could part the strands of the rope . . .

"Milady?"

The voice snapped her to attention. It was the boatswain, Jaime. How could she not have heard his approach? His thin frame bore the burden of exhaustion. Like them all. Did she look that bad? With her long hair tangled to her hips, dirty bare feet, and ragged underclothing, she imagined she looked like the mythical Medusa.

Talon's men had left her in peace since dropping a bowl of fruit at her feet earlier that morning. But that was hours ago.

Jaime's gaze slid from his resting captain to the frayed teeth marks on the rope. Slipping a knife from the leather sheath around his waist, he contemplated the wicked blade before touching her with his eyes. "For whatever reason, the cap'n seems to value you. Ain't figured it out, yet."

Her chin lifted belligerently. "What do you want?"

Jaime smirked at her thin show of bravado. "We've a need for the services of a wench." He sliced the rope binding her hands. "The boy will see to the captain's needs. You'll see to ours."

Regan's heart hit against her ribs. "I'll not go with you."

He yanked her to her feet. "Now I ain't the gentlemanly sort like the cap'n here. Seems you been handled with more respect than a Welles deserves."

Regan glanced over her shoulder at Talon. A panicked moment brought her near the brink of screaming. Logic set in. Jaime had untied her. Set her free. Absently, she rubbed her wrists.

Jaime pulled her into the hallway. Nearly colliding with the redheaded youth, she jumped aside as the urchin pushed past her with a pitcher of hot water and rags in hand. Their eyes briefly touched before he kicked the door shut in her face.

"Seems he's not so fond of ye neither," Jaime snickered.

She stared numbly at the closed portal. A box-winged cockroach skittered out of a crack beside the door, startling her.

Jaime smashed the roach into the wall with his palm. "Have ya ever eaten one of these delicate buggers?" he taunted, idly peeling the messy remains off the wall and flicking it in front of her nose.

Regan refused him the pleasure of intimidating her. "I imagine for someone of your ilk, anything is palatable."

He dropped it in his mouth. It took all the steely determination she possessed not to gag as he deliberately crunched and chewed smacking his lips with great vigor. Finally, she closed her eyes.

"The fine fare of many a dungeon, princess."

"That's . . . nauseating."

"Yer very bold with yer sentiment. But you've never been forced to live in chains. Have ye, princess? A man what wants to survive in this life will do anything to see it done."

Talon bore the marks of chains. A moment of anguish subdued her. Lifting her chin, Regan eyed Jaime's youthful features, from the tuft of his blond curly hair to his stubby boots. "You're not a man," was the worst she could think to say.

"Man enough to sail with Cap'n Drake."

" 'Tis an honor, no doubt, among cutthroats to sail with the lowliest pirate of all."

He pulled her down the corridor after him. "And soon we'll be the richest cutthroats on the Spanish Main. The cap'n is goin' after the lost treasure of Puerto Bello before Kendrick finds it."

Regan checked her pulse. Was Arabella to be used as some sort of pawn against Harrison? "Is that what this is all about?" she asked in disgust. "A hunt for some mythical treasure?"

Obviously miffed with her lack of appreciation for his black-hearted idol, Jaime aimed his snobbish silence at her.

It didn't matter. Drake would get nothing from Harrison. She'd burned the map.

The hall suddenly gave way to a vaulted foyer that reached thirty feet above the ground floor. Hot sunlight poured through the beveled glass above the stair landing. The shock of it stopped Regan.

Her gaze swept the aged splendor of the once grand house. Dust motes filled the air. A crystal chandelier tingled softly in the breeze that blew over Regan and smelled of sea and mold. A headless doll lay sprawled below on the stairs. In the palatial entryway, a clock stood sentinel, its brass counterweights tarnished black. It was as if the clock had died as abruptly as this house.

Something very tragic had happened here.

"This house was as grand as any belonging to the finest lords in England," Jaime said.

"They left so much behind," she said aloud. "Why?"

Jaime turned his eyes on her. "This be *his* house, princess."

Horror caught her expression. Jaime tugged her down the winding staircase, causing her to trip over her petticoat. She barely caught her balance. Her gaze remained fixed on the headless doll.

"The regular townsfolk stay away. They've left it be as it was since the day the soldiers came. His ma was shot in the courtyard trying to fight them off her little girl. They say their ghosts haunt this place. I don't believe none in spirits, but it's kept the scavengers away."

"Captain Drake didn't say anything." Her throat was raw.

"Why should he?" Jaime scoffed. "Everyone knows it was yer family what did this to him. But seein as how yer all honorable, you wouldn't know nothin' 'bout that, would ya, princess?"

Dazed, she desperately tried to assess Jaime's comment. She'd allowed herself to be humbled by him at the worst possible moment, when she needed her lagging strength to fight the strange hold Talon had on her. Besides, what did this boy know of the crimes that had convicted Drake and his family of treason? William Welles had been a respected man of justice. To blame Father for Drake's downfall was ludicrous.

"Drake is filling your head with lies." She summoned her principles to her defense. "He's using you for his own greed."

"Cap'n Drake didn't fill our heads with nothin'. I found out last night at the settlement." He kicked aside debris that littered the floor. A choking cloud of dust mushroomed with the violent movement. "And I've sailed with the cap'n long enough to know he don't do nothin' fer greed."

Jaime shoved her into a drawing room. "Here she is, mates."

A pair of legs stretched out and tripped her. Her palms smacked against the floor, painfully jolting her shoulders. Catching her breath, she lifted her chin. Through a waterfall of hair, she gaped at the sod that tripped her. He sat on a tattered high-backed chair. Two other men idled at a table, finishing a bottle of rum.

The look in their eyes turned her blood to ice. Regan felt like a raw brisket that had just been tossed at a pack of mongrels.

The man with his legs stretched casually wore a hat gaily festooned with a purple feather that matched his fancy claret doublet and buff breeches. His exaggerated finery contrasted with the other two buccaneers slouched at the table, who wore their wild-looking hair like crowns of barbaric glory. Baldrics crisscrossed their chests over leather tunics. Jaime appeared tame compared to this uncivilized lot. Until this moment, Regan hadn't appreciated the enormous influence Captain Drake exerted over his men.

Her mouth went dry. Unable to control the chill that shivered through her, Regan climbed slowly to her feet. She was grateful for the tangled mop of hair covering her thinly clad torso. In the heavy silence, she listened attentively over the pounding of her heart. The man with the silly feather swigged on a bottle of rum before wiping a ruffled sleeve across his mouth.

"Well?" he asked Jaime. "Can the wench cook?"

Jaime nudged her, making her jump.

Regan nodded, willing to say anything to end their obnoxious scrutiny. She knew more about herbs than she did about culinary skills. Which suited her fine. A healthy dose of that kind of knowledge would see them suffering after they finished eating anything she cooked.

"Count yerself fortunate the captain has put his claim on you." Jaime nodded to the men. "It's been a while since the lot of them laid eyes on a woman."

The old bewhiskered tar sitting at the table wagged a gnarled finger at her. "Why don't you move yer hair aside, missy. Give us a little look-see. There's no harm in a peek is there?"

"Don't think so, Harry," Jaime said. "The cap'n has his own plan fer this one." He pulled Regan out of the room into a back hallway that led outside. "And I doubt he's of a mind to share his wife with the scurvy lot of you," he called over his shoulder.

Wife! The earth could swallow Jamaica whole before she'd consent to matrimony with Talon Drake. Scuffled movement in the hallway arrested her attention as the men followed her through the door.

In a terrified rush, she pivoted. "Get away from me!" The smell of unwashed bodies filled the narrow confines of the hallway. She raised clenched fists, warning them off. "All of you!"

"Or what?" The old tar stepped forward, his thin angular frame crowding around Regan.

Jaime turned. "We agreed she'd cook, Harry. That's all."

"Ah, Jaime boy, would you deny us a little fun?" Harry picked at the strands of Regan's hair. "She ain't even showed us all what she's got hidden 'neath this fluff."

Regan shrank from his touch. Why hadn't she screamed upstairs when it might have done some good? The folly of her wisdom beat down on her in icy waves. "Don't touch me. I'm warning you."

"Have a heart, luvee. A man what's been at sea as long as I—"

Regan smashed her fist into his jaw, snapping his neck back with the force of her wallop.

Comical disbelief registered on Harry's face, but Regan couldn't have been more shocked than anyone else by her actions. Her fist stung. She drew it to her chest, poised to pummel the next man who dared touch her. Jaime crossed his arms and casually watched the standoff.

Harry rubbed his bristly jaw. "Don't that beat all," he muttered sourly. "The gal just about broke me jaw."

The claret popinjay sniggered. "I don't think she's got a fondness for ye, Harry."

"Aye," The other bloke agreed. "Like 'is bloomin' wife."

"Keep it up, men," Jaime said. "You'll be runnin' the bilge pump when we return to the ship."

Pondering Regan, Harry laughed and turned away. Talon was leaning with one hand braced against the door frame. His men instantly sobered.

At the precious sight of him, Regan couldn't still the leap of her heart. A clean white shirt hung haphazardly on his shoulders as if he'd just thrown it on. Without thought, she pushed past Harry and ran to him.

Wrapping her to him, he laid the full import of his gaze on his men. His heat embraced her. "Have I missed something?"

"I was just takin' the lady outside to the kitchen, Cap'n," Jaime rushed to explain. "We've a need for vittles."

Talon seemed to choke. "And have her poison our food? She's not to be trusted with a glass of water."

A furious flush heated her cheeks. He wasn't concerned at all for her safety. Regan spun around.

"Take her back to my room, Jaime," he said, looking at her. "I'll be up after I've had a few words with the men."

Jaime took her arm. Regan jerked from his grasp. But Talon remained in her path. Her gaze chased up to his face.

"You're to wash up." His gentleness made her breath catch. "The padre is waiting for us. He's been here all night."

"And what, pray tell, would the good padre want with me?" A bubble of hysterical laughter boiled up in her throat. "I've already been baptized. Perhaps 'tis you who should consider his services, milord pirate. For your funeral."

His narrowed gaze traveled over her face, then bluntly dropped to peruse her scantily clad body. "I don't need wedding vows to bind you to me, sweet. And bind you to me, I will. Be grateful I have scruples enough to marry you first."

Talon held Regan's stricken gaze. He felt a niggling regret to see the shadow of defeat in her magnificent eyes. But he would do what it took to crush the fight out of her. She could not defy him in front of his men and expect to survive with anything less than bloodshed. Her life depended on her obedience.

"Take her upstairs. And guard her," he warned Jaime, though his gaze remained fixed on his reluctant bride. "I'll be up in a moment."

She shoved away from Jaime. Talon watched the haughty swing of her petticoat as she swept past. Waves of dark hair cascaded down her back, emphasizing the curve of her bottom as she walked, and limped, he realized noting her dirty bare feet. Her father had never mentioned her injury. Was she in pain? he wondered. Talon brought himself up short when he realized he was staring.

His gaze landed on Harry and the other two men standing ill at ease as if they faced a firing squad. A possibility, when he considered their bawdy behavior. "Where's the rest of the men?"

"Mick, he's on watch," Harry volunteered. "Andy went back to the village. You been sick, Cap'n. We figured on fetching a doctor."

"Stay away from the girl, Harry. She's off-limits to the crew." Beneath his grizzled beard, Harry paled. "And join the Irishman on watch. If Kendrick discovers where Piers stowed the boat, a platoon of redcoats will be down our throats. Stay alert."

"Aye, sir."

Talon started to turn away. The room swam in sickening currents around his head. *Damn this infernal weakness.* After waiting years to see justice rendered, he realized he was nearer to being defeated than ever before. Very carefully, he straightened. Jaime was right. They needed a decent meal. Hunger was as perilous a predicament as any he'd faced. "Can any of you cook?"

His men grumbled their discord.

"Can you at least try?"

"Aye, sir." Harry shifted. "We've supplies enough if yer not mindin' the taste of seawater."

"We've all had worse." Talon turned away.

He had business to attend to. Pleasant business, he decided. A sense of satisfaction filled him. His future wife would not be the least bit happy about any of it.

A single candle lit Regan's prison. The only door opened into Talon's chamber. Growing more frantic by the moment, she paced within the precious circle of light. Gauzy spider-webs draped the ceiling and cast shadows across her wild imagination. Talon Drake's presence invaded the room as ominously as the darkness that enclosed her.

She wiped away fresh tears with the back of her hand. Lack of sleep and food mixed with the terrifying prospect of remaining this man's prisoner. For the first time in her young life, she felt utterly alone. Abandoned. How could she fight her family's most hated enemy? Her defeat was as imminent as the forbidding night.

An old rusted tub shadowed one corner of the bathing room. A faded blue primrose dress, matching stockings and slippers lay on the floor beside a bowl of water. A beautiful ivory inlaid comb had been set on top of the dress. Her wedding ensemble. The very thought mocked the dreams she held so close to her heart. Talon Drake would destroy those, too.

She rubbed her throbbing temples. She simply had to think. Where had Piers gone? She had to speak to him. Surely, the Frenchman would stop this madness with the truth.

Regan stopped pacing.

As Arabella, Talon considered her valuable. What worth would she have as Regan Welles? The daughter of the man who'd hanged his father. In a word? None. He'd give her over to his men. Hadn't he already implied as much?

Regan had oft heard tales of savagery among pirates. For over a hundred years, cities and ships along the Spanish Main had fallen beneath their brutal attacks. Talon Drake was a feared presence in these waters. His reputation had been forged in all the finest drawing rooms from Jamaica to England.

Her gut knotted.

Talon Drake had been a gentleman once. His late father a peer of the realm. Surely, the son possessed some civilized remnant of the past; he would not hand her over to his crew if she were his wife. Would he? Even if that wife was Regan Welles? Lord. She raised her eyes to the ceiling as she considered the possibility. She didn't know. She just didn't know.

"Damn you, Arabella." No sooner did Regan voice the words than she wished them back. She couldn't fault Arabella for running. Not entirely. Regan was ashamed to admit that she'd been ready to betray her cousin for the very same reason. What kind of person was she to wish Arabella here in her stead? To wish anyone else to suffer?

Father had detested cowardice. "Get a backbone, Regan," she snapped Father's words aloud. She was a Welles after all; she would find a way to fight.

The door clicked opened. Talon's frame filled the doorway. Her breath caught as if all the air had been sucked out of the room. In the lone light of the candle, she could see the glitter in his gaze. With just one passing glance of those silver eyes, he set her nerves on fire.

"Why aren't you dressed?"

Because she'd die first before she acquiesced to his will. "I need time," she whispered.

"Time is not mine to give, sweet." Talon moved into the confining space of the room. Only her fear of backing into the darkness kept her from retreating. He lifted a thick handful of her hair. "What am I to do with you, Arabella?" His other hand fanned her waist. This was not the hand of a coddled lord but callused like his soul. "You puzzle me. And few people do."

Her fists coiled against his chest, pushing against his pull. Another step and her thigh touched his. Captured as she was, Regan couldn't look anywhere but at his face.

"What kind of *lady* doesn't wear a corset?"

"Let me go," she forced out in a low panicked tone.

The heat of his body enveloped her. "I've met many a brave man in battle with less courage than you've shown," he said quietly. Suddenly trapped by the confusion in his emotions, she couldn't move. His palm tested the length of her rib cage, burning through the thin cloth of her chemise. He hesitated just below her breast near her heart. He had only to move his thumb.

"Please . . ."

His eyes caught in the candlelight. There it was again. That flicker of humanity. And she saw again the dashing stranger who risked his life to save his men. "I frighten you?"

He could clearly read for himself what he was doing to her.

"That's good." He released her. "Because if you ever defy me in front of my men again, I'll have you horsewhipped."

Regan's chest tightened in outrage.

"Do I make myself clear?"

"Yes, I understand . . . I understand you're a cruel, heartless barbarian. A coward who will terrorize a woman for his own greedy purpose. I understand that I hate everything you are."

A shadow of a smile touched his lips. "What? No punches to go with your soliloquy?"

"You were watching downstairs?" Her words faded to a wounded whisper. "And you didn't do anything?"

"No need. My men are still alive."

"Oh!" His amusement at her expense cast considerable strain on her temper. Regan kicked him. Twice for good measure. He did this to her: created a harpy out of her normally complacent character. "I should have sewed your mouth shut while I had that needle."

Talon dared to laugh. "You've clothes and water to clean yourself, Arabella. I'll expect you to be ready soon."

Regan was finished taking orders from this man. She grabbed the porcelain water bowl off the filthy floor. "Clean yourself, pirate!"

She tossed the water and drenched the captain solidly.

The look in his eyes froze her. His white shirt plastered to his chest, molding every sinewed ridge and curve to her shocked gaze. His hands came down on her shoulders and he pulled her to him. Her pulse spiraled. In an uneven exhale, Regan's head fell back and she met the emotions in his silver gaze.

His breath caressed her lips. "Shall I prove what a little liar you are, sweet?"

Oh! If only the rogue knew! The lie stretched beyond the boundaries of her identity to the feminine core of her body. If he kissed her now surrender seemed a likely probability.

"Tonight, my sweet." He rescued the bowl from her grip. His mouth broadened into a grin that bespoke much of what his eyes promised. "I'll have Jaime bring you more water."

Her fists clenched as he turned and strode from her prison.

She needed a weapon. If it was the last thing on earth she ever did, she had to find a way to thwart him.

Then the irony of her dilemma struck her.

Her gaze swung to the clothes. Her wedding ensemble. The arrogant, uncouth blackguard! Talon Drake thought he owned all the power. She did have a weapon, the queen mother of all weapons.

He was marrying the wrong Welles.

Chapter Seven

"Yer face be smooth as a whore's tit." Razor in hand, the redheaded urchin stepped back to survey his handiwork.

Tentatively rubbing his jaw, Talon considered the boy. "And what do you know of a whore's tit?"

"Oi knows plenty, Cap'n." Hitching up his baggy pants, the boy turned his attention to the fat padre sitting at the table. "And certainly more 'n that 'ol geezer. Why, 'e probably ain't never tossed a skirt. Or do ya tup 'em with their clothes on, Father?"

The padre coughed, spraying red wine over the remains of his lunch. "Now see here—" He wiped a sleeve across his mouth.

"Yer a man, ain't ya?"

"Someone should take lye to that nasty mouth of yours."

The boy thrust out the razor. "No one lays a 'and—"

Talon clamped the boy's wrist, startling the youth. For a moment, fear razed the blue eyes. Carefully removing the razor from the boy's grip, Talon applied it to the orange he'd been peeling. "What did you say you were called?"

"Oi told ya good 'an simple, Cap'n. Me name's Parrot."

"Your real name."

"Oi ain't got no name but Parrot. 'An don't ya be tryin' to civilize me with one, neither."

"Then Parrot," Talon said simply, placing the razor on the

wooden crates stacked beside the chair. "This is an old family friend. He's a priest. He doesn't toss women's skirts."

The boy's sullen scowl girdled the brown-robed padre who now sat at the table with his arms crossed over his ample chest.

"You have a dislike for men of God, Parrot?" Talon asked.

"Oi don't believe in no fancy god."

Talon could understand the sentiment. He sat back in the chair and split the orange into sections, offering most to the boy. Parrot hesitated then snatched it up. A nap, a half-decent meal, and a shave had served to fortify Talon's waning strength. Even his irritation with the delayed nuptials yielded to a half bottle of rum and the boy's copious entertainment.

"What were you in prison for anyway?" he asked, waiting for Parrot to finish the orange.

Defiance puffed the boy's skinny chest. "Murder." The priest's strangled croak drew his youthful ire. "Oi slit a man's bloomin' throat," he taunted. "Ain't sorry, neither. The bastard deserved 'is gullet split from ear ta ear."

Eyeing the boy's ragged canvas breeches and torn shirt, Talon chewed on a slice of tangy orange. "We all have reasons for the things we do, Parrot." The lad's wide eyes shifted nervously. "But you put on airs in front of the crew, and they'll feed you to the sharks."

The floor outside the drawing room creaked. A flurry of movement in the corridor alerted Talon to Arabella's long-awaited arrival. He looked past the urchin as two of his men ushered his errant bride across the threshold into the drawing room.

The shadows seemed to shift when she entered. Sunlight streamed through the tall windows framing her in its brilliance.

On someone else, the faded primrose muslin would have been plain. His gaze traveled appreciatively over her form. Shaped against the slim curve of her waist, the tight fitting bodice laced up the front cupping her full breasts. She'd plaited her hair and anchored it in back with the ivory comb he had Jaime purchase from the settlement store. Silken tendrils framed her oval face. A barely perceptive tremor in her chin stayed his gaze.

She looked fragile compared to the armed men who surrounded her, out of place among them all, like a dove in a nest of hawks.

A breeze stirred the room. In the grand entryway, the crystal chandelier quivered. The realization that he was nervous hit him soundly. Talon uncurled from the chair and offered his hand, regretting the impulse immediately. The civil gesture was reflexive, part of a simpler time when such behavior was symbolic of a gentleman. That man no longer existed.

Ignoring Talon's hand, she stepped past him. "Know before we start, Father," she coolly announced, "I am not here of my own will."

Talon's fingers closed into his palm.

"He is doing the right thing by you, my dear," the padre graciously interjected. "If there is a child—"

"A child?" Regan's gaze cut accusingly to Talon's. She hardly noticed when he took her hand firmly in his.

"Who knows what tonight will reap," he said, his meaning rife in the silver depths of his eyes. "A child is not unheard of."

The words turned Regan to stone. The scheme she'd hatched upstairs seemed suddenly filled with terrible flaws. With all her plotting, she failed to consider how she'd escape this other aspect of marriage. Consummation. The very idea defeated her nerve completely. She could not give herself willingly to this pirate. Not for any cause!

"On my honor, milord pirate, I swear you'll pay for this deed."

Talon bent over her hand. His gray eyes held hers. "The deed will be done, milady," he promised, stopping just short of touching his lips to her skin. "Your bloody honor be damned."

Regan sought to free herself but the muscles beneath her fingertips coiled with his grip. He tucked her arm beneath his.

The Padre cleared his throat. "I say we begin."

"By all means, Padre," Talon agreed. "Do proceed."

The priest made the sign of the holy cross. Regan stood rigidly in Talon's shadow. The breadth of his shoulders beneath the white Holland shirt blocked the light. He wore his clothes with the clean, casual grace of landed gentry. Shaven and more handsome than the archangel himself, but for the red scarf tied at his waist, he might have passed for civilized, untouched by pain or the burden of hate.

Conscious of the heat radiating from his powerful body and his hold on her arm, Regan's focus blurred. She felt strange, as if something inside battled to defeat her strength. Even the meal she'd consumed earlier did nothing to ease her roiling stomach.

The priest's words droned over her as if they'd been cut from the sacred pages of the holy book and dangled before her like some ghastly joke. She murmured the correct response at the appropriate times and would have been content to remain oblivious to the man standing like a pillar beside her, if only she could.

And then, "You may kiss the bride," rang through the room.

Regan kept her gaze riveted to the leaf-strewn floor. She hadn't heard those words!

"Milady—" Talon cupped her chin, turning her face. "—wife."

In rising panic, her fingers splayed the hard-muscled wall of his chest as if she possessed the power to move a mountain. To stop time. To run.

Talon covered her mouth with his, swallowing her gasp of protest. She tried to turn her head. Long fingers closed around the back of her neck, tangling in her braid, quelling her fight. She couldn't breathe. What was he doing to her?

He tilted her head, slipping his tongue between her startled lips, plundering her mouth with an expertise that robbed her strength. Tasting of rum and citrus, he filled the tight space of her senses, raking her will into oblivion. A low moan climbed unbidden into her throat. Sweltering heat pressed against her, making her knees weaken, until the hands that she'd raised to push him away, clutched the loose silken fold of his shirt for support.

Then Talon lifted his head. No longer mocking, his half-lidded gaze dropped to her mouth, drifting over her face to capture her eyes. Regan's heart hammered against her ribs, sounding like the very walls were crumbling around her. The impact of her surrender clawed deep enough to leave scars. He started to lower his mouth again.

She wanted him to kiss her again.

Someone was pounding on the door. "Captain!"

As if remembering that they weren't alone, Talon pulled his gaze from hers. Hushed words sounded from the hallway.

"Captain!" The dandy-dressed buccaneer snapped around, the execution of his manner a stark contrast to the claret ostrich plumes drooping from his hat. "A ship has anchored outside the lagoon."

Talon's expression hardened. He let her go. "Which ship?"

"The *Viper*, sir." The man offered the spyglass. "And she's flying the governor's colors."

Harrison had found her. Triumphant, she swung her eyes to Talon.

"See that my wife signs the documents," Talon snapped to Jaime. "And don't let her out of your sight." He walked past Regan, his stiff movement offset by the anger in his stride. He caught the glass in the man's hand and quit the room.

"Come child." The padre nervously motioned her forward. "We must hurry."

Jaime moved her to the table where the padre stood waiting. Two sheets of vellum lay opened before her. Talon had already signed his name to both. Regan stared at the bold signature scrawled with poetic flourish across the documents.

The beauty of the script struck her like a blow, encroaching beyond bounds that left her feeling strangely violated. A shield clutched within the outstretched claws of an eagle was embossed in wax beside his name, *the Fourth Earl of Sunderland*. It was the identical coat of arms on the silver amulet he'd worn around his neck and the same mark on the map she'd destroyed. A shiver of apprehension straightened her spine.

Who was this man of many faces? Her family's enemy?

"Stallin' won't help." Jaime's words startled her.

Regan snatched up the white-feathered quill from the table. This was war, she staunchly reminded herself, brutally relegating her misplaced emotions to their rightful place. Honor was naught but a handicap against this crew of kidnapers and their pirate captain.

Unlike the priest who watched for Talon's return, Jaime was content to antagonize her. He would know the instant she signed the document that she wasn't Arabella. What did it matter? The sham of a marriage would be short-lived. Harrison would find her before the day's end.

Hurriedly, she scripted her name beneath Talon's on each document. Dropping the quill, she stepped away. Beside her, Jaime stared at the vellum, satisfied that she'd fulfilled her duty.

He couldn't read, Regan realized. Not one letter!

For a strangled moment, she possessed the childish urge to flout that knowledge in his face. To laugh.

Talon entered the room, his expression grim. Ignoring her, he swiftly rolled the documents into a cylinder. "Get to Spanishtown by tonight, Padre." He stuffed one document into his sleeve and handed the other to the priest. "Register the marriage in my full name—"

"Milord," the priest lowered his voice. "What of the bedding . . . the law—"

"I know the law."

"Kendrick is powerful. There have been no banns posted. He can annul the marriage."

Talon looked at Regan. His gaze conveyed volumes to her benighted imagination. "He can try, Padre. Now go," he urged.

The priest reluctantly complied. "God be with you, milord." His affection and concern stamped across his somber expression, his brown eyes swept the men standing at arms in the room. "Even you, you son of a heathen," he said to the boy.

Parrot's chin lifted belligerently, but his eyes were less hostile as his gaze followed the priest's departure.

Talon turned to Jaime. "Are all the men accounted for?"

"Andy ain't returned from the settlement with the doctor."

"Damn!" His gaze hesitated on Regan; then his jaw tightened as he looked at Jaime. "Take her to the rendezvous point with Marcus. If he isn't there . . . you and the men stay low. I'll find you."

"But, Cap'n—"

"Go!" His eyes were fierce.

Regan numbly watched as Talon left the room. In her confusion, she remembered the hungry look in his eyes after he'd kissed her. Only the promise of escape kept her resolute. That, and the niggling sense of vengeance that would be hers when he learned the truth.

Braced between Jaime and Harry, Regan ran until her lungs burned. Gunshots faded with the distance. Her belly tightened. Every painful step that took her farther from Harrison made her more determined to fight her way back. But Talon's vigilant crew watched over her like she-wolves over a pup. Stern, yet gentle, they would not relinquish her from their sight, nor allow her to slow them down.

By the time they finally emerged from the logwood forest, deepening shadows, shaped by wind and trees, danced on the ribbed dirt. Behind them, a strange orange pall shimmered against the velvet sky, burning like dusk.

"The bleedin' bastards torched 'is 'ouse," Parrot said.

Talon's men stood in a semicircle around her. For one frozen moment, Regan stared. She tried to summon some feeling of victory. But could not. Profound visions of the once grand house decimated her conscience. Unnerved, Regan squeezed her eyes shut. *Think of Harrison.* But it was Talon's face that came to her now.

"Do ye think the cap'n found Andy?" Jaime asked.

Harry spat, "Andy ain't got the sense of a blamed goose. Probably found him a whore. More 'n likely get the cap'n killed."

Regan raked shaky fingers through her hair, forgetting she'd braided it. She flinched. The air, heavy with humidity, mixed with thirst on her tongue. Dizziness that had plagued her all day, wrapped her skull in a vise.

Finally, after they'd gone another three miles, she slumped beside Parrot against the rough-hewn bark of a spreading pimento tree. It cut into her back. She didn't care. She edged one toe and then the other beneath the torn leather of her ruined kidskin slippers and forced them off her swollen feet. Her stomach pushed against her ribs.

Parrot watched her curiously; his cotton-eyed gaze honed sharply on her hands. Regan tucked her palms beneath her bottom to shield their trembling. More noticeable than it was hours before.

Exhaustion had claimed her, but never like this. This was something else entirely. She'd made an effort to eat fruit and anything clse they could find along the trail. It couldn't be hunger. Regan closed her eyes to rest. She only knew that whatever strange ailment enveloped her, it stripped her of precious strength she needed to escape. And she had to escape if she were to live.

Some time later, Regan startled awake. Her blurry focus shifted from Parrot, lying with his red head nearly on her lap, to the man dressed in fancy garb squatting in front of her. The plume on his hat drooped over his eyes.

"Milady," he pleasantly addressed her. His leather boots creaked as he leaned a lace-cuffed elbow on his haunches and picked at his dirty nails with a knife. "Are you enjoying your royal sleep?"

Regan quashed the temptation to jerk his fancy black periwig off his head. Parrot sat up and rubbed his eyes.

"Leave 'er be, Charlie." Harry came to stand over them. Spiky brown hair menaced his pitted face, his fierceness a contradiction to the patience he'd shown Regan all afternoon. "She needs ta rest."

"We've been here too long already."

"Bloomin' 'ell, Charlie. We've done a good twelve miles. She can't go no farther. And neither can the kid."

"What are you, her bleedin' nanny?"

"Can't ya see she's sick?"

Charlie's head swiveled to Regan. Harry's observation shocked her. She'd refused to show weakness in front of them, even staving off their efforts to carry her when her shoes began to tear. Jaime had carried her anyway but not without consequences to his boyish features. Her elbow still hurt from cracking him in the cheek.

Charlie stood and glared at Harry with disgust. "One blow to the jaw an' yer bleedin' lovesick, Harry." He walked away.

Harry turned to Regan. His thick eyebrows amplified his expression. "I apologize, milady, fer our comely Charlie, here. Ya see he didn't have a ma to teach him proper manners."

"And yours did?" Charlie scoffed. "She was a bloomin' whore."

Harry ignored him. "Jaime's fetchin' some food. We'll all feel better with somethin' in our bellies."

"Harry," Regan whispered as he started to turn. "My—" she abruptly stopped herself from saying brother. She reasserted her thoughts. All pirates knew the value of a gold coin and she intended to take advantage of that weakness. "His Excellency is very wealthy. He'll pay for my release."

Beside her, Parrot made a rude conjecture comparing her unfairly to a female dog. He brushed the dirt from his breeches, showering her with fine debris as he went to sit with Charlie.

Regan dismissed the belligerent imp and bent her attention back on Harry, desperate to find some kindred ally to her cause.

"There's not a man-jack here who'd betray the captain, milady."

"Ah, a noble-minded buccaneer. It warms my heart, it does," Jaime mocked, walking out of the bushes behind her. He dropped a rat, two snakes and a skinny mongoose on the ground at her feet. "Dinner is served, princess." He gallantly bowed, his puffy eye clearly visible in the fractured moonlight breaking through the trees. "What will be yer choice of fare tonight?"

Regan eyed the disgusting heap lumped at her feet. She knew Jaime enjoyed provoking her. And that he was bound to get even with her for giving him a black eye that afternoon.

"Now that depends, oh great hunter," she replied. "Do you intend to cook your fine feast?"

His expression changed subtly. Obviously, their harried circumstances forbid a fire. Something he hadn't considered.

Regan climbed to her feet. She was dismayed to find the shaking in her arms had traveled into her legs. "I'm sure that anyone who enjoys the cuisine of roaches will not mind eating a raw rat," she said politely. "But me? I'll find some fruit if it's all the same to you."

Harry laughed at Jaime's red-faced expense.

Regan was grateful for their inattention. She could hardly stand. "We passed a stream just over there," she bluntly interrupted, nodding to the crescent-shaped grass dome where Charlie and Parrot were sitting. "I need some privacy."

Jaime shook his head. "The captain will have our skin—"

"Will ya give us yer parole, milady, not to run?"

"Criminy, Harry. Have ye lost yer brain?"

"Aye, he has," Charlie said.

Jaime threw up his arms. "She just tried to bribe ye."

" 'Av 'er swear on the 'oly cross," Parrot helpfully submitted. "No one breaks their word to God 'less they wanna roast in 'ell."

"Aye"—Harry turned. "—and we all carry a blessed—" A large gold cross, the size of a child's forearm, appeared in the dust with a metallic clink. All eyes went to the one who'd tossed it.

Parrot shrugged a thin shoulder. "Oi palmed it. The good padre probably 'as a dozen more where that one came from."

Peering at Parrot from beneath his brows, Harry picked up the cross.

"I give my word," Regan blurted out before he could make her touch the cross. Pain spiked her temples. Until a few days ago, she'd considered her word sacrosanct. Now blasphemous lies were burying her. She hated being Arabella. She'd descended to the ranks of a ruffian, shot a man, and lied before God, all in her grandiose scheme to battle an enemy who'd been weaned in the arena of warfare.

"In a pig's beady eye," Jaime smirked.

"I believe 'er," Harry said, and allowed her to leave.

Keeping her gaze shamefully averted, Regan limped to the creek and drank. Earlier, two of Talon's men had moved down the road to keep watch. She would have to be careful she didn't meet them.

Splashing water on her face and neck, she allowed the cooling drops to dribble down her neck and over her bodice.

She knew everyone was watching her. Except maybe Harry.

"Guilt is truly a warrior's enemy," Regan's muddled mind reasoned. God will surely forgive her this newest blight on her soul. She breathed the earth-scented air and lifted her gaze to the black sky. The stars would guide her. The Caribbean lay directly north. If she followed the stream, it would lead her to the beach. She lingered in the cool water, treading her hands in the current.

Looking down the creek, Talon's ominous specter hovered over her. Could she walk fast enough to escape in the darkness? She had to try even if it meant crawling on her knees to freedom.

The ground vibrated. Shocked to hear horses approaching fast, Regan hesitated. Soldiers! It had to be.

But in the darkness, she couldn't be sure. These woods crawled with society's refuse. She struggled against her damp skirts to stand. Her feet sank in the silt of the creek. Voices from camp seemed to fill the night. Someone was running toward her.

The muddled chaos spurred Regan to action. She struggled up the bank angling from the creek. Water splashed her clothes. The riders were approaching fast. She prayed they were friends, not foe. She needed to reach them. Her breath came hard and fast with her flight.

Footsteps behind her drew closer. She pushed harder. A muscled arm suddenly caught around her waist and hauled her against the familiar hard length of a man's body. With a cry of despair, she kicked out, flailing air as Talon squeezed the breath from her lungs. He was breathing as heavily as she was.

"Going someplace, Arabella?"

His presence spurred her to panic. "I have to reach them—"

"Not tonight, sweet." He clamped his other hand across her mouth and shoved her to the ground beneath him.

Chapter Eight

The ground trembled with the thunder of galloping horses sweeping down the low ridge. Talon clenched his jaw against the pain splintering his arm. He'd ripped his stitches. Heart pounding, he buried his face into his bride's silken mass of hair.

"Be still, you fool! Or you'll get us both killed."

She fought harder. Pressing her deeper into the soft dirt, Talon muffled her screams. Drunken banter preceded the deafening barrage as a half dozen horses passed only a few feet from where he lay sheltered in the darkness of trees. Shielding his wayward wife from flying clots of dirt as they thundered past, Talon tensed. Tiny rocks scattered. A bottle carelessly discarded clinked against his boot.

Smuggler's Cove lay directly ahead, a human cesspool that put Port Royal to shame even by pirate standards. There would be trouble if someone in that disreputable lot looked back and saw them. Talon wanted no part of a fight.

The noise faded, until the sounds of the girl struggling beneath him was all that remained of the roaring silence. In a furious maneuver, Talon turned his recalcitrant bride, entangling her skirts around his legs. "Out for an evening stroll, are we?"

"Get . . . off of me!" she choked and tried to hit him.

Talon grappled with her fists and brought them over her head, absorbing her struggles with his greater weight.

"You're a lot of trouble, milady wife." Her squirming had roused more than his ire. "I'm beginning not to trust you, sweet."

"Let me up! You're bleeding all over me."

"Aye, you've done a fair job of draining me dry."

"I . . . *will* . . . find . . . a . . . way to escape you." Her futile struggles died as she gasped for breath. "I swear I will."

In the moonlight that dappled the ground beneath the canopy of trees, he could see the hot glitter of her gaze. Sweet fire raked over him. Framed by the moonlight, she was exotically beautiful, her skin nearly pearlescent against her dark, wavy hair. "This isn't Spanishtown. You don't know what you're dealing with out here."

"I know exactly what I'm dealing with, Captain Drake. You've shown me more than I need to know on that account."

"That worthless lot would have killed you. And if they didn't, you'd wish they had by the time they finished with you." Pointedly ignoring him, she fixed her gaze rigidly on a spot over his shoulder. "Listen to me." He gripped her chin, snapping her eyes back to his. "This road is crawling with men who make mine look like patron saints. The garrison soldiers won't even come out here after dark."

"You and your men are the same as any other buccaneer who plies this coast. Whose hands I fall into make no difference. The end will be the same."

"Is that what you really think?"

Her eyes betrayed confusion. She looked away. " 'Tis what I know to be the truth. You act the rogue and claim that your intentions are more noble than theirs?"

"Aye," he hotly admitted. His gaze drifted down her throat. Her taut nipples pressed against the fabric of her damp bodice. "You've been a burr in my breeches since I first saw you. But have I plied that tight-laced mind of yours with visions of rape? I've not touched you."

"I do not wish to be plied by anything of yours, Captain Drake."

"Indeed." He grinned at her choice of words. Already the pain of his wound had receded as he found solace in her wit, or lack thereof.

"A first no doubt in your long line of conquests," she prodded.

He traced a finger around the delicate curve of her jaw and felt her shock at his touch. "Whatever gave you the idea the line was so long, Arabella?"

"I . . ." The sweep of her dark lashes bore distress. "Quit calling me that name. 'Tis unseemly to be so personal."

Talon could do naught but humor her. The strange request was no less peculiar than her complicated personality. "And by what name do you wish to be called, sweet?"

"Lady Welles to you, pirate."

"Not anymore, milady wife."

Her luminous eyes snapped to his. "I'll never be that."

His fingers threaded into her hair, pressing her into the pungent earth, telling her otherwise. "You think not?"

"Surely, you jest. You would . . . here?"

"Do I seem the type prone to humor, sweet?"

His mouth molded to her slightly parted lips, swallowing her strangled cry of protest. He intended only one kiss, to savor what he'd tasted in the drawing room, beneath the very face of their vows, but his carnal need was ruinous of that goal. She'd showed him passion then, astonishingly intoxicating, and he felt it now, dark and dangerous, cascading over him.

Her tongue fluttered against his, tentative at first, her cries mutating into a low groan. He probed the soft contour of her mouth. She tasted like springwater, hot like sunshine.

Coherency vaguely filled his senses. He broke the kiss to find her eyes trapped with confusion . . . then panic.

The air took on a charged hush.

Without warning, her knee caught Talon's groin. "Never, kiss me again, pirate!"

Pain shuddered through Talon. His vision blackened. She shoved against him. He rolled off her, doubling over on his side. In a flurry of petticoats, she scrabbled up the embankment. He reached out, snatching the hem of her skirt. With a cry, she went to her knees.

"Jeezus!" he gritted out, straddling her. "Where the hell did you learn to fight like that?"

She panted as she tried ineffectually to kick out. "My father wanted a son."

"How fitting that he got you instead."

Angry tears shone in her eyes. "Had I a sword, I'd run you through."

"When my back is turned, no doubt. A custom passed down through the family line."

"Son of a jackass! Bastard!"

He glared at his assailant, her voluminous eyes exquisite in their fury. "I am neither, girl." Talon climbed sluggishly to his feet.

"I know all about who and what you are, milord pirate. Custom indeed. You're the son of a condemned pirate and murderer."

"Am I, now?"

"I saw the execution warrant." She breathed hard as she crawled backward on her feet and hands to escape him. "I know why you hate us, why you've attacked and destroyed my family's ships."

Talon stalked her movement, ever close to wrapping his hand around her slim throat. "Have I put a notch in your family's ill-gained fortunes, sweet?"

"You have no conscience for what you do to people. For what you've done to us."

He paused just above her. "A grand sentiment when your family boasts the biggest slave trade in the West Indies." The shock on her face registered plainly. "You're a hypocrite, sweet."

"And you're a liar. Mother would never . . . we bank in sugar."

"That, too. And pirate's plunder, as well. My crew has yet to be disappointed for the small effort it takes to capture one of your ships—and sink her."

Furiously, she swiped the hair from her face. "You lie." Her wet gaze darted in panic. "Let me go. I'll see that you're paid well—"

"Your value cannot be measured in gold."

"Everything has a price. Even you, Talon Drake. What do you want?"

"I could ask for your soul and it wouldn't be enough, Arabella."

"Let me go. Please——"

Talon crouched above his bride. His boots creaked. Instinctively, she twisted away. "I'm not kidnaping you, Arabella." Rare humility suppressed his voice. He knew her pride and what it must be costing her to beg. "Your father came to me. I'm bringing you to him."

Her eyes wet with disbelief, she shook her head as if to deny his words. "I don't believe you."

"That doesn't change the facts."

"He would never turn to you. Not against Harrison."

Her naiveté incensed him. Perhaps because it made her appear less intelligent than he knew she was, and vulnerable when he knew she wasn't. "Kendrick tried to have your father murdered for the map he carries. When that didn't work, he decided to marry you as a way to blackmail your father. Your father found me in Tortuga. A fitting place for the likes of a Welles running for his bloody life." His eyes were dark upon her unsteady gaze. "But know this, milady wife. Your father owns more than my life at this moment. On his word, he holds the proof that will clear a grave injustice done to my family. Proof to set me free. You are my insurance, a reminder of the bargain between us."

Her expression stilled with shock.

"He came to me because he needs me to fight Kendrick. A battle I wage with no conscience for the consequences. I would gladly slit the bastard's throat. But if your father betrays me in this"—his knuckles grazed her skin, lifting the tangled hair from her face—"I have not earned my reputation through my gentle nature, sweet."

A single tear rolled down her cheek to break against his thumb. "You will fail, Talon Drake," she fervently whispered. "I'll defeat you. I swear I will."

By God, he'd suffered enough of her pride. Talon set his teeth and yanked her to her feet. He started walking with her in tow. Leaves scattered before each strident step. The pale moonlight lit his way. He ducked twice beneath low hanging branches. When he finally reached his men, who were clearly in a state of agitation waiting for his return, the girl sagged to the ground at their feet, her tattered gown flaring around her like a wilted flower.

"Don't let her out of your sight again. Do you understand?"

"She promised," Charlie sneered. "On a cross, she did."

It rankled him to know that his men had been so easily cuckolded. Wife or no, he wasn't foolish enough to bend or go soft in the head for the chit. He'd be damned if his men would either. "Put her on a leash if you have to. We'll move again at dawn. Wake me," he said, his annoyed gaze sweeping over each of them.

Even in the pale light, Talon noticed the black eye Jaime sported. His boatswain seemed intent on polishing his cutlass and refused to look up. Then his gaze fell on Harry who absently rubbed at the bruise on his whiskered jaw.

Talon didn't have to ask what calamity had befallen his men. He'd suffered more than the lot of them put together. "And I'll trust you to see that my charming wife doesn't plunge a knife in my heart while I'm not looking."

He straightened to his full height. The tenderness between his legs was nearly his undoing, but he refused the indignity of limping as he sought refuge in a quiet spot by the creek where he could clean his wounds . . . and contemplate what fate had decreed he suffer. Hours passed before he finally dozed. It seemed he had only just drifted to sleep when someone shook him awake.

"Captain, you must come with me."

A faint line of gray marked the horizon. "What is it, Charlie."

"Something's wrong with yer wife."

Sleep vanished. Talon followed Charlie. His new bride was lying beside a tree, curled with her knees pressed against her chest, her body shaking violently. Alarm coursed through Talon. He dropped to his knees beside her. Her brow was cool.

"What happened?"

"She's been like this all night."

He glared at his men. "And you didn't think to get me?"

"She wouldn't let us."

He'd never witnessed a more barbaric lot of men cowed single-handedly by a girl. "Get some water."

"She's not been holding a thing down, Cap'n. We've tried."

He placed a hand beneath her head. The girl's heavy-lidded gaze lifted to encompass him. "Go away," she groaned.

"Arabella." He looked up at Jaime. "We have to get her to Sulley."

"The settlement at Smuggler's Cove is less than a mile from here, Cap'n. We can get a room above the tavern."

Talon didn't want to take any chances going to that den of wolves with his young wife.

"Cap'n, if the *Fury* isn't waiting fer us . . ."

"Jaime, I can't carry her. Take her. Harry, find Marcus if he's at the rendezvous point. If not, meet me at Smitty's Tavern."

With a sidelong glance at the girl, Harry nodded.

"Cap'n," Parrot said after Harry left.

"Not now, Parrot."

"Oi've seen the likes of this before," he said, ignoring Talon's curt dismissal.

Something in the urchin's tone warned Talon to listen.

Parrot shuffled his bare feet, stirring up dust. "Outside the opium parlors at Port Royal . . . The streets be filled with those what need the drug and don't 'ave the quid to buy it."

Talon dropped his gaze to Arabella trembling in his arms.

"They calls 'em addicts, Cap'n."

Shaking violently, Regan could hear voices drifting from a great distance, like disembodied heads. Swirling. Torturous. Her stomach cramped, leaving her gasping for breath. The heat suffocated her. She was in a bed. Someone put a cool cloth on her forehead. She tried to tear it off but her hand was gently blocked.

"Save your fight, girl, for when you're stronger."

The voice seemed out of place among the chaos muddling her head. Her eyes opened. "Talon . . ." His dark hair was pulled from his face, as if hastily tied back with a thong. Shadows darkened his eyes with worry, making the silver gaze hauntingly beautiful. Regan touched her fingertips to his stubbled cheek, unaware that she'd done so until his eyes flickered with surprise.

Suddenly confused, she dropped her hand. A sense of urgency disturbed her. Did Talon endeavor to kill her now, for she would never betray Harrison. "Why don't you . . . get it over with?" she said weakly, aware that it took most of her strength to talk.

He brushed the damp tendrils from her cheek soothing the wet rag over her forehead. "I prefer to slay my victims standing up, milady. Not lying down."

He effortlessly secured his arm beneath her head. "Drink this."

She gripped his hand. "When this is over . . . what's going to happen to me?"

The look in his eyes brought her in check. "Swallow, Arabella."

A warm pewter rim touched her dry lips. Liquid dribbled over her chin. She grimaced, shoving the hand away. Still he held it to her mouth, forcing her to drink.

This wasn't like the broth Harrison gave her. This did nothing to ease the cramping pain in her belly. She shivered, but not from cold. Something soft wrapped over her. A blanket.

Somehow, she slept.

Dreams like tattered sheets of vellum tossed in her head. Bits of faded memories. She was running free, a child again. Sugarcane grew for miles in every direction, like spring grass higher than she could see. No limp crippled her. She could run. She could fly!

"Go, little monkey."

His laughter echoed behind her as she ran past him in her breeches through the fields to the beach. *"You make old Nicholas's heart ache to see you dressed so, chéri."*

"You're not so old." She laughed.

Taller than any who worked the plantation, his sun-bronzed skin gleamed with sweat. He was Mama's friend, a bondservant. And Regan adored him.

"What kind of girl wears pants?"

"The Rose has docked, Nicholas. Father is back."

Fitting that he got you instead.

Bawdy singing drummed her consciousness. The faraway sound of gunshots made her gasp. Wild with fear, she bolted upright.

Darkness surrounded her, consuming her. Something horrible lurked in the shadow beyond her vision. Terrified that it would find her, she frantically searched for an escape. She had to escape.

Warm hands were there again applying gentle pressure around her flailing arms, subduing her terror.

"I must find a way out . . . make the dark go away."

"Go back to sleep," the whisper coaxed and soothed. Deceptive, for it came from the darkness. "Nothing will happen to you."

"You . . . don't understand." Another spasm of pain gripped her. She gritted her teeth. Her stomach wrenched.

"She'll not be walking again. Infection has set in."

"Mama."

Mama held her, stroking her hair, easing the pain.

But the pain wouldn't go away. It never truly did.

"It . . . hurts."

Someone wiped the moisture from her cheek. Father didn't allow tears. *"Impudent child. You're not trying hard enough to walk."*

She would do anything to banish the disapproval from his face. "I'm trying." Had she not always done as he asked? Dusky shadows lengthened in the room, trapping the heat. Sweat coated her body. Harrison knelt beside the bed sponging her arms. *"Swallow. This will help your strength."* The sweetness made her stomach twist. Regan didn't want the tea. *"Your father is here. He will be proud if you walk. Do it for him."*

"Arabella," he called again forcing her to drink.

She opened her eyes at the name. "You left me," she whispered, drifting away again. "I was so afraid."

A little girl's weeping filled the space in her head. *"You're my only friend,"* Arabella whimpered.

Regan tossed. *"How could you leave me?"*

"I didn't know what to do. I was so frightened."

"Not your fault."

"Do not fear, little monkey. Old Nicholas found you. No harm will befall you. I pulled you from the cave."

Regan felt the tears. "But I'm afraid."

"I know," a voice whispered.

"It hurts," she gasped.

Strong arms wrapped around her. "It'll pass."

"Am I going to die?" She believed she would.

"Not while I'm here. I swear. Not while I'm here."

Weariness swept through her. She relaxed in the arms of the one who held her, an angel who'd come to take the nightmare away.

"The pain will pass."

She felt the steady thump of his heart against her cheek. His breath brushed the fine hairs on her temple. Protected within his strength, she was safe.

The beast in the darkness drifted back into the shadows. She was no longer alone.

Regan did as the voice bade.

Sometime during the night, the pain began to ease. Her fitful sleep eased into slumber. The first she'd had in years.

Regan tasted salt in the heavy breeze that caressed her. The sea was nearby. Light from a flickering candle danced over the rough-planked floor and cast shadows against the paneled walls. She lay in a clean nightgown upon a spindly four-poster bed. Sheets covered her. An armoire, a washstand, and a chair made up the other furnishings in the tiny room. Caught by a sudden gust of wind, the curtains billowed. Regan turned her head toward the sound.

He was there, haloed in moonlight, braced with his hand against the windowsill, staring into the darkness. Stubble framed his profile. The white Holland he'd been wearing had been exchanged for a black silk shirt that laced loosely up the front. Black leather breeches were tucked into his boots. He wore a kerchief on his head, looking much the way he did when she first saw him.

It shocked Regan to realize he'd turned his head. That he was watching her. The amber light illuminated the strange emotions in his eyes. "You're awake."

Was that relief she sensed in his expression? Mindful that he had his own agenda for keeping her alive, Regan dismissed his concern as nothing less than mercenary.

"Where am I?" Her voice cracked in the stillness.

He came to stand over her. Regan clutched the thin sheet to her neck, erecting a barrier that would protect her from his strong presence. She confronted him with a frown, barely contained by the strange comfort his nearness aroused.

"You're safe for now."

She wasn't on the *Dark Fury*, which meant his ship had abandoned the rendezvous point, leaving them stranded in some Godforsaken hellhole. Smuggler's Cove. She was too exhausted to contemplate escape.

"What's been wrong with me?"

"Maybe you can answer that better than I?"

Was there some cryptic implication in his tone? She felt like she'd been poisoned, but the accusation remained unspoken. "How long have I been here?"

"Four days," he quietly answered. "You've been very ill."

Color heated her face. The very idea that this man so intimately served her most base needs . . . A hand came to rest on her cheek. The contact washed over her. She didn't flinch beneath his resolute stare. But neither could she breathe.

"It's never been my desire to see you harmed, Arabella."

She was beginning to detest that name. She possessed the absurd want of hearing her name on his lips. Regan, the other cousin. The one of no value.

Then she thought of Harrison, her parents, all the reasons for fighting him. Like his kisses and his touch, his kindness was a decoy to lower her defenses. He cleverly twisted her in knots.

They were enemies.

Bracing a boot against the bed, Talon leaned an elbow negligently on his knee. "Do I detect a hint of malice, milady wife?" His crooked smile shocked her. "That's good."

He dismissed her to take his place in the chair beside the bed. He stretched his legs out.

"Talon," she blurted out. She no longer hated him, and that frightened her.

Their eyes met and held. A dark brow lifted waiting for her to speak. His eyes were gentle as if he understood her confusion.

She wanted to thank him for making her feel safe. For chasing the pain away. For standing between her and the darkness. He had done all of these things when no one else, except her mother, ever had.

"Go to sleep, Arabella. You've a long way to go if you wish the strength to plunge a blade through my heart."

Regan suspected she'd done just that already. She wondered if he'd regret not letting her die when he'd had the chance.

Chapter Nine

When Regan awakened again, Talon was gone.

Sunshine filled the tiny room, an unhappy combination with the muddy heat of an approaching storm, and Parrot. Regan flinched, unsure which bode worse for her health.

Parrot turned his attention from the ripe plum he'd just bitten. Regan could almost forget her discomfort as she watched him chew the juicy wad down without choking. A plate of fruit, cheese, and bread lay on the rickety table beside him. By the looks of what remained, Parrot had bored of her waking and indulged in the feast himself.

"The cap bid me ta bring ya lunch, he did," Parrot announced.

Regan considered her appetite. Prudence checked her animosity toward Captain Drake. For someone who was so bent on vengeance, he guarded her health with a protectiveness she was unaccustomed to feeling.

Parrot made no move to assist as she struggled with the pillows. The exertion drained her. When he didn't bring her the plate, she lifted her eyes and found him suspiciously eyeing her.

Crossing his dirty feet at the ankles, Parrot relaxed in the chair. "Oi ain't no bugger slave." He puffed. " 'Sides, the cap, he says fer me not ta coddle ya, being 'is prisoner 'an all."

"Did he?"

"The cap, he ain't known fer takin' prisoners. Usually 'e just finishes 'em off with a quick *svvt, svvt*." He emphasized, swiping a finger across his throat. "He must be savin' you fer somethin' special."

Caring naught for her night-clad state, Regan kicked the sheet off. Modesty prevailed only in society and she was too hungry for feminine outrage. Swinging her bare feet onto the floor, she waited for the room to steady a moment before she stood.

"So where is the great pirate captain?"

" 'E 'an Jaime went out. 'E left me in charge."

The boast made her laugh.

Parrot jumped to his feet. " 'E did, I say!"

"And I've sprouted wings." Regan reached for the plate of food.

A rusty knife point impaled the table inches from her thumb. Regan didn't jump. Nor did she stir as she removed her gaze from the blade to confront her assailant.

"Don't think oi don't know 'ow ta use it," he swaggered. "Oi've killed plenty."

Her brow lifted. "You know what I think?"

"Oi don't care a bloomin' turd fer what ya think."

"You're not so tough." Despite her weakness, Regan grabbed the hilt of the knife before he suspected her intentions. "You're not so mean, either. And you've never killed a soul."

Regan jerked the knife from the table. "Do you know how I figured this out?" she demanded, sliding a finger over the blade tip. "Because you talk too much, like a bleating lamb asking to get his throat cut." In a skillful maneuver, she'd learned long ago, Regan sent the deadly blade sailing end over end through the air toward the wall beside the door—

And in that fateful moment, the portal opened. She gasped.

The blade impaled the wall with a loud thwang, vibrating furiously in the chipped panel near Talon's head. A death knell, surely as his gaze grimly shifted from the knife to Regan.

Fear swallowed her breath as the weighty silence that followed sounded ominously. Even Parrot didn't breathe.

"Despite what you think, dear wife"—Talon tore the knife from the wall with admirable restraint—"I'm the only thing standing between you and that riffraff outside this tavern. That and a pocket full of gold promised the innkeeper until the rest of my men arrive."

Her own ire piqued, Regan drew an impassioned breath. "And who protects me from you, Captain Drake?"

In a movement too swift for Regan to counter, he strode into the room. Showing no remorse that he might have misjudged her even a small bit, he dragged her to the bed. "Stay!" he commanded, then glared at Parrot. "Where did she get this knife?"

Parrot seemed to wilt beneath Talon's glare.

"I took it," Regan declared. "When he wasn't looking, I snatched it from his belt. Being the *trusting* child he is, 'twas easy enough."

Talon seemed more interested in studying Parrot's ashen face than in responding.

"And when I heard someone coming, I was hoping with all my heart 'twould be my captor," she added with so much dramatic flourish that he finally gave her his attention. "I told you, milord pirate. I'd do anything to escape." The words were no lie and in that truth, she knew Talon believed her. Let him think she'd tried to murder him.

Talon closed the short distance between them. Irritation replaced his anger as he surveyed her anew. "It's good to see you've made a swift recovery, sweet. It saves me from having to worry anymore about you."

"The pleasure is all mine, Captain Drake."

"At any rate"—the intensity in his gaze sobered her as his glance touched her breasts then rose slowly to her face—"it *will* be tonight. I assure you."

He smiled and Regan thought she might die. His height, the width of his muscular shoulders did much to block the light and set her heart fluttering in sheer panic. What did he mean, tonight?

With marked humor in his eyes, Talon straightened. "A guard is posted at this door and one outside the window. Don't do anything foolish, Arabella. You can't escape." At the door, his glance lingered on Regan before he quit the room. It fairly cauterized every nerve in her body.

After a moment, movement startled her. Parrot stood beside her, plate of food in hand.

"Oi'll not be makin' much of a pirate to let a lightskirt get the best a me."

It shocked her to see humility in his blue eyes. "What kind of life is that anyway, Parrot. You can escape with me."

Moisture spiked his thick lashes. "Ya be loyal to the wrong man, milady," he said quietly. "Cap'n Drake, he be the bravest there is. Oi'd not betray 'em, on me death, to the likes of the guvnor."

"But you don't even know Harrison Kendrick. How can you be so sure of one man against another?"

Parrot wiped his eyes. "Oi feel it in me gut," he said, eyeing her steadily. "Likes oi feel it here 'bout you, too. In me gut. The cap 'an you be like two peas in a pod. The same sort."

To be likened to a pirate. "I am *not* like Talon Drake."

"Ya both 'as courage." Parrot looked down at his feet. A fly buzzed around his head. He swatted it away as he contemplated his dirty toes. "The cap, he saved me life in that prison." He paused. "Even bleedin' as 'e was, 'e didn't let 'em touch me. They flogged 'em. Not a word did he make. Not a word."

Remorse hit Regan and she bit back a gasp. That any man should be so barbarously treated appalled her. But she'd seen the lash marks on Talon and a part of his pain became hers whether she willed it or not. She'd put him in that horrid place.

She focused on Parrot. "Why were you in prison?"

"Thievin'." He shrugged. "Oi was hungry."

"They were going to hang you for that?"

"They was goin' to hang me to punish the cap, milady, fer helpin' me."

Regan felt the color drain from her face.

"Believe it as ya will, milady. But it be the truth."

She stared at her plate, confusion marking her thoughts, leading her to believe it a sight better to lose her mind than suffer the truth of Parrot's words. He was wrong. Harrison would never be so barbaric. More likely, the guards had doled out their own brand of justice.

"Ya best be eatin' yer vittles, milady," Parrot consoled as if sensing her turmoil. "One what comes off the opium is more 'n likely ta die of starvation as not."

"Wait!" Regan stopped Parrot before he turned away. "What do you mean?" He regarded her blankly. "About opium?"

"Comin' off opium 'as killed lots a folks. Oi know. It beggered me ma and killed her, and that be the truth of it, milady."

Appalled, she said, "You think I've been on opium?"

"Haven't ya?"

"No." Regan thought back to the occasional dose of medicine that Harrison supplied for her leg. *He would have told me if there were dangers.* Wouldn't he? "Why the very idea is ludicrous."

Parrot shrugged, clearly oblivious to her turmoil. "Milady?" he asked earnestly. "Oi do 'as a question fer ya, if it don't be a bother ta answer."

"Maybe. What's the question?"

"How'd ya learn' ta throw a knife like that?"

The bittersweet memory came unbidden to her thoughts. "A friend showed me." Nicholas. He'd died shortly after Father sent her to live on Martinique to recover from her broken leg. "He found I was in need of entertainment and took pity on me."

"And yer pa allowed yer interest?"

Clearly, Parrot was under the mistaken impression that Father cared anything about what she did. "It was definitely a way to get his attention," she admitted. "One always had to be creative."

Parrot's grin exuded boyish charm as if he'd just discovered a kindred spirit. "I'll be leavin' ya to be about with yer privacy, milady," he said brightly.

"Parrot—" She stopped him again when he reached the door. "Does Captain Drake also think . . . does he believe . . . about the opium, I mean?"

He shrugged. "The cap, 'e don't much share what 'e thinks

'bout nothin'. Oi only knows, 'e didn't leave yer side, milady. Not once."

Cramped in the room all day, Regan found herself mad with anxiety by the time dusk settled into night. Talon's words measured her torment in the galloping of her heart. She dozed often, rousing awake when someone delivered food and drink. She'd tried to engage Jaime in conversation when he brought her dinner, and failed. Harry delivered water, ignoring her. By nightfall, Regan stood at the window with her arms crossed, looking at the backwater town.

The streets twisted in no coherent fashion, giving way to clustered hovels. Naked timbers sprang forth from the bog; either remnants of burned down taverns or never completed buildings.

Regan pondered the fate of such outcasts who found their lives entangled here. And felt lost.

Her stomach tightened at the thought of never seeing Harrison again, that no matter how hard she tried somehow she'd cause his downfall. Her reflection watched her back from the glass. The flickering light of the candle on the table behind her framed her face. Disheveled hair lent an air of seductive charm she'd never seen in herself. Strange that her emotions were less on edge than she remembered.

Parrot's profound words would not leave her. *Comin' off opium 'as killed lots a folks. I know. It beggered me ma and killed her.* All day she wriggled in and out of denial. Parrot was wrong. She'd been ill. Nothing more.

He didn't leave yer side, milady. Not once.

It came to her suddenly and fiercely that a huge traitorous part of her had succumbed to Talon's guile and charm, pirate that he was. Regan leaned her forehead against the cooling glass. So many lies twisted the space of her thoughts, clouding the truth.

She was just too tired to think.

Perhaps she'd consumed too much wine with her lunch. Yet, her nerves were less frazzled now than ever before, even if her heart was not.

"Now, what do I do?" She lifted her head and stared at

her reflection, prepared to thrash her weakness to a nub.

Her eyes fell on Talon's reflection in the glass.

"Perhaps I can offer you some entertainment in your moment of boredom," he quietly offered.

Regan whirled. "Stay away from me!"

Talon reached above her shoulder and yanked the curtains shut. "Standing in front of the window is asking for trouble."

She tried to slide sideways. He trapped her easily with his arm. "Have you enjoyed your day?"

"In this rat hole, I've been quite entertained."

"I should have left the knife. You might have practiced your aim on the roaches. Hone the old battle skills, so to say."

"Obviously, I haven't a need to hone my skills."

"Feeling rather chipper, are we?"

Regan lost her ease. He tipped her chin and his heavy-lidded gaze focused on her fluttering pulse before lifting to her face. It took a moment for both of them to realize someone was tapping on the door.

"Come!" Talon stepped away from her as Jaime entered with a tray of food. "We'll be dining in tonight, sweet." He ushered her to the bed and tucked the sheet over her. "If you don't mind"—his white grin was very dashing—"I'd prefer to keep your charms to myself."

Regan yanked the sheet to her neck. "If you don't mind, I'll not share them with anyone."

"Ah, but I do mind."

"Hrummph."

Talon straightened. Harry stood in the doorway carrying one end of a huge brass tub. "Where do ya want the bath, Cap'n?"

"The end of the bed will be fine."

Regan's gaze fluttered nervously as Talon's men entered with buckets of hot water and filled the tub.

"How are the . . . newest arrivals," Talon asked Harry.

"Drunk."

"Encourage the barkeep to keep them that way."

"Trouble?" Regan asked hopefully. "Surely, the great Captain Drake isn't afraid of another pirate ship's crew?"

"Fear has little to do with caution. Despite what you think, dear wife, you're far better served in my company than theirs."

Talon checked the bath and directed Jaime on the placement of their small feast. Regan stared. She found herself mesmerized by Talon's movements, his height, and the sound of his voice. He laughed when Jaime presented him with a chessboard and pieces.

He turned to find her watching him. "Perhaps tonight you can put your talent for warfare to better use."

"You play chess?"

"I do possess other pastimes besides the general maiming of the populace."

"You're talents are astounding, I'm sure."

His slow smile sent her pulse fluttering, and it had little to do with fear. "Perhaps you're curious to learn just how much?"

The door shut and Regan nearly jumped from the bed in terror. They were alone in the room, enemies by right, engaged in combat to the death. He made her so hot she couldn't breathe in the stifled confinement of the room.

"I could take you now as my wife."

His voice was no more than a whisper. But the truth of it froze her. In her heart, his presence battled with her animosity. Regan sensed she'd be a fool to deny his tactical advantage, yet she would find a way to fight. He must know she would never submit to him willingly.

"Enough," he suddenly said. He poured wine into two goblets and offered her one. "Do you wish the bath first?"

Reluctantly she took the goblet. His fingertips touched hers, purposefully she suspected by the brazen look in his eyes, but it didn't lessen the frissons of pleasure that shot through her. She drank with much relish. More than was warranted.

"You're still a little weak." He gallantly stripped the sheet away. "Let me help you. The water is getting chilled."

Regan's gaze swung to the bath where steam rose and hovered like a vaporous cloud. "I don't want a bath."

"Don't tell me I've married a lady adverse to bathing."

"You're mocking me terribly."

Talon placed a booted foot on the mattress. His eyes twinkled. Her seditious mind observed him. Thick lashes framed silver eyes beneath one slightly cocked brow. The noble curve of his nose and sensual lips hinted boldly at the manner of his passions.

"It's not my intention to mock you. Come." He offered her his hand, as if the gesture signified a truce somehow. At least for the night. "You need a bath, if for no reason except that it'll make you feel better. I've even supplied you with a new nightdress."

He took her empty wine goblet and pulled her from bed, leading her with purpose to the tub. "Soap." He grinned handing her a ball of scented lye. "Compliments of Parrot. As is the wine," he added. "Now bathe. On my honor, I'll not intrude."

"Honor, indeed."

But Talon did as he promised. Turning the chair away from the bath, he faced the window and opened the curtains to the darkness. While waiting, he indulged himself in a slice of mutton.

Talon was correct. Lightly scented with spice, the water hinted of decadent paradise. She unfurled in its depths. Her long hair floated around her like silken kelp. One eye snapped open. Talon propped his boots against the windowsill. Clearly at ease, he crossed his ankles and sipped a glass of wine.

Regan closed her eyes, inhaling the steam. Her nipples hardened. She absently caressed her breasts, luxuriating in the sensuous way it made her feel. An inexplicable heat spread outward from her belly, sharpened by Talon's intimate presence.

Irritated, Regan sat up, splashing water over the rim. Talon continued to stare out the window, a picture of saintly patience.

She washed and scrubbed every inch of her body, including her hair, stealing periodic glances at the pirate only to find him true to his word. He still hadn't moved. Rivulets of moisture clung to the lead glass and Regan wondered why he didn't open the window and let in fresh air.

When she finished, she hastily donned the new nightgown.

"Your other clothes are clean and pressed," he said. "I'll bring them to you tomorrow."

Shyly, she joined him at the table.

Unlike Arabella, she couldn't think of a single witty response. They quietly ate and shared another glass of wine. Conscious of Talon's eyes on her, Regan kept her own averted. She felt the urgency to cover herself from his gaze, but sensed the uselessness of such an effort. He meant her to be half-naked or he would have delivered her clothes.

"You're very beautiful," he said quietly.

Compelled by his voice, Regan looked up. He raised the goblet to his lips and watched her over the rim. No one had ever told her she was beautiful. Such praises were always showered on Arabella to the point of obscurity. To hear the words now took her breath away.

He set the goblet down. "Are you a virgin?"

Regan's eyes flared instantly. "What kind of question is that?" The lively interest in his gaze made her nervously aware he knew exactly what manner of question he'd asked.

"Many things concerning you have piqued my curiosity."

Regan gripped her hands in her lap. She would not allay her nerves to him. "I also have questions for you, Captain Drake."

Their gazes held. "I imagine you do." He cleared away the dishes and set up the chessboard.

Regan watched his hands. Twice the size of hers, one bore a thin scar that curved into the black cuff of his sleeve.

He offered her the first move.

"Are you really an earl?" she asked the first question.

Talon moved his knight. "My peerage was never attained by the king. As my father's eldest son, I inherited the title upon his death."

Encouraged by the ease of his answer, Regan proceeded with another question. His raised hand stopped her. "My turn." His grin flashed white. "Unless you're afraid of my questions."

Trying to appear indifferent, Regan studied the board. "Ask what you want."

He moved another pawn. "How close are you to your father?"

"My father . . . loved me in his own way. But he never wanted a girl. After a while I accepted that."

Regan countered his move with a bishop. Talon's finger brushed over the queen, almost seductively as he contemplated her attack. Hair, the same midnight color of his head, specked his hands. Regan felt his gaze on her.

"Why did your father come to Jamaica?" she asked, suddenly remembering her next question.

"The king granted three thousand acres to anyone wishing to settle in the new colony. My father was the second son to a poor earl and didn't inherit the title until after I was born." He took her pawn, leaving her queen open to attack.

The move irritated Regan.

"I never lose," he said quietly, sensing her competitive bent.

Intent on the board, Regan captured his rook. Shamefully boastful, she smiled. "Neither do I, milord pirate." Her triumph bid her to ask another question while he was distracted. "Your father chose to stay in Jamaica? Why?"

"My father, much to his father's fury, married a Spanish noblewoman from Puerto Bello." He poured another glass of wine, drawing her gaze to the bottle, then slowly to his eyes. "Needless to say"—he tasted the wine, drinking in her gaze until she blushed—"I'm glad he remained stubborn over the matter, and in time, he did eventually inherit."

Talon handed her the goblet. With considerable, vexing effort, Regan returned her attention to the game. In the next move, he took her queen, the most powerful piece on the board. Still holding the goblet with the memory of his lips imprinted on its rim, Regan gaped at the catastrophe. Clearly, the man lacked principles of fair play. Setting down the goblet, she focused on what remained of her defense.

His black shirt was lightly laced and revealed his chest. She couldn't seem to dismiss him enough to concentrate. His elbows rested on the table, the casual strum of his long fingers marking time.

To retreat now would name him the victor. Suddenly, she realized she was enjoying herself. "I've been told stubbornness is the devil's trait."

"Stubbornness alone can keep men alive when nothing else can."

She knew he spoke of himself. "Someone a long time ago told me it was courage in its purest form," she returned.

He held her gaze. "It's dangerous. I welcome it in my friends . . . and respect it in my enemies."

"You have a lot of enemies, Captain Drake."

"Aye." His expression flickered strangely. "But none so formidable as you." He looked down at the board before she could respond. "Stalemate, milady wife." The barest suggestion of a smile pulled at his lips, forcing Regan to consider that he spoke nothing of the game. "You play chess well."

"I'm glad to see us in accord over something, milord pirate."

His eyes lifted. "I was told you didn't play."

Regan felt the blood drain from her veins. "There's a lot you don't know about me," she managed with aplomb.

Talon's silver eyes seemed darker, altering her pulse.

"All I know is that I wasn't prepared to get you."

The irony of his words filled Regan with dread.

"My bath awaits." Uncurling his frame from the chair, he towered over her. His eyes hesitated on hers before his hands went to the ties on his shirt.

Regan's heart leapt in perverse anticipation.

He grinned. "You can watch if you choose."

Snapping her mouth shut, Regan plopped in his empty chair and faced toward the window, unable to countenance the intoxicating heat swirling around her. She listened to the splashing behind her as he climbed naked into the tub. More wine and she felt her muscles loosen. After what seemed an eternity, she finally relaxed in the chair, and adjusted her senses to the night. The golden light from the room flickered in the glass . . . and Regan's gaze came to rest on Talon's reflection in the tub.

Her breath caught.

Leaning comfortably against the rim of the tub, Talon idled in the spice-scented water. Corded muscles rippled the sleek skin of his arms and chest as he laced his hands behind his head and watched her reflection with more than casual interest. Her temper boiled.

He'd tricked her!

While she'd been thinking kind thoughts of the miscreant, he'd been watching her bathe all along. The very idea!

Incensed beyond repair, she jumped up. Furiously, she jerked the curtains shut, whirling on her sneaky captor. Her gaze slid to the wall where his weapons were, and knew the moment she realized her mistake. He came out of the bath . . . every golden muscular inch of him, sleek and dripping, menacingly shaped by the flickering candlelight that glowed around him.

Maidenly shock paralyzed her. The rigid length of his arousal stretched tautly from a dark cloud of hair. She'd never seen a naked man before, or imagined such stark beauty carved from simple flesh.

Heat suffused her face, her body, robbing her of breath.

Her glance flickered to his eyes, faintly challenging, his wolfish grin easing into a slow smile.

She was trapped! No animal could be more terrified or more furious by his total lack of shame.

She leaped past him and reached for the pistol. Water sloshed a heartbeat before Talon grabbed her wrist. Droplets showered her.

"Bastard!"

Pinning her back against the wall, he jerked the gun from her hand, subduing her flailing fists. "You have much to learn of wifely behavior, sweet," he gritted out. "It's time I teach you."

Regan struggled. The water from his body soaked her clothes, molding the thin batiste to her like a wet glove. The masculine scent of him filled her senses. A fierce roar sounded in her ears.

Her breath came in pants. "You're a liar . . . milord . . . pirate. A liar!"

"I said I would not intrude. What word did I break?"

"You twist lies until they're truths. Even you believe them."

"And you hear what you wish to hear."

"Let me go!"

"No, milady wife." Hot breath mingled with hers. "Not

this time. Tonight you will be my wife in truth." His lips seized hers. She could not evade him.

Shamelessly naked, he braced her soft form between the wall and his body. His fingers threaded in her hair. He drank of her lips, consuming her struggles until there was naught but the tiniest voice to deny the pleasure that filled her core. He tasted of wine and steam, as intoxicating as the molten heat flowing between them.

"Deny me this," he whispered against her half-parted mouth.

She knew she could not. His hands dropped to the weight of her breasts, rubbing over her nipples. They hardened into tiny frissons of pleasure radiating through her.

Still the kiss went on and on.

Crushed against him, Regan's knees weakened. She wilted against his naked thigh. The tiny hairs prickled the smooth underskin of her leg. Her palms curled into fists as if to deny his power. As if to force her will to fight when she could not even raise a groan of protest. Seditious. He made her turn even on herself. Then her fingers went limp against the firm muscles rippling his arms.

Finally, he broke the kiss. Regan gasped for air. She felt the whisper of movement as he tore her nightgown over her head. He stared down at her intently, his heart beating against her palm, not nearly so fast as hers, but oddly unsteady. She tried to control the quivering inside her.

"Don't think for a moment I can forget who you are, Captain Drake." She was breathing hard and so was he.

His eyes remained steadfast on hers. "A sentiment I echo, sweet wife. You've tried to kill me twice."

"I am your enemy."

"An admirable one you are, too." He lowered his head and caught her bottom lip, sucking lightly. "And I suffer a need to know your passion. All of it."

His mouth caressed hers, hungrier than before. She tried to tear away. His kiss deepened, conquering her protests, scaring her senseless with a potent force she couldn't fight. She was dimly aware as his hands drifted to her hips, seeking and exploring, molding to her waist and breasts, down the curve of her back. Sensations stole through her. He cupped her bottom, lifting her higher on his thigh until she arched against his chest with dizzying euphoria.

"This . . . can't be happening."

He nuzzled the sensitive curve of her neck, her collarbone, his throaty groan joining hers. "Oh, but it is." The velvet whisper caressed her mouth.

His knee lowered. The floor creaked beneath her feet as Talon shifted her weight, going slowly to his knees in front of her. His hair brushed against a nipple as he bent to kiss her stomach and then her breasts, taking first one nipple, then the other into his moist mouth. Her hands wrapped in his hair. Cupping her bottom, he kept her standing while he teased her flesh beyond endurance. The wall scraped her back, but Regan lost herself to Talon's skilled touch and knew a shameless moment when she realized the world could shatter into a million tiny pieces and she wouldn't care.

"Talon," the whisper left her lips.

Talon felt the heat of her response, heard her faint gasps as he worked his tongue over her fevered flesh. He'd wanted to conquer her. His faceless demon, the devil that had destroyed his life. No mercy. The words rang over him now, a seductive reminder of the vengeance that warred in his heart. He'd not expected his young wife to respond to him. He'd not expected this dampening need that destroyed all else but the madness to bury himself deep within her.

Breathing an oath, Talon eased his hand between her thighs, the sweet musky essence of her filling his nostrils. He opened her to his probing hand and slipped a finger inside.

Christ, she felt hot.

Her strangled gasps filtered through his senses. "Talon . . ." The single word breathlessly broke, empowering him.

Holding her steady, he kissed the nether curls of her sex, tasting her fully on his tongue. She cried out, melting into his mouth and would have fallen had he not braced her with his hands.

Talon stood, lifting her, heedless of the pain in his injured arm as he brought her to the bed and pressed her beneath him.

"I can't . . . do this," she whispered.

"You can." He kissed her.

"Please . . ." Her voice became a plea against his mouth.

Talon lifted over her, looking into her misty brown eyes, half-lidded and drunk with passion.

"Stop. Oh, please stop!"

He could take her; she wouldn't fight him for long. But something stopped him. A nameless honor that refused him pleasures by art of force. She was his enemy. Mercenary that he was, he granted no quarter to his foe unless he was prepared to die for it. Yet, he knew instinctively what battle did to a body. It brutalized the spirit. Conflicting emotions warred, and the battle was not a gentle one. Taking her by force would destroy her.

The victor was the loser no matter which side won.

With her taste still strong in his mouth, Talon pushed himself off her. His gaze raked her firm body. He knew a harsh moment of regret that he possessed a single ounce of conscience denying him his right of conquest. A conscience was for people who gave a damn.

"Cover yourself, Arabella," he snapped.

She jumped at the command, willingly obeying him for once. Growling an oath, he dragged up his clothes and thrust them on, trying to ignore his wife huddled against the headboard.

Finally giving up all noblesse, he glared at her. His still active libido struck him as he prepared to depart from the room with some scathing comment appropriate to the occasion.

He could think of nothing—save the schoolboy notion that he wouldn't try so hard the second time. Inspired by this new insight, he looped the sash around his waist and gathered up his weapons before saying, "We'll be leaving here at dawn. If you can't walk, I'll carry you. Your new home awaits."

With a dashing bow, he bid his wife a fond adieu.

Chapter Ten

R egan tossed and turned, finding it impossible to sleep.
With at least an hour left before dawn, she finally kicked
off the sheet. "New home, indeed. The most notorious pirate
ship on the Main!"

She sat. Thick hair spilled over her in waves. Irritated with
the snarled mess, Regan snatched the comb off the stand
beside the bed to pick out the tangles.

"He mocks my captivity."

The ease, which he'd conquered her body tormented her.

Regan dropped the comb onto her lap and buried her face
into her hands. She'd never believed in such power between
a man and a woman. Hadn't Arabella been forever in and
out of love, as much as the seasons changed? Nor did Regan
believe that the perilous meandering of the heart could betray
her so mercilessly. Not her! That she wanted this man's touch
stunned her. Surely, Talon Drake, a skilled tactician, seduced
naïve virgins for sport.

"Curse you, Talon Drake." She glared at the bath, a plagu-
ing reminder of all that had passed, and shut her eyes against
the image of Talon's body, glorious in the golden candlelight,
mocking her still.

A thump sounded outside. Regan started.

Her door rattled. The noise was as blatant as the rain beating against the window. Her mind raced. Talon wouldn't dare
return to finish what he'd started this night. Feigning sleep

was out of the question. She'd have to be stone cold dead to ignore his touch.

Regan slid from the bed. Ready to defend her honor, she grabbed the stool beside the table, and rushed behind the door.

The minutes passed, and an inkling of self-doubt began to press against her thoughts. Could she smash Talon over the head? He deserved a cracked skull for everything he'd done to her. Eternal peril waited if she didn't have the courage to act. Talon Drake was dangerous. To her heart. To everything she believed in.

Regan stared at the door. Perhaps he'd changed his mind.

The latch jiggled again. Something broke the lock. Alarm raced through her. This wasn't Talon. She should scream. But the room was above a tavern. The thought of drawing the attention of a bunch of drunken sea rats aided her decision to remain prudently quiet. Perhaps the night visitor had the wrong room and would go away.

The door jolted open, letting in the clamorous noise from downstairs. The smell of rum and tobacco smoke assailed her senses. A large, bulky man crept stealthily into the room. Stark terror stopped her pulse. Regan smashed the stool on the intruder's bald head. Pain splintered up her arms. With a curse, the man stumbled to his knees and hit his forehead on the tub, crumbling.

The ugly sound of a cutlass sliding from its sheath alerted Regan to another man's presence. Still holding one pathetic piece of the jagged stool leg, she recoiled. A man rounded the door, nearly impaling her on the point of his sword.

The pirate's bearded countenance split into a broken-tooth grin. A mane of thick black hair framed his bristly face. Leaning a meaty fist against the door, he surveyed Regan with lust. "Blimey." The point of his cutlass eased down the front of her gown. "Lookie what old Weasel found? A lady fair ripe for me plucking."

"Then pluck this," Talon's voice sounded, "right between your eyes."

Regan felt her knees give. Her assailant stiffened as if he'd been shot. "If it ain't my old friend, Captain Drake."

"Old habits die hard, Weasel. You still slink in hallways like a stinking bilge rat."

The pirate turned his head to confront the voice. "You're a very popular man these days."

"Are you all right?" Regan heard Talon ask.

"Brings a tear to me eye," the pirate mocked, before she could answer. "Only you take a step, Drake, and I'll run the gal through."

"I'll blow your head off the first move you make. Back off."

"The *Viper*'s crew be downstairs. You shoot me, that bunch a blackguards'll be over you like maggots on a corpse. Maybe we can make us a bargain. Save us all our lives." His beak-like gaze slipped back to Regan. "The governor, he'd make a man rich fer bringin' his sister back."

Oh, Lord! A chill raked her spine. *Not now.* Yet, the lie had weighed heavily against her heart. She squeezed her eyes shut.

"What did you say?" Talon rasped.

"Seems he wants her back real bad." Weasel droned on. "But I figure I seen her first in that window." The man's pale gaze alighted on her with renewed interest. "Give me the girl. I'll see she gets back to the guvnor. No worst fer the wear you've given—"

Talon's fist smashed his jaw, sending him flailing backward over his fallen mate. "Bloody hell!" Weasel gripped the cutlass prepared to cleave his assailant. Talon's booted foot smashed his wrist. Crushing bone preceded Weasel's curdling cry.

Regan jammed a fist against her mouth to silence her scream. The pistol in Talon's hand swung around in cycloptic fury. Hate blazed over her. Certain that he meant to slay her, she longed for the dignity not to cry out. But she did.

"I'll shoot you, girl. God help me. You'll *not* raise arms against me again."

He thought she was going to attack him.

Regan dropped the puny weapon as if it burned her to the bone.

"Kendrick doesn't have a sister. Is he telling the truth?"

His knuckles were white on the weapon. "Answer me! Who are you?"

Regan clenched her hands. Courage stiffened her spine but could not make her form the words. Only a few hours before, she'd panted in his arms. Her deception bent her purpose, depriving her the gratification of seeing all his plans go to the devil.

"Answer me!"

Her head bobbed. "Yes."

"Christ . . . Yes what?"

"I'm his sister."

Downstairs in the tavern, the sound of fighting erupted.

"Do you hear that, Drake? Fighting," Weasel hissed. "We'll kill you, and still get the girl, you bleedin'—"

Talon kicked him in the jaw, silencing his taunt.

The fight in the tavern climbed the stairs into the hall. He looked at the pale girl, the mist that burned in her wide eyes, savoring her beauty even as he recognized the enormity of her treachery. "You have no idea what you've done," he whispered.

She'd beaten him at his own game. Talon retrieved the heavy cutlass abandoned on the floor. Testing his strength, he gripped the hilt in his left hand because he couldn't hold the weight of the weapon with his injured arm. He should leave her to these butchers. Drunken pirates would grant her no mercy. It wouldn't matter whose blue blood ran in her veins.

"Stay behind the door."

"And watch you die?"

"Isn't that what you've been waiting for?"

"Not defending me! I can use a sword."

Talon could imagine her skill once he turned his back. "If you move, so help me—" Sabers clashed in the hallway. He shifted his attention to the approaching battle. Shouts rent the air. Boot steps scuffed down the hallway. Someone approached. He would relish the fight. To hell with anything else. Let it be Kendrick or Roth.

Marcus filled the doorway. One baggy sleeve from his white shirt was torn. Panting from the fight downstairs, his brother's familiar grin joined with his relief. "Jeezus." Talon lowered the sword.

Marcus raised his cutlass in a dashing salute and clicked his boot heels. "Appreciative as always, big brother."

"Where's the *Dark Fury*? What the hell are you doing here?"

"Rescuing you, again, so it seems. Piers anchored the ship about a league north. Part of your crew is outside." He stabbed his fingers through his dark hair. "Hell, Talon, we saw the house burning. I'm sorry it took us so long to reach you."

"The *Viper* is nearby."

"Aye, and every militiaman on this island."

Talon's gaze swung on the girl standing rigidly behind the door. Marcus gripped the door and moved it aside, his soft oath shattering Talon's contact. Rumbling a vile sentiment, Talon quit the room, leaving Regan and Marcus gaping at the other.

No doubt existed in Regan's mind that this man was Talon's brother. Dark-haired and breathtakingly handsome, he was younger in age. But the similarity ended with their eyes. Jovial gray eyes separated him from Talon's hard-edged cynicism.

"Madam." He inclined his head and retreated after Talon.

Abandoned to the flickering shadows, Regan's gaze fell on the two prone bodies. Fighting erupted outside despite the pouring rain.

A feeling of despair crept over her, unyielding in its grip. Fear of Captain Roth's crew made her yield to Talon's undeniable strength. Even as she remembered his eyes, and the ruthlessness used to dispatch Weasel, she remembered more.

Memories that could not coexist with hate.

Sliding down the wall, she bent her cheek to her knees. She would stay and be glad for it. Not every man would be of Weasel's mettle.

"Milady!" Jaime burst through the door his arms overfilled with her clothes.

Regan jumped back to her feet to greet him.

"We have to hurry." He dropped the frothy bundle onto the bed. "He said I was to drag ya naked if I have ta."

Unexpected relief shortened her breath. Despising the tell-tale ache in her throat, Regan tremulously shook out her drawers from the pile. Jamie turned his back on her, his hard-lined countenance suddenly tainted with red. "Why Jaime," she couldn't resist needling, feeling a restless need to resume their familiar sparring. "I didn't know pirates could blush."

He snorted. Regan stepped into her drawers. Having the foresight to realize she could spare none of her scant wardrobe, she proceeded to dress over her nightgown.

"Soldiers are comin', milady. We must hurry."

Regan's heart thudded. Was Harrison with them?

She laced the bodice with shaky fingers. The knowledge that her brother might be near rushed dizzily through her. As she stooped to pull on a new pair of kidskin slippers, her bleak gaze hesitated on the unconscious intruders. Each wore a cache of weapons.

Lord, with Harrison so near . . . "Didn't Captain Drake tell you never to turn your back on me?"

Jaime spun. Instantly his gaze fell on the barrel of the pistol pointed at his head. She told herself that he should have known not to trust her.

"I need to escape, Jaime. Just move aside. Please."

"Will ye kill me then to see it done, milady?"

"You must move aside." Where was the cocky arrogant bastard who'd taunted her with rats and cockroaches? "Don't you understand? I can't go with you."

Outside a bell tolled. Gunshots punctuated the rumbling thunder of the storm. Movement behind Jaime stirred her gaze. Parrot stood in the doorway. "Mum, fer meself, I'd as soon leave this place with ye than without. But fer 'is sake, if ye don't make up yer mind, it won't be matterin' none if ye shoots 'em or not."

Strength deserted her. Jaime would accept death over the dishonor of her escape. "Curse you . . ." She let the threat hang in the air. It was the least he deserved for all the misery she would endure because of him. "My blood is on your hands."

For once, Jaime remained speechless. He took the gun from her outstretched hand, then moved aside to allow her unfettered passage.

They descended the back stairs. Once outside, Regan stopped. Dawn framed the blackened clouds. She shivered in the slashing rain. All around her, chaos roused the town.

Talon was mounted on a horse, shouting orders to others near the stable. The wind whipped his dark hair around wide shoulders. Regan kept her head high even as she felt ill. Gallows' dancers all of them. And she'd put Jaime's life over her own. Fool that she was.

"Madam."

The voice spun Regan around. Marcus stood behind her, his white shirt plastered to his chest by the steady rain. Though his voice held a playful lilt, his eyes noted her seriously, before shifting to the merchant Talon was arguing with.

"There's a bit of disagreement," he said as if they were on a pleasant riding excursion and not running for their lives.

"Over the horses?" she scoffed. "Why not just steal them?"

Her sarcasm changed Marcus's manner. "Or we could just kill the merchant and be done with it. Hmm?" Motioning toward the horse snorting unhappily at his back, Marcus lifted Regan into the saddle and climbed behind her. "But my brother, pitiless bastard that he is, doesn't suffer for a lack of conscience. The man is an old friend of our family. He aided Talon. Kendrick will burn the tavern to the ground. The merchant won't leave."

Fury flushed over her. "You make Harrison to be a monster."

Marcus spurred the mount forward.

"Where are we going?" Her voice emerged in panic as he galloped past Talon and another score of men mounted double on rangy horses.

"It'll be a race who can reach their ship first." The wind dragged his voice away. "Us, or Roth's crew."

Regan turned to look at him. With much flourish, he amplified his enthusiasm. "I love a good race!"

They traveled for hours over wet terrain unbroken by civilization. Talon remained far behind, allowing Marcus to lead the way to the ship. Hot mist clung to the ground in places where the rain finally stopped. Then Marcus crested a hill and the world opened with breathtaking ease before her.

Below in a protected lagoon, *Dark Fury* rolled in the swell. The wind had picked up a knot since morning. Even from this distance, she could hear the crash of breakers against the shore.

Talon rode up. A firm grip on the reins steadied his nervous mount. Winded, with tousled hair, Talon fastened his gaze on the ship, before his head lifted and he scanned the Caribbean beyond. Just over the grassy berm that horseshoed the lagoon, dark clouds boiled on the horizon blending with endless pewter-colored sea.

"Hurricane weather," Talon said over the wind.

"What are you planning?"

Talon's gaze shifted to Regan. The cold steel of it touched her deeper than a knife.

"The plan hasn't changed," he told Marcus. "We still have to get Arabella away from Kendrick. I only hope it isn't too late."

Chapter Eleven

Wind buffeted the waves, nearly laying the longboat on its side. Someone steadied it against *Dark Fury*'s rocking hull. Marcus caught Regan's hand as Talon lifted her to the ratlines hanging over the side of the ship. Unfazed by the ship's dizzying height, men clamored up the ropes like a horde of monkeys. Even Parrot managed the task with artful speed. A wave crashed over her. She gripped the rough hemp. Her life depended on not letting go.

"Do you wish a sling to help you board, milady?" Marcus yelled.

"We've not the time," Talon snapped and proceeded to climb.

A morass of uncertainty swallowed Regan. Hampered by heavy, wet skirts, climbing had never presented her with such dubious consequences. Not since she had broken her leg and learned to walk again did anything challenge her so determinedly.

"Today would be nice time to start," Marcus shouted when she didn't move.

"Today would be a nice day to drown!" Regan lifted her eyes skyward. Talon was already high above her. Even injured, he possessed the powerful grace of a cat. She felt lost.

Regan reached hand over hand and started to climb. Finding purchase with every step, she slowly scaled the wall of rope. The sea banged her mercilessly against the hull, smashing her knuckles. Wet skirts wrapped around her legs. With arms trembling from fatigue, she reached down and tried to untangle herself.

"Take my hand!"

Regan focused on a pair of black boots. Salt spray stung her eyes. Her blurry gaze lifted past a muscular thigh and fixed on Talon's face. His eyes were dark with worry.

"Dammit! Take my hand."

Too terrified to remove one finger from her deathlike grip on the rope, she didn't budge. Talon descended, his face intent as he yelled again for her to grab his hand. He could drop her and no one would ever question that he'd committed murder.

But Regan knew she couldn't remain where she was. Her illness the past week had robbed her of much strength. Tearing one hand from the ropes, she stretched her arm out. The sea dipped again. Regan's other hand slipped. For a terror filled moment she flailed, then was swinging from Talon's grasp high over the water. His enormous strength kept them from falling. Like a pendulum, she dizzily rocked, until Talon lifted her beside him.

Their eyes met. "Put your arms around me," he warned her unnecessarily, his voice tight with pain. His injured arm twisted in the thick hemp.

Someone from the deck grabbed her wrists and hauled her over the side. She pitched headlong into Piers. *"Chéri."* He pulled her upright. "You give Nicholas a fright."

Regan's thundering pulse stopped at the familiar memory. She lifted her gaze to scan the tattooed visage, and wondered helplessly if she'd suddenly conjured up a ghost. Surely, fatigue rendered her incapable of coherent thought.

"By God! Where is she? Where's my daughter?"

Regan stared in disbelief as Uncle Robert pushed through the men. Lord. Talon hadn't lied. Robert was here. Suddenly, more than anything, she wanted to shrink into the ship's planking.

Talon climbed over the side. With staggered breath, he braced his palms on his knees. His head lifted at the sound of her uncle's voice and he straightened. Robert stopped in front of her, his puzzled gaze growing dark. "What the—"

Talon pulled Regan past the crew. "Not a word, Robert. Not one damn word!"

"What do you mean? Not a word. Where's Arabella?"

"Piers!" Talon called, "If he disobeys me again throw him overboard."

"The hell, you say . . ." Robert stammered, his gaze darting to Piers. "All right." Robert glared at Regan. "Not a bloody word."

Talon shifted his attention to Marcus, who seemed amused by his tact. Obviously, they both shared the same sentiment concerning Robert Welles. Then Talon's gaze touched on every face, lifting to encompass the men in the shrouds.

The clank of ratchet and pawl could be heard as the long-boat was pulled aboard. Rain drizzled against the deck. A hundred and fifty feet up the masts, colorful pennants snapped in the lusty wind, a vigorous contrast to the crew's silence. Almost a hundred men lined the deck and shrouds.

"Welcome back, Captain," someone yelled from the fore-castle. The crew stirred as a steady rumble of ayes followed.

The ship careened, throwing Regan backward with the roll. Talon steadied her in front of him. Like heat to ice, his body pressed against her backside. She gave herself over to his protective arms. His warmth fed strength into her limbs and without admitting it, she was grateful he spared her the in-evitable confrontation with Robert.

"The *Viper* is in the offing, men!" Immediately the deck came alive. "Up with the main!" The black mainsail unfurled and bloomed against the stormy sky. "Set course north by northwest. The helm is yours, Marcus. Take us out of here."

Turning on his heel, Talon shoved open the oaken door that lead down into the stern galley. He lifted her over the twelve-inch coaming that prevented water from spilling into the living quarters. No lamps lit the narrow corridor. He pulled Regan inside a room, then kicked the door shut behind him.

Without a word, he dropped his grip around her waist and walked to the desk back-lit by the huge stern galley window that framed the entire tail wall of the room. Outside rain pummeled the filigree panes, reflecting like crystalline tears on the thick, blue Turkish carpet that covered the wooden floor. The room smelled of aged leather and spice. It smelled of *him.*

Regan shivered as she briefly assessed Talon's quarters. Elegantly paneled in dark wood, it reflected the image of a man she was only beginning to glimpse. A massive square-poster bed built into the bulkhead behind her faced the window. Bookcases, filled with intricate gold-leather volumes, shared another wall with the desk. Beautiful lacework cabinets housed bottles of fine brandy, Dutch blue and white delft, and crystal glasses, all bracketed in place by a thin copper bar. The room bespoke nobility.

A half dozen wooden lanthorns attached to rings above the cabinets banged the wall with the ship's rocking movement. The creaking motion made Regan queasy. Disheartened, she looked at Talon standing behind the desk watching her. Everything about him was hard and cold, except his eyes. His eyes burned. A document she recognized as their marriage certificate was spread out over scattered charts, as if he'd just read the signature scrawled so intimately below his. An awful lump closed her throat.

Scurried footfall above invaded the silence. The ship veered to starboard. Talon rode the movement with the graceful skill of his station. Regan had long since lost her sea legs. She hit against the bed and sat abruptly on the mattress. Her pulse throbbed. She was exhausted, emotionally drained. Even of fear. There was naught she could do to escape his rigid scrutiny.

Talon leaned with his hands braced on the desk. "What kind of foul trick have you dealt me?"

For all her pretense to bravery, Regan couldn't stop the tears that blurred her eyes.

"Did you think to find me content to be deceived by yet another Welles? You risk everything with this act of stupidity."

"Stupidity!"

"Aye!" He slammed his fist onto the desk. "You lied to me."

"*You* kidnapped *me!*"

Clawing a hand through his hair, Talon whirled to the

window. "You should have told me who you were." His voice seemed filled with ache and vulnerability.

She didn't want to feel for him. Bristling with the injustice of it all, Regan jumped to her feet. "You ruined my life the moment you stole into Arabella's room. Should I have revealed your mistake then? Would you have tossed me over the balcony? Considering your fondness for my family, you'd more likely have slit my throat."

Talon turned his head to stare at her.

"Or should I have said something after you threatened to give me to your men as all *valueless* cargo is shared among sea rats? Perhaps, I've endeared you to our family cause and you would forget your vengeance long enough to allow me to leave your company unharmed after I shot you. All of that aside, milord pirate; did you think I could sacrifice Arabella and see you destroy her? If I have ruined your plans . . . then I'm glad!"

"You test me, Regan. God's teeth, but you test me."

The sound of her name on his lips shocked her. Unable to summon the voice of restraint, her aplomb vanished in a mist of rage. She despised the intimacy he forced on her.

"Nay, milord pirate. You test me. Beyond all that is human, I have endured your wrath upon my family. You killed my parents, Talon Drake. Attacked and destroyed their ship. You murdered them!"

His expression darkened.

"Perhaps my father wronged you in some way." She gritted her teeth, palming her temple. "Lord only knows how little I understood him, how much I needed to understand him. But Mama . . ." Tears bloomed and flowed over her cheeks. Despising Talon for bringing her to this shame, she swiped at her face. "Mama didn't deserve your wrath, or hatred. She didn't deserve to die. She was beautiful and kind. I loved her more than anything in the world. You killed her." She whirled looking for something to throw. "You murdered her. Now you would go after Harrison. He's all I have left."

Talon came around the desk, a firestorm bearing down on her, wracking her imagination with horrible images of retribution. She screamed and swung her fists. He caught her flailing arms. She kicked out but connected only with her wet skirts. "I will not allow you to hurt him," she sobbed. "I will not!"

Talon held her firmly, subduing her fight. Desperate to vent the rage harbored so deep in her soul, she fought until he forced her back against his chest, until her sobs melded with the creaking timbers of the ship.

"I hate you," she choked, unable to bear the strength of his arm beneath her breasts stilling her fight as if she were no stronger than a gnat. He'd stripped her of pride. She felt naked. Exposed inside and out. "You ruined my life. I lost my home. My mother. Even my brother changed. You took them all away from me."

Pulling her down with him on the bed, he trapped her in his lap. She fought him until huge sobs wracked her body. She hated his power over her. But his heartbeat against her ear was as palpable as the life force that surrounded him. She buried her face against his wet shirt. Frightened by the intensity of her emotions, her lack of control, and the old desperation that enveloped her to feel love, she clung to his tenderness. She needed him.

God had damned her, stealing everything and cursing her with feelings for the very man who committed heinous crimes against her.

Talon smoothed the salt-dampened hair from her face and waited for her tears to ebb. In time they did, and Regan sniffed, wiping her face with the wet hem of her skirt.

"I cannot change the past, Regan," he whispered against her hair. "God help me if only I could for all our sakes."

She shook her head, wishing to hear none of it. "Just send me back to Harrison. Let me forget this nightmare."

"I can't do that, Regan."

She sat up, blinking the tears back. "But you must."

"There's more at stake here than you know."

Icy darts stabbed through her. "But you can't keep me here. Is it because of that?" Her arm swung toward the desk. "The marriage?"

Tapping at the door intruded.

"Answer me!" Panic made her desperate. He had to send

her back. "The marriage was never consummated. And I'm of no value to you."

He set her off his lap and came to his feet. The knock on the door became more persistent.

"Kendrick must want you back badly to send his whole militia after me. Why, Regan?"

The question stole her guard. Clearly, he expected a revelation. The years of exile on Martinique no longer mattered as she realized her brother risked all finding her. "He's my brother. Would you do any less for yours?"

The silver eyes met hers. "I'm not Harrison Kendrick."

A fist beat against the door. *"Capitaine!"*

"Come," Talon called.

"I'll fight you," she whispered passionately.

The door opened. Piers's huge frame filled the entryway. He regarded them equally. "You are needed topside, *Capitaine.*"

Behind him an elfin man squeezed into the room, and Sulley burst through the door like an exploding cork. "Milord," he gasped. "They weren't going to let me in."

Talon grinned. "Sulley. It's good to see you safe."

"Aye, milord." He rubbed his arms and regarded Piers pointedly. "Despite the efforts of some."

"Have you seen to the boy?"

He sniffed indignantly. "The little guttersnipe is with Cook."

"Let him eat, Sulley. He needs it."

Talon turned back to Regan prepared to face the brittle anger sizzling in her eyes. Instead, her gaze was riveted to Piers. Unable to dismiss the discomforting notion that the two somehow knew each other, he made a mental note to talk to Piers later.

"Sulley, see that my wi—see that Lady *Welles* removes her clothes to be dried. If she doesn't, come on deck and get me."

Dismissing her outrage, Talon turned. He saw Robert standing behind Piers. "I want to talk to you, Robert. Now."

Talon left Sulley in the room with Regan. When Piers shut the door, Talon ordered a guard posted. "And see the deadlights bolted over the window. With the storm a brew, things will get rougher." Not to consider Regan's impetuosity for trouble. He knew her well enough to realize she'd risk her life to escape.

"Leave us a moment, Piers."

His quartermaster ducked out of the narrow passageway, leaving Robert to receive the full brunt of Talon's violent gaze. A distinguished man, even in his fifties, Robert Welles possessed intelligent brown eyes and the skinny bearing of a politician. Talon would not forget the man was once a formidable foe.

"You didn't tell me Kendrick had a sister."

Robert grunted. "He can't stand the sight of the chit. Had her shipped off to some uncle on Martinique the last I knew."

Talon felt a new surge of fury. Not that his young wife could maintain loyalty to a maggot like Kendrick, but that anyone should abuse that love so blatantly. "Then tell me why Kendrick wants the girl back so badly. Is it her wealth?"

"Regan's father willed everything to Harrison." Robert shifted uneasily. "Harrison was his stepson. The boy was like his own."

Disgusted, Talon sought fresh air on deck.

"I still hold you to our bargain, Drake," Robert called before he gained the steps. "Our agreement was that you marry my girl in exchange for my deposition."

"I'm well aware of our agreement, Robert."

"Without my testimony to the king you and your brother will remain hunted until you die. You need me."

Talon slowly turned. Something in his eyes made Robert blanche. "Kendrick has my beautiful Arabella as hostage," he blurted. "He'll do anything to get my map and keep me under his thumb."

The irony of the situation struck Talon like a blow. He gripped Robert by the collar shoving him against the wall. "I should have known you needed me too much to betray our bargain."

"Betray you! You're the only man who can fight Kendrick." Robert raked a shaking hand through his thinning brown hair. "When you're finally cleared, the crown will try to hang me, Drake. I need you to protect us. Arabella needs the protection of your name. You know what happens to families of convicted felons. God help me, I watched what they did to you."

"Better, Kendrick and his sister to save your own neck."

Robert had the decency to look abashed.

"And what of the treasure, Robert?"

The man swallowed. "I need that gold, Drake. Would you see my family impoverished?"

"For all your noble airs, you reek of treachery."

"Kendrick is your enemy. Not me! Never forget he murdered your mother and sister," Robert hissed as if Talon needed reminding of those facts. "And it was he who arranged your escape from prison. It was no accident that you sailed directly into Spanish hands. That galleon was *meant* to find you and your brother. I didn't do that to you. Kendrick did. He is mad with greed. Mad enough to kill Arabella if I go to the authorities!"

Unable to stomach any more, Talon gained the stairs to the deck, and threw the outer door wide. Wind buffeted him and caught in his shirt. Stepping over the coaming, he forced the door shut.

Piers and Marcus stood at the rail. Talon went to stand beside them. Sea air cooled his temper. Flying spray drenched him.

Marcus handed him the eyeglass. "She's weatherin' on us."

Talon took the brass scope. The *Viper*, canted over sharply, sliced through the churning sea a good knot faster than the *Fury*. Talon snapped the glass shut. Lifting his head to the sky, he measured the force of the gale. The *Fury*'s taut rigging vibrated through the surface of the deck. He didn't trouble with the notion that Captain Roth's maneuver was potentially fatal or that he would have to match it or risk being fired on.

"Kendrick must be on board. That would explain Roth's unusual stupidity," Marcus said.

Talon thought of Kendrick's sister imprisoned in his cabin. Immediately the thread of his concentration snapped. Even being back on his ship did little to tame his errant thoughts. But dismissing Regan Welles was like ignoring a toothache.

He tried to comfort himself with the realization that she made a valuable hostage. That he could use her somehow. Kendrick seemed intent on getting her back. For now, Talon would thwart that goal for the supreme satisfaction of beating Kendrick at his own game.

A moment elapsed before he recognized the distant hail from the crow's nest. "Sail ho!" Talon saw his lookout pointing eastward. Wedged between sea and sky, white sails tipped the horizon.

"A British man-of-war," Marcus said over the wind.

Talon estimated the time until dark. Blowing from east to north, the wind pushed *Dark Fury* away from Jamaica. "We'll stay on this tact for now."

Marcus's startled gaze focused on Talon. "The devil knows, we owe Roth and Kendrick. But even your talents can't bring that man-of-war to heel, big brother."

Piers, who'd shown remarkably more sense than Marcus in figuring Talon's gambit, slapped the younger man on the back. "No more talk of battle, *mon ami*. The *capitaine* has a plan. Let us fill our bellies and get some rest. Come nightfall there will be time for neither."

Chapter Twelve

Regan awoke with a start. Darkness enclosed the cabin. Nauseous from the ship's plunging passage, she struggled to prop herself up on her elbows. Instinctively, she sensed the direction of the ship had changed.

Sweeping the coverlet off her body, she tumbled out of Talon's bed. Heedless of her state of dress she found the door and flung it open. Only then did she breathe. In the faint amber light from the narrow corridor, Jaime slouched against the wall asleep. Obviously set to guard her, he'd succumbed to exhaustion instead.

Balancing herself against the rocking ship, Regan tore a wooden lanthorn from its mooring on the wall. She stepped over Jaime's legs to the stairs. Talon had not returned to the cabin. Lord. She needed to know what was happening.

The wind ripped the door from her hands. It banged wildly against the bulkhead of the quarterdeck. The hot gale sucked her breath away, tearing at her hair and clothes. An amber sphere of light from her lanthorn pooled in a circle around her feet, reflecting foamy rivulets streaming down the wet planking. Braced against the door's solid planking, she pushed it shut.

Despite the storm, the deck teemed with activity. Somewhere in front of her, Talon's strong voice pealed through the darkness.

His scarlet sash whipping in the wind caught her eye. Then

she could see him, a defiant specter, legs carelessly braced as the ship rode the waves. Regan's heart raced. Nothing protected him from the fury of the sea. He stood tall and formidable, his wide shoulders filling the dampened folds of his shirt.

She felt the ship begin to lie over to port. Her mind cleared. The *Fury* was heeling round back to Port Royal!

Sulley had informed her earlier that the *Viper* pursued them, clearly confident that Captain Drake would elude the threat. Cloaked by darkness, *Dark Fury* was invisible. She imagined they were passing directly across the *Viper*'s bow. No one would know because the storm blocked all light from the moon.

Part of her admired Talon's cunning and the ease with which he executed such daring. Then her mind plunged, struggling desperately for some recourse. They were heading back to Jamaica. He'd not altered his plan to kidnap Arabella.

Regan didn't understand this ungodly alliance between Talon and Uncle Robert. She only knew it boded ill for Harrison and Arabella.

"Keep her as near the wind as she'll lie, helm!"

"Jesu, we're cutting this damn close, Talon," Marcus barked from the quarterdeck above her.

"Right down their bloody throats—" Talon turned, the reckless grin vanishing abruptly when he saw her. His savage gaze dropped to the light in her hand.

Her heart hit her ribs.

Time froze, staring back at her with startling clarity. The light. She realized its significance at once. If she could make a beacon, the *Viper* might see them.

Foreboding rooted her to the deck. More light meant creating a fire. A seaman's worst nightmare: her only chance in the darkness. If someone from the *Viper* just glanced this way.

Furiously signaling toward her, Talon yelled to Marcus on the quarterdeck. The ship continued to veer steeply. There was no time to rationalize her act. Talon forced her into this position.

Regan moved away from the stern galley door, knowing if she didn't, she'd forever regret her cowardice.

She threw the lamp.

The lanthorn split on a pile of coiled robe. Flame burst over the wet hemp. Suddenly the *Dark Fury* plunged, sending Regan to her knees scrabbling for a handhold. A mass of seawater swept over the bow, racing aft down the length of the ship, drowning the fire. Spitting out salt water, she stared aghast, her success vanquished by the wretched darkness and fear of being swept overboard. Hair whipped her face. Then someone grabbed her waist, lifting her back to her feet. She stared up into Talon's blazing eyes.

"Goddamit, girl! What are you trying to do? Kill us all?"

"Captain Roth will see through this ruse," she yelled back in the shrieking hell that dominated the world around them. "You'll not make it to Port Royal."

"You're bloody mad!"

The ship's movement yanked her legs out from under her. She screamed, and clung to Talon's neck. His hand slid over her spine to her bottom. Her eyes grew wide when she hit full against his hardened frame. His eyes burned into hers. Above the din of the wind and waves, he yelled for Marcus to take the helm. His other arm coiled around her waist as he half-carried her toward the stern galley door. Jaime's fearful face suddenly appeared in the companionway. He flinched as Talon cursed him.

Then the stern galley door banged shut behind her. Once out of the wind, the ship's groaning timbers drowned her shrieks. Talon dragged her back to the cabin. Darkness shrouded them. She screamed as he lifted her and tossed her sprawling onto the bed.

"Do you know what fire does to a ship?"

Regan flinched against the raw fury in his voice. She heard the strike of flint. Talon's large shadow wavered and took shape as light fluttered from the lanthorn beside the desk. He came to stand over her, and Regan scrambled to her knees.

"By Christ's wounds—" He gripped the bedstead. "—you've shot me, tried to stab me, burn my ship, and kill yourself. You're an endless battle, Regan. A bloody menace to mankind."

"And what would you do in my place? Sit meekly by and watch someone you love destroyed?"

Talon's eyes glittered. "Unlike you, milady *wife*, I wouldn't have failed."

"Ohh!" The taunt struck her like a blow as vicious as any delivered by Father. She hit him, splitting his lip.

Before she realized the rashness of her actions, Regan rolled off the bed in a flurry of wet petticoats. Talon reached her before she got to the door. "Smart, Regan." He lifted her off the floor, kicking and screaming. "Where do you think to run on a ship?"

"Anywhere but here with you!" she screamed.

"In the hold, perhaps? With water rising to your neck?"

"Yes!"

He fell with her to the bed. With a vicious curse, he grabbed her flailing wrists. "Then it's a tomb you prefer to me."

"I prefer anything to you, pirate."

"Anything?" Holding her hands above her head, he pinned her to the mattress, while ripping the chord from the gauzy cloth that draped his bed. "That can be arranged, Regan."

"What are you doing?" She struggled for air beneath his weight.

"Don't you ever tire of fighting?" With his thigh wedged between her legs, Talon wrapped her wrists in the tassel chord and bound her to the headboard.

"You can't do this. Not in this storm."

"Watch me."

"What if the ship goes down? What if it sinks?"

"Then you'll be the least of my problems." His silver eyes drove into hers, warning her that he'd reached his limit. "A proposition I'm beginning to fancy, Regan. You might have killed everyone on board tonight with that fool stunt."

"You'll not reach Port Royal. The *Viper* will find you."

In the shadows of his stubbled face, his teeth shone a mocking white. "Ah, yes. I forgot. Your hero, Captain Roth."

"Not a pirate who kills and maims."

The fury outside raged in his eyes "Your lover perhaps."

"More than you'll ever be, milord pirate!"

The steady beat of Talon's heart thumped against her chest. His damp hair fell over her face, touching her skin. She could lose herself in those silver eyes, she realized suddenly, desperately aware of the razor sharp line she trod between surrender and survival. Between truth and betrayal.

"Regan." His low voice caressed her cheek. "What would you have me do with you?"

Tears ruined her courage. "Send me back."

"You're my prisoner, Regan. My hostage, and whatever else I feel like. I'll grant you no more leniency. You'll not threaten the lives of my men. You'll not raise arms against me." He held her furious gaze. "So help me God, you ask only to get hurt if you continue to defy me."

"Please." Her entreaty seemed to soften his expression. His eyes encompassed her face, then dipped lower to the swell of her breasts.

The wet cotton of her chemise molded to her bosom. Regan sought to catch her breath. Dewy beads of seawater dropped from his forehead and trickled over her bottom lip. He laced his fingers in her hair.

"It seems we're at an impasse, Regan."

His mouth opened hungrily over hers, taking her lips in a devouring kiss. She could not fight. Or draw air enough to breathe. He tasted of the sea, of salt and wind. He was the essence of power and freedom. Regan wanted to touch him, to feel the blistering heat of his body. His tongue trailed a leisure path down the curve of her neck to the sworl in her ear. Liquid heat erupted through her.

"For your own life, quit this foolish fight, Regan."

She wrenched away. "I . . . will not stop fighting you."

"Your body tells me differently, sweet."

"You're my enemy." The choked words fell around her.

"I am not your enemy."

"Can you bring back those you've killed?" she whispered passionately. "You already said you couldn't change the past. You ask that I give you my life, and that of my brother's." She shook her head. "There can be no surrender between us. Ever."

"Would it matter if you knew I didn't kill your parents, Regan?" he quietly asked. He caressed her hair. "Would it matter enough to cease this fight against me?"

Tears suddenly stung her eyes. "Are you telling me you didn't attack the *Rose*?" Her eyes narrowed with vehemence when he denied nothing. "Then you would be a liar, sir, as well as a murderer. I will not listen to anything you have to say."

"And what do you know of truth, Regan? You're a bloody Welles." He pushed off the bed. "I do have other things to do before we reach Jamaica other than to coddle you."

"Talon?" The single light threw his shadow against the wall. She couldn't hide the tremor in her voice. "You won't hurt Arabella?"

Talon leaned with predatory ease against the bedstead. "For all your noble sacrifice, Regan, you bought your cousin a few weeks, and you didn't save your brother at all. When this is over, he'll still hang for the murdering bastard he is."

Then he left, slamming the heavy oaken door behind him.

Regan shut her eyes and prayed tomorrow would never come.

God never answered her prayers.

When Regan opened her eyes daylight pressed between the deadlight slats bolted to the stern galley window. The ship was riding anchor in choppy seas. Through the bulkhead, she could hear the rhythmic pulse of the bilge pump working overtime.

Sitting up, she rubbed her wrists. Someone had untied her during the night. Her dress lay over the chair. Regan slipped out of bed. Her chemise and petticoat were stiff and reeked of seawater.

Dropping to the trunk beside the wardrobe, Regan opened it. The strong smell of lavender wafted over her. She gasped at the luxurious items folded neatly. Silken undergarments, petticoats, a veritable reservoir of rich feminine apparel, apparently belonging to Arabella, no doubt, courtesy of Uncle Robert, who'd had the foresight to see his daughter fashionably attired even on a pirate ship.

With a snobbish tilt of her chin, Regan opened the armoire. Hanging beside Talon's shirts, an array of frothy dresses swung on wooden hangers. The intimacy of the scene assaulted her.

If everything hadn't failed so miserably, Arabella would

be standing here in her stead. His wife in truth.

The unbidden thought of Talon touching Arabella the same way he'd touched her knifed through her. She slammed the door shut.

Impatient to be out of this room, Regan lowered her ragged dress over her head and laced the bodice. A sound at the door alerted her. Sulley entered tray in hand. He saw her and paused.

"I must see Uncle Robert," she announced imperiously. Regan wanted no kindness from this man and would set the boundaries now. "Where is he?"

"He's not here, milady." Sulley walked past her and set the tray on the desk where it rattled. "Been gone since dawn."

Some of the starch left her spine. "I don't understand."

"The cap'n, he sent him ashore with Marcus to fetch the Lady Arabella."

"Your captain must be mad. Is he planning on attending another dockside hanging?"

"His Excellency is on the *Viper*, milady. The lady's papa will arrive for a visit. A simple ruse. Wouldn't you say?"

She didn't want to think of Harrison, or Captain Roth, whether or not they'd seen her signal last night. "Where are we, now?"

Sulley blocked her path. "I'm sorry, milady," he said kindly.

Regan eyed the frail-looking man, measuring her chances of pushing past him.

The thin, wiry man watched her back. "I've spent five years on this ship, milady. You'll not find it a simple thing to best me."

Regan's haughtiness had the opposite effect she intended. In truth, she couldn't keep it up. She turned her attention to the tray richly laden with fruit. "There's a boy on this ship."

"Aye," Sulley sniffed. "Parrot, he is."

She lifted her eyes to Sulley. "Is he being treated well?"

"He's not moved from his bunk for a full day, milady."

Regan felt her breath catch. "Has . . . has someone hurt him?"

"He suffers seasickness, milady." His pale blue eyes glimmered. "Not that it's not deserved." He chuckled.

"Please Sulley, take me to him. I'm sure he needs this food more than I."

"The cap'n says you've been ill and you're to eat." He pulled out Talon's heavy leather chair the other side of his desk, allowing Regan no choice but to sit. "I've brought a comb and some water for ye to freshen up. I'll be back to take ye to the boy."

After Sulley left, Regan forced herself to eat, glad that she did. Afterwards, she struggled hopelessly with her tangled hair, finally dismissing the curly mess, intent on seeing Parrot instead.

True to his word, Sulley returned and took her to the boy across the companionway. Slightly smaller, the cabin belonged to Marcus.

The room smelled of sickness. Regan knelt beside the pallid boy. His heavy-lidded gaze opened. "Oi don't think much of this pirate life, milady," he mumbled. "Me thinks, oi'm better suited to prison."

"It's called seasickness, Parrot," Regan reassured him, dipping a rag in a bowl of sloshing water beside his bed. She laid the rag over his forehead. "Have you tried to stand?"

"Oh no, milady. Oi'd as soon die as stand."

"Nonsense." She turned to Sully. "We're going on deck."

"I can't allow that, milady."

"Then let me speak to your captain."

Sulley stood uneasily in front of the door.

"Are you prepared to strike me, sir?" she demanded. "Because if you're not you'll have to stand aside. Or perhaps your captain doesn't care how his crew treats women."

"Oh, no, milady," Sulley rushed to reassure her. "He'd have the head of any what harmed ye."

"Oh?"

"He said if there's to be any harmin', he'll do it himself."

"Really!"

"Aye, mum. Said the words hisself."

Regan spun back to Parrot. "Up," she said.

"Oi don't wants to be goin' nowhere, milady," he protested.

"Where's your spunk, Parrot?"

"Sure as God's balls, oi barfed it up, I did."

Suppressing a smile, Regan made him stand. "You're going on deck, Parrot. You need the fresh air. Walking will help."

With Parrot braced against her shoulder, Regan turned her attention to Sulley. "I'll not run, Sulley. Or cause any trouble. Please, I know my word isn't much. But Parrot needs to go on deck."

Sulley finally opened the door. "I'll take ye to the cap'n, milady," he compromised. "It's his orders I be followin'."

Parrot moaned when Regan started forward. "Ya be a mean-hearted woman, milady. Oi thinks yer tryin' ta kill me is all."

Regan laughed. The rocking movement of the ship made her steps wobbly. "That has crossed my mind this past week, Parrot. But I think I've developed a fondness for you, despite your best efforts."

They made it up the stairs and onto the deck. The ship pulled at the length of both her anchors. Spars and blocks banged in the wind. Cannons lined the deck, held secure by chains.

Men tended to the rigging. Talon wasn't on deck.

Cupping her hand over her eyes to block the glare of the patchy sunlight, she suddenly gasped. *Dark Fury* lay siege to the bay, in full sight of Port Royal, just beyond the range of the fortress guns. Among the bobbing masts in the harbor, only two flew the British flag, a small naval sloop and a brigantine, neither, which seemed eager to confront the *Fury*'s massive guns.

"Cowards," she grumbled, then reluctantly conceded some wisdom to her fellow countrymen. No captain in his right mind would attack a square-rigger twice his size.

Regan sat Parrot safely atop a roll of coiled hemp, warning him to stay out of the way. She straightened. Across the bay, she could see Harrison's house high atop a hill. The churning surf pounding the beach appeared nearly phosphorescent, strangely alive. Regan cast her gaze over her shoulder to the dark clouds rippling the horizon.

"How long does he intend to hold Port Royal hostage," Regan inquired. "With a hurricane coming. Surely he must know the danger to any ship still in harbor."

"Ships have been leaving all morning, milady."

"Fellow pirates, no doubt."

Even more so than Tortuga, Port Royal boasted the biggest pirate refuge on the Spanish Main. Even as she voiced the sentiment, a captured Spanish galleon swept out of the bay under half sail. Men dressed in baggy canvas pants lined the rigging, waving and hollering in a most festive manner. The *Fury*'s crew returned their shouts with equal spirit. But she noticed none left their posts beside the cannons.

She saw Piers standing on the quarterdeck, his huge arms crossed over his chest as he watched the ship pass. Recognition seized her again. Nicholas? But the Nicholas she remembered as a child was not this man with his fearsome countenance and swirls of raised cicatrices. Was it? Nicholas if he still lived would not have left her seven years ago without a word.

"Come, milady. The cap'n is in the galley." Sulley directed her across the deck to the door beneath the forecastle.

She climbed down a ladder. In the dim light of the room, she could see men bent over bowls of porridge. At her noisy entrance, most blinked back the light to stare. Returning their scrutiny, she searched their sullen faces for the one she sought. And found him sitting alone, asleep, his head lying across his forearm on the table. He still gripped a mug. Coffee sloshed over his hand.

Regan's heart caught. Talon's vulnerability struck her.

She realized suddenly, the crew seemed intent on protecting their captain's solitude. Regan wondered again how one man commanded such loyalty from this hard breed. The pirate Drake possessed a strange code of honor. He could have slept in his own bed or beaten her soundly for her stunt last night with the fire. Any other man, including her own brother, would have flogged her back to ribbons for what she'd done. He could have let her fall from the ratlines to drown and been finished with her. He knew her identity, tasted her betrayal, and still he'd kissed her with passion.

She pulled her gaze from Talon's dark clad form. "Don't

disturb him," she said quietly. "I'll go back to the cabin if you insist."

Sulley probed her with interest. A gust of wind swept against her when he opened the door. Parrot was still sitting where she'd left him, talking with Harry and Charlie. He already looked better.

"Give me your word, milady," Sulley said, closing the door. The wind whipped his shirt and brought a sting of moisture to his pale eyes. "That you'll stay out of the way. Ye won't try to escape."

Regan captured the length of her hair, dragging it over her shoulder. Unable to relinquish Talon from her thoughts, her gaze stretched across the choppy sea to encompass Harrison's house on the distant hill. Even now, Arabella was probably on her way. Tonight, Regan would be banished from his room, while Arabella shared his bed.

She swallowed the ache. "I promise, Sulley. Let me stay up here with Parrot."

He didn't move. Regan found him watching her with compassion-filled eyes. "He's a good man, milady," he said as if reading her thoughts. "Proud to a fault."

Her attention captured, Regan waited for him to say more.

"Every man jack here owes his life to him in some way. Like him, most were pulled from the galley of a Spanish ship. Some were bondservants or navy seaman pressed into service and just wanting to go home . . . like the captain. They'd die for him, milady."

In the face of his actions against her family, Regan tried to reconcile his character to the man who now captained the *Dark Fury*.

"What happened to him, Sulley? To make him the way he is now?"

"I was his father's steward, mum." He walked her beneath the forecastle deck overhang, out of the blunt force of the wind. "Served the family my whole life." He looked away and focused again on the sky. "They took us all. The cap'n was a privateer in King Charles's service. Proud he was."

Sulley spiked a hand through his white hair. "Like his father he was falsely imprisoned for piracy, milady. He'd a hanged if not for the Lieutenant Governor, Henry Morgan hisself, interceding, sending him 'an Marcus to England to beg a King's pardon. 'Bout cost Morgan his job. He was accused of protecting pirates."

"But Captain Drake didn't receive the pardon."

"For all Morgan's efforts the cap'n never made it to England. The Spanish captured his ship. The cap'n and Marcus spent the next four years imprisoned in a Spanish dungeon in Puerto Bello, until the Spaniards made the mistake of taking them out to die on a slave galleon."

"Sulley?" A horrible sense of foreboding warned her not to delve where she didn't understand. "Who murdered his family?"

"When next you see yer brother, ask him the truth, milady."

"Wait!" He couldn't leave her like this. "Tell me what Uncle Robert has to do with this?"

Regan drew back, suddenly terrified of what he would say. "On his testimony, the cap'n will finally see his family's name cleared, and yer brother hanged for treason, milady."

Clenching a fist to her belly, she watched dismally as Sulley left her on the deck.

Talon must know that destroying Harrison would see her ruined as well. She was William Welles's daughter. The law did not aid treasonous families; it eradicated them, as he was well acquainted.

"Damn you, Robert. What is your game?" She shielded her eyes from the sun's harpooning glare and looked toward Harrison's house.

Who was right?

Where was the truth?

Chapter Thirteen

"Where is she?" Talon filled the doorway of his cabin. Sulley struggled to straighten with the tray in his hands. "She's with the boy. On deck, milord. She gave me her word not to escape," Sulley yelled as Talon wheeled away.

Her word! Like hell. Didn't anyone ever learn?

The wind nearly took the door from his hands as he stepped out onto the deck. Piers leaned against the bulkhead beside the door, his arms crossed over his chest. "She is very beautiful, *oui*?" he casually said as if he'd been waiting for Talon to emerge.

He followed Piers's gaze.

A stabbing sensation gripped his body. Regan stood in the wind atop the forecastle deck, hands clasped to the rail, hair blowing wildly behind her. More radiant than the sun, she could have been a pagan goddess, one with the tempest embracing the storm-tossed sea. She had only to lift her arms into the purple twilight and he was sure the wind would give her wings.

She smiled at the boy standing beside her. He realized she wasn't alone. Half his crew idled around enjoying her company.

"She's been up here most of the day," Piers said. "Harry took her and the boy on a tour of your ship."

"Jeezus, Piers. And you let him?"

"We took great care to remove all weapons, especially near the powder stores."

"These men are pirates, not bloody monks, Piers."

"They will not harm her, *Capitaine*. Or they answer to me."

Piers's strange attitude over the girl betrayed more than Talon cared to know. He faced the big man. "You knew, didn't you? You knew all along who she was."

Piers uncrossed his bulky arms and sided Talon with a glance not the least apologetic for the deception. Talon felt like smashing the man in the face.

"I owed a debt to her mother," Piers said, as if that simple explanation should justify his actions. "I had not seen the girl in many years. I thought she was safe on Martinique. If you knew her as I, you could not have left her on that beach."

"Dammit, Piers, why couldn't you just tell me the truth?"

"You were not prepared to hear the truth, *mon ami*."

"I bloody married her. Do you know that?"

"Oui," the big man grinned, clearly amused. "But no consummation, I will wager." Piers read Talon's expression and laughed. "You would have had to force her, *mon ami*. You may hate her, but you would never hurt her."

But Talon didn't hate her. And therein lay the problem. He shoved his fingers in his hair. He'd slept most of the day. His eyes felt gritty. "Robert doesn't know about the marriage, Piers."

"It is wise to keep your own council on this matter until you have him well under your gentle care. But if you want my opinion, you are better served staying married. Once my *chéri* accepts the truth and stops trying to kill you, she will make a fine wife. The girl has passion."

Fiery passion molded every perfect inch of her body. Talon had tasted it in her arms, her words, and in her staunch loyalty to her family. Even if she didn't threaten to cost him Robert's testimony, he couldn't trust himself around her. She'd riddled his restraint with so many holes, he felt like a bloody sieve.

"Why hasn't she recognized you?" Talon asked.

"I do not look the same." Piers shifted his stance, regarding the subject of their conversation with an implacable frown.

"Her life has been hard. I do not wish to see her hurt any more. When I left Martinique, I was a man very much in love with her mother, angered with the world for conspiring to keep us apart. Angelique was the kindest woman alive and the most courageous. She fought her husband's policies in every way. But she would never betray him with another man. And I was a bond servant." He sighed dramatically. "Alas, it was my own passion that drove me to leave without saying goodbye."

Piers didn't say more. Talon didn't ask. He had to work through his own demons concerning Regan Welles and wasn't about to volunteer advice to Piers.

"Do you think Roth saw the fire last night?" Piers asked.

"Maybe. He would have waited until daylight to make a move, when they discovered we slipped their snare. We bought maybe ten hours."

Piers eyed the approaching darkness. Talon knew he was thinking that their time had run out long ago.

Talon looked toward the scattered lights of Port Royal and beyond the hills across the bay. "Where the devil is Marcus?"

Feminine laughter grabbed his attention and his gaze shifted to the upper deck. His men needed to find something else to do.

Determined to set them on their tasks, Talon crossed the deck and climbed the stairs to the forecastle. Regan turned. Her brown eyes lighted upon his approach. Blindsided by the sheer force that hit him, he stopped. A moment passed before he realized his men were waiting expectantly for him to say something.

"Don't the lot of you have something to do?" he snapped.

Possessiveness crept over him. He didn't like sharing any part of his bride. Especially with his too-eager crew. The men glanced uncertainly between them. Harry, being the wisest, hastily left to attend his job. The other men followed.

Talon turned to Regan. "It's time to go below, milady."

"Truly, Captain. I've done no harm. Your ship still floats."

He checked the urge to follow the swing of that slim hand and settled his gaze on Parrot instead. His mood lightened somewhat. "You're looking better."

The boy grunted. "Oi ain't dead if that's what ya be meanin'."

"Nobody ever died of seasickness, Parrot." He grinned. "At least not aboard this ship. Why don't you get something to eat?"

Parrot glanced at Regan as if to seek advice on the wisdom of eating a meal. Talon felt oddly befuddled by the attachment. Hell, he felt left out.

"Oi be seein' what there is, then," Parrot agreed.

"You've won a friend," Talon said after the boy trudged away.

"Does that shock you, Captain? That I might have a friend?"

"In him?" He laughed. "I considered him a good judge of character. But alas even he is not immune to a pretty face."

The wind brought a blush to her cheeks. He admired her flawless oval face and rose-tinted skin. She set his senses on fire. He thought of her tied in his bed all night, and him barred by necessity, unable to sample what was legally his. Knowing she could never be his, not while they were married, with Robert holding a damn ax over his neck, and the whole of his future at stake.

She pulled her thick hair around her shoulders to hold its flyaway strands. "I did attempt to seek your permission to be on deck today, Captain. Have you rested well after your bout of pirating?"

Lifting a strand of her hair, his gaze raised back to hers. He had a need to fluff her silken feathers. Her composure annoyed him. "Is Arabella anything like you, sweet?"

Defiance blasted him. "You're a man. You'll be able to answer that better than I soon enough."

"Will I?" He edged a booted foot beneath her flapping skirts. Her feet were small and delicate compared to his. "Is she a virgin, too?"

"Why . . . of all the . . . I don't know."

His finger flirted with the pale curve of her shoulder. Her ire fully aroused, she physically removed his hand. "Captain Drake—"

"The girl you spoke about at the convent was you, not Lady Arabella."

Nodding, she faced him squarely. "Mama's brother is a priest at the orphanage there, where I teach with another girl.

Our students are of all races, including slaves that have escaped from the colonies." She lifted her chin. "Mama was a very active abolitionist, Captain. My family doesn't deal in slavery."

With a snort of derision, Talon quit ogling her cleavage. He leaned against the rail. His shirtsleeves snapped in the gust.

Harrison Kendrick was the biggest single importer of human flesh in the West Indies. Regan's feelings bid him to keep his tongue. He lacked the heart to inflict further pain in her life.

"You've been away from Jamaica a long time, Regan."

She hesitated. "Martinique is my home now. I'm taking my vows upon my return . . . and never leaving again."

He crossed his arms over his chest. Harnessing her spirit in a cloister, was that not sacrilege in itself? It was unimaginable thinking her a nun. "Won't your recent nuptials interfere with your life of solitude?" He couldn't resist needling.

Her head snapped around. "Must you be so crass?"

"Sugarcoated reality serves the very young or the very old, Regan. You can't hide from the world."

A fine eyebrow arched. "Such cynicism. Men of your breed would not understand faith or the kind of peace it brings to your heart."

"And what breed am I?"

"You're a pirate."

"Pirating is an occupation. I prefer to think of myself on less ignoble terms."

"A thief, perhaps."

"From your jaded point of view, no doubt. My men would beg to differ. We're skilled tacticians of war."

"Murderers."

"You're very free with your sentiment, Regan. Has it occurred to you that if I possessed half the traits you've labeled me with, you would not be here . . . alive?"

Her gaze faltered. But not for long as she reclaimed his with a sanctimonious tilt of her chin. "Don't you ever get tired of it all?" she asked, her soft voice full of accusation.

"Every damn day of my life." He placed both hands on

the rail and looked across the storm-tossed sea, feeling every bit of its energy whirling inside. "I want to end this battle so Marcus can have a life. So I can wake up in the mornings and know that semblance of peace you banter about so freely."

"Peace . . . with Arabella?"

He cocked a brow at her sudden inquiry and the fierce emotion behind her words. Her luminous eyes caught the light.

"Perhaps I won't give you an annulment," she pretended bravado, and he laughed.

"A dangerous threat in the company of killer pirates, milady."

"I don't know why Uncle Robert is doing this—" She whirled to the rail "—but it won't work."

"And you accuse me of lacking faith."

"Gold is the only voice that moves Uncle Robert."

"Considering he's a Welles, are you surprised?"

He recognized shock that could only come from seeing the truth or at least part of it. She knew her family was a bunch of gold seekers, but she didn't know the extent of that greed. Or did she?

"Then . . . this *is* about the treasure of Puerto Bello."

Talon frowned. Her conclusions were all wrong.

"Captain!" Charlie pointed from his position in the ratlines above the deck. "Look! There's Marcus. On the beach."

"Thank God," Talon whispered.

"Sail ho! To the larboard, Cap'n," Jamie cried from the lookout. As one, the crew seemed to turn. "The *Viper*. She's veering straight for us!"

Regan ran to the port rail. Stepping beside her, Talon pulled the brass scope from the sash around his waist and put it to his eye. Barely a moment passed. He snapped the glass shut. His gaze swung toward Marcus, who was just putting off in the longboat from shore.

"They will be here before Marcus, I think," Piers said gravely, appearing at his side. "A very bad thing, *mon ami*."

Talon went to starboard and watched his brother's longboat battle the surge. The past sennight was a sure testimony to the failure of this whole disastrous plan. What else could go wrong?

He shouted over the wind to Harry standing ready at the guns. "Load the cannons with chain shot! Ball and powder standing by." He stepped away from Regan. "Piers, man the capstan. When Marcus nears, start raising the anchor. And pray we can get the hell out of here."

As the longboat approached, Regan glimpsed Arabella between the men manning the oars. Her cousin's fondness for adventure showed readily in her wracking sobs. Regan recognized Arabella's mother. Her stomach rolled. So, Uncle Robert had brought everyone back. Right into the mouth of a British blockade. He was a fool.

Ratchet chains vibrated through the hull as cannons were realigned. Below deck, the gunports slid open. High on the forecastle, Regan clung to the rail as she followed Talon with her gaze. He continued to shout orders, clearly forgetting her in the wild fray. His control contrary to her mounting terror, he prepared for battle. Last night's ploy was doomed to disaster. Men would die because of her.

No longer eager to embrace the *Viper*'s company, she started to swing around, and gasped. A second pyramid of white sails formed on the horizon miles behind the *Viper*. A British man-of-war!

"Looks like she veered in this storm," Talon shouted to Piers, studying the slow progress of the second ship through his glass. "Her main sail is splintered."

"A pity she is so damaged," Piers solemnly agreed. "She will miss the fight. Not so your *Capitaine* Roth."

Regan stared. In a billowing white cloud of canvas, the *Viper* plunged steadily nearer over the tossing sea, her gunports opened even in the dangerous swell of the sea. Flapping fiercely in the gale, the governor's colors flew high on top the mainmast.

Harrison. In the fading light, she saw him standing in his golden finery on the forecastle deck, his glass trained on her. She felt the sting of tears and knew at once everything that had been said of him rang of lies. He risked his life to seek her out, to get her away from Talon, as he always protected her against father's wrath. He tried to protect her still. He loved her.

Unable to bear the thought of looking over the *Fury*'s deadly cannons aimed at him, Regan turned away. And met Talon's gaze. In the storm-ridden twilight, his silver eyes flashed. The brass scope clutched in his scarred hand rapped against his thigh.

"Captain!" The lookout shouted over the wind. "They want to talk. They've raised the parley banner."

"In these seas?" Talon met Regan's gaze then looked over his shoulder to gauge the longboat's choppy progress. "Kendrick may be mad. But he's just bought us the time we need." He cupped his mouth and yelled to raise the white banner. "What are our navy friends in the harbor doing?" he called to Piers.

"You do not want to know, *Capitaine*!"

His gut kicked. Fear. Lifting his gaze, Talon studied the sky. The wind had picked up considerably during the day but the full brunt of the storm had yet to reach them. In an hour, it wouldn't matter whether a hurricane sank them or not.

"They're lowering the longboat, Captain," Jaime yelled. "It's the bloomin' guvnor hisself!"

Talon swore. "His heroics don't make sense."

Regan whirled and gripped the rail. She wiped the moisture from her eyes. "You don't know him as well as you think."

"You're wrong, Regan." He turned his attention to the other side of the deck. "How long before Marcus gets here?" he yelled.

The ship plunged suddenly, lying over. A mass of water washed over the bow. Without her sails, the *Fury* floundered against her cables.

"How long?" Talon shouted again to Charlie.

"Now, sir! Now! We're lowering the sling."

Before he could grab her, Regan swept past him down the stairs to the main deck. He didn't need to be worrying about her. With the sudden shift of wind, the storm had become more unpredictable.

"Cap'n," Charlie shouted. The sling wavered in the wind. Talon could hear a woman's shrill screams.

Regan leaned over the rail. Talon jerked her back. "Get below!"

"I'll not go!" She fought his hold. Before Talon could direct one of his men to take her, Arabella's sodden head reached the top of the deck. The sling lifted her over the rail.

"Regan!" she screamed in holy terror. "Oh, Lord. Help me!" She dangled above the deck, eyes huge in her face as Charlie lowered her.

Regan broke his grip and embraced the hysterical girl. Talon's eyes riveted to Arabella's face, recognizing her as the maid on the beach who'd abandoned Regan to his mercy.

He stared, unprepared for the impact of his emotions. Even then, Regan had tried to protect the chit. These people didn't deserve Regan's loyalty.

Marcus was the first to climb onto the deck from the longboat.

"We've got problems," Talon yelled.

His brother wiped the wet hair from his face. "Do tell." He grinned, shielding his eyes from the wind. He stared at the *Viper* barely fifty yards beyond the bow. "Is this your idea of retiring in flame and glory, big brother?"

"Would you rather that I'd left your sorry hide to their mercy?"

"The weather has worsened. Maybe God is on our side."

"Don't count on it." Talon took Marcus to the port rail. "A visitor is about to arrive."

Marcus swore. He searched out Regan still huddled over Arabella. "She must mean a hell of a lot for him to risk his neck like this."

"And I can guarantee it's not brotherly love."

Kendrick's longboat slammed against the ship's side. He clamored up the ratlines. Four men remained behind, their combined strength needed to keep the longboat moored solidly to the rise and fall of the *Fury*.

No one stepped forward to aid Kendrick as he climbed over the rail. "I've come to negotiate for my sister, Drake," Harrison announced, his formal request absurd in the face of one ship looking down their cannons at them and three more British warships clawing their way closer.

Everyone on board the *Fury* seemed caught in the drama of the moment as Kendrick's gaze swept the deck, stopping on Regan, whose face had lifted from a sobbing Arabella.

With a cry, she released her cousin. One hand braced on the cold iron of a cannon, Talon leapt to intercept her. He took her arms, pulling her away from Kendrick.

She fought him. "You can't do this to me."

Talon was furious with himself for allowing her anywhere near the bastard. Regan turned in Talon's arms. The heat of her passion pressed against him. With his arm coiled around her shoulders, he continued to hold her against him. His other hand went to the pistol in his belt.

"She's staying with us, Kendrick."

Harrison took a step forward. Piers restrained him.

"You can go free. I'll give you anything."

"Anything, Kendrick?" He handed Regan off to Marcus. "How about the lives of my mother and sister? How about my bloody life back?"

Kendrick's gaze sought Regan's, then abruptly lifted to find Robert on deck.

"Did you think I couldn't get my daughter back, Excellency?" Robert taunted gripping his wife and daughter. The wind whipped the wet lace on his collar. "What weapon will you use against me now?"

Kendrick's gaze swung to Talon. "I'll fight his accusations for the lies they are, Drake. He can prove *nothing* against me."

"And I'll do you one favor, Kendrick. Though, God knows, you don't deserve it. I'll let you leave this ship alive."

"My sister belongs to me, Drake."

"She's a bloody Welles. She's mine until we reach England."

"Bastard!" Kendrick railed, slipping out of Piers's grip.

Talon blocked Kendrick's swing and smashed him against the rail.

"Stop it!" Regan's screams pierced the wailing wind.

"Why don't you tell her what kind of man you really are, Kendrick."

Piers pushed between them as Marcus grabbed Regan and dragged her away. Her furious screams drowned out Talon's voice as Marcus hauled her below.

"She thinks you're some sort of bloody saint, Kendrick. She doesn't know what you did to a nine-year-old girl."

Kendrick ran his hand over his mouth, where a drop of blood beaded on his lip. "Your plan will fail, Drake."

"You don't risk your life for anyone? Why is Regan so important to you?"

Eyeing blood on his fingers, Kendrick lifted his gaze. If eyes were indeed the window to one's soul, Talon knew Harrison Kendrick's spirit was blacker than hell.

"She's my beloved sister, Drake," Regan's brother said with more contempt that Talon could stomach. "The love of my life."

"Get him overboard," Talon yelled to Piers.

"I'll kill you, Drake—"

Harrison went over the side.

Talon didn't care if the man dropped into the sea. He turned and shouted orders to his men manning the braces. Seconds opened into minutes. *Dark Fury* seemed to yawn as if rousing from a long hibernation. Looking up in the darkness, Talon could see her sails unfurling in the wind.

He spun around to face Robert and his terrified family. "Jaime," he called. "Put Lady Arabella in my cabin with Regan. Lock Robert and his wife in Marcus's room."

The ship lurched drunkenly and began to roll in the swell. "Port your helm, Piers!"

The *Viper,* as if sensing Talon's bent, aimed a volley of cannon over the stern.

"Harry!"

"Aye, sir."

The *Fury* had awakened. "Fire as you bear."

"Aye, sir!" the gunner shouted and waited only a moment before giving the order to fire on the *Viper.*

The guns roared consecutively, vibrating through the hull of the ship as the *Fury* delivered a crushing broadside to the *Viper*. The wind swept away the powder smoke; he could hear timber splintering and the distant crash of mizzen chains and sparring.

He'd taken his one shot; the answer Talon dreaded came in a wrath of fury.

The lethal broadside ripped into the *Dark Fury*, tearing her to pieces. Hellish screams rent the darkness. Regan pounded on the cabin door. Masts cracked and splintered, crashing violently to the deck overhead. Festoons of rigging slammed against the deadlights bolted over the galley window. The din of cannon fire deafened her.

"Oh, God!" How could anyone live through this? She slammed her hands over her ears. "Talon!" He was on deck.

Blast after blast tore into the *Fury*, unceasing in its fatal madness. Suddenly the *Fury* careened to starboard, spilling her back into the room. The deck exploded into action again as Talon brought the ship into the wind. The stench of powder filled the room. Through a wet fall of hair, Regan saw her cousin. Arabella had fainted in a pile of gray silk.

Praying that a cannonball wouldn't tear through the stern galley, Regan dragged her cousin's sodden form onto the bed. Somehow, the cabin had been spared the anguish of destruction. Absurdly, Talon's bed seemed the safest place to hide from the wrath of the battle. Nearby in another cabin, she could hear Arabella's mother screaming over the shrieks and bellows of the men on deck.

Urged by the gale-force wind, the *Fury* should have plunged away from the storm of cannon fire. But wreckage trailed behind them, weighing like an anchor. Smoke rolled through the cabin. Regan thought of Parrot somewhere on board. Maybe everyone was dead?

Talon's shouts answered her fear. Her heart, already beating at a frantic pace, hit her ribs. He was directly above her on deck. She could hear the sound of axes furiously hacking. The rigging against the window came loose, as someone cut it. Cannon shot boomed over the creaking masts straining against the wind. The ship picked up speed.

Regan no longer screamed. She curled against Arabella on the bed. Caught in the darkness, she couldn't breathe. In the face of what Talon endured, her fears were inane.

How could he maintain his sanity?

And in that fateful moment, Regan knew a danger more

perilous than all the guns in Port Royal. Dangerous because she had to restrain the force of her heart, to stop from running to Talon and throwing herself into his arms. To feel his strength, the tenderness he'd oft yielded to her even when she'd not deserved a morsel of his affection.

He did not mold to her perceptions of a maddened killer. Lord! She didn't want to see him die!

Chapter Fourteen

Hours after the cannons ceased firing, Marcus moved Parrot and Arabella's parents into the main cabin with Regan and Arabella. Regan met him at the door. Her relief that Parrot survived the battle was short-lived in the face of the storm that now hammered the ship. Only one thought existed beyond her meager space of life.

"May I see the captain?" Regan asked Talon's brother.

"He can't leave the deck, milady. I'm sorry."

Huddled on the bed, Regan flinched as waves lashed the deadlight slats bolted across the stern galley windows. On the deck above her, Talon battled the storm. While she battled the memory of burning silver eyes when he'd told her he wanted peace.

Peace. God's gift to a repentant soul. Isn't that what Father Henri always said? A spark of conscience suddenly grabbed her, refusing to let go. Talon's observation about her family's greed had touched the truth.

As soon as the thought erupted, Regan discarded it. For all her doubts, she couldn't tolerate disloyalty. Yet, fealty could not shield truth. Some nameless sense of despair cracked her resolve. But it wasn't Harrison's integrity that she questioned. Her gaze lifted.

Hunched over Talon's massive desk, Robert buried his head in his hands. His tangled hair and torn blue jerkin were pitiful reminders that they all suffered from their confinement. Regan could scarcely keep herself from flying at the man with her nails barred. He deserved no less for bringing them to this end. Including Talon.

Regan poured over Robert's motives vigorously. During the next few miserable days, nothing her uncle said or did escaped her notice: his nervous pacing, his pickled conversations with his wife, which always ended in bickering. Only Arabella evaded his temper. And Regan grew no closer to learning his purpose.

Clearly, Robert needed Talon's protection while he cried foul to the king. Arabella had to be but a pawn. Her cousin's marriage to Talon would protect Robert. Only Talon had expected treachery and took the burden of marriage upon himself before Robert could change his mind. But why did Robert agree to this madness in the first place? Only one reason alone lasted her scrutiny.

Gold is the only voice that moves Robert.

Her very own words. And Talon never answered her that day on deck when she practically accused him of bribing Robert with the infamous treasure of Puerto Bello. Father's lifelong ambition. His greatest failure. She glared at Robert.

"You're not about justice, are you, Uncle?" It had been so long since anyone spoke. The lethargy in the cabin seemed to vanish at once as all eyes turned on her. "You've sold us out, haven't you, Uncle Robert?"

"Please, Regan. You mustn't upset him," Arabella whispered.

Regan climbed to her feet. "This *is* about gold."

Robert glared at her with such venom, Regan felt violated. "Aye, this has always been about gold. More riches than you can imagine."

"Tell her the truth, Robert," Arabella's mother shrieked. Robert faced his wife huddled in the corner of the cabin. "That man up there on deck has every reason to hate us. Then tell *me* how you can force your baby to marry someone who would as soon slit our throats?"

"Can you even tell the truth, Robert?" Regan gripped the bedstead for support. "One that's not tainted by greed."

Robert's pallid expression darkened. "Your father hanged Brendan Drake. And that's the bloody truth of it!"

The horror of the admission was unexpected. Regan recoiled in shock. But Robert wasn't finished. He came around the desk. "He hanged Drake's father on trumped-up charges, wiped out the whole family for crimes of treason. You wanted the truth, Regan? There it is. You're the daughter of a cold-blooded murderer."

A sick wave of terror gripped her. "I don't believe you."

"Regan," Arabella pleaded, drawing her from Robert's path.

"All Brendan Drake had to do was give up the maps' secrets. Our scheme was flawless. Brendan Drake had married a Spanish noblewoman in Puerto Bello, long before we ever heard of a treasure. The ease of the accusations brought against her for spying bore the sentiment of the times. She would have hanged if—"

Regan shook her head. "No . . ."

"Your father conceived the plan."

"You let those people die. You helped destroy Talon's life." Her voice was a whisper. "What right do you have to condemn Harrison and me in your stead?" He had no rights at all. None! "By your own admission, *you're* the one guilty of treason. You'll not destroy me for your own crimes. Nor my brother. He's the governor of Jamaica. He's above suspicion."

"Harrison," he spat in contempt. "Even when he left you in that convent after your parents died, you continued to be his strongest supporter."

Confusion gripped Regan. "He had no choice."

"Why? Because you're a cripple? And he's embarrassed by the sight of you?"

"Papa!" Arabella cried.

Regan backed a step from Robert's wrath. "Is it true then?" she whispered. "Did Captain Drake really murder my parents?"

"They deserved to die!"

Hot tears blurred her fury. She wiped them away.

"Harrison will be next. I know things that will destroy him."

"It's too late for your grand scheme, Uncle."

Parrot jumped between her and Robert. "Don't be sayin'

nothin' foolish, milady. Not without the cap'n bein' here."

Robert shoved the boy into the floor. He slammed his head against the wall. "Parrot!" Regan leaped to his side. She reassured herself he was all right, then faced Robert with more courage than she had ever challenged Father. "Arabella can't protect you."

"No, milady." Parrot clutched her torn sleeve, rending it further. "Don't say it. He's mad, 'e is."

"Captain Drake didn't trust your bargain."

Robert's face swelled with red passion. "What are you saying?"

Her chin lifted. "He thought I was Arabella and took matters into his own hands. Talon is married to me."

"Goddamn slut!" Robert slapped her.

Regan hit the floor. The room blackened. Still, she lifted on her palms and glared. "Where is your great plan, now?" she taunted.

Her uncle's hands closed around her throat.

"Robert!" Arabella's mother cried. "Are you mad?"

Regan struck out but couldn't stop Robert from choking her. Parrot beat against his arms. Arabella started screaming.

Robert's scarlet countenance wavered unmercifully before her. "I've spent the last year in hell running for my life because of Kendrick." He shook her. "Curse your father for everything he did to me. Curse your brother."

Clawing at his fingers, Regan tried to breathe. Her hands groped for his collar. Arabella's screaming faded. The sound of the storm disappeared in the high pitched whine that began to blanket her in darkness. Robert was choking the life from her.

"Curse you, Regan. You'll not thwart me!"

Then Robert's weight disappeared followed by the sound of smashing glass. His body hit the dinner tray on the floor. Someone lifted her from the screaming maelstrom.

Talon's angry voice rumbled against her cheek. "You touch her again, Robert, and so help me, I'll kill you."

Assailed by the familiar scent of sea and rain, Regan closed her eyes. "Talon." Her throat hurt. He held her tight against his chest. "My father . . . he did this to you."

"Put her in Marcus's cabin for now," he told someone, his

voice like ice. "I have business to attend to here."

Her eyes opened. She didn't want him to let go of her. "Take me home . . . to Martinique," she rasped. "I want to go home. Please."

"Christ . . ." His bearded face scratched her temple. "If only I could, Regan."

He handed her into Piers's arms. His gold earring caught the light. She reached out and touched his cheek. "Nicholas?" It made perfect sense that he should be there as if the years had not taken him away.

"*Oui*, little monkey."

"Is it true? Was my father . . . evil?"

"I am sorry, *chéri*."

And then his voice faded into blessed darkness.

Sunshine awakened Regan. The bright light slanting across her face came from a patched hole in the upper hull. The room had endured cannon shot. She flinched at the shattered remnants of a desk and a wall of bookcases. Scorched spines and bits of dampened vellum fluttered in the breeze coming through cracks over the port window. The room smelled of kelp and gunpowder. From the other bunk across from hers, someone stirred.

Parrot watched her with sleepy eyes. "Ya look a painful fright, milady," he offered in his usual blunt wit.

Regan lifted a hand to her throat. She tossed the thin counterpane off and steadied herself against the ship's movement. "The storm's abated." Her voice rasped. She tried to stand and decided it wiser to sit for a moment. "How long have I been asleep?"

"The night, milady. They brought us down some gruel."

"What happened to the *Viper*?"

"No one knows. Fer now we lost her."

Her gaze fell on the tray. "Was Sulley here?"

"No, mum. It be someone else."

She needed to speak to Sulley. He would know the truth of Robert's accusations. After forcing herself to eat something, Regan braided her hair, caring little that it looked crooked. With Parrot beside her, she opened the door to the companionway. Sunlight wedged through a gaping hole in the ceiling. She sloshed through brackish water and a net of mizzen chains to reach the stairs.

"Milady." Parrot ran after her. "Oi don't think it be such a good idea to go on deck."

Pushing open the stern galley door, Regan stopped. A gentle breeze tugged at her hair. Framed against a perfect turquoise sky, the welcoming Caribbean sun shone upon the carnage on deck.

The foremast was gone, snapped off twenty feet from the deck, trailing canvas astern. Leech lines entangled with the main topmast. Most of what remained of the sails had been jury-rigged to the masts. The deck was so littered with debris that it was impossible to negotiate a path.

"Where's Captain Drake?"

" 'E's been working to clear the decks, milady. And fix what needs fixin'."

Regan gaped at the wreckage. The whole ship needed fixing!

"Lady Regan—"

She spun at the sound of her name. Marcus walked toward her, his gray eyes serious. His tattered clothes revealed raw scabs. Unable to stop herself, she lifted a hand to the wound in his hair.

Marcus aimed her back down into the stern galley. "This is no place for a lady. Now down with you," he prompted. "If you must do something, clean my cabin."

"You're hurt—"

"I'm all right. And so is Talon," he quietly answered reading the concern in her eyes. "Now go." Clearly not trusting her to obey, he walked her to the cabin.

Regan hesitated. "I must talk to Sulley. He hasn't been by—"

Marcus's expression softened. "Sulley is dead, Regan."

"I . . ." Tears misted her eyes. "I'm sorry."

"So are we all. He was a good man."

Parrot took her hand and pulled her back into the cabin. The door shut behind her. She dropped onto the bunk, unaware as Parrot nudged her back and tucked her into bed. "Sleep, milady," she heard him say before her eyes closed to the tears.

Sometime later, Parrot nudged her awake. A bowl filled with lumpy gruel sat on a tray beside the bunk.

"The cap said to eat it, milady," Parrot urged. "Ya need yer strength like the rest of us."

She did as the boy bid. Again, she went on deck, intercepted this time by Jaime, who was intent on aiding the ship's carpenter and almost missed her as she emerged from the stairs.

"Let me do something," she pleaded as he escorted her back down the companionway.

"The cap'n would have my hair if I let ya on deck." He saw the room and suggested she clean it if she wanted something to do.

Not to be deterred, Regan again left her cabin that evening. She almost screamed when a bewhiskered Harry met her at the top of the stairs, dinner tray in hand. "Come, milady," he directed. "The cap'n be adamant that you stay below."

"Truly, Harry. I'm not an invalid. I wish to help."

"Orders, milady."

"Then why won't he at least see me?"

"He's a busy man, milady. Maybe tomorrow." He glanced at the cabin and groaned. "Ya want something to keep ya busy, milady. I'd say you have a job right at yer feet."

Regan slammed the door.

The next morning she cleaned the cabin, directing Parrot to carry everything not attached to the bulkhead on deck and toss overboard. In her view, the room couldn't get much cleaner.

Again, she went on deck, determined to raise a fist to the next man who stopped her. Piers saw her. She stiffened.

"Little monkey." He grinned.

Irritated by the twinkle in his eyes, her gaze narrowed on his smiling face. "I haven't anything to say to you, Nicholas," she snapped. "And if you try to take me below, I'll . . ." she eyed his bulk. "I'll hit you."

Undaunted, he laughed. "Why would I keep you from the deck?"

"Captain's orders?"

"The *capitaine* has been in a most foul mood," he agreed. "But even he cannot be everywhere at once. What is it you wish to do?"

Relief spilled over her. "Are there many wounded?"

"Too many," Piers said.

"I have medical skills that can be of use to your surgeon."

Looking at the ring of bruises around her neck, he rubbed his smooth chin. "You are well then, *chéri*? This will not be easy."

"Quit coddling me, please. Yes, I'm all right." She waved a hand at the stretch of endless sea. "And I'll not jump overboard. I'll not burn the ship. And I promise not to kill anyone."

"*Oui*, you are well enough," he chuckled. "Come with me."

"Where is Uncle Robert?"

"The *capitaine*, he has chained him in the hold."

"Has anyone checked on Arabella and her mother?"

"*Oui*," Piers said. "The *capitaine* is caring for them."

The sting to her heart jolted her. Talon hadn't so much as peeked in on her.

"Your cousin is very beautiful, *oui*?"

"So I've been told." Numerous times her whole life, Regan wanted to snap, but quickly swallowed the vixenish sentiment. This predicament was not Arabella's doing.

"The *capitaine*, he is a formidable man, *oui*?"

Too formidable, she considered.

"But he is only flesh and blood. He risks his life on the testimony of one man."

Regan didn't want to hear this. She had her own problems to consider. She looked at Nicholas. All the old hurts surfaced. Her chin lifted. "You gave up your right to council me long ago when you ran away, Nicholas. I don't wish to discuss this matter."

Regan knew her words cut. Thick-skinned as he appeared, the man was still human. She wanted to ask why he left Martinique those many years ago without saying good-bye. But the past had already harmed her irrevocably. She wanted nothing more to do with it.

"Just take me to the men, Piers."

The practice of medicine at St. Mary's did not prepare Regan for the reality of war. Nothing could. Hours later she stepped from the hold and made it to the rail, sucking in great breaths of air to salve the violent heaving of her stomach. Doctoring was a wretched job, better suited for men accustomed to violence or those with iron bellies. Through a blur of tears, she looked down at the bloodstains on her surgeon's apron and tore the cloth off.

"Piers warned you it wouldn't be easy."

The horrible apron still clutched in her hand, Regan whirled. Talon sat on a crate, dipping a rag into a bucket of water and watching her. His shirt lay at his booted feet. Moonlight shifted in the breeze, catching the gentle play of emotions on his face. Shadows glinted in liquid silver eyes that surveyed her disheveled hair and tumbledown appearance. He looked rough, disreputable for the battle he'd waged, and her heart raced over emotions near the point of total collapse.

"Don't say it, Captain Drake. I can't bear your criticism—"

"Regan—"

"—not now. Not when all the sky is falling down on me and . . . and—" She glared at her soiled hem. "And I've ruined my only gown."

"I'm not criticizing you, Regan." Water sloshed as he wrung moisture from the cloth. She stared at the play of his muscles, nearly bronze in the moonlight, before lifting her bewildered eyes back to his face. His brow arched at her perusal and he dropped the rag back into the bucket to give her his full attention.

She dashed the traitorous tears from her face. "Then what?"

Talon was a stranger to gentleness, but a part of him softened as he witnessed her distress. He should have hauled her out of the hold when he'd first discovered her recklessness, but Piers stopped him. And his men needed her. He'd watched her enough that day, struggling to aid the surgeon, fighting to be brave, to know that she'd survived the gruesome task longer than most men.

He stepped over a crate to reach her. "What you've done today isn't easy, Regan. You don't have to go back down into the hold."

"I don't need you to tell me I'm weak or that I failed."

He wiped the tears from her face. "You're not weak," he whispered, his lips inches above her temple, "and failure isn't in your nature." He heard her sigh and was surprised when she yielded to his arms to cry out the remainder of her distress. But his pride couldn't relent to the protector in him and finally he forced himself to step away. It was insane to desire attachment to her, when in the end he would end up hurting her.

Regan looked up as he moved to retrieve his shirt. "You're hurt."

"No worst than usual, sweet."

Clearly, alarmed at the dried blood on his arm and shoulder, she ran to his side. "Why didn't you ask for help? Of course, you wouldn't. The captain of the *Dark Fury* is as invincible as his ship."

With a glance, Talon measured the cost of life and damage around him. "Not so invincible. I barely got us out alive."

Her eyes fixed on his. "I'd say that counts for something." She pressed him onto the barrel beside the bucket of water. Bedeviled, he simply stared as she proceeded to tear the second tier of her petticoat into a bandage.

"It doesn't look like you need stitches."

His gaze lifted from her delicate hands to her face.

Regan clutched the remnants of her petticoat to her chest like a shield. "I don't mean to be so bold."

"I hadn't noticed that you were."

A blush stained her cheeks. Her fingertips trembled against his skin, and he found solace in watching her face as she attended him. "It's a shame we're enemies," he said when she finished.

"Maybe we don't have to be." Her voice was quiet. Hopeful.

He brushed the hair from her face. "A long time ago I would have courted you. Probably even grown fond of you." The declaration stunned her as much as it did him. He laughed at his own foolishness but his insides kicked in turmoil as he let his gaze fall on her mouth. The memory of her taste sent heat coursing through him. "You're right. Fondness is too tame for what I'd have felt."

She smiled. "No one ever wanted to court me before."

He realized that he had truly grown to like her. That she was far more than he expected in a woman. "Unfortunately, it wouldn't have worked out for us. I couldn't have abided your family."

The anguish in her face made him regret his words. "Greed turns all men into liars and murderers, Captain Drake. What my father did was unforgivable. But no less than what you're doing now."

His curt laugh ended on a nasty oath. He hadn't been speaking about her father. He'd been thinking about Kendrick. "Jeezus, Regan. For someone with intelligence, you lack the simple wit to see truth."

"The truth?" Those brown eyes he'd found so alluring a moment ago snapped to his. "Which version of the truth should I believe, today, Captain Drake? Robert's? Yours? Father's. Which one do I choose when gold can turn lies into any truth you want."

"A lie can never be truth."

"I only know that Harrison risked everything to come for me," her quiet voice intruded. "He risked his life when I have nothing to give back. No one has ever loved me like that."

Talon clenched his jaw. He knew if he said one damn thing, he'd only let loose what remained of his temper.

"Don't you see? He can't be guilty of Father's crimes against you. Harrison is not the man in the picture you've painted. But you?" She wrapped her arms protectively around her. "You seek the plunder of Puerto Bello. The bribe Robert is taking to speak in your defense."

"You err in your assumption about a lot of things, Regan."

Her eyes flared passionately. "How many more ships will you sink? How many more people will die before this nightmare is ended?"

"This nightmare?" He came to his feet. She retreated a step. "You've been living in a bloody convent. Don't talk to me about nightmares, Regan. Not until you've spent years in a Spanish dungeon. Without sun or air, fighting rats as big as a man's forearm for every morsel of food thrown to you. Rotting inside with your own bilge and stink, and roaches by the thousands. Until even a Spanish slave galleon is heaven compared to living in the sewer of a dungeon. If I regain what is mine by preying on the thieves who stole it, then so be it."

"And what of my brother?" she whispered.

"If the courts don't take care of His Excellency, I will."

"Then you must fight me as well, Captain Drake. You know that."

"Fight you?" He laughed, then clamped his jaw as if that were enough to check the rush of frustration. "Christ, Regan. You're spoils of war. I own you."

Chapter Fifteen

During the next week, sounds of carpenters and sailmakers filled the hot quarters that housed the wounded men below deck where Regan toiled daily to exhaustion. The work tore her mind from Talon. Spoils of war, indeed! Such arrogance from the unprincipled pirate measured his base character completely.

And yet his very proximity to her on this ship made her weak all over. That was the lowest humiliation of all.

By the end of the second week, the fresh water ration had to be cut. The ship was fast running out of provisions. Regan could scarcely do more for the injured than keep their wounds clean.

More than once, Arabella tried to approach her, but Regan couldn't stomach her cousin's calm acceptance of their plight enough to hold a mature conversation.

Ever fresh looking, wearing a beautiful gown, Arabella drew every man's eye in the evenings when she ventured on deck. Not that Regan cared for the attentions of every man on board. Nor one man in particular. She glimpsed Talon often with Arabella as they shared a meal on the quarterdeck. It was the only time she saw him not bent over some task, or fixed high in the rigging repairing the shrouds. Like all men, he obviously found Arabella pleasant company, and he hadn't spoken with Regan since that night on deck when she'd wrapped his wounds. Their truce had lasted an hour too long as far as she was concerned.

Regan eagerly spent her time with Parrot, away from Talon's simmering glances, away from his towering presence. Even Marcus had become a regular visitor below deck in the evenings when she would read to the men from Talon's selection of books.

By the end of the second week, she was giving reading lessons to most of the crew, her most ardent pupil being Jaime. "Ya tricked us all," he told her, clearly impressed with her cleverness, which she no longer considered so clever. Then he'd told her he believed in fate and some such nonsense.

But Regan believed in nothing.

She thought of that now as she stood on deck bathed in moonlight, the breeze caressing the heat from her face. She'd lived the last few years in a haze not to see the trouble beneath her very nose. Pride inched her chin up. The past weeks did hold some pittance of a reward. Somehow, her limp had become less noticeable, the pain less severe. And no one treated her like a cripple.

The clangor of pumps drifted over the water lapping against the ship's hull. The one functional mainsail billowed as it caught the breeze. Regan lifted her face to the sky.

"You look in need of company." Marcus intruded on her solitude. He leaned back against the rail, stretching his long legs, crossing them at the ankles.

Regan followed his line of vision as he watched Talon and Arabella walking the main deck below. She turned away. "You're rather chipper."

"I've had a blasted headache since you took out my stitches."

"If you have a headache, sir, consider blaming the real source." She glared pointedly at the chatting couple below. Arabella looked breathtaking in maroon silk that caught the glimmer of moonlight.

Regan brushed her hands across her dingy skirt, removing the soiled surgeon's apron with disgust. She didn't consider what her hair must look like. Thankfully, at least she'd washed it in the rain today. She dropped the apron in a basket behind her filled with other filthy items she needed to clean tomorrow morning.

"You and every man on board have been ogling Arabella until your eyes should pop out. I'd have a headache, too."

He laughed but when he spoke his voice was serious. "She is a bit of fluff," he admitted with a grim smile. "But I find myself thinking of her to distraction."

"She has taken to her new circumstances well." Too well, Regan decided, considering she was in love with Harrison a few weeks ago.

"She misses you," Marcus said, studying her.

The comment didn't demand a response. She wasn't about to get into a debate over Arabella's perceived loneliness. Not with Talon ogling her cousin like tomorrow's sunrise.

"He's not as indifferent to you as he seems, Regan," Marcus said, reading her mind with uncanny ease.

"Who?"

"You know who I'm talking about." He shifted and turned to face the water. "He's always watching you. Even now, I'll wager he has his eye on us up here." His handsome face tilted slightly. She saw the mischievous twinkle in his gray eyes. "I should kiss you."

She laughed. "You'll do no such thing, Marcus Drake."

"I've been thinking about it since you came up here tonight."

"Marcus—" Alarmed by the sudden look in his eyes, Regan moved sideways. "Surely you jest."

He grinned. "When's the last time a man kissed you? I see," he said, reading her shocked face. "So big brother has made his mark."

"Mark, indeed," she sniffed, "He's a black-hearted rogue."

He placed a hand over his heart. "Spoken like a woman in love."

She choked. Marcus was like a wolf baying at the moon. His absurd charge . . . well, 'twas absurd, that's what it was.

"You underestimate yourself," he said, ignoring her unsubtle outburst. "You're very beautiful in an indecent kind of way."

"I most certainly am not," she said unsteadily.

"Just the sort of woman my older brother would fancy if he ever decided to grow attached to anyone."

"You mean he's not got an armful of swooning maidens at every port?"

"My brother doesn't lack for attention," he admitted, "but no woman has ever been on this ship, in his bed." He lifted her thick braid and entwined it around his fist before she could respond. "You shall not escape, me pretty." He laughed, tugging her against him. "And me thinks, my brother needs a lesson in humility."

Her hands splayed his chest, catching in the fine hairs beneath his opened shirt. "Don't you dare, Marcus."

"Ah, but I am me brother's, brother." He grinned wickedly, maintaining the game. To her horror, he pulled her full against him. "A kiss, my sweet."

"Marcus . . . you must be ma—"

His mouth slanted over hers, a chaste mockery of his passion. She kept her eyes opened, glaring cross-eyed at him until he finally pulled back to survey her face.

"I'm insulted."

"I should slap your brutish face. What must everyone think?"

"I only care what one man thinks." He chuckled.

Regan was tempted to look over his shoulder. "Marcus," she said on a more serious bent. "Why discourage his marriage to Arabella?"

Marcus sobered. Regan almost regretted bringing up the subject.

His sighed. "We've lived like this for more years than I care to count," he said quietly. "Talon is driven. He's done what he's had to do to keep us both alive." He slanted a glance toward her, turning to face her fully. "He needs Robert. No matter the cost."

"So he trades gold for your lives."

"He would trade his soul to go before King William with proof to reclaim our lives and honor. Nothing else has ever mattered."

Regretfully their conversation dimmed, and after a half hour, Marcus left. She glanced hastily around the deck. Talon and Arabella had gone below. The vision of golden hair spread over his pillow, his mouth teaching her cousin's the magic of love, created a wretched conflict inside that made her physically ill. Regan never felt her aloneness more than at that moment.

She left the deck and went below. Since her recovery, Parrot had moved from her cabin. Tonight, she would miss his chatter.

A door clicked shut, and suddenly Talon stood in her path. His presence filled the companionway sucking away all the air. She didn't have to look past him to know which room he'd just left.

"I see you haven't wasted any time?" The shrewish words were out before she could pull them back. She didn't think to consider that Arabella shared the room with her mother.

A dark brow lifted. "You speak to me of not wasting time? I should laugh."

Marcus had been right. Talon *was* watching them. A surge of gratification charged through her. "Try not laughing too hard, Captain," she said airily, "I'd hate to think you might actually enjoy yourself for once."

His hand reached the wall behind her, blocking her retreat. "Did you enjoy his kiss?" His finger lifted to caress the fading bruises that ringed her neck. The masculine scent of him filled the sultry space between them. "Did you, sweet?" he cajoled.

Tiny frissons quivered through her nerves. "Yes. And I think I shall enjoy more."

His other hand braced against the wall, caging her between his powerful arms. "And I think you're a liar, sweet." His mouth touched the moist skin above her temple with soft menace. "But then I'm not surprised. It runs in your blood."

A rush of color burned her cheeks. Driven by her own pride and what little remained of her family honor, Regan shoved against the hard wall of his chest. He would take everything from her, goad her to shame. "Get away from me."

He toyed with the end of her braid, slipping the thong away. "Stay away from Marcus."

She wanted to strike him.

"Be warned." He quelled her with a look. "I've only allowed you on deck because you've been of use to my men, Regan. Don't tempt me to lock you in your room."

"You strut like a peacock with my cousin, then threaten *me* because I dared kiss your precious brother? Why should you care?"

"I care about Marcus. Stay away from him."

She felt the horror of tears. "I won't."

His eyes narrowed with dark enmity. Gripping her by the arm, he pulled her around him to her cabin. Opening the door, he forced her inside, stopping abruptly as he noticed the stark bareness of the room cast in shadows by the single brass light hanging on the wall.

His frown took in the patched ceiling.

"Jeezus, it's hot in here."

Regan stiffened. Only a lout could be less observant. "I haven't the luxury of your room, Captain Drake. It's always hot in here. That's why I enjoy going on deck when I can."

His gaze fell on the port window.

As if coming to a decision to enter her domain, he walked the few steps to examine the portal. The gentle rocking of the ship closed the door behind him. Unlike Regan, he didn't seem to notice the insidious click.

Rolling up his loose sleeves, he proceeded to wedge the vexatious window open. The movement of his muscled forearms mesmerized Regan, trapping her feet to the planked floor. Rusted iron scraped against wood. Talon finally resorted to brute strength, forcing it open with his shoulder.

The cabin filled with fresh air. The tropical breeze caught the folds of his black silk shirt and carried the seductive scent of orange blossoms. Her heart was thunder in her ears.

"We're coming upon Tortuga." Bracing his elbow against the bulkhead, he bent to peer out the window. He seemed reluctant to leave. "We'll be hauling the *Fury* into shore to finish repairs. You'll be able to get off the ship."

From the scuffed tips of his jackboots, past his leather-clad legs to the sash tied around his waist his masculine presence dominated every inch of her thoughts. The room was too small for them both.

He turned to face her. "What? No words of gratitude?"

She bit down a nasty retort. "Aren't you worried I'll escape?"

"The island is not known for hospitality," he said, straightening to his full height. "If you run away you'll probably never be seen again. I'd advise against it."

"I should think you'd be happy to get rid of me."

He closed the space between them. Blood rushed to her face making her heady for lack of breath.

"Rid of you?" His palm cupped her cheek. "No, Regan—"

"Don't touch me." She took a careless step backward and sat abruptly on the bunk. Talon followed her down as she scurried away.

He braced his hands on either side of her face against the pillow, the heat of him burning in his eyes as they trapped and held hers. "What happens if I touch you, Regan?"

She gasped, willing herself to resist him, knowing at once, she could not. "You're a bastard, Talon Drake. I hate you for doing this to me."

His indulgent mood vanished, replaced now by a dark, seething hunger. Somewhere in the haze, she heard water lapping against the hull, the masts creaking in the breeze.

"And I'll tell you again—" His breath was hot over her lips, burning through her like blue flame. "—You're a liar."

He kissed her, joining his mouth to hers, savoring her lips with a savage urgency that drank the very life force from her lungs. A groan built deep in his throat. The kiss deepened. Hard and fierce, he plied her mouth, opening her to his tongue. He tasted like rum, drowning her senses until he was breathing for them both.

"Deny me, girl," he whispered huskily, relentlessly perusing her lips, compelling her to respond. "Deny this attraction between us."

The passion in his voice trapped her. Sensations engulfed her in fire. Talon dragged her against him off the bed, his powerful legs balancing them both against the gentle roll of the ship. His heart raced with hers.

"Say it, Regan."

"I . . ." She could not deny him.

Her head lolled back. He gripped his hand on the back of her neck, burying his face in the silken fall of her hair, easing his hands through the half braid that unraveled as easily as her body beneath his touch.

"Fight me, Regan." He possessed her mouth drawing out her breath. "Or by God, you're mine."

"Talon . . ."

His name on her lips was magic, and she said it again and again relishing the liquid music. His mouth traveled over her collarbone to catch her whispered words in a ravaging kiss. He pulled her dress over her head. Her petticoats whispered to the ground, leaving only her shift and drawers, a frail barrier to the heat of his touch. His knuckles skimmed her stomach. Fire seared her skin, burning where his roughened palms touched. A throaty groan answered hers as her fingers fumbled clumsily beneath his shirt, reveling in the soft black curls that covered his hard chest.

Talon lifted the shirt away, his muscles flexing with impatience, rending the tender fabric; then she was lost again to his hungry kiss, oblivious to the gentle swell of the sea, the shadows, and her own near nakedness. Cradling her bottom against his thigh, he arched her back over his arm, heatedly sucking each nipple through the silken chemise, making the thin cloth wet and hot against her sensitive skin. She cried out. Featherlike tremors rippled through her, stroking her skin with seductive promise.

"Regan . . ."

Slowly, Talon lowered her to the bed. Air grazed her skin. He removed her drawers. Stunned, Regan panted for breath. She perched on her elbow, her wild hair falling over her face and shoulders, dazedly watching as Talon removed his boots and pants. She saw him from behind a sheen of tears in all his magnificence, a powerful nemesis, a foe. Her heart weakened her, made a muddle of her will.

Talon must have glimpsed the conflict in her eyes. His fevered gaze gentled as he knelt between her knees and pressed her back into the mattress, taking her mouth again, smoothing her hair, and kissing the wetness from her face. "Stay with me, Regan." His voice was hoarse against her mouth. "I need you."

"I need you, too," she cried in a whisper, understanding none of the madness between them, frightening her beyond all else.

Hunger simmered in the silver heat of his gaze. His palm eased beneath her shift, slipping over the curve of her hips to her breasts, joining his other hand as he pulled the shift over her head. His dark head lowered first to one hard nipple then the other as if the hunger within him could not be assuaged.

Regan pulled the thong from his hair. Silken strands shivered over her ribs. His palm trailed over her flat belly, his mouth lifting back to hers, catching her cry as his finger eased into her. Nerves rippled. He caught her moans, drinking passionately from her mouth, burying another finger into her moist heat. Ablaze, eyes half-shut, Regan arched, drawing him deeper.

He caught her bottom lip between his teeth, gently suckling. "You feel . . . so ready," he rasped, dragging a hoarse cry from her, "so . . . good." He withdrew his fingers, bracing himself aloft. Her feminine scent touched her senses, mixing with the heady taste of his kiss and the race of her emotions. "I want to know your pleasure." His shoulders rippled with power as he slid a hand beneath her bottom lifting her to him. "All of it, sweet."

Lord, she could not fight the white-hot surge of fire that drove him inside her. Pain shattered the misty passion that enveloped her.

"Talon!" Her nails dug into his hips. "Please . . ."

"The pain will pass," he rasped against her temple.

"Oh, please—"

"I swear, I would not hurt you for the world. It'll pass."

Crowded words broke on a dry sob beneath his mouth. "What have we done? Oh, Talon . . ."

Long fingers laced with hers as he brought her hands over her head. " 'Tis too late, Regan. For both of us." He sank into her softness, swallowing her whispered moans, until her body took all of him. Regan soared with shameless hunger. His husky voice formed into half-broken words over her mouth. "So . . . tight."

He dipped his head and laved her breasts, moving his hips

slowly at first until his powerful body rocked against hers, measuring her response to the searing rhythm tearing at the ragged edges of her control. Her breath came in pants. Finally releasing her hands, when she wanted him as she'd wanted nothing else in her life, he seemed to know the exact moment of her surrender.

Fostered by the thread of passion linking their bodies, she clung to him. Sensations swirled and dived, the feel of him driving into her, stealing all that she was until she gave herself completely to his carnal domination, losing herself to his body.

She cried against his mouth, consumed by the powerful need to meet his solid thrusts. To know more of this savage need surging over her body, raking her nerves, and finally draining her soul.

Talon muffled her cries of pleasure, surrendering to her passion, answering the madness with her name on his lips. He needed her. Her touch. Her essence. The raw yearning of it surged through him, wrenching a groan from deep inside.

Stiffening, he shuddered and spilled himself deep within her, fusing reality into oblivion. And finally darkness into nightmare.

Chapter Sixteen

Regret—the ungodly result of a conscience—hit Talon with the crushing force of a broadside.

What price would he pay for this act of lunacy?

Regan's hair fanned around her in a waterfall of ebony silk. Her wet gaze, raw and uncertain, searched Talon's face. She made him reckless and eager. Poor traits for a man who survived by keeping his wits intact.

He lifted a fine strand of her hair. "You're a pirate's treasure, sweet. It's been a pleasure. But one I already rue."

Regan's body stiffened in response. "You're the worst kind of thief for what you've stolen this night, Talon Drake." Her harsh whisper hinted of pain. She struggled against him. "Get off."

The harsh words abruptly banished any charitable thoughts he harbored in her direction. She made him feel like he'd betrayed her somehow. What did she have to lose now? Nothing. Hell, she'd won.

"Don't play the bereaved maiden, Regan." He eased from between her thighs. "I didn't hear any complaints from that lovely mouth a few moments ago."

She snatched the counterpane over her body, sliding back against the wall. "I'm neither bereaved nor a maiden any longer, Captain."

Talon shoved his legs into his breeches.

"And you didn't hear any complaints because you weren't listening."

Slowly, he turned to face her. The lanthorn light cast her skin in a creamy glow, highlighting her tousled hair. Awareness of him shone in her liquid eyes, fired now with pride. "Shall I prove again what a bad liar you are?" he parried, distinctly more at ease with her anger. It wiped away all trace of her vulnerability. He leaned his knee on the bunk and a dark brow lifted. "Hmm?"

A discernible tremble evident in her chin kept her tears in check. Suddenly he needed to get away from her.

He bent and retrieved his shirt and boots, dressing hastily. But when Talon's hand went to the door, ready to swing the heavy portal wide, something stopped him. That small part of humanity residing deep within, that made its appearance just often enough to annoy the hell out of him. To throw him off course like a bad compass.

He leaned an arm against the door. What could he say? He'd never known a woman like her. Passion and innocence. Heat to thaw a man's heart. She touched him in a way nothing ever had. He didn't want her thinking this moment had meant nothing to him.

"Regan—"

"Don't worry, Captain Drake. I'll still grant your annulment."

He shifted to face her.

"But only if you take me back to my brother. Ransom me if you will, but you *will* take me back. Or I'll grant you nothing more than what you've stolen this night. Which is more than you deserve."

Talon leaned casually with his back against the door. He ached to strangle her. "We're going to Tortuga, sweet, to repair the ship."

Her tongue darted over a mouth still ripe from his kisses. "Then leave me there. Any place away from you will suffice."

"Something to consider," he managed pleasantly. "Leaving you behind in that cesspool would certainly end my dilemma."

Turning away from her, Talon shut the door with scant restraint. He wanted to rip it off its hinges. Unable to reconcile himself to what he'd done tonight, or the primal emotion Regan evoked in him, he stopped to catch his breath.

He'd bedded the hot-tempered wench and should be free of this insane want of her. But Regan had done him no favors this night. Indeed, he still wanted her badly enough to realize that she was more dangerous than all the navies of Christendom put together. He *should* ransom her to Kendrick. The man wanted her back badly enough to risk his life. What did it matter that his reasons smelled as noble as bilge water. She was a Welles. Her loyalty would always lie with her brother. They deserved each other.

He left the companionway. Talon knew one thing at that moment; he would play the pawn no more!

Once on deck, he grabbed an ax that had been used to hack away debris still cluttering the deck. He went below into the hold. A single port window opened to the night, letting in the breeze. Robert's hastily constructed cell had been made from a stall that housed livestock. A pungent supply of straw lay piled in the corner. Chains rattled. Robert's shadow moved in the darkness.

"Drake? What are you doing?"

Robert's fear lent Talon a macabre sense of satisfaction. "At the moment?" He raised the ax then slammed it down with a whack, severing the thick length of chain bolted from the planked floor to Robert's ankle. "I'm changing our agreement."

"You've not met your side of the bargain, Drake."

"You're in no position to argue technicalities, Robert."

Dragging Robert on deck, Talon ignored the curious stares of his night watch. He ducked through the stern galley door. "I want your deposition, Robert. And I want it now." He pounded on his cabin door, then shoved it open. It slammed into the bulkhead.

Arabella and her mother screamed. Ignoring them in bed, he jerked Robert to the desk. "You'll begin your story, as you told it to me six months ago. As you'll tell it to the king."

Movement raised Talon's gaze. Regan stood framed within

the doorway, her beautiful face white with apprehension.

"Your daughter will marry Marcus," Talon said.

The mother burst out in tears. "Momma," Arabella protested.

"No!" Regan ran into the room. "There'll be an annulment."

Talon leaned against the corner of his desk. "Quite the contrary, Regan. I've decided I find marital bliss to my liking."

Regan swung on Talon, brown eyes flashing murder. "I'll not do this. I'll turn you in myself at the first port for the ten thousand doubloons on your bloody head."

Talon stood and faced Robert. "Whether you fill out that deposition or not, your daughter belongs to Marcus. But consider this"—he braced his palms on the desk—"if you don't, the sharks can finish what Kendrick started."

He snatched Regan by the arm.

"You can't do this!" She hit him, and dragged her bare feet to keep him from pulling her out of the room. "Marriage is sacred—"

Talon slammed the door behind them. "So sacred, you lied before God?" He pulled Regan out of the companionway up the stairs. She was still shouting at him when he reached the deck. "Man the wash-deck pumps, Jaime," he ordered.

Clearly baffled by the strange command in the middle of the night, Jaime did as he was told.

"You tricked me!" Regan shoved against him.

"Me?" He laughed. "Now isn't that the proverbial pot calling the kettle black."

"Tonight was your fault!"

"Aye." He stalked her. "My fault for taking the wrong bloody Welles in the first place. And again for falling victim to your twitching skirt, to your eyes, and the promise of your smile. A smile eagerly bestowed on every man in this crew but me. My fault for watching you every day, wanting to touch you, knowing I could make you my wife at any time, to hell with the bloody consequences."

Regan's back hit the quarterdeck wall. She was speechless, unable to utter a single scathing word in her defense. He'd stolen her voice, leaving her a breathless heap of matter. She heard the squeaking sound of a pump. And suddenly frigid salt water gushed from a huge sprocket over her head dousing her soundly.

Talon held her gasping beneath the water. "Something to cool your temper, sweet *wife*."

She screamed then sputtered.

His hot mouth caressed her lobe. "You lied to the priest, Regan. So suffer the consequences of your deception."

His mouth covered hers, melting against her lips. His hands slid to her bottom, lifting her against him, molding her pliant body to the scorching heat of his embrace. She shook her head, refusing to heed her body's traitorous reply to his touch.

She would not respond. She would not!

Her fists twisted in his wet shirt. The water befuddled her, seductively cooling her heated skin, racing over her face and hair, down her bodice in silken rivers. His hand crafted a blaze up her spine and tangled in her hair. She tasted salt water on his tongue.

Finally, Talon lifted his head. His wet hair slicked back from his face, the night shadows marked his stubbled jaw, making him devastatingly handsome, dangerous to her heart. He met her gaze, blinking back the crystal droplets cascading down his face.

"Soap, my dearest nun?"

Dazed by the strange words, Regan looked down in his hand and saw a skimpy ball of lye. Another glance told her he wasn't alone, that half his crew stood gawking at them, including Piers and Marcus leaning with arms crossed against the capstan. Jaime chose that moment to quit pumping. The seawater trickled to a stop, leaving only the creaking sound of masts to fill the heavy silence.

Pride snapped her gaze back to Talon's face. Furious tears stung her eyes. He'd not kissed her. He'd conquered her so all his men could see her humiliation.

Her palm cracked against his cheek.

Talon caught her wrist before she could whirl away. Slowly, deliberately, he pressed her hand to his mouth. "Go to bed, Regan."

She recognized the silver flame burning in his eyes. She'd

seen it often. It touched her now, not with cruelty, but compassion.

"Tomorrow will be a long day."

Regan jerked her hand away. "What day hasn't been overly long since I met you, Captain Drake?"

Once in the companionway she flew to her room and hurled the bolt home. With his kiss still burning on her mouth and hand, Regan wiped the one across the other, unmercifully seeking to rid herself of his presence on her body. But the tenderness evident between her thighs measured her loss completely.

Regan vowed to find a way to Martinique. Father Henri would know what to do. He knew the pirate Drake for the crime he'd committed against her parents.

To hold Talon accountable for her grief lent Regan a measure of self-righteous strength to fight him, her sanctuary against the horrifying crimes her father had perpetuated against him. Compassion for Talon's plight did not mean tolerance for his crimes. No matter the righteous cause. Vengeance was merely another name for murder.

But her body betrayed her, doomed her to peril.

Regan twisted away from the door. She missed her home. She missed her friend, Sarah. Next to Arabella, Sarah had always been her closest friend. They were teachers at the mission school, sharing girlish dreams of love and adventure.

In two months, Sarah would be taking her final vows. Regan intended to join her.

Regan awakened to the stifling heat. And groaned. The sun shone on the sea with an eagerness that baked the room. Nothing stirred the air. The rapid clank of the wash-deck pump told her the crew was hard at work watering down the canvas, hoping to harness the stingy breeze. Talon's voice rose above the din. For a long time, she listened, letting his voice wash over her body.

In disgust, she finally turned into the shadows and slept half the morning until Parrot pounded on the door.

"The cap says yer to eat, milady," he yelled through the door. "I'm ta fetch him if you've a mind to be difficult."

Regan wrapped herself in the counterpane. She threw the

bolt back and swung open the door. "Oh, really, Parrot." She stood aside and curtly motioned him inside. "Are you on his side, too?"

"From the way I sees it, milady, there's only one side." Parrot set the tray down on the empty bunk. "And it ain't yers."

"Out!"

Unabashed Parrot sauntered past, stopping before she could throw him out of the room. When he looked at her, it was not with the cocky eyes of a boy, but someone far wiser than his years. More than once Regan had seen that look.

"He ain't so bad, milady."

"You just don't know, Parrot."

"Oi ain't so blind as you, milady. The cap, he gots a fancy fer ya. Any fool can see it. And oi've seen enough of men to know 'e's not one ta give 'is heart ta just anyone."

Parrot left Regan gaping after his bedraggled form. She shut the door, leaning heavily against its support. Sweat beaded on her chest and brow. She remembered the cold shower beneath the wash-deck pump. She remembered more. Felt the erratic leap of her pulse . . . and heaved a frustrated sigh.

"His heart! A heart filled with vengeance."

She tried to shield herself from the tight knot of pain. Deep down, he was as alone as she was. But the past marked them, tainting their hearts, their dreams, and their lives. Reminding her again that time could never heal anything.

Regan attacked her chores with zealous intent. If she couldn't remove Talon from her mind through will alone, then she'd do it through exhaustion. Singlehandedly, she cleaned the forecastle deck of the last of debris. Stretching her sore back, she kneaded a fist against her hip. Heat beat down on her face. She looked at the sun. It was time to make her rounds below deck.

Gripping the water bucket, Regan jimmied open the rain barrel. She set the ladle aside and dipped the bucket inside. It scraped bottom, forcing her to lean into the barrel. The wind lifted her skirts. Regan jerked out and hit her head. A pair of strong hands gripped the bucket before she could drop it.

"You're a distraction to my crew, wife." Talon's voice shot her startled gaze to his face. He handed her the bucket. "Next time ask me to get the water." His eyes stoked the fire in her blood.

She gritted her teeth. How she longed to show him indifference! He wore no shirt. The burnished ripple of skin measured more than his strength and drew Regan's gaze with memories that made her blush.

"I am not your wife."

His laughter invited her ire. She despised the ease that he made light of her turmoil. He touched the bump on her forehead, and she swatted aside his hand. "There is such a thing as divorce, milord."

"On what grounds? You were the one who lied."

"You won't let me forget that, will you?"

"Not until I decide what to do with you."

She whirled. Talon caught her waist and spun her around. She slammed against his body with a heady gasp. Her fingers pressed against bare flesh and muscle. The bucket dangled uselessly in her other hand. Despite her fully clothed state, she could feel the burn of his nakedness. His eyes probed her flashing gaze. "And don't think a locked door will keep me from deciding, sweet."

"Oh." She pushed away. "Let me go."

But that night before the sun even set, she fled to her cabin. Talon's trunk sat against the bare wall. She slammed the door. Her hand clutched the dead bolt. With a sob, she let her fingers drop. Heart hammering in her ears, she undressed and slid beneath the counterpane. Nerves stretched taut, she waited. And waited.

Talon didn't come.

Nor did her torment end with the daylight. Regan felt his eyes on her all the next afternoon, watching her from the top castle platform as she read to the men or did the laundry. Once, she raised her eyes to watch him as he moved further up the shrouds to work. As if sensing her regard, his hands stopped in their task and he looked down at her. Her thoughts fragmented. It wasn't fair that he could hold such power over her that a mere glance could leave her breathless and scarcely able to focus.

Her stomach pulled. Regan refused dinner on deck and ate in her cabin. Light rippled the water. She stood at the port window and weighed the night. The bloated moon mocked her sanctuary. The stars only reminded her of his eyes. She rubbed her temples.

"What's happening to me?" she murmured hoarsely.

In her dreams, she trailed her hands pensively across her breasts up the slim column of her throat. His very memory mocked her body. Betrayed her will.

Fingertips traced her mouth and the ridge of her lips where he'd kissed her. Where his tongue teased and tormented and made her burn. In her dreams, his hands replaced hers. And something inside turned from ice to liquid heat. Something she couldn't name.

He was a pirate, black lord of the seas, and she could not raise arms against him. He was the candlelight in the cave, the warmth in her blood, a part of her being. In her dreams, he was there beside her, his name a whisper on her lips, his kisses a brand on her soul.

"Shh, sweet," his rasp came from the light to caress her mouth, her neck, her breasts, the very core of her being. The length of his body stroked hers with the sweet vibrancy of a tempest. In her dreams, there were no boundaries. No lies. No pain. Naught that could hurt her, and so she returned his embrace.

And awakened in his arms.

When he entered her this time, she felt only searing pleasure, a need so great it could not be measured by his touch alone. She clung to Talon, her soft cries swallowed by his kiss.

Afterward, Regan slept curled against him, but before the night watch signaled the change of crew, he left the cabin.

Hot tears threatened. Regan rolled over onto her back. She'd lain in bed with her enemy and felt naught but passion in his arms.

Desperate to be out of the cabin, Regan washed and dressed.

The sun had yet to rise. On the eastern horizon the first stark shade of coral blossomed and began to send fiery tendrils across the sky. The air smelled of the sea. And of peace. It smelled of Talon.

Gripping the rail, Regan drew in a deep cleansing breath. She'd never witnessed anything so spectacular as a Caribbean sunrise.

"It takes your breath away."

Talon's voice spun her around. His eyes bore no hint of his usual amusement. A somber figure dressed in black, he stood less than an arm's length away. His hair was tied away from his handsome face. The faded moonlight caught in his eyes as his gaze roamed her flushed face. He moved behind her to the rail, and together they looked over the awakening sea colored to a pale opalescence as if they were truly man and wife. His strength wrapped around her and melded with the very air that she breathed. He made her forget who she was. And Regan desperately needed to remember.

"This is my favorite part of every day," he said. "I usually spend it aloft."

Regan looked past his shoulder to the top castle platform. A sense of awe washed over her, fired by the strange warmth of Talon's presence. She wondered what the world looked like through his eyes.

"When I was a child, no tree was too high to climb," she shyly admitted. "I touched the sky. And dreamed of adventure. It was never enough to be on an island where the seasons never changed. Nicholas understood that about me."

"He's very loyal to you."

She sighed, aware that her life's journey had blessed her with the knowledge that Nicholas lived. She'd not behaved kindly to the man who'd been better to her than her own father. "Nicholas was a bond servant," she said. "He was right to get away when he could."

Her thick braid made a rope down her back. He touched her hair and slid his hand over her hip. Her stomach pressed against her ribs. His hand hesitated against the scar on her outer thigh.

"How did you survive it?" he asked. "The fall? Your leg?"

"When life is the most dark, light comes only from the

hope in your heart. You grab on to that and never let go. That light often opens into many windows."

"You have a strange religion, Regan."

"Without hope, there is no light."

Talon held her gaze as if he searched her very soul for the truth in those words. Then his eyes hooded and he was lost to her. Amusement replaced somberness. He was again the pirate captain.

With a roguish grin that tossed her wit to the wind, he remarked, "It's a long way to the top castle platform."

Her gaze swung aloft. He didn't remind her of her limp or question her ability to climb. A childlike surge of enthusiasm suddenly enveloped her. "I can do it."

Leading her to the ratlines, Talon wrapped strong hands around her waist and lifted her into the shrouds. "If you're going to fall, do it now."

"I'm not going to fall." If she took the climb slowly, there'd be no danger of entangling her feet in her skirts. She gripped the tarred hemp and started climbing.

Talon climbed beneath Regan.

The frayed hem of her dress brushed his head, indulging him with a glimpse of her shapely backside. A quick glance below assured him that none of his crew could see what he could.

He should be hanged on the yardarm for allowing her to take this dangerous climb. But something in her face betrayed that same reckless hint of spirit that so often drove him. Talon had seen it frequently, and until now never knew quite how to harness it. He could hear her laughter with the dizzying sway of the ratlines.

Jamie was on the top castle platform peering northward when Regan popped her head over the side. Stunned, he helped her stand, gaping at Talon as he followed.

Regan breathed reverently. "Look. The sky is so clear."

"I'll stand watch for now, Jaime," Talon said, taking the brass tube from Jaime's limp hand.

"Aye . . . I'll be going down then." Jaime's wide gaze locked on Regan who was flushed beautifully with excitement. "You'll be all right, milady?" He almost fell over the rail backing away.

"Oh, yes, Jaime." She pulled her gaze from the top of the mast still some sixty feet above her and watched him clamor over the side. She leaned over the wooden rail. "I suppose I've shocked him."

Even wearing that rag of a dress, she glowed. She never complained, he realized. She worked harder than any ten men did.

His wife's luminescent eyes lifted to encompass the world. "Oh, Talon," she breathed, "Look." She swept past him, her skirts brushing his legs. "It's so beautiful."

That he'd given her this gift filled him with a strange sense of possessive pride.

"There's the Orion belt. And the moon in the same sky as the sunrise. Listen—" She pivoted. "I've never heard such heavenly silence."

"Some say the space of time between the darkness and dawn is so quiet you can hear the stars."

Regan slanted him a grin. "And what do they say, Captain?"

Grimacing at his foolishness, he clasped his hands behind his back and cleared his throat. "It's not exactly words they speak." With an effort, he stepped away from her. "My mother was a devout Catholic. She put us to bed with tales of silver-haired angels. She used to say that when the earth slept, the angels kept watch."

"The stars—" A light came into Regan's eyes. "—are all silver-haired angels."

"And the time between night and day before the world awakens, you can hear them sing." How many years had he forgotten his mother's words? "My sister never stopped believing," he heard himself whisper.

Memories he'd made himself forget surfaced. For the first time in years, he felt his little sister's presence wrap around him. As he stared into the sky, he could almost believe she lived among those glittering stars. He could almost believe in peace as if the past had suddenly slipped away.

"That's a very beautiful story, Captain Drake."

Regan's face came into focus before he realized he was staring down at her. That she thought him—the worst kind of fatalist—incapable of such whimsy was obvious. "Is it so strange that I might have had a prior life?"

The light went out of her brown eyes and she averted her gaze. "I imagine even thieves and murderers were once children who suckled at someone's breast. Even you, Captain Drake."

Talon popped open the brass tube and proceeded to scan the horizon. Since dawn yesterday four new ships had appeared. He scanned to gauge their distance. But his mind was bent on Regan's words.

He tried to remember his other life. And couldn't. He was pirate, murderer, and thief. All she said he was.

Her father had done this to him as much as he'd done it to himself. The demons inside would not rest until they either destroyed him or he destroyed his enemies. There would never be any compromise. No halfway. Especially with her. And he'd lived this side of his life for too long to think he hadn't sacrificed a chunk of his soul for the promise of justice.

"When I was a boy," he finally said, lowering the glass, "I always thought tomorrow would go on forever. It was a shock to wake up one day and learn it doesn't. That the world could change, and all the wishing and wanting can never bring back those you love."

Regan didn't respond, and he turned, surprised to find her watching him. "I'm truly sorry," she whispered.

Talon handed her the glass. Her blank stare encompassed his hand. "Take it. You wanted to be close to your brother."

Her eyes raised in alarm. "What do you mean?"

"The *Viper* is out there." She snatched the glass away. Her eagerness irritated him. "Dead in our wake. She won't be going anywhere for a while."

"The governor's colors aren't flying."

"Even Captain Roth isn't stupid enough to sail into Tortuga with the governor's colors flying."

"Do you think they'll really go to Tortuga?"

Talon leaned a hip against the rail. Her distinct profile silhouetted the sunshine to the east. "Do you worry for me, sweet," he asked, "or him?"

She lowered the glass. "Why should I worry about you,

milord pirate? You're quite at home among these cutthroats."

"The *Viper* is not unknown among the good people of Tortuga."

"And what's that supposed to mean?"

"He outguns every ship in this port. Including mine. Your precious brother will be safe enough."

Regan's gaze hung uncertainly on his before she drew herself up. Her brevity lacked conviction. The distress he glimpsed in her brown eyes was clearly for him.

Chapter Seventeen

"Have ya ever seen the likes of this place, mum?" Parrot asked, standing at the rail beside Regan. His eager gaze swallowed Tortuga.

Regan had never seen a more wretched place in her life. Unlike her little island home of Martinique, the pirate port of Tortuga bustled with humanity. The filthy waterfront offered taverns aplenty. A breeze carried the taint of brine and sewage.

She found Talon easily, his height setting him apart from the riffraff swarming the docks. Her pulse quickened. A red kerchief bound his dark hair. Beneath a sleeveless tunic, powerful arms were bared to the sun. He stood among a group of men haggling over barrels that lined the walls of a warehouse. He'd wasted no time since their arrival yesterday refitting the ship and filling the stores. Supplies had been arriving hourly. He'd filled the hold with barrels and crates, timber, and livestock for food.

At this rate, they'd be leaving Tortuga soon. Again, Regan's eyes skimmed the two dozen ships anchored nearby, hoping she'd find the *Viper* among them. Had she missed her brother's arrival last night?

Regan turned back to the dock as a red-clad whore swaggered up to Talon. She froze in indignation. The blackguard seemed to catch the attention of every twitching skirt in Tortuga. Only this one, he didn't turn away. He gripped the hilt of his sword, moving it slightly, as he bent over the dark-haired girl and handed her something. It looked like a note. Regan couldn't see for sure.

Their cozy exchange irritated her. "Surely Captain Drake could have found someplace else to go for repairs." Martinique for example. Any enemy of England and Spain would certainly find haven there. And she wouldn't think twice about jumping ship.

"We ain't aimin' ta stay, milady." Jaime stopped and lowered his load onto the deck. He stepped beside Regan against the rail. "Piers and some men are out looking for a mapmaker what lives here. We'll be meetin' them three leagues north in a few weeks. Our ship should be repaired by then."

"A mapmaker?" Regan said the words absently. "What ever for?"

"Someone what sailed with the captain's father years ago." At her puzzled glance, Jaime straightened. "I thought you knew."

"Captain Drake's quest for the treasure is no secret, Jaime."

"Your uncle's map isn't enough. Cap'n Drake needs more."

"Robert has a map?" A chill swept down her spine.

"Aye, milady. There were two maps."

And she'd destroyed one. On the quarterdeck, Arabella's laughter intruded. Uncle Robert stood with her and his wife. Talon had finally allowed him on deck under guard. Where would Robert's loyalty lie if they couldn't find the treasure? What would happen to Talon then?

"The cap's comin' back," Parrot said.

Regan's pulse skipped. "Would you go to the galley and fetch lunch for the wounded?" she managed with indifference. "I'm sure they're hungry."

"Oi ain't that lightskirt cousin of yers that can be ordered about, milady. Ye can say, please."

Regan felt a twinge of guilt over her shabby treatment of Arabella. Her cousin had gone so far as to make herself useful in the hold most mornings helping with the wounded. And Regan knew Arabella, never having seen a sunrise in her life, hated mornings.

"*Please*, Parrot," she sweetly gritted out. "Now?"

Mumbling something appropriately rude, he left. Regan bent to the task at hand. The wounded had been moved from the hold and lay sprawled on deck in the sun. She knelt beside Charlie to swab his forehead with fresh water brought on board that morning. Charlie had lost a leg in the battle at Port Royal. His scarred, ashen features had not improved in three weeks.

She laid aside his silly hat with the claret feather. He valued the thing like gold. She always made sure it remained nearby. "Have you ever considered going into the planting business when this is over, Charlie?" she casually broached the subject. A common topic she shared with all of her patients. "Sugar, maybe. Or tobacco."

Skeptical blue eyes lifted to hers. "What would be the profit in that, milady?"

"At least there's honor in being a planter."

"Honor in slavery?" His raspy voice expressed shock. "Have you seen a plantation, milady?"

"But Charlie, to steal from others—"

"Where do you think the Spanish get the gold?" The topic filled him with life as if he knew firsthand the horror of the inquisition. "They steal it from the Indians, that's where. The ones they've murdered or enslaved. It seems to me any ship of Spain be fair pickin's for another thief stronger than they are."

His befuddled reasoning silenced her. "Who am I to argue your logic, Charlie?"

"You can still keep preachin' to us, milady." His lopsided grin warmed her. "We don't mind. It's sort of like attending mass."

Regan wrung the rag out and regarded him fondly. "I'll remember that."

Once, her fear of being cast to the mercy of this bedraggled group made her marry Talon. But they were only boys, most barely older than she was. Indeed, she'd foolishly cast her fate with the most rapacious of the lot. Talon Drake.

Her breathing quickened. An overpowering urge to defend him defeated her anger, and though her body rebelled against the memory of his touch, her mind remembered all too well the beautiful story of silver-haired angels. His tenderness for his sister betrayed the pirate and exposed the man she imagined he once was. She sensed loneliness about him, kindred to her own. Marcus knew it was there. He'd tried to tell her that night on the deck.

"You've been a bonnie good sport lookin' after us," Charlie sheepishly replied. "Especially considerin' how we treated you."

"I would do no less for any other, Charlie."

He touched her wrist. "But no one else would do it for me."

Regan checked the bindings on his leg. She didn't want to like these men, but she'd shared their pain and their suffering these past weeks. And somehow they'd become as real to her as Talon. Men with souls, lost and wandering. Men who could never go home again. "Didn't anyone take care of you, Charlie? When you were a child?"

"I don't suppose none of us here ever had the likes of a mother. Not the kind you had."

"My mother?"

"You've a kindness about ye, milady. And it didn't come from the man yer father was."

Caught off guard, Regan swallowed. "My parents are dead."

"Aye," he said quietly. "I was there when the *Rose* went down."

Shock stilled her gaze. Charlie's words tore the wound open all over again. How could she forget the ilk of these men?

"The captain would have taken off the survivors—"

"Charlie, please." She couldn't take the pain. Not now when she'd found herself drawn to the very man who'd killed her parents. Regan picked up the basket of sun-dried bandages.

He clutched her sleeve. "You'll be reading for us tonight, milady? Jaime said ye been learnin' him the letters."

"You're welcome to join us, Charlie."

"Thank you, milady. I will."

Regan turned to flee below. Robert's bedraggled form blocked her path. Alarmed, she scanned the deck for Marcus.

"He's with my daughter," Robert said. He reeked of rum.

"What do you want, Uncle?" Her arms ached and she felt the prickle of sweat where the sun burned into her back.

"I . . ." His stance shifted. "I wanted to talk to you."

Regan dropped the basket.

"I'm not an evil man, Regan."

"Evil?" She laughed. "Or good? I find the thread between the two very thin. You must understand my lack of charity for you, Uncle."

"Nothing has gone as planned."

Eyeing what remained of Talon's prized ship, she swallowed the sharp retort on her tongue. "We're in port, Robert. We should all escape while we've a chance. Before it's too late."

"And go where?" he said tiredly. "I need Drake's protection."

She stiffened. "Unlike you, I don't need Captain Drake's protection against my brother. What I *need* is to get off this ship."

"A bad idea, milady wife," Talon said from behind her.

She snapped around and found him leaning against the mainmast. Heat washed over her. Thoughts unbecoming a lady prowled the nether regions of her mind.

"And I thought you were finally adjusting to my hospitality."

"I have work to do, Talon."

Catching her hands in his, he stopped her from reaching for the basket. "I'm giving you the day off." His breath stroked her cheek.

"You mean you're locking me in my cabin."

"No." He politely lifted her fingers to his mouth and kissed them. "I *mean* I'm giving you the day off."

"Captain!" the lookout called, pointing starboard.

Regan felt Talon's arm tense. Beside her, Robert swore. Whipping around, she sighted the square-rigger crawling into Tortuga harbor.

The *Viper!*

Even from this distance, she could see the damage to the *Viper*'s masts. Holes pocked the canvas. Her bowsprit and top mizzen sails were missing. 'Twas a wonder she sailed at all.

Talon turned to Jaime who was standing at the rail. "Take my wife below."

"But you can't—"

"Go below, Regan."

Visions of Talon caught in a barrage of cannon fire threatened to ground her in panic. "Are you expecting trouble?"

He tipped her chin and kissed her nose. "Only from you, sweet."

"Talon—"

But he'd dismissed her. Calling for Marcus, he leaped up the stairs to the forecastle deck.

Work on deck stopped as Talon's crew watched the enemy's approach. The *Viper*'s crew also halted their work in the shrouds. Some had dropped to the deck and lined the rails. Animosity stretched taut between the two ships. Regan imagined even the people in Tortuga holding their collective breaths, silenced by the notoriety of two such formidable enemies within firing distance of the other.

Captain Roth stood tall on the quarterdeck, glass in hand, garbed in tan breeches tucked into thigh-high boots, his white silk shirt fluttering in the faint breeze. His gaze was fastened on the *Fury*'s prow. Talon stood braced against the fractured foremast.

A gentleman's salute mocked Roth's arrival, igniting a chorus of smirks among the crew. What the *Dark Fury* lacked in gun power, her captain certainly made up in bravado. Regan resented his arrogance as if the stakes he played for were less than his life.

She barely noticed when Jaime took her arm and guided her through the stern galley door.

Angry voices sounded from her cabin. She heard Arabella's mother yelling. Confused, she stepped forward. "What's happening?"

"Cap'n's orders," Jaime said. "Yer ta be moved to his room."

Regan stared aghast. "But what about—"

"Yer cabin has bunks enough to make 'em comfortable."

Two crewmen, clothed only in canvas breeches, passed carrying a brass tub into Talon's cabin. More men followed, hauling buckets of water. They nodded politely.

Jaime beamed. "A bath, milady."

Regan felt her pulse quicken. Even the *Viper*'s dramatic arrival was momentarily forgotten. "For me?"

"Captain's orders. Fresh water, too."

The stern galley door opened. More men entered carrying packages wrapped prettily in a fluffy red bow.

She recognized Harry's bristled countenance beneath the feminine accruements. He beamed handsomely. "Clothes, milady."

Stunned, Regan followed the line of men. Her arms crossed tightly against her midriff, she stopped just inside the cabin.

Harry laughed at her reticence. "Cap'n says ta throw yer current wardrobe away. He's sick 'a lookin' at it."

Her spine stiffened. "Is he now?"

"Picked these out hisself, milady. First thing yesterday." Harry eyed her shrewdly. "I think he got the measurements right."

Heat colored her face. "I'll have none of his generosity. He can give it to Arabella." She swung away, only to plow into Jaime.

"It won't do ya no harm to enjoy the bath, Lady Regan," he bid.

Miserably uncertain with herself, Regan slid a glance sideways at the tub. How long had it been since she'd enjoyed a freshwater bath? Her gaze touched longingly on the packages piled on the bed, then touched the shabby state of her gown. She didn't know how many more washings it could take before it dissolved in the salt water.

While she pondered her decision, the door closed. The outside bolt slid into place. Whirling to the portal, she beat her fists furiously. "Damn you, Jaime! Harry! I'll get you!"

She heard muffled laughter. Pressing her ear to the door, she listened as they climbed the stairs and left. Traitors! Regan turned to face the room. With her back against the door, she glared at the tub set invitingly near the filigree window.

A beautiful rainbow shimmered on the floor through the glass.

The window!

Regan ran to the galley window and stretched out. The noisy town lay to her distant right. Far below, garbage bobbed in the murky water against the ship's dark hull—too far to jump without making a huge splash, even if she was inclined to dive into that cesspool.

Regan shut her eyes. Confusion rocked her. It wasn't cowardice that kept her from leaping. No matter where her loyalty lay, it wasn't enough anymore to blindly run back to her brother.

But neither did she trust Talon. His every action was suspect. Even this bath. Irritated, with her lack of a viable plan, Regan pushed herself back into the room. And screamed.

"Nice day." Talon leaned with his leg propped against the stern galley to look past her out the window. "Admiring the view are we?"

"Of course I'm not admiring the view."

He caught her elbow and pulled her toward the bed.

"What are you doing?" Her heart hammered.

"It's dangerous for you here in Tortuga, Regan." He shoved aside the packages and sat her down. "That jump alone is enough to kill you. Or are you that desperate to escape my cruelty that you would risk life and limb?"

Regan sat on her braid and her movement made her flinch.

"Besides—" Talon released her braid. His voice had grown tender. "You'd probably hang yourself on your hair if you jumped. There's a lot of rivets on the way down."

The man led a despicable life. He was a thief and a murderer. A skilled liar. And yet for all that, her feminine side rebelled against her logic. His touch proved more perilous than any jump.

She sprang off the bed and hit the armoire. "I want you to leave."

"I came down to make sure you take a bath and change."

"Keep your plunder, Captain Drake."

Talon slipped a wicked-looking knife from his boot. "For some reason, I knew you'd say that. I even imagined you'd **try to escape.**"

"But I won't!"

His brow lifted skeptically. "Now, Regan." He wagged the blade in front of her. "We both know what your word is worth." He advanced a step, his buccaneerish grin as lethal as the knife.

Surely, he didn't mean to kill her. "But I won't escape—"

"There's a man on guard above the window. If you so much as stick your head out he'll signal the guard outside this room and you'll be tied to the bed." His eyes grazed the length of her. "Which for myself, I wouldn't mind."

Regan dodged past him. His arm whipped around her waist.

Talon made quick work of the rag she wore, stripping her naked. "How dare you! Get your hands off me!" He threw her over his shoulder. She pounded furiously on his back. "What are you doing?"

He bent to slip the knife back into his boot. "You smell like my men, Regan. Not an enticing proposition." He lowered her into the tub, dunking her thoroughly.

She came up sputtering for air. By the time she wiped the water from her face, he was dousing her with scented oil. Orange blossoms.

"I like my women smelling sweet."

"I'm not your woman."

A bar of soap splashed in the water over her belly. "You have three hours to be back on deck. Nicely attired, smelling like a tropical flower. I wish to dine with you."

"I'd rather dine with the livestock."

He knelt beside the tub, his boots creaking. And she went still. His hand slid beneath the weight of her hair to cup her head. "If you're not dressed"—the jagged warmth of his breath tingled her lips—"I'll accept that as an invitation to skip straight to dessert. And join you down here."

Shock encumbered her speech. A callused thumb traced a drop of bathwater down her face. She wanted his touch, was stunned by the power of that need and the hunger in his. Several moments passed before her cloudy mind registered his sudden frown.

He released her. "I'll see you soon, Regan."

Talon pivoted away from the tub and quit the room.

Shutting the door behind him, he leaned against its solid planking. "Christ," he said on an exhale. That troublesome piece of baggage had ruined him. He thought of her constantly: the swell of each perfect breast in his hands, the downy curls between her thighs, the way her luminous eyes could read a man's soul, spinning a bond between them. Another moment and he'd have had her on the bed.

"Tough day, Captain Drake?" the melodious voice interrupted.

Arabella stood poised at her door ready to enter, obviously stopped by his unorthodox exit from his room.

His eyes narrowed on her beautiful face. "Tell your family, dinner will be served topside." He'd be damned if he were going to dine with Regan alone. "Three hours."

Arabella's gaze lifted to the door. She smiled knowingly as if she'd read his thoughts. He strode up the stairs. "Oh, Captain?" she called after him. "Thank you for the lovely dresses you purchased for Mother· and me."

"Thank Marcus," he said without turning. "You're to be married before we go to England."

Regan slumped over the desk and stared at the hourglass she'd removed from one of the curio shelves. The face blurred. She took another swig of rum and shuddered.

Three hours, she scoffed, and flipped the timepiece again. She'd show him.

Tapping at the door lifted her head. Arabella peaked inside, her blond curls bouncing merrily. She met Regan's suspicious glare. "Everyone is waiting," she announced.

"Go away, Arabella."

Looking regal in apricot satin trimmed with ivory lace, Arabella swept into the room. She walked around the desk, noting first the new silky chemise Regan wore, then the disheveled state of her hair still uncombed from her bath. Lifting the bottle of rum, she shook it as if to verify its contents. And burst out laughing

"Oh my God! I've never even seen you drunk before." She sniffed the bottle. "Black Rum. Hmm. Very bad for you, Regan."

"Do you think?"

She set the bottle down and beamed. "Let's get you dressed."

Blatantly ignoring Regan's foul mood, Arabella turned toward the bed. "Oh, Regan," she cooed, digging through lacy drawers, stockings, nightclothes, and petticoats Regan had unwrapped and discarded. "Look what he bought you." Arabella lifted a royal blue velvet gown before settling on the citron taffeta. She swung around to face Regan. "You'll wear this."

Regan blinked. She wanted to lash out at her cousin's noisy interference, but another part wanted to . . . "Why are you here?"

A blond brow lifted in reprimand. "Frankly, I'm tired of you ignoring me." She shook the dress out. "And someone has to see that you make it through this whole affair intact. You obviously lack the sense to know what's good for you."

"How dare you judge the choices I've been forced to make."

"What?" Her hand flew to her chest and fluttered. "Me judge the honorable Regan Welles . . . Drake? Never!"

Regan stared into the glass cupped in her hands. "What do you care what happens to me?"

"Because I love you, Regan."

"Oh, please." She didn't want to hear this.

"You're my family. You stood beside me even when I left you in that cave, when I was too frightened to go in myself." She knelt beside Regan's chair, her gown flowering dramatically around her. "Because you're the only real friend I ever had."

Regan straightened. "I told you, the cave wasn't your fault."

Arabella's blue eyes welled with tears. "And I'm sure you meant it. But don't you see? Maybe if I'd gone in with you you'd never have fallen and broken your leg. They'd never have sent you away."

"If you'd gone in with me you would have fallen, too. The cave was unsafe. The whole floor collapsed."

"I left you on the beach that day. I've lived with it every **second since.**"

Regan jumped to her feet and stumbled. If Arabella had been remotely honorable and not abandoned her on the beach that day, she'd be the one married to Talon now.

Irrational jealousy filled her. "Oh, stop it!"

"Listen to me for once."

Regan plugged her ears. She preferred her anger. Didn't Arabella get it? Anger made her strong. "Go away."

Arabella wrestled Regan's hands. "You're going to hear me out."

They both stumbled over a box and sprawled across the floor, knocking the breath out of Regan. She found herself straddled.

"You're drunk, cousin." Arabella giggled.

"And you're having too much fun," Regan choked unable to break Arabella's grip on her wrists. "What's wrong with you?"

"I'm happier than I've ever been. And you could be, too."

"With a pirate? Are you bloody mad? What future is that?"

Arabella slammed her wrists against the floor. Her long blond ringlets wilted over Regan's face. "Follow your instinct for once. Talon Drake is not your enemy."

Regan spit out the golden strands of hair. "Get off me!"

"Not until you promise to get dressed."

Regan met the determined blue orbs and knew a sudden ridiculous urge to cry. "You're a bully, Arabella."

The observation brightened Arabella's face. "Why, I think that's the nicest thing you've ever said to me, cousin."

"Let me up."

Arabella smiled sweetly, clearly enjoying her superior position. "You still haven't promised to get dressed. Or to be nice to me," she added as an afterthought.

The absurdity of her plight snatched Regan's guard. Arabella had somehow finagled a victory from their scuffle. The room swirled. "I think I'm going to be sick."

"I don't recommend that you throw up, Regan. It'll be a most unpleasant experience in your present position."

They were ten years old again, untouched by tragedy, alive and forever in trouble. Regan giggled. Soon Arabella was sprawled on the floor beside her. They both laughed until tears streamed from their eyes. Regan tried to lift on an elbow, but caught her hair. Arabella saw her struggle and laughed harder falling back against the pair of scuffed boots that had suddenly appeared.

"Captain," she gasped.

Regan's head tilted back and her gaze followed the stout length of well-muscled thighs, over the black Holland shirt, to settle intrusively on the most mesmerizing eyes she'd ever seen. Her heart made a reckless thump in her chest. "Has anyone ever told you how beautiful you are?" she said.

Talon's delectable mouth curled slightly. "Not recently."

Clearing her throat, Arabella struggled to sit. "We're almost ready, Captain. We've had some things to discuss."

"You Welles's have the damnedest way with family discussions."

Regan mustered her dignity. "We are most passionate, Captain."

Talon's gaze remained gently attached to Regan. "We're waiting dinner for you both. When you're ready."

It seemed to take him an effort to turn away and leave.

Regan rolled on her belly to better assess the doorway, as if Talon lingered within its frame. Her heart beat a strange cadence against her ribs. Her skin still burned where his eyes had touched and no voice of logic raised its ugly head to shatter the illusion.

"Arabella?" she entreated. "I want you to make me beautiful."

Chapter Eighteen

Talon remained on the forecastle deck throughout dinner, ignoring the revelry below. Night had descended, blanketing the bay in a velvety morass of stars. Overlooking Tortuga harbor, his men lined the shrouds in various stages of watch. The water glowed with the amber warmth of small lanthorns, reflecting from the deck. He could see the *Viper*. And they could see him. He'd made sure of that.

He'd also made sure the merrymaking concealed any noise his men made swimming across to the *Viper*. The success of his plan depended on carrying it off undiscovered.

The music started again. He flinched. Christ, his men were bad. But at least they were loud. With hands clasped behind his back, he turned to survey the small dinner party on the main deck.

Arabella danced with Marcus in a flourish of ungainly steps masquerading as the minuet. In the shadows, Robert sat with his prune-faced wife away from the festivities. Talon's gaze fixed on Regan sitting alone at the table tapping fingers in time to Arabella's steps. He swallowed the strange force of emotions that threatened. Like a dozen other times that night, he stared.

Curls that tumbled from the pile atop her head framed her face. A wealth of yellow taffeta flowed over her chair, opening around her like a vivid sunflower in bloom. Its fitted neckline bared her shoulders, accentuating the sensuous curve of her breasts. Her beauty rivaled the sultry tropical night.

Talon considered how different the two cousins were, how unsuited he was to the younger who lacked passion, the kind Regan inspired—once tasted, never forgotten.

Behind him, his hands clenched into fists as he felt the first formidable tinge of cowardice for what he planned to do. The need to purge her from his life now became an act of deceit. Even now, with the *Viper*'s arrival, the pact was being made. He'd given the note to a young girl that afternoon to be delivered upon Kendrick's arrival detailing the terms for the trade: a governor's pardon for he and Marcus in exchange for Regan.

Talon was bartering his bride to the devil.

His gaze shifted to Robert slumped in the chair. A bottle of rum a day had made his features gaunt. Tattered rags covered his wasted body. Talon believed in the success of Robert's plan months ago. Now, too much depended on the testimony of a man who'd sunk to the depths of a drunk. Talon needed that pardon. Or he and Marcus wouldn't live long enough to seek an audience with King William.

Regan was his wife, but she was still a Welles.

Tomorrow she'd have her wish and be gone from him.

So, why hadn't he just told her his plan? Because deep inside he knew he'd found something remarkable, something good within her that touched him in a way nothing ever had before. He didn't want to witness her eagerness to leave him for a vile man like Kendrick. He didn't want to let her go. But knew he must.

Talon watched as Marcus stopped in front of Regan. "Dance with me, me beauty." Marcus elaborated with a bow that caused Talon to roll his eyes. He listened as they argued the merits of dancing.

Squaring his shoulders, he turned back to the rail, where the world opened before him with a sprinkling of glittering stars. And a new kind of darkness he'd never seen before. The notion lingered that he could travel that endless sky and it would never be far enough from her.

• • •

"I can't, truly, Marcus." Regan felt inept not being able to dance, even to nerve-scraping music as that, which hovered over the deck. " 'Tis unseemly," she pleaded. "I've never danced in my life."

"Your rejection hurts, milady," he said, taking Arabella back in his arms. "Perhaps I can bore you for another dance, my dear."

" 'Tis no bore, milord." Arabella laughed as he swept her away.

Regan's breath caught. Looming tall before her, Talon stood in the shadows next to the mainmast. The moonlight shaded his face but she could feel his gaze hot against her skin, melting through her.

He stepped into the lanthorn light, and she met the fire in his quicksilver eyes. The sea breeze tugged at his hair. "Everyone should dance, Regan. At least once."

She wanted to deny her ability, but the words didn't form.

"If you don't step on my feet, I'll not step on yours." He offered his hand. "May I have this dance, milady wife?"

Regan's heart pounded heavier than a drum. He held her gaze. And somehow the music suddenly seemed less horrid. Regan placed her smaller hand in his, teetering as she made an undignified attempt to stand. Talon wrapped his other hand around the curve of her waist. It didn't matter how he held her, only that he did.

"You'll have to forgive my orchestra," he said quietly, his breath hot on her ear. "I had no time to audition their talents."

The heat of him passed through the barrier of her gown. "You've gone to a lot of trouble, Talon."

His eyes never left her face. Contrary to her awkwardness, Regan felt him move skillfully to a rhythm that had nothing to do with the noise being played, and breathless, she followed in step. He'd danced this dance long ago. Perhaps in a gilded ballroom with a pretty girl in his arms, a worldly future ahead, dreams to follow.

What had Talon's dreams been? she wondered, then closed her eyes. Her pulse drummed in her ears. She didn't want to think of that now. Not of his loss, or the pain he'd endured. Let tonight stand alone, just for them. She wrapped her arms around his neck.

Eyes closed, she lifted her face drunkenly to the stars and drifted on moonlight. He smelled of bay rum and the salt-scented breeze. He filled her senses. Touched every nerve until she tingled. He was the man she'd glimpsed when they'd climbed to the top castle platform. The enigma that was Talon Drake. Strength and softness.

Something carnal seeped through her. She was acutely aware of his every hardened inch. Opening her eyes, she found that they'd stopped in some shadowy recess beneath the quarterdeck.

Talon's silver gaze fixed on her. He wore a strange expression that had nothing to do with the unholy lust burning in his eyes. "You test my nobility, Regan. Meager as it is." His hands tangled in her hair. "What am I to do with you?"

Sinfully happy and fully aroused, she nuzzled his warm wrist. "Should I suggest to the pirate Drake what he could do?"

A corner of his mouth lifted. "You're foxed, sweet."

"Am I?" She traced her finger along his bottom lip thinking she'd never seen such delicious lips. "Then I would stay this way."

"Why?" His husky voice enveloped her.

Regan lifted on her toes. "Because I can tell the rest of the world to go to the devil. Because I think you're beautiful and I want to kiss you." She touched her lips to his. He seemed shocked by her ardent assault, and she pulled away to gauge his strange response. "Don't I smell flowery enough, good sir?"

"You're drunk, Regan."

"Totally. And although you've ignored me all night—" She gripped his shirt collar and arched against him. "—I'm still throwing myself at you."

She boldly kissed him. For a space of a dozen rapid heartbeats, she felt his resistance. Then his hands moved up her spine and curled in her sleeves, her hair. His lips softened over hers. Passion swelled between them. With a muffled groan, his kiss rapidly changed. Grasping her head with both hands, he thrust his tongue between her parted lips, savoring her with savage intensity. Clinging to his powerful body, she moaned, unable to comprehend the strange, wonderful delirium that had taken hold. She floated.

His hand found her breast and her head fell back from the sheer force of his touch. He dragged her against him, leaving a hot trail of kisses down her neck. Crying out incoherently, she arched against his thigh, needing to ease the fiery ache building inside.

"Regan," he rasped, breaking the contact to nuzzle her hair. He kissed her again, a long languorous mating. "We are not in the most private of places."

Her blood gushed through her veins in a deafening roar. "Maybe you know someplace better," she whispered breathlessly.

With a strangled groan Talon plucked her off her feet and carried her back to the main deck. "Wake me later," she heard him tell Marcus.

Head resting on his chest, she listened to his beating heart and not the tiny voice that berated her shameless display before her family. Then she was in Talon's room on his bed, her eyes closed to the swirling sensations inside.

Suddenly mindful that she was alone in the darkness, she called out. He leaned over her, kissing her. "I'm right here, Regan."

Her arms wrapped around his neck. She reveled in the muscles rippling beneath her splayed hands. Giving a little sigh her hands fell away. "Am I your wife, truly?"

Talon's eyes darkened to a smoky gray. His hand spanned her belly, raising to cover her breast before curling into her hair and tilting her face. "Regan—"

Her heart jolted at the intensity in his eyes. "Don't you want me, Talon?"

"Aye," he whispered against her mouth. "More than you know."

"Is that so bad, then? To want me?"

"Tomorrow will be different."

Regan glimpsed indecision in his eyes. Had she hurt him? "I don't want to think about tomorrow. Only tonight. Please—"

His mouth moved over hers. "Aye," his words echoed

faintly and to her ears, not without regret. "Only tonight, then."

A long, sensuous kiss followed. Unbridled by logic or conscience, hunger drove her passion, unlike anything else in her life. He removed her clothes. She absorbed the cascading wealth of sensation roiling over her naked body everywhere he touched. He wrapped his fingers in her hair, kissed her lips, her cheeks, and the curve of her neck. His groan rumbled against her throat, mating with hers as she rolled herself on his body, her hot breath fanning across his furred chest.

"Dear Lord—" She tossed her head back. Her hair fell in a silken waterfall over Talon's thighs. His hands cupped her breasts. Her voice hitched. Reacting instinctively to his touch, she bent and kissed him, drawing him tight against her mouth and body until she felt him lift her, turning her on her back. Her hair fanned wildly around her. She met his burning eyes as he poised above her and touched the heated juncture between her thighs. His fingers stroked her with icy hot fire, blinding her with sweet sensations.

His chest heaved with shallow breaths as if he'd been running. "Touch me." His husky voice pressed against her mouth.

The wind kicked up, carrying the wet-scented breeze of rain through the cabin. The ship gently rocked. She could hear the faraway roll of thunder and it vibrated in her veins.

Savoring the languid heat of his body, her hands roamed feverishly over hot flesh, finally taking his erection in her hands. His throaty growl lifted her eyes to his, hot and burning with desire. He kissed her again grasping her bottom. She cried out as he slid into her, filling her completely. So completely. Her breath caught.

"Love me, Regan," his voice was ragged. "For tomorrow as sure as the sun rises, you will hate me again."

She wanted to say that she would never hate him again. Pleasure rippled through her and her thoughts shattered. His words became hers, incoherent whispers at first until she heard them over his breathing and the gentle unrelenting assault on her body.

"Love . . . you," she rasped repeatedly with each mounting crescendo that drew him deeper inside, pitching her higher.

He mated with her as if it were their first time, their last time, thrusting deeper, dragging her arms over her head, lacing his fingers with hers. She whimpered and arched, carried aloft by his sensuous movements, his name a small cry on her lips. She clung to him, confused by the terror of her emotions, dissolving, melting her fear of tomorrow. Her breaths came in pants, shallow and dizzying, and finally shattering around her like glass.

Talon joined his mouth to hers, riding her, straining. He arched his head back, catapulting her into the brilliant light where she rode the sensual tide until he shuddered, until his mouth found hers again, until he fell against her, spent at last.

Regan twined her arms around him, frightened by this drunken need to hold him, to ease the hunger in her heart.

He kissed her temple. "What am I going to do?" Easing out of her, he pulled her into his embrace and dragged the counterpane over their sated bodies. "Tell me, Regan. Tell me."

The lanthorns in the cabin were no longer lit. In the safety of Talon's arms, Regan closed her eyes. Outside, rain began to fall, drifting gently on the tropical breeze.

"You make the darkness go away," she whispered against his heart. "That's all that matters, Talon."

Light tapping on the door intruded. Talon stirred. Wind billowed the curtains. He gently untangled himself from Regan's arms. She didn't move, and he covered her. Stepping into his breeches, he went to the door.

"The missive arrived five minutes ago," Marcus said. "Roth has agreed to meet you. The Lion's Inn. Dawn."

"Where's Kendrick?"

"Didn't say."

Eyeing Marcus who clearly noted his undressed state, Talon scraped his hands through his tangled hair. "Is everything else ready?"

"The men swam back from the *Viper* before midnight."

"Any word from Piers?"

"He doesn't expect you to wait for him. He'll meet us later at the appointed place on Hispaniola."

Talon hesitated. The galling reality of what he was about to do hit him, and for the first time in his life, confidence failed him. "All right, then. Ready the longboat. I'll be on deck in a few minutes." He shut the door only to find it blocked with the toe of Marcus's boot. Talon's eyes shot up.

"Have you told her?"

"The decision is already made. One that you and I both made."

"Jesu, Talon. Everything's different now."

"Nothing's changed, Marcus."

His expression fervent, Marcus looked away. A lock of dark hair swept across his face. "My whole life you've spent protecting me. You've taken care of me, taught me to captain a ship. You've picked me up when I didn't want to go another day. I survived these past years because of you. Let me do something for you," he pleaded. "I release you from this insane quest. We can find another way."

Glaring furiously, Talon leaned a fist into the door frame. The other gripped the portal latch with such force, he felt it jar lose. Their future, Marcus's future, depended on the success of this transaction. "Remind me again that we're entrusting our lives to that drunken man in there." He nodded curtly toward Robert's cabin. "And tell me why I don't have to do this. There *is* no other way and you damn well know it." Christ. He couldn't trust himself to say more.

Talon shut the door on his brother.

Braced against the door frame, his hands formed two hard fists against the solid portal. Marcus's bootsteps faded. He regretted the disappointment he'd seen in his brother's eyes.

By God's blood, he was a fool to torment himself in this way. The Welles family had destroyed him, ripped the very fabric of his life from beneath him. He should feel no regret. Regan's loyalty lay with her brother, and Kendrick wanted her so bloody bad, he'd just agreed to give Talon what he wanted. A pardon.

Talon had won the first battle.

So, why did it feel like he'd just lost the war?

• • •

Smiling, Regan turned into her pillow. Her body ached all over. Her mind a fuzzy recollection of fragmented emotions and memories, she lifted on her elbow. Talon was gone.

Blowing hair from her face, she stared groggily around the room. Pale gray light revealed the first hint of dawn. Packages and clothes littered the floor. Her bath remained as she'd left it yesterday. Crawling out of bed, she kneaded her temples. The sound of a boat being lowered into the water drew her to the window.

Her heart stopped. She saw Talon, his black shirt unlaced to the breeze, and Harry beside him looking half drunk. The other men in the boat she'd seen often working the shrouds. Regan's gaze searched the shoreline. Rickety skiffs lined the beach, lying on their sides. The pier was practically empty, as was the thatched marketplace. Where were they going?

Then Talon's voice carried over the quiet morning breeze, and every intimate memory last night came crashing down. Whirling back into the room, she shivered. "Lord, what have I done?" Shamed by last night, by her continued weakness, by her love, oh yes, by her love, her gaze fell on the bed and tears filled her eyes.

He'd murdered her parents.

And yet, for all his talk of vengeance, he looked at her with a tenderness that burned to her soul.

Her heart beat the painful truth. His raw courage drew her to him but it was the depth of his compassion for people: his brother, his crew, for a boy who had faced the gallows that finally bent her heart. Knowing the man, his flaws had become less real. And understanding him, his motivations for the things he'd done, she understood less of hers. Loyalty to Harrison was no longer enough to keep her away from Talon.

Resentment flared. She blamed God for throwing her into the jaws of the lion, casting doubt into her life, marring her with horrible guilt and the inability to see the truth. She knew only that Talon's damning accusations against her family would destroy Harrison.

And still, she found herself wanting to believe in Talon.

"Lord," she raised her eyes. "Surely, you've struck me down with a lightning bolt of stupidity." Nothing else could explain losing her heart to a pirate. What next? Her very soul?

Fear of imminent dishonor lent momentum to her decision. She couldn't stay a moment longer. The conflict weighed too heavily in her heart. Away, she would seek the truth.

Regan padded to the window. The *Viper* was moored a hundred yards away. The shore was closer. With the exception of a few fishermen, the beach remained lifeless this early in the morning.

She dragged the heavy mahogany chair to the door and propped it back against the latch. Then she proceeded to the bed and began shredding the linens, tying them in clever little knots.

No one would hear her descent into the bay.

Chapter Nineteen

Smoke filled the tavern with a hazy stench. The room reeked of sweat and urine. Despite the early hour, men in various stages of drunkenness filled the tables. Talon's presence at the Lion's Inn stirred the lot to life. A thick slab of wood, cut from the trunk of a huge mahogany, stretched over two barrels and served as the bar. A barkeep, busy swabbing a row of pewter mugs, nodded as Talon and Harry passed to the back of the common room.

Talon breathed in the stink of the place. What was he doing in this cesspool? He felt like a callous sonofabitch. Nothing was simple. Not that anything had ever been simple in ten years.

"Top a the mornin', Cap'n." A man blocked Talon's path, his one blue eye narrowed shrewdly.

"Smitty," Talon acknowledged.

Smitty was the town crier, an ambitious toad who needed no reason to start a fight.

"Seen that fine craft of yers," he expostulated, rocking back on the heels of his silver-buckled shoes. A leather doublet, missing half its buttons, opened over his protruding belly. "Rumor has it yer responsible for the shape Roth's ship is in."

Talon's dark brow lifted. "What do you want, Smitty?"

"A surgeon went out to the *Viper* last night. The governor a Jamaican hisself, bless his black soul, is ailing from injuries suffered during your send-off a few weeks ago at Port Royal."

The news caught Talon's interest.

"It surprised us he had a sister," Smitty continued. "Musta had her tucked away. Hear tell she's a comely sight—"

Talon shoved him aside and walked past. Discussing Regan with the man would only cause him to draw his sword. Talon found a table in the shadowed corner. Adjusting the length of his scabbard, he sat with his back to the wall and stretched his legs out. The wooden chair creaked, protesting his weight.

"A bloody pox he is," Harry spat.

Smitty never ran around without his henchman. Talon scanned the taproom, but found the one-eyed man gone.

The tension didn't leave him.

Images of Regan wavered before him, more beautiful than the sunshine. That he should wax poetic over any woman warned him anew. He admired her steadfastness, eternal defiance, and loyalty. God in heaven, what he wouldn't give to own even half of her allegiance.

She was no part of Robert's plan, yet Talon knew the equation would no longer work without her. He had to let her go. For Marcus. For the future. For her. She'd robbed him of his senses if he thought there could be another way.

"Do ya think Roth'll show?" Harry asked.

"He'll show."

"Never made sense. Him being the type to work fer Kendrick."

"Roth would slice your throat if he thought you deserved it."

"Do you think the governor is really ailing? Will Lady Regan be safe?"

Safe? The notion was absurd. Kendrick was a cold-blooded killer. His gut crawled.

Talon sat up.

To hell with it all. Regan belonged to him. He wasn't letting her go. "Come on, Harry. We're getting out of here."

"Cap'n Drake." Slapping down two pewter mugs of foamy brew, a buxom brunette bent over the table. Her dingy white blouse hung from one brown shoulder, and tucked loosely in a ruffled red skirt stuffed in her waistband. The scent of sex clung to her thighs.

Impatient to be gone, Talon nodded. "Clarissa." Black curly hair framed a pert face now lined with exhaustion. The last time he'd spent here at the tavern, he'd brawled over the whore, and lost if he'd recalled the night correctly. He'd been too drunk to care either way.

"I ain't seen ya here fer a while. Heard tell they granted you a pardon. King William hisself."

"I'm working on it, Clarissa."

Her chin lifted. "Hear tell ya got yerself hitched. A fine one to be sure. Tall, long dark hair, a regular mermaid—"

Talon slapped a gold coin on the table. "Get some rest, Clarissa." But when she snatched up the coin, he caught her arm. "Wait. How do you know what she looks like?"

"Why, Captain," the maid laughed, "she just climbed down the backside a that devil ship a yers."

Regan heard the clank of chain behind her. A longboat was being lowered from the *Dark Fury*. Marcus's shouts pulled her around. She bobbed in the water, her thin chemise billowing around her hips, swirling with her hair. She steadied herself in the gentle swell.

Marcus furiously paced the deck. Regan glimpsed Talon's temper in his younger brother. "Don't be a fool, Goddammit," he yelled. "Get back here. It's too dangerous."

Regan twisted around. How could she explain that it was more perilous for her to stay? That she was being ripped apart.

She'd have to swim fast if she was going to beat the longboat to shore. The cool water felt good. Despite her leg and the fading remnants of a nasty hangover, Regan swam. Fast, she realized as her heart beat erratically with the pace. She drew in deep breaths, plunging her arms into the water, gliding across its oily surface. Marcus's shouts faded. The pier stretched out before her, attached to wooden pilings buried into the harbor's silty bottom. Salt water stung her eyes. Regan could hear the slap of oars behind her. Frantically she swam, clawing now at the water.

The pilings loomed before her. She reached out to pull

herself over the wooden trestle onto the pier and grappled, searching for a hold. Suddenly someone seized her hand, dragging her from the water. She stumbled forward into the hardened length of a man's body.

"Captain . . . Roth!" Her breath came in huge gasps.

"Lady Regan." Dark eyes grazed her dripping form. "What an unexpected surprise."

His eyes trained on the approaching longboat, he stepped around her. Regan grabbed his sleeve. Marcus was outnumbered. "Don't hurt them, please. Let's get out of here." Before Talon saw her.

Roth seemed amused as he assessed the approaching war party. The boat stopped rowing fifty feet out, the swell edging them toward the beach. Marcus stood in the boat and watched them. The sunrise blanketed the sand in a soft amber glow. Last night's rain freshened the air. Regan shivered despite the warm breeze.

"Please," she urged again. Thankful Roth had somehow found her. But she wanted to leave. Needed to leave. Now!

The breeze ruffled his blond hair. "And I thought to defend your honor, Lady Regan, from these ruffians." A roguish grin split his handsome features as he touched his fingers to his head in a salute to Marcus. "Nice to see you again," he called.

"Dammit, Roth. Let her go."

"Obviously she prefers my company to that bastard brother of yours." His voice grew serious. "Tell Drake he can go to hell. I'm taking the girl back to her brother."

Roth turned with her. His dark gaze fixed on his men and she became conscious of their stares. With her chemise sucking to her like a glove, her lack of foresight to bring along more clothes became blatantly obvious. Roth ordered his men to back off.

"You're a lot of trouble, Lady Regan. Drake was a fool to let you out of his sight." He yanked his shirt from the waistband of his buff breeches, his muscles rippling as he shrugged it over his head. "Unless you intend to cause a riot, this will have to do for now."

Regan noticed other men gathering nearby. The scurvy lot looked none too friendly. His hand on the small of her back,

Roth hastened her off the wooden pier. He lifted her onto
the beach, over flotsam littering the white sand. Four of his
men formed a semicircle behind them. The other one walked
a few paces ahead. Her feet made sucking noises in the wet
dirt.

"You've a lot of guts, Lady Regan," Roth said conversa-
tionally, taking her mind from the men gathering near the
marketplace. "You blew Drake's plan all to hell. I was going
into town now to discuss your trade."

Regan stumbled. Roth caught her elbow. "Milady—?"

"Talon was going to trade me?"

"Your brother wants you back badly enough to grant
Drake a full pardon. I was on my way to make the arrange-
ments right now."

She stopped. "But . . . he'd have told me."

"I'm sorry, Lady Regan."

And he was. She read it in his dark eyes, nearly black, a
stark contrast to the blond hair swept recklessly over his
brow by the warm breeze. She'd known Quentin Roth for
nearly a year and during all that time while he sailed for her
brother, she'd never seen him sorry about anything.

Numbly her gaze dropped to the sheet of folded vellum
he held out. Unable to hide the tremble in her fingers, she
opened it. She recognized the script, had seen it on the marriage document.

Regan read its brief inscription. Talon Drake was selling
her off. He'd wooed her with kindness. Seducing her, devouring her like the predator he was. The bath, the new
clothes. He'd simply cleaned her up for her brother. To think
she'd accepted for one breathless moment that nonsense
about being his wife.

Lies! Everything had been a lie. He'd merely found a
quicker means to an end through her. Regan's fist closed
around the paper crushing it. How last night must have made
him laugh.

"Harrison agreed to this pardon?"

"Obviously you're worth a lot to your brother."

Her view of the world rapidly declined into a tailspin.
"And what worth might that be, Captain Roth?"

"Captain," one of Roth's men called out. "We got trouble."

Roth's head snapped up. "Damn!" He edged Regan behind him.

A mob marched toward them. They fanned open, boxing Roth against the sea. He drew his sword, revealing his intent to fight.

One of the motley lot swaggered forward. "Now the way I sees it, Roth—" The pirate locked thumbs in his belt. "—we all 'av a right to the bounty on that girl ya be hidin'. She's Kendrick's sister."

"Aye," Roth agreed. "That she is mates."

"She'll bring a pretty quid on the block for those what can afford her if Kendrick won't pay hisself."

"Can't argue with your logic, Smitty."

Smitty grew furious. "That pretty smile of yers ain't gonna be so nice if ya don't hand the chit over. Yer outnumbered."

Movement behind the men stirred the mob. "Think again, Smitty." Talon's icy tone seized the unruly crowd.

Smitty whipped around, his face a pale mask as his men melted away. Braced with his legs apart, cutlass drawn, Talon loomed before him. "Kendrick's sister belongs to me," his voice rose over the crescendo of voices. Eight of his crew divided the brunt of Smitty's mob, sucking their enthusiasm to a belligerent grumble.

"This ain't none of yer affair, Drake."

"She happens to be my wife. And I'm not of a mind to share her. Especially with you Roth. The deal's off."

Regan gripped Roth's arm. "I'm not going back—"

"Lady Regan . . ." Roth shoved her behind him.

Smitty laughed. "I'd say that leaves her fair game, Drake."

"It won't be so easy, Smitty," Roth warned.

Cutlass lifting, Smitty reeled around. "Easy enough, Roth. You ain't Drake."

"Get her out of here, Roth!" Talon leapt into the mob. The clash of swords resonated through every terrified nerve in Regan's body.

Roth shoved her away. "Marcus is behind us. Run like hell. Drake won't reach us in time."

Horrified, she hesitated, her gaze hanging on Talon as he parried two men who came at him with cutlasses.

With a wild banshee cry, Smitty attacked Roth.

"Run!" Roth slammed his cutlass against Smitty's.

Regan whirled. Her bare feet dragged in the soft sand. Roth stopped the second man who dived for her. Their clashing steel measured the ferocity of the fight.

And Talon was in the midst of the fray.

She wanted to turn. But running steps dogged her. She leaped rubbish littering the sandy beach, crested the final berm, and slid down the length of its backside, clawing at the green things growing in the hill to stay balanced. Breathless she swept past the pier. Her lungs burned. Marcus saw her and was shouting for the others to push the longboat back out into the waves. His eyes sliced to a point beyond her. She could hear men curse as they slipped and salvaged their balance down the sandy berm.

Marcus drew his sword and ran toward her. "Don't stop!" she heard him yell as he lunged past, sweeping his sword down.

Metal clashed and rang. Then she was in the water, stumbling, dragged down to her knees by the undertow. Hands gripped her waist. Marcus lifted her over the waves toward the boat. "Get her back," he shouted to Jaime.

A pistol fired from the beach. Marcus's grip slackened and Regan splashed into the water as he stumbled forward.

A startled look of amazement crossed Marcus's handsome features. His gaze slid downward to the white shirt plastered against his flesh. A dark crimson circle blossomed on his side. "Christ . . ." Gray eyes lifted to Regan's horrified gaze. "I've . . . been shot."

He dropped to his knees in the water. Screaming for Jaime, she caught Marcus beneath the shoulder. They both went under the surf. Above her, she heard shouting and a blunderbuss explode. In the heavy surf, Marcus slipped from her grasp. Lungs burning, Regan desperately grasped his shirt. Someone pulled her out of the water.

Coughing, she clung to the side of the longboat as it bobbed further out. Her hands were covered in blood. She clung to Marcus's bloody shirt. "He's still out there!" she screamed.

Musket shot splattered the water. Jaime dragged her over the side of the boat then dove into the water.

Tears blinded her. "Find him, Jaime!"

On shore, two more men waded into the waves. Regan searched for a pistol to fire. The two men left in the boat battled the surf to keep from tipping.

"Lady Regan." Jaime caught her shoulders. Water mixed with blood from a wound on his scalp dripped from his hair. His chest heaved.

She fought Jaime's hands. "Let me go!" she screamed.

"He's dead." Jamie's voice fell to a choking whisper. "Marcus is dead."

Chapter Twenty

Cutlasses flashed, ringing noisily as Talon drew back into the marketplace. Roth blazed a path toward him. The crews of both ships began to scatter Smitty's men. Straining to catch sight of Regan, Talon leapt onto a trestle table. A savage cry resounded, swinging him around to meet a pirate's charge. He leapt the sweep of a flat sword, upsetting the table with his weight. Colorful pottery shattered to the ground around his feet. Bowls and cups rolled in all directions.

The fight spread into the thatched stalls scattering vendors and early morning patrons. Chaos ensued into fisticuffs. Talon tried again to sight Regan. Too many people lined the sand berm. Frustrated, he covered Roth's advance, ending back to back with his nemesis as the fighting disintegrated into a free-for-all.

They ducked into a back alley out of the fracas. "Like old times, Drake," Roth chuckled ruefully, lifting an apple from a fruit bin.

Talon's sword swung around. He faced Roth, brandishing the steel point in a slow figure eight. The cobblestone alley reflected heat in the hot tropical sunlight. Sweat coated Roth's bare chest, a furious reminder where Talon had last seen the man's shirt.

"I'm not letting Kendrick have her back."

Eyeing the cutlass, Roth's brow lifted. He bit into the apple consideringly. "Is she really your wife?"

Talon stabbed at the fruit bin behind Roth, impaling a papaya. "In every way."

"Kendrick doesn't know."

"Damn Kendrick!"

Roth carefully wiped the juice from his swollen lip. Someone had gotten in a lucky hit. "I'll follow if you try to leave this harbor. I've been ordered to hunt you down. You're a dangerous man, Drake." He chewed the apple methodically. "Everyone wants you dead."

"And yet, I'm still alive." He bit into the papaya, spitting out the peel. "You work for the wrong man, Roth."

Roth's gaze dropped to the papaya. "Why didn't you kill me?"

"Why didn't you take Regan and run?"

An unspoken truce. Long ago he and Roth had shared the same length of chain on a Spanish slave galleon. The same thirst. Hunger. Pain. But time carved separate paths. Next time they met, it would be over the point of a sword.

There was no time for Talon to greet his crew. Once on deck of the *Dark Fury*, a hasty nod confirmed that Regan was on board. He'd deal with her antics later. The anchor had been raised. The ship was already under way when Talon leaped the steps to the quarterdeck.

"Headsail sheets, men. Bring her about." He lifted the spyglass to his eye, focusing on the *Viper*. "Follow me if you can, you bastard." He smiled to himself. The moment Roth tacked the ship around, the drogue they'd shackled to the stern last night would render the rudder useless, leaving the *Viper* to flounder.

Long enough for the *Dark Fury* to escape.

It had taken most of the night under the noise of their festivity to complete the task. Proof of the handiwork would soon make itself known. Talon turned to Harry. "Get Marcus up here."

Talon raced to get his ship under way. If their plan failed, they needed a head start. He'd not surrender the *Fury* to Kendrick. The thought of a battle fostered his need for haste.

His gaze lifted to check the wind in the sails. His crew seemed laggard.

Irritated, Talon shouted at the men in the shrouds. Jaime wasn't at the helm. Where the hell had Harry gone? Talon yelled again, pulling two men off the mizzen to man the mainsail.

A thunderous crack sounded from the *Viper*. The plan had worked!

Talon swung around bringing the spyglass back to his eye. The *Viper* yawed, her main beam sweeping over, sending men scurrying to the helm. Though not outright basking, Talon indulged a grin. Roth wouldn't be following them anywhere.

Where was Marcus?

"Captain," Harry said quietly.

"By God, it worked, Harry." Ordering the *Fury* on a course to larboard, he prepared to make a dog-legged turn past the fortress guarding the bay.

"Captain," Harry said again, his voice subdued.

Talon lowered the brass tube and snapped it shut. He turned to Harry. "What is it?" His attention fixed beyond his gunner to the men standing ill at ease behind him. Had a mutiny occurred during his absence? Then his next thought retracted to Regan. "Where's my wife?"

"She's in the hold. But Cap'n—"

Talon left the quarterdeck.

"Cap'n!" Harry called.

Marcus's bloody shirt clutched between them, Regan huddled with her arms wrapped about Arabella's wracking shoulders. Sobbing, Arabella buried her face against Regan's shoulder. They were brought down to the hold in case of a fight. Now, Regan waited for the sound of cannon fire. The ship seemed to be picking up speed.

A clamor on the stairs brought her head up. Talon stooped beneath the beam. His stark gaze fell on her. Her breath caught. She couldn't control the strangled sob that welled in her throat. Pain wracked her, devastating what remained of her control.

Marcus would be alive if not for her.

And at once, she hated Talon with every ounce of her being. If only he'd been honorable with his intentions. He'd betrayed her with his deceit. Now Marcus was dead.

Horror dawning in Talon's eyes, his gaze dropped from her white face to the bloody shirt clutched in her hands. Like a blind man, he pushed past the men who crowded the hold over a wounded Jaime. Talon tore the shirt from her hands. His scarred hand lingered over the small tear made by a lead ball that killed Marcus.

Talon's pain knifed through her soul.

"We tried, Cap'n," Jaime rasped.

A bandage swathed his skull. Swallowed by the stench of reality Regan shrank into the shadows against the bulkhead.

"We must go back," Arabella cried. "We must."

"We tried to find his body, Cap'n," Jaime said. "I swear."

Talon lifted the boy by the collar and slammed him into the bulkhead. "You left him to die?"

"They shot him. He was already dead. I had to get Lady Regan away. I had to."

His fists loosened on Jamie's shirtfront. Talon released his boatswain and stepped back. "Get everyone out," he spoke softly. *"Now!"*

Screaming, Arabella fought the hands that dragged her away until she finally fainted. Harry carried her out, Talon's men following somberly behind.

Staring at the bloody shirt in his hand, Talon didn't move. His pain was a black, living thing of wretched grief, held in check by years of abuse and a life that allowed for no weakness. Regan bit into her fist to keep from calling his name.

Drawn to her movement, his head snapped up, the hot silver flame in his eyes dulled by a thin film of moisture. "How?" His voice cracked. "How did it happen?"

"The beach." Regan's voice caught on the horror. "He was in front of me. I'm . . ." She stepped into the amber pool of lanthorn light, her hands twisting for courage. "I'm so sorry."

Talon's gaze registered her attire. Sanity flashed with rage. Still wearing her chemise and Roth's shirt, her very presence brought back the whole of her escapade. He took a menacing step toward her, filling the space of the hold, his height and fury engulfing her.

Only that morning she'd recognized her love for him. And then she'd run.

He stopped scant inches from touching her. She wished only to touch him. To dispel his horrible pain.

"So help me God, if you touch me now . . ." He stared at Marcus's bloody shirt. All that remained of his brother. All that remained of their past. The last of his family.

"Get out, Regan!"

Her gut wrenched on a sob. She ran past him to the stairs. Desperately, she shot a look over her shoulder at Talon.

Silent tears raged over him. They stripped her bare, peeling away the hardened layers of anger, past the shining bob of injustice she dangled before her daily as a reminder of his treacherous deeds. All which she struggled now to recall but couldn't remember.

Talon Drake, the man, touched her soul with a hunger that made her quake. If she could have traded her life for Marcus's at that moment, she'd have leaped the fires of hell to see it done.

It was her fault that Marcus died. And hers alone.

She deserved whatever dark fate Talon dealt her.

No words of mourning were spoken as Talon wrapped Marcus's shirt around a fist-sized cannon ball and sent both to the bottom of the sea. His words were brief. Wracked with pain. Furiously shrugging off the condolences of his men, he climbed to the crow's nest to escape them all. He didn't come down until *Dark Fury* weighed anchor in a hot, secluded bay on Hispaniola, the island across from Tortuga.

Working in an emotional void, Talon immediately firmed up the defense of their sanctuary made almost invisible by the two headlands of rock and forest. The crew used supplies purchased in Tortuga and cleared away forest to repair the ship.

Then three days after their arrival, he put Harry in charge and disappeared into the tropical jungle.

At night Regan slept alone in Talon's bed and wondered what had become of her soul to lose herself so completely to grief. She lacked the will to find a way back to Harrison, or even to Martinique where sanctuary for her beleaguered heart awaited. Black-and-white choices no longer existed and she surrendered to a perfunctory madness, sweet in bliss and short on reality, where Talon loved her, the inanity of it making her laugh.

Robert drank himself into a stupor, daily. Arabella didn't move from her cabin. On the eighth day near dusk, the lookout sighted the *Viper* on the horizon.

Still Talon didn't return.

Food was plentiful. Regan and Parrot combed the forest perimeter daily, gathering fruit in an excuse to search for some clue that would lead to Talon. " 'E's gone, milady." Parrot's cryptic tone smothered her. She didn't need the negative conjecture. She needed hope.

"He often goes away by hisself, milady, when he needs ta think," Harry reassured her later. "Give him time. He'll be back when he's ready."

Harry would know. Talon loved the *Dark Fury*. He'd never abandon his ship.

Regan cleaned his cabin. She moved the clothes he'd bought for her beside his in the wardrobe. His masculine scent clung to his shirts. She held a sleeve against her face, closing her eyes.

Her whole life yawned over a dark chasm and all she could do was moon over clothes and dreams that could never be.

She would have to face Talon when he returned. Eventually.

Gathering her arms tightly about her, she kicked the armoire door shut. Fighting nausea, her fingers dug into her sleeves. Marcus's death would always remain between them. Just as her parents' death anchored her in reality.

By the time Piers walked into camp two weeks after their arrival, Regan had already forced herself to resume some semblance of activity. Barrels were heated in huge pits dug on shore and she'd been helping with the task of melting pitch.

"He didn't find the mapmaker," Jaime informed her a few moments later. Squatting in the sand, he ripped out handfuls of sea grass from its tuft. "The cap'n's ruined."

Regan shut her eyes. She'd burned the second map. The one Father stole. Lord. What had she done to Talon? "But you still have Robert's map," she finally said.

"That map we got ain't worth pig's spit from all I hear."
Jaime nodded to Robert snoring in a hammock strung between two trees. "And to think he staked his bloomin' life
on that treasure, fer the good it'll do him now."

When Regan's gaze slid to Robert, she felt only dread.

Jaime left and joined Piers. The big man's expression
darkened as Harry relayed Marcus's death. The tragedy she'd
caused.

Thoughts of treasure vanished.

Regan brushed her skirt off, and looked toward the azure
sea. Having long since abandoned her shoes, she walked a
careful path among the scattered seashells. She ran along the
beach until she dropped to the wet sand, oblivious to the swirl
of sea foam wrapping around her feet. Behind her the palm
trees clicked with the force of a sudden gust. A storm brewed
overhead.

The desperation to scream pounded in her chest.

Then Piers sat beside her, and it was as if time had never
taken him from her. He wrapped her gently in his brawny
arms and allowed her to cry into his leather jerkin. "Was I
wrong to try and escape to my brother, Nicholas?"

"You have suffered through a lot, *chéri*."

"I was afraid of what was happening to me," she said,
wiping the moisture from her eyes. "I should hate Talon for
what he is."

"You are mad to care," he agreed.

"He kidnapped me."

"*Oui*, he did."

"Made a wreckage of my life."

"And you were very happy with your life," he commiserated.

"You mock me, Nicholas." She burrowed her toes into the
sand. "He lied about . . . about keeping me as his wife."

"Naturally, you were honest when you married him."

The poignant observation hurt. She was seeking validation
for her actions, not a censure of her integrity.

Piers stared at the *Dark Fury* rolling in the swell, protected
within the vast lagoon. "There are not many men I would
give my life for. He is a good man, *chéri*."

She felt the fury flash in her eyes. "You say that knowing he killed Mama. I don't understand the logic of your emotions."

Piers shook his head. One arm rested on his knee as he looked away. "He did not kill Angelique. He did not sink the *Rose*."

Regan swallowed with difficulty. This couldn't be. "He so much as told me . . . Captain Drake was there," she insisted.

"*Oui,*" Piers agreed. "The *capitaine* was there. We waited for the *Rose* nearly two weeks. But he did not sink her. He needed your father alive." Finally, seeing how sick she looked, he sighed. "It has been too long that you have believed in the lie, *chéri*."

Helplessly, she came to her feet. "Don't you know what I've gone through because I believed him guilty of Mama's death?"

"Because you wanted to believe, *chéri*."

"He could have told me." She paced furiously. "All this time—"

"Could he?" Piers shook his head. "I do not think so."

Her hands trembled. Piers had no idea what he'd done to her. He'd shattered the one barrier she'd erected against Talon, fragmenting every defense she possessed.

It changed everything. Yet nothing at all.

"The *capitaine* bid the *Rose* to surrender," Piers said quietly. "She was under gunned and would not survive a battle."

"Then what happened?"

"Two Spanish galleons attacked us before we could board her. We could not defend her, though we tried. We could not. The *Rose* was destroyed. The *capitaine*, he blew both galleons to splinters. But the attack left him injured for nearly six months. If not for Marcus, he would have died of his injuries."

Regan cradled her head in her palms. "I've been such a fool."

"No, *chéri*. You are not a fool. Only blind."

Blind! The slight was too kind.

Talon allowed her to believe him guilty of that heinous crime. But she should have known. It was not in his character to commit murder. And then she remembered the times he'd tried to tell her. The times she wouldn't listen. Because she wanted him to be guilty!

It was so much easier to hate him.

But even that had been a lie. He'd crippled her heart from the beginning, the moment he'd put his men's life before his own.

After Piers left, Regan stood alone on the beach, her skirt tucked in her waistband. The edge of the jungle trembled in shadows. Birdsong danced in the trees. She shaded her eyes and searched the hilltops beyond the plush rise of green. "Oh, Talon. Where are you?"

From his position high on the ridge, Talon watched her hand fall away. Dappled shadows veiled her face, but could not hide the defeat measured by her stance as she looked at her bare feet and finally back to the sea. Hidden within the dense shade of the slope overlooking the endless expanse of aqua sea, he sat on the spongy ground against a rotting stump of a once magnificent cotton tree. His wrist drooped over one knee, the bottle in his hand dangling.

He could see her clearly, a small figure on the empty shoreline. His gaze raked her mop of curls and length of bare calves. He had yet to see her looking less than a fragile waif, her seductive pull more potent than rum. He cradled the vision, and for the briefest of moments surrendered to something other than grief, closing his eyes, breathing the scented breeze faintly tinged with orange blossoms.

Even as he despised what she had done to him, he had to admire her tenacity. The strength of her will. Her fierce loyalty, as misguided as it was.

He brought the half-emptied bottle of rum to his lips and swigged, tasting the fire. The primal roar of his heart filled his head. "Blast her." He drew in a ragged breath. Lost in his own self-contempt, his anguish was a palpable thing. Raw. All consuming. Suffocating. Obliterating the tenacious grip on his control.

He'd lost everything. His name. His future. Including her.

Marcus's death cleared him of civil responsibility. The hard-won sanity he'd built these past years vanished with his brother into a watery grave. Talon swigged the bottle deeply.

It no longer mattered whether he lived or died.

Chapter Twenty-one

The next day, Regan forced Arabella to go with her and Parrot to gather food. Her cousin was wont to wallow in solitude these past weeks, a tragic circumstance for someone who thrived on human contact. Regan was determined to get her out, as much for Arabella's grief as her own.

"I don't blame you for what happened to Marcus," Arabella told Regan after they'd been walking for hours. They'd not spoken about the tragedy. Sinking to the ground, Arabella's apricot silk skirt flared around her. "You didn't ask for anything that's happened."

Her cousin's insight brought a spasm of tears to Regan. She sat next to Arabella in the shade. Parrot dropped against the rock beside them. The pungent scent of dead leaves filled the glade.

Arabella laid her head in Regan's lap. "What will I do now?"

Regan smoothed the blond curls from Arabella's face. "I have a friend at the convent. She says that God opens many doors. But the choices granted us sometimes are not those we choose."

"Is she a saint? This friend of yours?"

Recalling Talon's poetic vision of the stars, she smiled. "Perhaps a silver-haired angel. Sarah's blind. Mama brought her to Father Henri soon after I arrived."

"And what door will open for me, Regan? I've lost everything."

"If we get back to Martinique, maybe you can teach." Regan nudged the dozing boy. "Parrot can be your first student."

He made a rude noise.

"I don't have your prowess, Regan. I'd as soon the little darling stay with you."

"Oi'm thirsty," Parrot announced, ignoring the jibe.

Arabella sat up and blew a curl from her face. "I wonder where we are? Do you think we're lost?"

"It's a bloomin' island." Parrot stood and smacked the dirt from his canvas dungarees. " 'Ow lost can a person get?"

Regan looked up through the canopy of branches to gauge the position of the sun. "Listen—" Arabella gripped her wrist. Even her sense of drama couldn't allay the trodden leaves crunching beneath the step of someone's approach. "Someone's coming."

The rustling stopped. Had the intruder heard their voices? The silence grew ominous, harsh and penetrating, even to Regan who thrived on adventure better than most.

"Pirates, milady," Parrot rasped, edging behind Regan.

Rustling started again. The gait of the approaching intruder seemed more treacherous. Arabella climbed to her feet. "I think it's time we leave."

Too late. The thicket shuddered.

A scaly green head, the size of a man's fist, emerged from the undergrowth. Arabella screamed.

The lizard's spiny throat fan sprang open.

Panic drove Arabella against Parrot. Heedless of the local insect life, they whirled headlong into the scrub. Their raving departure sent a swarm of colorful birds soaring into the sky. The dragon loped past Regan, pursuing the excited crash and tumble.

Following on the tail of the lizard, Regan bit back laughter. The trees thinned and opened onto a sandy berm dotted with golden clumps of sea grass. Arabella was jumping madly, as if a fire lit her drawers, shaking her hair and screaming, "Spiders. Get 'em off! Get 'em off!" Her head snapped up at

Regan's approach. Her frantic gaze dropped to the lizard watching her a few feet away. A flick of its forked tongue sent her screaming into the water.

Parrot crumbled to the sand, chortling like a sick goose. Regan dropped next to Parrot. The absurdity of the situation, the pain of the last weeks, everything conspired to make her feel like a lunatic. His guffaws sparked her own.

Men shouting down the beach from camp lifted Regan's head. Arabella's screams brought the troops out in force. Wiping the tears from her face, she sat up to find her cousin. Sopping wet, hair drooping, she stood knee deep in water, hands on her hips, glaring at them.

Regan fell into another fit of laughter. Noise behind her warned her to check their nasty dragon. Laughter died in her throat.

Talon stood at the wood's edge, feet braced in the sand. Sweat dampened his black silk shirt. A dark beard ringed his face, yielding her a view of stark silver eyes an instant before his gaze sliced up and down the length of beach.

When he looked at her again, Regan labored to stand. "You came back," she whispered when his gaze finally came back around.

"Were you hoping I wouldn't?"

The anger in his voice hurt her. "I'm sorry. We must seem so crass. It's just that—"

A dozen feet away the fearsome lizard snoozed contentedly.

"Marcus is dead, Regan. He doesn't mind your laughter."

Talon's men trudged toward them, breathing heavily from exertion. Seeing their captain, they slowed. "Sorry, sir." Harry bent over, hands on his knees. "We didn't know . . . you'd returned. We heard screamin'—"

"So did I." Talon had not taken his eyes off her. With a disgusted shake of his head, he looked at the fat green lizard, then walked past Regan toward camp.

Seeking absolution from his thoughts in work and seclusion, Talon avoided Regan for the next few weeks. Her very presence impaired his judgment. He didn't trust her, didn't trust **himself.**

After what happened to Marcus, he'd never wanted to see her again.

Moonlight dappled the sand, drifting in rhythm to the salt-scented breeze. Hands resting on his hips, he watched the *Dark Fury*.

Moored in the secluded bay, she moved idly in the swell. The crew had patched her hull and repaired the three towering masts with timber cut from the forest. Silhouetted against the white disk of a pagan moon, the spindly reach of her masts and crosstrees stretched gracefully into the sky. She would sail tomorrow in better condition than she'd been in over a year—without Marcus.

A chill grated his belly. Casting his gaze to the heavens, he knew he trespassed on thoughts best left alone.

Someone walking in the water stirred his solitude.

Annoyed by the intrusion, Talon deliberately ignored the individual's approach. Roasted boar sizzled over the fire pit built in the sand berm behind him. Beneath the palm trees to his left, Talon could hear voices. Their volume had risen since Robert laid the worthless treasure map on the sand for all to poke over.

"Ain't ya the least bit interested, Cap?"

Parrot stopped directly in Talon's line of vision, forcing him to relinquish his gaze on the *Fury*. Parrot's pale skin looked luminescent in the moonlight, his eyes bigger as he surveyed Talon.

"Lady Regan is of a mind oi should come bother you."

Talon's irritation showed. "And why should Lady Regan care?"

"She said ya have the look of loneliness about yer face."

He resisted the urge to find her in the shadows beneath the palms. "You can tell her I prefer my loneliness."

"She says it's bad fer ya, Cap. And I'm of a mind to agree."

"Is that why you've been dogging my heels all week?"

Parrot shoved his thumbs in his waistband and kicked a pebble around in the water. "Oi had me a sister once," he finally said. It was all he said. Talon understood. Someone he loved was also dead. "Oi been wantin' ta tell ya, is all." He started to turn away.

"Your sister was your only family?"

"Oi'm of a mind ta think the ache never goes away."

The moonlight caught Parrot's face, softening the angles of his jaw. His lashes, thick and dark, fringed expressive eyes, eyes that for the first time lacked guard. Something about the boy's face demanded scrutiny.

With an oath, Talon tilted Parrot's chin, noting the feminine slant of his . . . her mouth, the smooth, lightly freckled skin, astonished he hadn't caught it before now.

But then he'd been distracted by other things.

"How long were you going to wait before you told us?"

Parrot's full mouth tightened in belligerence. But Talon was stronger. Parrot couldn't pull her chin from his grip. "Never if oi had a choice of the matter."

"How old are you?"

Her lower lip thrust out defeating her pride. "Sixteen."

Jeezus. "Where have you been sleeping?"

"Jaime's been seein' me safe. Not in the way ya be thinkin', neither."

"I see." Talon dropped his hand and stepped back to look her up and down. Her ragged canvas dungarees and soiled shirt did wonders to aid the disguise. But she'd gained enough weight these past months that she could no longer hide the hint of feminine curves.

"You ain't plannin' on doin' somethin' about it, are ya?"

"Like what? Stake you to the ground and torture you?"

Parrot crossed her arms in disdain. "Like put me in a dress."

For the first time in weeks, Talon laughed. Perhaps it was the unlikely image of Parrot trussed in a steel corset, ribbons dangling in her hair, her freedom squashed to a pulp by moral society.

Talon couldn't help but think of Regan, how different she also was from other women, how unique her pride and defiance of custom.

How suitable her character was to his.

"A pirate ship is no place for you, Parrot," Talon said.

She regarded him mulishly. "You gonna get rid 'a me, Cap?"

"No." He put his arm around her stiff shoulders. "I won't

let anything happen to you. But you can't keep your secret forever." The rising voices in camp turned peevish, drawing him around.

"Oi think ya best be getting' back, Cap."

Talon stopped outside the circle of firelight, aware that Robert's drunken slur dominated the petulant mood of his men.

"I'm telling you she's lying," Welles voice carried.

Dressed in the rosebud silk gown Talon had purchased in Tortuga, her dark hair flowing to her hips, Regan looked ethereal in the midst of his battle-hardened crew. His men revered her next to sainthood and would never harm her, but Robert was another matter.

Regan faced Robert's bullying without flinching. "These coordinates mean nothing." Her quiet tone commanded the full attention of each man present as they strained to hear her words. "No such place exists on the Spanish Main."

"So you say."

Talon moved into the ring of amber light and his crew's murmurs quieted as every eye settled on him. Thirty of his men milled about the camp, trying to glimpse the map. The others were either on guard or lay out in pallets around the boar pit. He stepped past Regan, aware that she watched him. He could hear her breathing. His gaze held hers before he forced himself to stare down at the map spread out on the sand.

He'd looked at Robert's map many times in the past months. Three golden bells expertly created graced the top left corner. Below this someone penned the navigational symbol: *10:14;56 degrees north.*

Regan was correct. Yet, something suddenly seemed familiar about the combination of those numbers.

"We can't find the treasure for ourselves because we don't have both maps," Robert persisted. He swigged deeply from a bottle. It sloshed as he pointed it at Talon. "What about it, Drake?"

Talon eyed the older man, his florid complexion marked by dark shadows beneath bleary eyes. Eyes void of reason. Talon considered Robert's grip on reality.

"I've seen the other map," Regan suddenly replied.

All eyes seemed to shift onto her. Shame stirred in those luminous coffee-colored eyes but she didn't drop her gaze.

"These markings—" Her finger trembled as she pointed to the drawings on the side of the map. "—are the signature of the mapmaker. But this map is a twin to the other in every way. They could be nothing more than navigational charts."

"Is that true, Drake?" Robert demanded.

"She's correct about the symbols," Talon said carefully not taking his eyes from her face. Her logical observation twisted through his mind to the point of madness. He'd questioned the very same thing but believing in the treasure lent strength to his purpose. That his father had been murdered, that his own life had met ruin for a mythical treasure, measured his loss absolutely. For one insane moment, despair slipped his control.

"Damn you, Drake!" Robert threw the empty rum bottle into the fire where it shattered. "There is no treasure. She knew what you were about all along." Robert kicked the map, sending it close to the fire. "Do you know what I've lost because of your lies?"

"Do tell." Talon put his fists on his hips, felt his fingertips rub the hilt of his cutlass. "What have you lost?"

"Everything. I can't go back home, ever. I needed that gold."

"Should I cry, Robert?"

"Mock me as you will, Drake," he sneered. "I don't have a price on my head. Tell me, Captain, who'll be living a year from now?"

The crew erupted, silenced only by the ominous scrape of sword against scabbard. Talon leveled the blade at Robert's worthless throat. The man cowered beside his whimpering wife. Arabella stood behind them, blue eyes flaring. Talon warned her with a look to stay still.

Regan grabbed his arm. "Don't do this, Talon."

Drunk with rage and astonishment, Talon stared at her. He wanted to throttle her. To hold her. Kiss her. All the while fighting the grip on his temper so he didn't slash the lot of them to shreds. Fate decreed their lives to his hands. His enemies. His curse. And all he'd done was shield them. Even now, he knew they needed his protection. The irony of it cost him his composure.

He owed them nothing. Leaving them to the mercy of this empty countryside was better than they deserved. More than had been granted Marcus.

Talon yanked her arm, dumping her in front of Robert. "You want to get back to your brother so badly . . . he can bloody have you."

Regan twisted around to face him. "What are you going to do?"

"I'm leaving you behind, something I should have done before you got Marcus killed."

Jaime stepped forward. "What happened wasn't her fault, Cap'n."

"The hell it wasn't." He swung his cutlass around to face his men. "If any of you has a problem with my decision, then fight me now." An unnatural hush settled over the camp. He walked the circle of his men. "What? Not a champion among the lot of you?" He looked down at Regan. "It looks like you're staying with your beloved family. And you—" His furious gaze landed on Robert's mottled face. "—I don't need you or your bloody depositions. I'm doing this my way from now on."

Regan scrambled to her feet, hair whipping wildly around her shoulders. "You can't!"

"You think not?" Talon threw the cutlass into the soft sand at Regan's feet where it vibrated with the force of his fury. "Watch me."

Talon turned, dismissing her, the final insult to a heart he'd flayed to ribbons. Indignant with her own sense of mottled rage, Regan dragged the cutlass from the sand and chased after him.

"Coward!" She swung the sword in an arc bringing the weight of the blade in front of her.

Sidestepping her charge, Talon whirled in amazement. She pivoted to face him, blocking his escape. Anything to keep him from leaving her again. The moonlight glittered in his eyes, the first spark of life she'd seen in weeks.

"You would run me through, Regan?"

Her chest heaving, she gripped the ivory hilt of the cutlass with both hands. Fear crawled over her at the savage look in his eyes. "Nothing less than you deserve, Captain Drake."

"For the murderous thief I am, no doubt."

"No, milord pirate." They circled each other, the weight of the cutlass heavy on her arms. " 'Tis your blasted lies."

"A bold accusation from the wit of the greatest liar of all."

"You would have sold me away. After . . ."

"After bedding you?" he said helpfully. "I should have given you away. The bargain would have been mine."

Tears blurred her eyes. "You could have told me your plan."

"And ruin the fun you were having?"

"Bastard!"

"Now is that any way for a future nun to talk?"

She thrust the sword at him. "I'm your wife."

"Piers," he called without taking his eyes from her. "Bring us two rapiers. If my saintly *wife* wishes to run me through, then she deserves a fair chance of success."

The heavy sword was exchanged for a lighter rapier.

"Guard your flank," Piers casually instructed as if her life, her mortal soul weren't in danger of being torn from her chest.

Talon sliced the air, testing the grip of the hilt. Eyeing Regan, he stepped back into his stance. "I'm going to enjoy this."

How long had it been since she'd dueled with rapiers? Not so long that she couldn't wipe that arrogant smirk off his face.

Regan wrapped the length of her skirt around her forearm to keep from tripping. Knees bent slightly, she raised the steel point in perfect repose.

Two steps, she met his parry. They battled around the clearing, the metallic click of rapiers the only sound in the silence. Talon's men expanded their ranks to give them space. Regan's weapon glided against his. Hilt to hilt, he held her gaze, sweeping away reason.

"I'm impressed, sweet." Amusement edged his voice.

She wanted to crack him over the head. She whirled away,

parrying his attack, recalling everything Piers had ever said, but she'd been a child then. Talon blocked her thrust, repeatedly sidestepping her attack and finally slipping her guard.

The tip of his rapier sliced the top button on her bodice. "But you're too careful, sweet. Too trusting of the wrong people."

She found herself breathing hard with the exertion. "Are you speaking of yourself, Captain?"

Eyes hard upon her, he swept beneath her cut and struck again, skillfully slicing her bodice without marring the white skin of her shoulder. She gripped the severed cloth and whirled as he deftly moved toward her flank. He toyed with her. That was obvious now.

Modesty having no place in warfare, she released her bodice. The pale curves of her breast surged forward, threatening to spill over her chemise. He hesitated, and she attacked. The tip of her rapier severed the top laces on his shirt.

His eyes burned into hers. "Touché, wife." His weapon touched hers lightly. "But I told you before, I never lose."

"No!" She shoved her rapier against his. "The almighty pirate Drake quits instead."

Talon slashed up, nearly stripping the rapier from her grip. "Have you learned nothing, Regan? Would your pride see you slain?"

"Better that than bend before a coward."

She lunged. Talon pressed her blindly backward, driving her with the solid force of his attack. The scope of his ability shattered her defense. Her feet danced in retreat as she warded off his greater skill, convinced he would slay her.

Panting, she slammed against a palm tree. Talon was upon her, wedging his knee between hers, his rapier entrapping hers above her head. Her chest heaved with the exertion of her fight, her breath mingling with his.

Waves broke on the beach a few yards away. Talon's mouth hovered inches from hers. "I didn't get my reputation for my gentle nature, sweet. Ruthlessness is strength."

The heat of his muscled body encompassed her. "It's cowardice."

"Power."

"Without honor." She brought her knee up but, anticipating her move, he tripped her over his boot.

Regan let loose of her rapier and threw her slight weight against him, her momentum shoving him backward. They both went tumbling over a piece of driftwood, rolling down the soft berm in a tangle of limbs and petticoats. She fought him, twisting and kicking, trying to extricate herself only to end beneath him, wrapped in her skirts, panting so hard her lungs nearly burst.

Regan felt the drumbeat of his heart against her breast.

"I should hate you." He breathed into her sweat-dampened hair. "You're a Welles and I can't get you out of my head."

"Oh God, Talon. I've been so afraid . . ."

"You were never from my sight," he rasped against her temple.

Tears glistened in her eyes. "I love you."

His head lifted and she looked into crystalline eyes, filled with disbelief, stark in the shadows of his bearded face.

"I thought I'd never see you again," she whispered.

He cupped his roughened palms around her face and kissed her. Life sparked in Regan's chest, soaring with her pulse. Passion filled her, reminding her of the endless nights she'd dreamed of his touch. Her arms entwined around his neck. She returned his kiss with a fervent hunger matching his own. Through the maze of pulsing emotions, she was aware that they were alone on the beach.

"Join me, Regan. Fight this battle with me. At my side."

Anguish swept through her. She could not watch Talon die nor could she watch him destroy Harrison.

Her brother had only been nineteen and just back from Cambridge when Talon's family was arrested. He should not be held accountable for her father's crimes. There had to be a way to save Talon and Harrison from each other.

He rolled off her. "Christ, Regan—" He grabbed a handful of dirt and flung it in the wind. "You never give up do you?"

He'd misread her silence. Regan twisted to her knees in front of him. "Don't you understand?" she beseeched, touching his hands, but he pushed her away and climbed to his feet. "You can't run from the authorities forever. Roth will never stop hunting you. This is about me, too. About finding the truth."

"The truth?" He stared down at her. "You've been staring at it for years. You still haven't seen it."

Regan came to her feet. Sand spilled from her hair. "You speak of truth? Why didn't you tell me the Spanish sank the *Rose*?"

With an oath, Talon walked away.

"Talon!" The roar of the waves drowned her voice. Regan ran after him.

"You wouldn't have believed me, Regan."

Breathless, she gripped his arm. Furious muscles coiled beneath her hands. He spun around, eyes glinting so savagely she staggered back. "You don't want me as an enemy, Regan. You either stand with me or against me."

"But Harrison's my brother. You ask the impossible. What if I can find proof to clear you? There must be something."

"Everything disappeared years ago. Robert was my only hope to see this through in a court of law." Vulnerable for the split second he shut his eyes, he looked away. "When Marcus was alive, it was worth risking my life," he said quietly, facing her with condemning eyes. "Now, I don't particularly care how justice is served. But justice *will* be served."

"I know my family did horrible things . . ."

"You can't say it, can you?" He pressed her back into the sea. Water swirled around her ankles. "Your family is a bunch of two-faced murderers." His violence stunned her. "I'll take you to Martinique, Regan. If that's what you want. Just stay the hell out of my life."

Chapter Twenty-two

Leaning against the rail on the forecastle deck, Regan watched Hispaniola slide away until it became a tiny bluish smudge adrift in a bank of turquoise. Voices on the main deck distracted her. Arabella and Parrot were pointing at something in the distance. *Dark Fury* was fast approaching a school of flying fish.

"Hang on, milady!" Jaime shouted from aloft.

Gripping her hair in one hand, Regan turned, whipping her gaze past Jaime in the crow's nest to the tops of the masts magnificent under full sail. Having caught the trade winds, *Dark Fury* began to lie steeply on its side.

Talon's voice carried from the quarterdeck where he stood with Piers amidst a rainbow spray that framed the bow. Watching the newly rigged masts with a captain's careful eye, he directed orders to those who manned the sheets. His black silk shirt caught the wind rushing around him. Regan had never seen him more invincible than on the deck of his ship.

Pride for his skill mingled unfavorably with jealousy that something could command his heart so completely. That she would never feel anything from him but the passion of vengeance.

Regan listened to his voice as he drove the *Fury* headlong into the wind. Seizing the moment, she released her hair and clung to the rail behind her, feeling bold enough to fly.

Talon's voice faded in the excitement around her.

He was watching her. She felt his gaze like she did the burning sun on her back, and slowly, her head turned. She looked directly into his eyes, and for one breathless instant time stood still, closing the distance between them until she scarcely noticed the Neptuniun wonders around her. Abruptly, he turned away, a scowl marring his handsome features as if he was annoyed to be caught staring. And hated her somehow for making him weak. Fury and tenderness. A flawless contradiction. Yet, he bore them both equally.

She'd come to know him so well—this valiant man who fancied death a fitting alternative to failure—and she possessed a staggering need to keep him alive.

"I love you, milord pirate." She said the words aloud.

And vowed to spend the weeks ahead proving it, bridging the world between them, praying that her love would be enough to make him stay.

That night when she blew out the light in the cabin and crawled into bed, she realized that she slept in the dark. For the first time in ten years, since her accident in the cave, the light of determination overshadowed childish fears. And as Martinique's golden, crescent-shaped beaches and wild craggy cliffs loomed on the future horizon, determination became hope.

Somehow, she'd reach him before they reached Martinique.

But the next week proved him more elusive than the wind. Talon didn't want to contend with her. He didn't sleep with her in the cabin. During the day, he'd simply vanish for hours, belaboring her attempt to find him. Once, she saw him in the galley, but she could not confront him in front of his men. When he at last tired of her efforts to seek him out, he took to the shrouds. And to her eternal frustration, evaded even her gaze. She'd learned quickly enough that she could scour the reams of heaven and hell and she'd not catch Talon unless she sprouted wings.

"How long can he stay up there?" Regan said, coming to stand beside Nicholas on the main deck.

"Him?" Piers followed her gaze the hundred and fifty feet up the mainmast. "Longer than all of us, *chéri*."

"I'm worried for him, Nicholas," she said miserably. Her chest ached with a tightness that bespoke more than her fear that she'd lost him completely. For no matter how she tried to convey her heart, he wanted nothing more to do with her.

"*Oui, chéri,*" Nicholas agreed. "Marcus's death has hit him hard. He will not let it go."

"He won't let anything go."

"He is most stubborn."

Yes! Well, so was she. Regan moved forward to the shrouds. She started to lift herself into the ropes. The wind hit her with a lack of consideration and she shook the hemp furiously.

Piers put a hand on her arm. "No, *chéri*. This climb is not for you. He will be angry to see you try."

"At least that would be something."

"Unless you are one of his men, *chéri*." He chuckled. "The *capitaine*, he has not been fit company for even the beasts in the hold."

"I love him, Nicholas. I won't lose him."

"You will do him no favor if you get yourself killed."

But Talon had the disposition of flint. She wondered if he'd miss her at all.

Reluctantly, she gave up her vigil and went below just in time to hear someone scream. The foretelling crash of a lanthorn came from Parrot's new quarters. To the curiosity of everyone on board, Nicholas had vacated his cabin for the boy when they'd left Hispaniola.

Regan ran to the door, stopping abruptly at the sight of Arabella straddling Parrot on the bunk.

"Get the bloomin' witch off me," Parrot shrieked.

"Show me!" Arabella shook his shoulders.

Having discovered firsthand Arabella's aggressive nature, Regan stepped into the room ready to leap to Parrot's defense.

"Show me!"

"Oi'll not, ye bloomin' tart!" Parrot bucked but Arabella remained firmly attached like a tick to a dog.

What had happened to Arabella's sweet nature? "Show you what?"

"His breasts."

Regan burst out laughing. "Arabella!"

"Don't you *Arabella* me. I know a girl when I see one. Look for yourself. Hurry. I'll hold him . . . her."

Parrot stopped fighting. "Get yer bloomin' arse off me. Oi'll tell you."

"Swear." Arabella insisted. "Swear you won't run again."

Regan stood over them, her pity-filled gaze falling on Parrot's flushed face. Thick lashes raised and revealed accusing eyes. Beautiful eyes, Regan considered as she studied the light blue orbs. "I'd swear if I were you," Regan suggested.

"On a toad's balls, oi swear!"

Arabella rolled off. She crossed her arms over her bosom, her gaze triumphant as she awaited the revelation.

"All right! Oi'm a bloomin' skirt. Are ye happy?"

"My God." Regan sank to her knees in front of Parrot.

"You'll not be puttin' me in dresses."

"Of course not," Arabella sweetly rejoined.

But Regan knew better. Parrot was a doomed soul. Nobody loved playing dress-up more than Arabella. "Talon knows, doesn't he? That's why Nicholas gave you this cabin?"

"The cap woulda figured it sooner but fer all the hubbub. Jaime knows."

"But why have you been hiding?

She shrugged. "Me ma was bent on keepin' me a boy and oi didn't see no reason to change. Oi still don't," she warned them, and much like Talon's reaction when he'd discovered the truth, Regan laughed.

That night Regan arrived on deck for dinner eagerly hoping Talon would be present. During the last few hours, she'd worked her unruly hair into something presentable. She knew her royal velvet gown contrasted vividly with her skin and set off her eyes. If she couldn't win her husband one way, she'd attempt another.

"You're late," he curtly informed her.

Her vanity, which had never been so profane as when she glimpsed herself in the mirror before coming on deck, wilted. Taking the only remaining chair, furthest from him, she thanked Piers for helping her sit. They ate the meal in peace. Talon didn't provoke her, and Robert, sitting next to his wife, remained coolly aloof, which suited Regan. Arabella's parents were predisposed to rudeness that only Talon's presence held in check.

"We need some gaiety on this deck," Arabella cheerfully said, breaking the droll mood surrounding dessert. "Let's play whist."

Whist was a game that took extreme mathematical skill. In answer to everyone's blank stares, Arabella said, "It was Marcus's favorite." She shot Talon a nervous glance. "We played often."

"Really, Arabella," her mother snapped. "Don't make a fool of yourself. We've had enough of that from your father."

"For your information, Mother, I'm not as dull-witted as you think." Her prim nose lifted. "And I don't have to pretend to be so feminine." She looked at Regan for affirmation. "Do I?"

That was exactly what Regan was aspiring to be. Feminine.

"Do you know something else?" Arabella announced, clearly on a feisty bent against her parents. "I can converse in Latin. I even know about stars and navigation."

"I've never heard such nonsense from you, Arabella."

"Why, Mother, did you know there's a *North Star*? Isn't that so Captain Drake?"

Talon seemed amused by Arabella's newfound emancipation. He pointed helpfully to a glittering orb in the night sky, barely discernible through the sails. "I believe there it is."

"I can name every constellation in the sky tonight." She proceeded to spout them all. "They're in different places depending on the time of year. Marcus told me."

The stars in different places!

Arabella's words struck Regan. Something about the two maps. The one she'd seen on her brother's desk pictured Orion's constellation. Her pulse leapt. Did it coincide with the numbers on Robert's map? A date perhaps? What land mass did Orion's belt cover in October?

In the background of her thoughts, Regan sensed the argument had shaped into war. Soon someone would start throwing something. Arabella's mother suddenly bound to her feet. Her dark hair was rolled back into a stern bun, robbing her of the softness of beauty.

Her sharp glare encompassed Regan. "This is your fault my daughter is acting like some ill-mannered hoyden—"

Arabella promptly jumped up. "Really, Mother!"

"—always wanting to be like you, though heaven only knows why."

"None of this has been Regan's fault, Mother."

"She's been nothing but a disgrace to this family, with her highfalutin morals. Why, she's nothing but a—"

Talon slammed both fists on the table. "Enough!" Eyeing the elderly Constance and Robert, he came to his feet, towering over them all. "I don't know what it is with you bloody Welleses, but I've had it with the lot of you. You can stay in your rooms until we reach Martinique. Then you can kill each other as far as I'm concerned."

"You can't do this," Constance wailed.

"I just did, madam." Issuing orders to have the table and chairs cleared from the deck, he stormed off to attend some captain's duty.

"Well," Arabella affected a pretty moue. "If I'm going to be condemned to prison, I'm moving in with Parrot."

Constance gasped. Her gaze swung to the boyish urchin sitting at the end of the table, and she promptly swooned.

Looking from Regan's shocked face to Parrot's, Arabella casually asked, "Whist, anyone?"

Regan awoke that night with a start, jolted by nightmares that evaded her memory's grasp. Nausea plagued her again. The seas were rougher tonight. Outside the stern galley window, darkness blended with the sea, broken by a flash of distant lightening. Dawn was still hours off on the horizon.

Talon was at the desk, contemplating the glass of brandy cupped in his hands. Light from the lanthorn above his head spread around him in an unwelcome glow, embracing his dour mood. Yet, her heart leapt. It was the first time he'd come near her in weeks.

Hair spilled over her shoulders as she struggled to sit. "Talon?" His gaze lifted to her voice. "What are you doing here?"

"You've plodded my every step. Now my presence disturbs you?"

Wearing only her shift, she stepped out of bed. "No, it doesn't disturb me." She could hardly breathe for his presence. His clothes were damp and smelled of rain. Papers cluttered his desk. "What are you doing?"

Clearly, he suffered displeasure to have her so near. "I'm making it easy for you to get a divorce, Regan."

Her heart slammed against her ribs. "But I don't want one."

"You can get a divorce, an annulment. It matters little to me. You've been nothing but trouble. I'll be glad to get rid of you."

Stepping to the desk, she snatched the wretched document from his hand. He was mad to think she was so weak-kneed that she would not fight him. Dread pirate, indeed! He cowered from matters of the heart like a fledgling rabbit.

Without looking at the papers, she ripped them into confetti. "And you, Captain Drake, are a liar." Her eyes remained fixed on his as she dribbled the pieces over his head. "You shall miss me."

Talon pulled her across his lap, his angry mouth stopping within inches of its descent. "So you wish to play the whore of a pirate."

She was beyond the pain of words and would not be provoked. "I'm no whore."

"But I'm a pirate."

"And I'm your wife."

His mouth touched her hair. "Your vows were a lie, Regan."

"I'm still your wife." Her persuasive whisper sent a tremor through him. She felt it.

As if realizing he'd underestimated her, his expression grew stark. The graphic proof of his desire, pressed against her hip, empowered her to act recklessly. Regan draped her arms around his neck. She kissed his stubbled cheek, inhaled the scent of soap and abandoned herself to his turmoil. "And the way I see it, *sweet*," she emphasized the endearment for good measure. "If you wish to end this marriage, you'll have to postpone your plans of revenge while you seek to petition a safe colony. Like Martinique. 'Tis French and offers a haven for English pirates. You may seek your divorce there."

A look of astonishment passed over his features.

"I've decided to keep you, milord pirate." She tossed his words back in his face, words he'd once used to taunt her. Her voice grew serious. "And if I can keep you alive along the way, I will."

Talon stood abruptly, dumping her on the desk. "Get it through your thick skull, Regan. I don't need to be saved. Especially by you." He stalked out of the room, slamming the door.

Regan eyed the portal, pondering her own reckless insanity. Snatching up the bedsheet, she followed him.

On deck, lonely in its emptiness, the sound of tackle banging lightly against the shrouds drew her gaze skyward. Thunder rolled over the predawn sky. Even under reduced sail, the *Fury* flew with determination before the southeast wind. The air smelled damp.

Regan scanned the darkness. Only the helmsman and watch were awake at this hour. A flash of lightning revealed Talon in his hammock beneath the quarterdeck overhang. It swayed furiously as if he'd just thrown himself into its stiff mesh.

The advancing storm concealed her approach.

His forearm was flung across his eyes. Staring down at his features, she touched his stubbled cheek with liquid tenderness. His fingers wrapped around her wrist, startling her.

"What are you doing here, Regan?"

"Come downstairs, Talon. To bed."

The grip on her wrist tightened almost painfully. He shoved her hand away and put his forearm back over his eyes. "Stay away from me, Regan."

"I should douse you beneath the wash-deck pump, Captain Drake." He stared up at her, his expression unreadable in the darkness. "But I suppose the rain will suffice. I recall that cold water has a way of cooling a temper."

He replaced his arm over his eyes, shutting her out. "I recall that I was a fool then."

Pain tempered her pride. She swallowed both. "Not as

much as you are now. You know I care what happens to you."

"Spare me your sentiment, Regan." His voice was tired.

She touched his hand. "Deny that you care for me, Talon."

"Care?" In one swift movement, he was out of the hammock, towering over her, backing her against the bulkhead of the quarterdeck. "I would care for nothing more than to strangle you."

"Because I'm responsible for Marcus's death? All right—" She gripped his wrists, forcing his fingers around the slim column of her neck. "—no one can see. Who will stop you from killing me? Lord knows you deserve your revenge. You've suffered. You hate me. You hate my family. Do it!" She lifted her chin, presenting him with her throat. "You'll rid yourself of one Welles."

His eyes tore into hers. Furious. Stricken.

"Do it for Marcus. Then there are three more of us. You can kill us all."

His hands lifted to cup her face, then tangled in her hair. "Christ, you didn't kill Marcus. I did."

The ravaged words tumbled in a whispering plea from his lips as his head bent over hers and finally in a last desperate attempt to separate, he pushed her away, and fell against the bulkhead. "Just leave me the hell alone!"

Overhead thunder rumbled. "Talon—"

Talon didn't need her contemptible pity. "Get away from me, Regan." He raised his face to the sky as the first raindrop touched his parched skin.

And at once, his strength crashed in on him.

He slid down the bulkhead, burying his face against his fists.

Regan went down with him to the deck, wrapping him in her arms, the sheet around her body shielding them both.

He could taste the fresh scent of her hair and skin, her sweet breath whispering over him. Shutting his eyes, he soaked up her touch until he surrendered completely to the soothing promise of redemption. Her hands caressed his face; her gentle words his soul, leaving him to believe in the promise of life that once stretched before him like a rainbow into eternity.

Rain splattered against his arm and struck the deck in musical cadence quickening to the pulse of his heart, until the sky opened.

Regan pulled his head against her chest, anchoring him against her with strength that belied her small frame. And for the first time since he was a babe, he gave himself to the comfort of another's arms.

And cried.

They were lovers. They were enemies. He needed her, and it struck him that his grief was for more than Marcus. It was for himself. For the stolen years he'd lost. For what might have been. For his mother and sister and the horror of watching his proud father destroyed, his body picked clean by crows. The knowledge that he'd failed and might never know the taste of true freedom again.

The emotions ravaged him. Seared him as violently as any firestorm, leaving behind devastation that couldn't be measured by sight alone. Marcus's death left him scrambling to shove the charred pieces of his life back together and somehow go on.

"Come to bed with me, Talon," Regan gently coaxed.

The rain had stopped. How long ago? A few minutes? An hour?

They were both soaked. Dressed as she was, Regan needed to go below. He lifted his head to tell her this and found himself buried in her liquid eyes.

He kissed her deeply, aching to touch her soul.

Her lips flowered beneath his, her breath hot as her tongue found his in a velvet caress. Burying his fingers in her tangled hair, he twisted her around until she was caged in his lap and he felt the full bounty of her body beneath his hands. Her arms wrapped around his neck, melding her to him.

Primal need surged through Talon, tearing away the thin veneer of humanity that separated him from his animal brethren. "Regan," he rasped. Her mouth covered his, kissing his lips, his stubbled cheeks, the column of his neck. "What are you doing to me?"

"Loving you, Talon."

She ran her hands beneath his sodden shirt. He closed his eyes, lifting the shirt free from his body. The salt-scented breeze touched his skin. He pressed her back against the sheet, following her down, covering her mouth with his, devouring her. If any men watched in the darkness, he hoped they had the decency to turn away.

Regan's wet chemise molded to her skin. He suckled her sweet breasts through the soft material, his hands shaping to the pliant contour of her hips. She arched, pressing against him until he hurt with the need to sink into her warmth. To know more than her desire. To take more than her body.

He fumbled clumsily for the laces on his breeches as Regan kissed him to distraction.

"You're too slow," she rasped, freeing him.

His arousal filled her hands. He closed his eyes, his control tempered by steel that was fast melting beneath her touch. His voice mingled with her hot breath. He kissed her again, tasting her lips, and the sweet melody of her groans. He caressed her breast, her waist, her hips; he couldn't get enough of her. He opened his mouth to her hot, wet invasion. How expert she'd become at unleashing the primal force between them, rendering control but a useless word to add to his battle-scarred library of cast-off emotions. Finally, he parted the moist, silky curls between her thighs and entered her, sliding, sliding deeper as she lifted to absorb all of him.

His powerful need for her raced with his pulse, wrapping around his senses until his ragged breath came hard and fast with her movements. Tension gripped the thick muscles on his arms, obliterating all else. He rocked against her. She clung to him with wild urgency, her whispered cries captured by his hungry mouth until passion sent him soaring. Wracking release catapulted through him, tearing him, driving him harder and harder against her, and he knew in a moment she was with him all the way. That she'd always been with him.

And as he fell against her sated body, he wondered how it could have taken him so long to discover the sweetness of surrender.

Chapter Twenty-three

Marital bliss occupied Talon during the short days that followed. In the evenings, the sunset belonged to him as he shared this part of his world with Regan. Even the darkest thunderheads became glorious shapes in the sky to be marveled. He and Regan conversed about everything and nothing at all.

In the cabin, wrapped in his arms at night, she talked about her home on Martinique. The orphanage where she spent most of her life after her accident. Her friend Sarah. Her mother's family. Talon listened with infinite tenderness, amazed by her fortitude. Unhampered by the hardship fate had dealt her, she'd built a life from the scraps of defeat. Though, she would never see it that way.

"Where did your father meet someone like your mother?" Talon asked Regan one night a week later.

"In France. She was a widow visiting her family at court. Father was an ambassador for King Charles." Regan curled around to face him. "Does it make you uncomfortable talking about my family?"

He brushed the hair from her beloved face. "Everything about you is a new experience," he admitted without rancor. "Until a few months ago, I didn't even know you existed. Why did your brother leave you in Martinique?"

"After my parents died, Harrison felt I needed more care than he could give me," she finally replied, clearly embarrassed to admit that she could be so much of a burden to her brother. "It was everything to Harrison to follow in Father's footsteps. His political aspirations were his life."

"Your parents left you nothing?"

"Harrison's taken good care of me, Talon, the best he could. I have no regrets."

Regret? The sentiment tore through him. Her misplaced love for the man tested his truce with Regan as nothing else could. Talon turned her over on her back, trapping her between his arms. "Tell me, Regan. Is it for me, or your brother that you worry? I don't know what to think about any of this. About you."

Her radiant gaze surrounded him. "Three months ago I wanted to shoot you. Now, I'm throwing myself at your feet. The heart does naught for logic and goes to great lengths to confuse me as well."

"I was not prepared for this. For what you do to me. For reminding me that I can feel and know life again. You've stripped me of all that I am . . . and still I want to know more of this gift you've given me."

"Make your home with me, Talon," she said simply.

It came as a shock for him to realize the taut thread he walked between domestic peace and war. That he wanted to stay with her. Wanted a home, children, everything that went with life.

His mouth crooked in an attempt to combat his own confusion. "And quit?" he said lightly. "Be accused of cowardice?"

"I know what I said. But I don't want you to die, Talon. I would selfishly steal your life for myself."

Talons held her close to his heart. For a moment, peace was his. And he could barely cope; it hurt to the point of madness.

She'd shattered the order of his life.

A shriek in the hallway made Regan look up from the desk. Talon was already swinging his legs over the side of the bed. She'd been guarding his sleep and groaned at the disturbance that had been steadily building in volume the last hour since sunrise. Another scream, raised voices, and a thunderous slam of a door confirmed the discordant mood of Talon's other passengers.

He stepped into his breeches. "Sounds like a bloody war."

Regan beat him to the door. "I'd leave them alone," she said casually. "Besides," she ran her fingers over the hardened ridge of muscle that formed his stomach, "you're not dressed. And I'm not of a mind to share you with Arabella."

Talon leaned a hand against the door. Her pulse quickened at the wolfish grin that lifted the seductive corners of his mouth. "I can see we have an authority issue between us, milady wife."

"Arabella is exerting her independence. This is good for her." Regan laughed when Talon lifted a skeptical brow. "She's moved in with Parrot and has yet to inform her parents of Parrot's true gender. She's enjoying torturing them."

"And you grew up with these people?"

"For the most part, I grew up with our servants."

"That accounts for the sanity."

The argument escalated between the rooms and Regan grimaced. "I'm sorry they woke you."

His dusky gaze anchored to her chemise-clad form. "Don't be."

"Thank you . . . for your patience."

"Strange words coming from my kidnap victim."

In one ironic moment of madness, he'd changed her life forever, blessed her, as if fate bid it so. He was blind not to see the perfect sense of it all.

"What are you doing up?" he asked.

She suddenly remembered her purpose. "Where's Orion's orbit in October?" she asked, having puzzled all morning over the numbers on the bottom of Robert's map: 10:14;56. Talon would know. The stars were a primary source for navigation.

"The Panama," he answered easily. "Why?"

Puerto Bello is near Panama!

She dipped beneath his arm, but he caught her and swung her around before she could sweep past him to the desk. "Regan—"

"What if there was a treasure and it never left Puerto Bello?"

Talon seemed to study her face half-hidden beneath tumbled curls. On impulse, he kissed her freckled nose. "I've had enough Spanish hospitality to last ten lifetimes, Regan," he said carefully.

"But your mother was Spanish. You said so."

"Puerto Bello is still a death sentence to me."

"You must have family there."

"I never knew my mother's side of the family. I never wanted to."

"Why not, Talon?"

"Not once during the time Marcus and I were on trial for our lives did any of them step forward. To console. To comfort. To defend. My mother's life meant so little to them. Her sons lives meant even less."

"Their own flesh and blood?" she was aghast.

"My mother was disinherited from her family when she married my father in Puerto Bello. My Spanish blood has only been a curse."

Noting the breakfast tray on the desk, Talon walked across the cabin. Light from the beveled window spilled across Robert's map. Pouring a cup of coffee, he ignored the map and looked out across the sea. "Why the sudden interest in the treasure, Regan?"

Her mouth went dry. She could not bear this abrupt change in him. Or imagine the pain he'd gone through in his life. "That gold could build us an island fortress."

He looked at her. "A prison."

"It could buy you a pardon, Talon."

"So could you, sweet. And I wouldn't have to die to get it."

With the sudden memory of Tortuga, the words shocked her. But he was right. Why hadn't she thought of that?

"No," he said reading her mind. "I knew it wouldn't be long before you figured it out and tried to do something idiotic."

"But this isn't idiotic."

"I won't send you back to Kendrick. I couldn't even do it the first time."

"Why not?" she said, keeping an open mind. "It would settle everything. I wouldn't stay gone for long."

"He would find a way to keep us apart. No, Regan. Risking you settles nothing. A pardon doesn't change the past."

"It makes you free."

"Free?" He mocked the notion. "What is freedom if I sacrifice you to get it? What is freedom if I have no name to give my children? No honor—a conviction of treason forever over my head."

"What is honor if you have no life?"

"Honor is everything to me, Regan."

Her throat tightened. Despite her anguish, she understood his pride only too well. It was all that he was; it was all that he had left. "Then you'll know why I must to go to Harrison. I have to try."

He set down the coffee cup. "You won't go back to Kendrick."

She fought a rush of frustrated tears. "But why not? Harrison won't hurt me. You're wrong about him—"

Talon placed two fingers against her mouth. "Don't ever defend him to me again, Regan. Ever."

"Why do you hate him so? I don't understand."

How could he explain why he didn't trust her life in her brother's hands? Would she believe her brother capable of the filthy crimes he'd committed against Talon's sister?

"I swear that no matter what happens you'll never be dependent on him again," he said.

"What are you talking about?"

His lips pressed together as he looked away from her searching gaze. Until now, he hadn't known how to tell her he was leaving her on Martinique.

Realizing the full import of his words, she gave a half-hysterical laugh. "I see."

"I can't stay with you, Regan."

"You can't? Or you won't?"

God help him, but he'd not fought ten years to lose now.

He had to leave her. For her protection. He was a criminal wanted by the English crown, an enemy of Spain. Kendrick still lived and deserved more than any one on this earth to die. But in seeking justice, he'd hurt her. In seeking his name, he'd destroy hers. She'd lured him from his purpose, defeated him with nothing more than the promise of peace.

Already he'd lost the ability to think straight.

Clutching her arms to her, she whirled away from him, her eyes darting around the cabin. "I suppose I'll need to pack, then. We'll reach Martinique tomorrow—"

Talon felt his heart twist.

"I . . . I've nothing to pack my things in." He heard the break in her voice. "You won't mind if I take your sea chest. Clothes are so hard to come by. But then I'll be with Father Henri—"

"Regan," he dragged her to him.

"You'll not have any trouble from the authorities there." She ran a hand through her hair, wincing as her fingers caught a tangle. "The governor is Mother's cousin. I know him. A slovenly man, actually, not in the least nice—"

"Please, Regan. Don't make this harder than it already is."

With a sob, she hit her fists against his chest. "I can't go with you. You ask that I stand aside and do nothing to help. You ask that I not see my brother. You ask the impossible! I hate your stubbornness, for going away to die. I hate you!"

"No, you don't, Regan."

"I do!"

He held her tightly. The hot flow of her tears dampened his chest, tearing him in half. Christ, he was a fool. The pain of it sucked his breath away. He didn't want to leave her. He loved her. Perhaps he'd always loved her. Only he didn't recognize it until that night she'd taken him in her arms and promised salvation with only her touch. He kissed her tenderly, tasting her tears.

She clung to him, kissing him back with the force of her anger. "I would do anything to keep you with me forever, Talon."

And Talon would give her anything to make her happy, except the one thing he couldn't. "The future isn't mine to give, Regan," he whispered over her anger. "It never was."

The French town of Fort-Royale was built around the turquoise waters of the bay. Crammed with colorful markets and shops, the seaside community bustled with life, unspoiled tranquillity within a backdrop of verdant forests and an old volcano. On the hill overlooking the harbor entrance, a huge French fort stood sentinel.

Nausea rolled unpleasantly in Regan's belly. Nervous agitation, she finally decided, at the thought of leaving the *Dark Fury*. The French inspectors from the garrison had arrived an hour before. On deck, Regan kissed Charlie farewell and smiled as he made an effort to walk on his new peg leg for her. Piers proved more somber. Arabella was already on shore with Parrot, and while Talon was busy with the inspector, she made Jaime row her to shore.

"A ship is leaving for France tomorrow," Arabella breathlessly announced when Regan reached her. It hurt to learn her cousin wouldn't be accompanying her to the mission. "Talon has already purchased passage for me and my family."

Regan stared, aghast. "He's letting Robert go?"

"Papa isn't any use to him. I pray that his deposition will open an inquiry." Her cousin hugged her. "Talon has seen to it we'll be taken care of."

Regan pulled out of her arms.

"He gave me a thousand pounds sterling and enough jewels to make the queen green with envy." She whispered conspiratorially, "He said the money belonged to Marcus. And, he told Papa in no uncertain terms that if he touched one pound of it without my permission, that Harrison would be the least of his problems."

"When did he do this?"

"This morning. You were still in bed, cousin. Now go. Quit worrying for us and for your husband. He'll be back once he realizes he can't live without you."

Regan burst into tears. If only Talon did love her. Arabella made a grand production of comforting her, clearly at ease with their role reversal. "I never get to do this for you," she said, patting Regan on the back.

"I've become emotional, lately."

"Parrot is adamant you're with child. We've a wager—"

Regan's head lifted. "What?"

Arabella leaned over and whispered. "That does happen sooner or later. And with him—" Her gaze found Talon on the quarterdeck of the ship, his tall form accentuated by a white linen shirt and black breeches tucked into boots. "I'd gamble sooner than later."

"I . . ." Regan sniffed. Heat baked every inch of her skin. When was her last menses? Two months? The realization she could be carrying Talon's child made her pulse surge.

"We're ready to take you to the inn, milady," Harry said, stepping forward to offer Arabella into the carriage he'd just brought around. "Yer parents are waitin', Lady Arabella."

"God be with you, cousin." Arabella hugged her again, then made a spectacle of herself waving from the carriage as it clattered down the cobbled street and disappeared in the swarm of townspeople.

Jaime and Parrot stood beside Regan. She managed a brave smile. "Well," she said, trying not to imagine Arabella really leaving. "What do you think of my home?"

"Oi imagine it's like any other island," Parrot grunted.

Regan looked out at the *Dark Fury* subdued in the gentle swell by its moorings. Talon was still speaking with the French inspector.

As if sensing her stare, Talon looked up. She met his agitated gaze over the man's uniform hat. Clearly, he was perturbed that she'd left the ship. She turned away. The afternoon heat penetrated her yellow taffeta gown. Sweat trickled down her back.

Jaime took her elbow. "You don't look well, milady."

"I need someplace to sit. To wait for Harry to return."

He guided her across the street to a shaded cobblestone alley where a café opened to the hills. It faced away from the harbor. Away from Talon.

"Parrot will fetch something refreshin'. I'll wait fer Cap'n—"

"No. I want to leave the moment Harry returns."

Jaime and Parrot exchanged an uncertain look. "But, milady—"

"Please, Jaime. Just do as I say. It'll be easier this way."

After they left, Regan closed her eyes. Struggling to hang on to some semblance of calm, her mind drifted to the breeze and the music filtering from a tavern a few doors away.

Pregnant. The thought excited and frightened her at once.

Lord, could life get any more complicated?

"Hello, Regan."

The soft-spoken words dropped Regan's heart. Her eyes snapped open.

Harrison lounged indolently in the chair beside her. She hadn't even heard his approach. Her next gasp was one of shock. Hideous scars marked his once handsome face where grapeshot had torn through part of his cheek. A dark patch covered one eye, an ugly contradiction to the blond periwig that curled stiffly to his shoulders. His long-ringed fingers strummed the table.

"You're surprised to see me."

She opened her mouth to speak. He wore a red velvet doublet ornamented with flashy gold ribband that reached to the tops of his silver buckled shoes. One leg stretched oddly out in front of him as if it hurt to bend. "My God, what happened to you?"

His one eye darkened. "I've been waiting here for weeks, Regan. Recovering from wounds—" He took her hands. "—but please. I don't want to talk about me." Looking around the square, he said. "Pleasant island. I'm surprised I haven't found the time to visit more often."

Her heart beat at a frantic pace. Harrison must know the *Fury* was docked. Why was he so calm? Something was amiss. Then Regan remembered that Mama's family was also his. That her half brother was a political figure of great importance.

Talon was in trouble.

"Let him go, Harrison." Her fists clenched in his sleeve. "You have no authority here."

Harrison drew back. "Roth said you were in love with the man."

"Yes, I'm in love with him. I'm married to him. His child grows inside me. You will not harm him. So help me—"

"If he fights us, he'll die, Regan. I can do nothing for that. He's dangerous. More dangerous to both of us than you know."

"You can't hurt him!"

"Will he give up his sword without a fight?"

She knew he wouldn't.

"Do you wish to save him, Regan?"

"Oh God, yes."

He studied her face, then urged her back into the seat. "There *is* something you can do." A snap of his fingers brought them two glasses of wine a few moments later. "See that he drinks this."

She was ill. "Is . . . is this drugged?"

"Thirty of my men surround us, Regan. The French authorities will not intervene. Drake *will* die if he fights us. At least this way he's guaranteed a fair trial in Port Royal."

Regan stared at the wine. Tears blurred the burgundy liquid to blood. "He won't come. We already said our good-byes."

Harrison laughed. "You underestimate his feelings for you, sister mine. He's already on his way."

Her head snapped up. "No."

"Make up your mind, Regan. Does he live or die?"

"You offered a pardon once—"

"He was a fool to renege on his word."

"But he brought me back here. He didn't have to do that."

"A fair trial, Regan."

Could that be possible? One judged by the Admiralty Court this time? That's what Talon wanted, wasn't it? She closed her eyes.

Harrison caressed her cheek. "You've been through a lot, Regan. When this is over, I'm taking you home."

She wanted to shout that she was home. That he'd ruined her life by asking her to betray Talon. Regan shoved Harrison's hand away.

His arms opened in supplication. "I risked my life for you, sister mine. I am not the criminal here." He stood without his usual flourish. "No matter. I'm glad you're safe, Regan. I've missed you."

Torn by her little girl worship of a brother that could do no wrong, all the years of her life crumbled to her feet. He'd suffered hideous injuries because of her and she'd not thought to offer comfort. He'd come for her. And she'd treated him like dirt.

Oh, why did you have to find me? Why?

Chapter Twenty-four

Talon leaped from the longboat before his men could tie it off. He couldn't get to shore fast enough. The inspector had been meticulously slow in registering them, but with the cannons of that fort staring down at the bay, Talon was reluctant to square off with the little tyrant.

"Did she already leave?" He rushed past Jaime.

"She didn't feel well, Cap'n," Jaime informed him following at his brisk pace. "I sat her in the shade to wait fer Harry."

Talon scanned the crowded square. His men were nowhere to be seen. "She's alone? Jeezus, Jaime, you know better than that. Harry should have been back with the carriage. Go check on it."

Talon was relieved when he found Regan. She was sitting in the cool shade of a balsa-wood tree, dark head bowed, fingers tightly laced around a glass of wine. Her uncovered hair fell over her face and bodice. She looked fragile enough to break.

She'd waited for him. "Regan?"

Luminous eyes, bright in the shade against her yellow gown, encompassed him. Moisture clung to her dark lashes. She was probably upset over Arabella leaving. Hell. What was he saying? He was to blame for her tears.

The need to take her into his arms struck him. She had

that power over him, to move his emotions. He wanted to wipe the sadness from her face.

He was still staring down at her when she spoke. "I ordered wine for you," she beckoned softly. She nodded to his glass when he didn't respond. "I'm sorry. I thought you might need some refreshment, after . . . Did everything go well?"

Talon tore his eyes from hers and looked around the square. Vendors hawked their wares beneath thatched roofs that would blow over in the first gust. He felt tense. Then decided his own awkward feelings put him on edge. He sat in the chair across from her. His sword scraped the cobbled walk.

"I had problems with the inspector." He studied her pale oval features over the rim of his glass and ached to see the warmth in that cinnamon gaze, the way her eyes would light up when she laughed. "It seems the French fortress with five hundred men and fifteen thirty-two pound cannons aimed down my throat isn't enough to convince them of my harmlessness."

Velvet eyes plucked at his heart. Clearly, he'd failed at humor. But then he'd never been good at humor. At a loss for further words, he drank the wine and grimaced. It tasted too sweet. Hell, what did it matter? A whole bottle wouldn't be enough to quell his mood.

Finishing the glass, he idled back in the rickety chair and gazed at her. "Jaime said you weren't feeling well. Maybe you should eat something before you go to the mission."

"I'm not hungry."

"That doesn't surprise me, Regan," he said irritably, "you're not very good at taking care of yourself."

"Talon—" Her voice wavered.

"You've enough money in the chest to go anywhere you want. Ill-gained plunder, so to speak. It belonged to your family. I'm sure you'll put it to better use."

"Stop it!" Her gaze floundered. "Why are you talking like this?"

"Because you've forgotten who and what I am."

"I know what you are. You're good and decent—"

He was suddenly furious. It was folly to come. He'd blun-

dered to think he possessed the ability to let her go. Before
he took her into his arms, he stood. Where the hell was the
carriage?

"Jaime and Harry will see you safely to the mission, Regan. I need to get back to the ship."

Regan left her chair. "Why did you even come on shore,
Talon? For once why didn't you just leave?"

He didn't like the accusation in her eyes. "Because, I
thought . . ." What had he been thinking? A dull throb began
just above his eyes. He'd been angry at her departure, worried that she'd come to shore alone rather than face him ever
again.

The sound of the carriage rattling toward them drew him
up. "You're home, Regan. Go back to your uncle Henri. Go
back to Sarah where you belong. This is a nice island. Stay
and make it your home."

Tears spilled from her eyes. "I thought coming here . . .
we'd have a chance. I thought everything would be different."

He rubbed his temples to clear his head and forced himself
to focus on her face. "I can't make it different. I just don't
know what else to do, Regan."

She buried her face against his chest. "Oh God, Talon.
You should have left us in Tortuga."

The broken words swept over him. Warned him a moment
before he felt the weakness go through him. "Regan, what
the—"

Roth stepped around the carriage. "Captain Drake."

Talon's body acted reflexively, but he couldn't move with
Regan in his arms.

"You're surrounded, Drake," Roth quietly warned. "If you
fight, they'll kill you."

Regan clutched him. "Please, listen to him, Talon."

Talon looked down into her pale, terrified face. He remembered the too sweet wine. "What have you done?"

The carriage door swung open. "What I asked her to do,
Drake." Harrison's hideous visage filled the narrow point of
Talon's vision. A part of his mind that wasn't dulled recoiled.
"Yes," Kendrick hissed. "Take a good look. You did this
when your ship fired on the *Viper*." He crawled forward.

"She's my sister, Drake. You don't think she owed you her loyalty, did you?"

"No!" Regan gripped his shirt. "It wasn't like that."

"You poisoned me?" Talon hated that his voice sounded incredulous. That it shook with fear or rage. He didn't know. He couldn't comprehend anything beyond her betrayal. Shoving her against her brother, he staggered backward. His gaze sliced to the top of the carriage. To the man wearing Harry's clothes . . .

The pirate's mouth eased into a black-toothed grin. "Jolly good day, Cap'n."

"Weasel!" With all his strength, Talon drew his cutlass.

"You can't fight them," Regan pleaded. "They'll kill you."

His gaze swiveled to impale her. Overpowered from behind, Talon lost his sword. It clattered over the cobblestones. He slammed his knuckles back into a man's sweaty face, feeling bone crush beneath the impact. He kicked out, dislodging his other captor. Then a fist smashed into his jaw, snapping his head back. A punch in the ribs dropped him to his knees. The rocks tore his skin. And he fell forward on his palms, spitting blood from his mouth. Blood spattered his white shirt.

"Leave him alone!" he heard Regan screaming.

Someone grabbed a handful of his tangled hair, jerking his head up. He focused on her face, the terrified luminous eyes that still dared to speak her love.

She'd betrayed him. How could she?

He spit a mouthful of blood. "My ship?" he rasped to Roth. At least he could trust the man to see that his crew wasn't butchered.

Harrison answered him. "Impounded, even as we speak, Drake. The *Dark Fury* belongs to me now. I won, you bastard. All these years. Now you're mine. Like your sister. Remember your sister, Drake?"

Talon's murderous gaze sliced to Regan. She was shaking her head, white knuckles buried against her mouth. Tears filled her eyes. She would pay somehow. He'd rise and snap her neck if she moved a foot closer. His beautiful, treacherous wife.

She staggered back against the force of his stare.

"You better hope they kill me, wife." His savage words slurred with the drug she'd fed him. Life was seeping from his muscles. "If they don't there won't be a place this side of hell for you to hide."

And then the ground came up to meet his face, taking the light from his life.

Regan remembered nothing of the carriage ride to the mission. She awoke later to the darkness, feeling the horrible relentless surge of more tears. Her breath caught on a scream before her hands registered the soft cotton of the comforter wrapped around her body. She wore only her chemise. The soothing scent of vanilla and lemon calmed her racing heart.

She knew where she was. She must have fainted, not to remember where they'd taken her.

"Sarah?" she called, daring to hope. She was home with Father Henri, in the small room she shared with her friend. Her hands ran along the night table for the lamp. Nothing. A three-legged stool was next to the bed. She groaned. Her head ached as if someone laid a hammer to her skull. "Sarah?"

Rustling movements followed from the other bed. Sarah dropped onto the stool. "Thank the Lord. Your brother gave you something to calm you down. You've been asleep nearly the whole day."

"Where's the lamp?"

"Your brother said you'd scream when you're ready to come out."

The tremble in her voice betrayed shock. "Harrison said that?" He knew more than anyone how she hated the darkness. Only, he hadn't reckoned that her only fear now was for Talon. Nothing else mattered.

"Sarah—" Regan sat on the edge of the bed. Sarah's silken hair draped over Regan's knees. In the daylight Sarah's white blond hair glimmered nearly as silver as her eyes. "You've no idea what's happened since I last saw you."

"Sir Kendrick has thought of nothing but finding you and this man Drake."

"Has Harrison hurt anyone?"

"I've been caring for him . . ."

"Has he hurt you?"

Sarah had come to the convent ten years before, brutalized and battered: a child of nine, her sight destroyed by the same horrors that had stolen her memory. That Harrison would dare touch her . . .

"He's capable of great wrath." Sarah's evasive words died to a whisper. "Father Henri has begun to fear him. But it is for this Captain Drake that we worry."

Regan's eyes closed. She'd handed him Talon's life. "Oh, Sarah. What have I done? There will be no trial," she whispered.

Approaching bootsteps outside the door stiffened Sarah.

"Don't make a sound." Regan hustled her to bed, then slid the stool in the way of any intruder who entered their room.

The latch clicked open.

Faint light wedged into the room from wall sconces in the dank hallway behind the door, silhouetting the bulky body of a man. His sour smell preceded him.

"Weasel!" Regan raised up.

The pirate hitched his canvas trousers. "You remember me, do ya, missy?"

"One doesn't forget the smell of bilge."

"I'm not so fergettin' neither, missy. Just ask yer cap'n."

She couldn't conceal her shock. "What have you done to him?"

"Give 'em a bloomin' 'eadache I did, the size he gave me." He swaggered into the room and tripped on the stool. His weighty momentum carried him forward and he sprawled over Talon's trunk that someone put against the wall. Wood splintered with the impact.

Regan shot past him.

"Bloody bitch!"

She ducked into the second doorway and down the stone staircase, directly into Captain Roth's strong arms. Screams echoed down the cavernous hallway. She kicked out. Roth swung her aside just as her pursuer exploded out of the doorway. Cursing, Weasel skidded headlong into the wall.

Roth's grip on Regan tightened as she struggled to escape his hold. "You were told to bring her to Kendrick. Not attack her."

"She bloomin' nearly killed me."

Roth's brow lifted skeptically. "Get out of here. I'll take her to Kendrick myself."

After Weasel left, Roth set Regan out of his arms. He wore a leather doublet buttoned over fine white Holland, buff leggings and boots. His cool glance took in her lack of attire. "It seems we have an affinity for meeting like this, milady."

"You bastard." Regan slapped him. "They're beating him to death and you're letting them."

Roth rubbed his cheek, his obsidian gaze raking her appreciatively. "You pack a wallop, Lady Regan."

"Harrison promised that Talon wouldn't be hurt."

"Captain Drake has not been a model prisoner, Lady Regan. But as far as I know my men haven't touched him."

"Then what about Harrison's men?"

"I'll check on it."

"Where's Talon's crew? Some of them are injured and need—"

"They're being cared for. I promise. Now—" He swept out his arm. "—since you haven't a problem running about half-dressed, I'll take you to your brother without further wait."

Harrison sat in the spacious dining hall at the end of a huge mahogany table, set with silver platters of roast chicken, fruit, yams, and cubes of cheese. More food than families on this island would see in a week. Tapestries decorated the walls, adding a bright splash of color to the simple decor. The doors behind Harrison were open to the tropical breeze. Somewhere in the darkness outside a dog barked.

"So this is where you've made your quaint little home all these years." Harrison swirled the wine in his glass, studying her carefully over its rim. He wore a dark periwig tonight, the same color as the black patch over his eye. He looked evil and for the first time in her young life, she was confused by the image she saw.

He set the glass down and lounged in the chair. "I always knew our family riches would be wasted on you. You've no appreciation for what money can buy."

"I know what it can't buy."

Candles on the chandelier fluttered casting long shadows

over the table. "Sit down, Regan. Dressed as you are I wouldn't want Father Henri to happen by and keel over from shock."

"What have you done with everyone who lives here?"

"Done?" He laughed that absurd laugh of his. "Why they're all in bed I suppose." Harrison fingered the sterling ware beside his plate. "I visited dearest Arabella and her family this afternoon," He lifted the butter knife and seemed to study its scrolled design. Without realizing it, Regan gripped the back of a chair. Harrison leaned toward her. "They've already left for France. But not before Robert swore on paper that Drake perpetuated your kidnaping and other crimes against me."

"But that's not true!"

"Come here, Regan. Sit down. You look in need of nourishment."

Roth moved her to the seat beside Harrison before taking his stance in front of the opened doors. A stack of vellum had been carefully laid out next to a plate of steaming food.

She had to think, but hunger defeated her. Conscious of Harrison's scrutiny, she ate the food. She'd endure anything at the moment for a bite to eat. Even his cruelty.

Halfway through the meal Harrison removed the plate. She nearly groaned to see it go.

Harrison handed her a glass of wine. "A toast, sister mine." He raised the glass. "To my generosity. I've decided to strike a bargain with you."

Alarm and hope mingled painfully in her stomach. What could she possibly have that he'd want?

"Drink up, Regan. You'll like what I have to say."

The wine was drugged. She knew that. Still, anticipation, fear, bid her to sip, if only to make Harrison tell her this bargain.

The familiar syrupy taste rocked her, and all the years she'd been drinking her brother's wine, his coffee, his special medications came crushing down on her. Parrot had been right. He'd been feeding her opium little by little. And she'd been such a fool not to see it.

She must have made some sound, because Harrison

touched her trembling hand and set the glass down. "Your withdrawal must have been unpleasant. I often wondered how you endured."

She was vaguely conscious of the need to remain strong, but anguish ravaged her emotions. "How could you do this to me?"

"You've not been well, Regan. Not since your accident."

"I trusted you."

He ignored her. "I've got a pardon here."

Her gaze drifted to the rolled parchment at Harrison's elbow. The wax bore King William's seal.

"Sign these papers, and this—" He lifted the parchment. "—will go to Drake."

Regan snatched the document. Hands trembling, she unrolled it. Her eyes welled with tears. Finally, she looked up, incredulous. "This was signed by King William two years ago. You kept it from him. You've been a part of the conspiracy against him from the beginning."

"You're too sentimental, Regan. I'm not willing to hang for something done ten years ago. Are you?"

Her expression disbelieving, she dropped her gaze to the other papers and read. She read until rage mingled with tears. Desolation replaced pride. Lord, how she'd been so naïve, in need of love that she possessed no defense against this kind of insanity.

She owned everything. The Welles empire, all its vices and crimes. She owned it all. Father's will had given her sole possession of the horrid legacy and on Mama's written request the fortune would revert to the orphanage before it ever went to Harrison Kendrick, her own flesh and blood.

"It would have been mine. Should have been," Harrison's voice drifted. "But for one mistake. One mistake and I lost it all."

Regan's throat burned. "They both disinherited you. Why?"

A deadly silence fell over him. Regan was too hurt to care.

"You've been poisoning me all these years with your lies and your drugs, tucking me out of your way while you robbed and pillaged." She read the list of ships in her family's name. Known pirate vessels. Smugglers. Slavers. "This is why you wanted me back. You need me alive."

"In a few months you'll be twenty-one. You're to be in-firmed. There are sanitariums in England that handle cases like yours. Everyone knows the fragile state of your mind, sister mine. That's why I had to leave you here when I went to London."

A pitiful laugh kept her tears at bay. "My heroic brother."

"You've always been a simple fool. Now I've discovered you're in league with Drake. I'll need to go to the king, and plead for your life. Of course, he'll demand adequate com-pensation for the years you've robbed him of his just due. As your guardian, I'll make sure you rest comfortably for the rest of your short life."

"You're not my guardian."

A snort of disgust, and Harrison snapped, "Fetch the cap-tain, Roth."

Heart hammering, Regan caught Roth's expression as he lifted his eyes from the pardon and looked at her. He wore a strange, almost shocked expression. Almost as if he were ill.

Harrison waved his hand dismissing him. "Go, Roth."

Regan felt Roth's hesitation before he left the room. It was clear that he didn't trust leaving her to Harrison. But some-thing else had flickered in those dark eyes and as her gaze hung on the empty doorway, she considered his loyalty to Harrison.

Harrison dug beneath the pile of papers in front of her. "An annulment, sister mine. Lacking only Drake's signature. You should have heard your captain's tender endearments when the drug wore off. I've no doubt he'll sacrifice you for the chance of a pardon. He almost did it before. He'll go his happy way like he did when your father imprisoned him. Only this time it won't be a Spanish galleon waiting for him when he leaves."

"You're . . . insane!"

"Drink the rest of your wine, Regan," he said tiredly.

She glared at the nasty glass. With a flick of her hand tipped it over. "Go to the devil, Harrison."

"Now, look what you've done, Regan." He reached for the bottle of wine. The one he'd been drinking out of all night.

"You know I never ask anything twice, sister mine."

"Quit calling me that."

Harrison wrapped his hand in her hair and jerked it viciously. "You're being unreasonable again, Regan."

"I'll not drink it!" She tried to shake her head. The bottle hit her teeth, sloshing warm liquid over her chin. It dribbled in tiny rivulets down her neck and chest.

"I'll bloody drown you in it if I have to."

Despite her best efforts, the wine drained down her throat, burning as it went into her lungs. She swallowed more to keep from choking. Harrison shoved her head against the table. She slumped over gagging.

"Now, sign." He forced her fingers to grip the quill.

Regan poised the quill over the vellum. Heart raging, she wrote in bold unmistakable scrawl: *Go to hell.*

He ruefully sighed. "Why do you always insist on being difficult, Regan?" He slapped her.

Her eyes filled with the shocking horror of his brutality.

"I really hoped you'd cooperate." He knelt beside her and gently thumbed the blood from her lip. "I'm sorry you made me do this."

Movement in the doorway snapped him up. Talon faced him. Standing between two of Kendrick's men, his hands and ankles fettered, he towered above his guards, his defiance savage. A bloodstained cloth wrapped a wound on his head. The once elegant white linen shirt was ripped, exposing the muscled flesh of his shoulders and arms. But nothing broke the pride in his reckless stance or the hard, chiseled features on his face.

Weasel shoved him into the room. Any other man would have sprawled. Hate festered in his silver gaze as it fixed on Harrison, then dropped to Regan, trapping her with such intensity that it sent her gaze floundering to her lap. Hair shielded her face. Pride bid her to conceal Harrison's brutality.

Sickening horror besieged her. She could never face Talon again with the appalling reality that she'd been so wrong about everything. That she'd ever defended her corrupt family. That her whole life had been one monstrous lie.

She pressed a fist to her belly, frozen by the realization

Talon would never know the truth of their child. Debilitating pain swept over her. She would not give in to tears. Not to be mocked by her brother or by Talon, who would consider Harrison's betrayal a just reward for her treachery.

Blessedly, the drug Harrison gave her was beginning to take effect. She noted a strange sense of boneless euphoria settling through her body. Voices floated with little clarity around her, but she recognized Talon's mocking tone as he read the annulment papers Harrison set on the table in front of him.

"You're welcome to her," she heard Talon's sarcastic words. "But she'll be a widow soon enough. And I'd as soon the stigma of my name stick high in your royal craw." The rattle of chains followed as he tossed the quill back at Harrison. From the side of her vision, Regan could see where blood caked his wrists.

"Perhaps you misunderstood what I'm offering." Harrison reached over Regan's shoulder and lifted Talon's pardon.

Mesmerized by the play of light on the crystal, she watched a drop of wax spatter the fine linen tablecloth.

"What have you done to her?" Talon demanded.

"My sister can be rather trying, as you might know."

Regan could feel Talon's gaze. Then his attention fell to the parchment Harrison gave him.

The night went silent.

"You sonofabitch."

"I admit it's a little late in coming." Harrison volunteered the quill again. "The pardon is yours if you sign."

"It's mine if I don't."

Harrison ripped the paper from Talon's hands. "You can rot, Drake."

Weasel's powerful blow from behind sent Talon to all fours. Hair hanging in his face, he lifted his head and met Regan's wet gaze. It pierced him, and the ground beneath him seemed to tremble with her pain. Her chest rose and fell rapidly against the thin cloth of her . . .

She wore only a chemise stained with wine as if someone had poured it over her face. Fresh blood pooled on her swollen bottom lip. His fevered gaze sliced to Harrison. The primal surge to commit murder raised Talon back to his feet.

Someone grabbed his arms and dragged him backward. He'd kill them!

"Back off, Weasel." Roth drew his sword. "Enough of this madness!"

"Enough, indeed." Harrison raised his pistol and fired.

Chapter Twenty-five

Regan awoke in bed. Sunlight spilled through the window that looked out onto the courtyard. Heat suffocated her. Cursing Harrison for drugging her, she staggered to the chamber pot and retched. Sarah held her wracking shoulders, until Regan finally collapsed against the chest on the floor. Talon's chest. She clung to it.

"Harrison shot Captain Roth, Sarah." Regan gingerly touched her swollen lip. "My brother is insane."

Sarah sat on her heels, hands folded around a Bible in her lap, a habit she manifested when frightened. "He has Father Henri and the other sisters confined. Do you think they'll be harmed?"

"God, yes. I need my clothes." Regan flung Talon's chest open to retrieve her clothes. "We must get help." The smell of mold and age assailed her. She stared at Sarah's belongings. She'd forgotten that Sarah had a chest. Shocked, she realized it was an exact duplicate of Talon's. Regan lowered the chest lid and glimpsed the strange insignia carved into the cracked lock plate, barely visible beneath years of tarnish.

A chill swept over her. Remembering the sterling amulet Talon once wore around his neck, she ran her thumb over the metal plate: a shield clutched within the outstretched claws of an eagle.

Regan twisted around. Sarah was foraging through woolen robes and underclothing in her armoire. Regan sat on her knees, dizzy with anticipation. "Sarah, has anyone ever gone through this chest?"

Sarah's muffled words sounded from the armoire. "Father Henri has the key. I've got clothes in here."

Weasel must have broken the lock when he fell on the chest last night. Regan propped the lid and rummaged through the contents. Mostly navigational books and journals. They were too moldy to know for sure. A child's dress. A frayed Bible. Her hand stilled over a doll's head, torn from its body, one sightless blue eye cracked. The memory of a child's headless doll half buried in the rubble at Talon's plantation house drove through her.

Regan pulled out the Bible, her fingers trembling as she flipped open the torn and cracked pages. The leather cover was thick, but before she could question what was buried inside, her gaze stopped. Golden scrolls rimmed the worn page:

John Brendan Drake wed to Mary Francis y Diego

October Fourteenth,

Sixteen hundred and fifty six in the year of our Lord

Puerto Bello

The numbers on the map: *10:14;56.* They weren't navigational coordinates. The names of Talon's family blurred behind tears. She brushed her finger lovingly across his. Then touched Marcus's name. Two more children had lived and died in infancy. Sarah's name was the last addition on the page.

Mama must have known.

All these years she'd protected Sarah's identity. Yet, never buried it. It was almost as if she meant everything to be found. Only Sarah never regained her sight or her memory. Never read the Bible. Never knew anything but the name Mama gave her when she brought Sarah to live at the orphanage on Martinique.

This trunk, the Bible was her only link to the past. Her link to Talon and stories of celestial angels with silver hair.

Her link to life. Regan clutched the Bible and lifted her gaze heavenward.

Talon's sister is alive!

And on the tail of one thought another followed, perhaps less significant, but this one brought her to her feet.

"I know where the treasure is!"

Sarah dropped a handful of clothes on the bed and whirled toward Regan's voice. "Regan, have you gone daft?"

"Sarah." Regan wrapped Sarah's fingers around the Bible and gently squeezed as she guided her to sit. "You must find a way to get this book to Talon Drake or to Father Henri. Do you understand? No matter what happens, you must make sure they get this. Now hide it, while I get dressed."

"Truly, Regan. What is this treasure you're talking about?"

"The maps meant nothing. The symbols on the edges were the clues. The church bells, the mission. That treasure never left Puerto Bello. I was right!"

Regan dressed in Sarah's woolen habit. She quickly braided her hair, tucking it beneath the collar. "I'll be back with help."

She would find a way to free Talon if she had to dig beneath the outer walls to do it. Regan pressed her ear to the door. Her heart beat too loudly to hear anything. Harrison would post a guard. She needed to reach the stairway and get to the widow's walk on the roof. How many times had she and Sarah sneaked up there after dark, to share in the cooler nights and listen to the wind? A huge tree with thick branches draped over the roof from the courtyard.

She opened the door. "Harrison!"

He leaned with one hand braced in the doorway, thrumming his ringed fingers against the wood. Dressed in a scarlet jerkin, his ruffled cuffs shivered elegantly over his wrists. "Do tell, sister mine. Aren't we full of chatter?"

Regan's heart leapt in panic. Lord, how long had he been standing there? Behind Harrison, Weasel lingered with two other men, big burly fellows with dark hair, colored handkerchiefs about their thick throats and pistols in the waist of their breeches. They carried Talon's chest between them. Her clothes.

Regan swung her gaze back to Harrison and found his

interest on the Bible lying beside her bed. Sarah's worn Bible. He limped over and stooped to pick it up. Regan glanced swiftly at Sarah. Bless her. She'd hidden Talon's book.

"Though for the life of me I can't figure what a Bible has to do with anything."

"What are you talking about, Harrison?"

"Do you really think me so doltish that I can't listen through a door, Regan?"

In the daylight, his skin looked waxen next to the black periwig he wore. Sweat beaded his brow. Her gaze dropped to his leg as he limped back.

"So, you know where the treasure of Puerto Bello is? A secret kept hidden for over twenty years."

Pride stiffened her back. "Let Talon go and I'll tell you."

Moist fingers clamped her chin. "Sarah, dear," he said over Regan's shoulder. "I'll be taking my sister away now." He eyed Regan. "It's unbecoming, a high government official of the crown, to have any association with a lynching. I've decided Drake will be taken into the courtyard and hanged from that huge useless tree that makes a bloody mess all over the cobblestones. Father Henri can bury the body."

"No!" Regan gripped her fists into his collar. "You promised!"

Harrison shoved her. "There you go imagining things again."

He swung his fist. Regan ducked. He hit the wall. His bellow was still ringing in her ears when Weasel finished the job.

Talon braced his palms against the moist stone wall. He'd long since lost track of time in the windowless cellar. The darkness buried him. Black as pitch, the storeroom smelled of aged flour, spices, and mildew. Water dripped somewhere, mocking his thirst with an aching ferocity that closed his throat. He leaned his forehead against his shackled wrists.

She'd betrayed him. And he could think of naught but her abuse at Kendrick's hands.

With an uttered curse, Talon slid down the wall to the ground. Mortar scraped his taut shoulders. He drew his knees to his chest as close as the length of chain allowed. The movement shot pain through his legs. Hunger and exhaustion claimed his strength. Never one for helplessness, the feeling shocked him.

The rattle of chains stirred the inky darkness, and Talon's attention abruptly shifted to the back of the storeroom. "I don't know what's worse," Roth groaned, "your pacing or my goddamn headache. Don't you ever sleep?"

Talon didn't understand Roth's sudden heroics last night. Fortunately, or unfortunately, depending on Talon's cynical frame of mind, the man survived Kendrick's poor aim with only a gash to the head. "Shut the hell up, Roth."

"Or what? You'll break your chains and smash my face? They've got you bolted to the bloody floor."

Chains rattled with Roth's movements as he struggled to his feet and stumbled over something. They were both blind in the darkness. "If not for Lady Regan, Kendrick would have killed you in that marketplace two days ago, Drake. Whether you want to see the truth of it or not, she bought you time. Hell, she bought you your friggin' life."

Talon's laugh was ugly. "That's bloody rich." She'd bought him a rope. "I'd as soon die with a sword in my hand than strangle to death on her goodwill."

"You're wrong about Lady Regan, and you're wrong about me."

"Jeezus, Roth. What do you care? You work for Kendrick."

"Kendrick!" Chains clanked with his furious pacing. "I sail for the crown. I always have. I went back to England when we parted company years ago. After Kendrick said you refused your pardon, King William sent me to hunt you and a score of other pirates down. You were the only one left. It took a mere girl to finally crush the mighty captain of the *Dark Fury*. And a Welles, at that."

As if sensing Talon's violent bent, Roth quieted. "You saw her face last night?" Roth let the ugly silence hang. "I'll wager my life she's been less cooperative than you."

"Shut up, Roth." It was better to pretend he hated her. Hate he understood. It was his only weapon against his emotions when he had nothing left inside with which to fight.

Only, he didn't hate her.

The image of shimmering curls, an impish smile, the warmth of her touch flowed against the background of darkness. And he knew a desperate loss. She'd rescued him from the precipice of hell, gifted his life with sunshine more valuable than gold.

Then traded his life for Kendrick's. She was a victim of her own treachery . . .

"I found out last night, Kendrick has control of her fortune. That's why he's fought so hard to get her back."

Talon's head lifted.

"He's been drugging her. Mounting a case against her sanity. If not for your untimely interference, his plan would have worked."

The memory of Regan's illness, her dismal state last night, twisted like a knife in his gut. She'd loved her brother enough to die for him, and this is how Kendrick repaid her loyalty. What kind of monster could hurt her like that?

But he knew Kendrick. Knew exactly the kind of monster he was. The brutality his own sister suffered at Kendrick's hands still haunted Talon. Her battered body had never been found.

"Ironically her fortune belongs to you, her husband," Roth said. "Kendrick needed that annulment to protect himself from your legitimate heir."

Talon felt the breath leave his lungs. "What did you say?"

"You don't know, do you?" Roth's voice came out low.

"Why don't you tell me?" he rasped.

"She told Kendrick she's carrying your child."

Talon fell before his emotions. He was so shaken, he almost cried out. "And I was going to leave her."

"She would die for you, Drake."

He pressed his hands against his temples to still their trembling. "Ah, Christ. What have I done?"

He'd handed Kendrick her life and that of his child's.

The world seemed to fall away. In that moment, he knew he'd lost everything. His bitterness broke him. He'd die never having believed in her completely. Never having told her he loved her, failing her as appallingly as he did Marcus, his crew, and his family, chasing a past he should have buried years before. He'd lived in hell, clawing to undo the horror, never obliterating the enemy—his memory. It plied him with hate, seductively promising peace in vengeance. Yet, peace was forever beyond his reach, a fantasy, until Regan touched his soul.

One vision died to spark another. It would never be enough again to sail the blue Caribbean, to conquer the phantoms of a long lost dream. He'd give it all away for a moment's peace. A life filled with laughter.

A life with Regan.

His fists clenched. If is were the last thing he ever did, he'd find his way out of here. To her.

Then he'd rid the earth of the festering sore that was Harrison Kendrick.

The metal latch on the door moved.

Talon's head shot up. Immediately alert, he crouched, ready to spring. From the darkness, he heard Roth do the same.

Talon embraced the familiar rush of adrenaline. With no thought or conscience, he gripped the length of chain that bound his wrists, curling it around his fists. Ready to smash the man's skull.

Rusty hinges creaked. "Cap?" Parrot's small voice stilled him.

"Jeezus, Parrot!" In the darkness, Talon could see nothing. He could have killed her.

Keys jiggled. Parrot's small hands touched his chest. "Oi've come ta fetch ya out of here, Cap."

Instinct warned Talon that Parrot wasn't alone. "Where's the guard?"

"The bugger's upstairs, Cap. Got 'em a fancy-sized headache."

Taffeta rustled in the darkness as Parrot knelt over Talon's shackled feet. "What the hell are you wearing?"

Parrot snorted. "A bloomin' dress. And oi've I mind ta leave yer arse, if ya utter a word a insult, Cap. You didn't think the guard would fall fer the wiles of a boy did ya?"

Talon grinned. Parrot always did possess a way with expression that lightened the worst of moments. "How'd you get down here? It's pitch dark."

"Oi ran into someone what knows this place."

"The boy must be talking about Sarah," Roth said.

The shackles fell away from Talon's ankles, then wrists. He rubbed his chafed hands. "Where's Kendrick?"

"He took her, Cap. He took Lady Regan away."

The hinges on the door creaked. "Please, Captain Drake," a small feminine voice whispered. "You must help her. She said something about a treasure—"

"The treasure of Puerto Bello?" Roth cut in.

"She gave me a Bible and said that I must get it to Captain Drake. She said she knew where this treasure was. Then Sir Kendrick came in. She wanted to trade you for the treasure. They got into a terrible argument. Someone hit her—"

Talon gripped her arms. "Who hit her?"

"There was another man. I remember the smell."

"Weasel," Roth hissed.

The thought of Regan in Weasel's hands—"How long ago?"

"Sir Kendrick still has men upstairs," Sarah's voice broke. "I must get you out of here. They mean to hang you both."

After Parrot released Roth, Sarah led them into the hallway through a maze of darkened corridors. "There's a tunnel that leads outside the walls."

"What about you?"

"Father Henri has escaped to fetch the authorities. I'll hide with the others until he returns. You must go. We've horses in the stable. Your man, Jaime, is waiting outside for you."

Jaime was alive. "My other men—"

"No good," Roth said from behind him. "They're at the fortress."

The girl stopped, then moved into a curving stairwell. Leaning against the wall, she lifted on her toes. "There's a door up there."

Stooping beneath the wooden ledge, Talon bent his back into the trapdoor. Roth joined him.

"Hurry," Sarah whispered.

The wood cracked, then splintered. Light flooded the stairwell, tearing into Talon's head. Roth climbed out first.

Talon's gaze fell on Parrot dressed in a gaudy gown of red taffeta and black lace. The fitted bodice displayed feminine curves that even his feral imagination could never have conjured. Her short crop of red hair hugged her piquant face.

With hands braced on her hips, she snapped, "Are ya gonna stare yerself ta death, Cap. Or get me out of here?"

"You've ruined your image, Parrot." Talon lifted her into Roth's surprised grasp. Then he was looking into Sarah's sterling silver eyes, and his expression froze. Recognition climbed just beneath his skin. "You're Sarah?"

The girl grabbed his hands. "You will not let Regan die." The hood of her habit fell back. Silver-blond hair framed her face. She was looking at a spot over his shoulder. Talon realized she was blind. "Take this with you," she pleaded.

His gaze dropped to the canvas bag she pressed into his hands. She'd been carrying it attached to a strap around her shoulder.

"Now, go," the girl urged.

"I'm not leaving you here alone."

"I must get back to the children."

"Cap," Parrot rasped. "Hurry!"

He twisted again to face Sarah. But she'd already spun away. "Don't worry about me," he heard her whisper.

Talon slung the canvas bag over his shoulder. Roth helped him climb out. Sarah disappeared before Roth shut the trap-door.

Jaime was already mounted and waiting in a stand of trees about fifty yards away. Two jittery horses stomped the ground behind him.

The pungent breeze touched Talon's face. The sun warmed his skin. They were outside the mortar wall built around the compound that housed the three stone structures. Red-gable roofs were stark against a blue sky. Talon turned. Mountains bracketed the valley. A rocky hill sloped into a verdant valley waist high with sugarcane. In the distance, Talon could see the sparkling waters of the bay, the white fortress on the hill overlooking the town. He stopped cold.

In a sickening moment of disbelief, he watched *Dark Fury* sailing under half-canvas out of the bay. He stepped away from the wall. A brisk wind whipped the scarlet sash around his waist.

Kendrick had taken his wife *and* his goddamn ship! "Where's the *Viper*, Roth?"

Roth moved behind him. "In a bay north of here. Finishing repairs. It'll take the day to get there."

Talon cursed. Time was everything.

A shot rang out. Mortar splintered the wall behind him. Two men were racing from the direction of the main entrance, waving cutlasses. "Run!" he yelled shoving Parrot forward. Roth grabbed her arm. More shots followed, pocking the ground at their feet.

Jaime met them with the horses. "Kendrick's men are behind me."

Roth flung Parrot onto the back of a dapple-gray mare and swung behind her. Talon mounted the black. The horses burst into the clearing. Without breaking stride, they leapt a wooden fence leaving Kendrick's hounds far behind.

All afternoon, they rode, resting at intervals where water and grass ringed the hills. The sun burned Talon's back bared from the stripes he'd received at Weasel's hand. Perfect turquoise skies defied the savage storm brewing beneath the thin veneer of his control. Every long minute that passed took Regan further away.

When they finally stopped for dinner, he removed the canvas bag from his shoulder and threw it on the ground. Lying back against the soft earth, he listened to the lull of conversation as Roth talked to Jaime and Parrot. Behind him, the horses slurped from the stream. They'd been driven hard and needed rest. He needed to sleep, but dark images nagged at his head. Regan with Weasel. His ship and his pregnant wife in Kendrick's hands. The treasure.

Talon's eyes opened. How could Regan figure out the puzzle of the treasure? A puzzle people searched for years to unravel. He sat up. Absently his gaze fell on the canvas bag.

Talon withdrew an aged Bible, turning it over in his hands. A chill crawled over him, then slowly swallowed every inch of his soul. He felt the press of hope and reality collide.

"Regan . . ." He held the familiar Bible in the moonlight. "What did you find?"

Chapter Twenty-six

Regan became aware of dizzying movement, then timber creaking. The pungent scent of straw opened her eyes. An unmucked stable couldn't have smelled worse. Her head whirled. Voices above drew her gaze to the timbered ceiling. Lord, she was on a ship.

Her memory came rushing back. Heart racing, Regan struggled to her feet. How much time had passed? Had Harrison hanged Talon?

She couldn't perceive Talon's death. It wasn't so. It wasn't!

Hampered by the heavy robe, she caught herself on the bulkhead. The pale amber glow of a lanthorn fell over the stall. Harrison had put her in an animal pen. At once, she recognized where she was. Talon's ship. She was on the *Dark Fury*.

"Harrison!" Damn him. He'd pay for what he'd done.

She screamed and pounded on the barred doorway. Chickens squawked, sending feathers floating over their crates. She didn't care if she riled the whole lot and they keeled over of fright.

A cumbrous door creaked. She stilled. Heavy-soled boots descended the ladder into the hold. Regan's stomach dropped when Weasel's whiskered face gained the lanthorn light.

"If it ain't her highness roused from her royal sleep."

Refusing to heed his despicable presence, she stiffened her spine. "I demand to be taken to Harrison."

"Now, you ain't got cause to be orderin' me about, missy." Pudgy fingers jerked the door open. "Seems to me, yer no better than the likes of those chickens. Just ripe fer me pluckin'."

"What do you think you're doing?"

"I've a mind to see what got Drake in a bleedin' dither." He eyed her rudely. "Never thought it'd be a skirt what finally took that one down."

"Don't touch me." Regan's back hit the wall. She gagged on the stench of his unwashed body.

"Oh, but I will." Weasel's bulk covered her. "I been rememberin' everything about you since that first night Drake cracked my jaw." He gripped the back of her scalp. Fleshy lips fumbled over hers "If yer real good, I won't be sharin' ye none with the others."

Hands groped her breasts. Regan felt his erection stiff against her belly and thought she would retch. He would not do this thing to her. She had to fight for her baby, for the memory of Talon's touch. Weasel would destroy it all, and it was everything she had left in the world.

Ruthlessly, summoning her strength, she forced her hands to roam his belt, catching first on the pistol. It wouldn't budge.

"Aye," he grunted. "Ye like old Weasel do ya?"

Like a sack of vomit, she wanted to hiss. Her other hand hit the icy handle of a knife. She withdrew it and slid the sharp edge between his legs.

"Bloomin' hell!"

"So help me, you make one move—"

"I'll break yer bloody neck, missy."

Regan pressed the blade higher.

Weasel threw his hands up. She slipped the gun from the sling on his baldrics. "Now take me to my brother."

Regan's outrage kept her focused until she gained the main deck of Talon's ship. Her gaze lifted to the night-shrouded masts. A full moon emptied its pale light over the dark canvas. The masts creaked and swayed in majestic grace, a mockery to the horror of his absence.

Oh, Lord. Could he truly be gone from her life? Seeing part of his crew in chains, she turned her face away before anyone could glimpse her torment. Desperation seized her. Closed around her. It took every ounce of control not to shoot Weasel in the face. Then at that moment, she found Nicholas lashed with his arms outstretched to the ratlines. His vest hung in tatters.

With a cry, she flew barefoot past Weasel. "Nicholas, what have they done?"

One swollen eye cracked opened. "You have found your way free, *chéri*. We didn't know what they would do to you."

Swinging the pistol around, she yelled, "Cut this man down!"

"Ye can't be fightin' all of us, missy," Weasel growled.

"Now!" She slammed the point of his knife into the wooden step of the mast. "Cut him free."

Regan couldn't keep the tremble from her hand as she held the gun taut. Men stopped working, and the deck grew silent. Kendrick's henchman held Talon's crew at bay with pistols and swords. Tears filled her eyes. "So help me, I'll shoot you, Weasel. I will."

Another glance at the pistol convinced him. Clearly, he wasn't about to be the first to die for Harrison's cause. He jerked the knife from the wood.

"Harrison ordered Talon hanged before we left Martinique," she told Nicholas as Weasel sawed through the ropes.

"I know." Nicholas's left arm fell free. He sagged to the deck.

Regan shoved her tears back with the heel of her hand. "Why are you on this ship? I thought you were imprisoned at the fortress."

"Kendrick needed a crew. And you are very beloved, *chéri*. Most of the men on board are here because he had you."

"Oh, Nicholas . . ."

"They would help you if they could." His other arm fell free and he crumbled to his knees.

Regan dropped beside him. Her gaze swung around the deck. These men would die because of her. They couldn't fight. Without weapons, most of the crew would be dead before they accomplished a successful mutiny. Her mind worked frantically. "Harrison will have everyone hanged unless . . ."

The treasure. Yes, she could somehow use the gold as leverage. If it existed, she knew where to find it.

Would Harrison risk a political scandal by sailing into Puerto Bello? Knowing her greedy brother, for wealth, he'd risk God's wrath. Once the gold was on board, pirates—being notoriously rapacious by nature—would not be long tamed by Harrison's will. They would revolt. Nicholas would win.

Raising her voice, she spoke to every man on board. "I know where the treasure of Puerto Bello is."

A low murmur grew over the wind.

"And if any of you hurts this man, so help me, you'll not get an inch of my cooperation in finding that gold." She glared at Weasel. "Now, take me to Harrison."

When Weasel opened the door to Talon's cabin, nothing prepared Regan for the sight and smell that greeted her. Books were strewn over the floor as if someone had thrown them in a vengeful fury. Clearly, Harrison had been in a frenzy looking for the maps. The room was a shambles. Harrison's slumped form on the bench in front of the stern galley window froze her. Light from the lanthorn flickered from its wooden ring above the desk and shone on the muzzle of a blunderbuss pointed directly at her chest.

"Regan," he called drunkenly, "please enter."

Weasel ripped the weapon out of her hand. "You're not so smart, missy." He shoved her into the room. "Wait till you come out."

Harrison lowered the gun and an empty laudanum bottle dropped to the floor. "Have you come to pick my bones clean, 'ere the reaper finds me, sister mine?"

As Regan approached Harrison, her numbed gaze dropped to his outstretched leg where the elegant satin pants had been cut away. A wound festered on his swollen calf. Two black flies gorged themselves on the dead flesh that colored the skin.

"Drake did this to me. I thought the break had healed. The surgeon would take my leg." He gripped her wrist, startling her with his strength. "What would you do, Regan?"

She cringed at the horror. Taking a limb was no small endeavor. He would be conscious during the surgery.

His gaze softened over her face, touching on the bruises. "I've been cruel," he said quietly. "I'm so sorry."

Regan summoned her anger. This man had murdered Talon, drugged her, lied, cheated, and thrown her into the darkness of the *Fury*'s hold. She would not remember their past. She would not!

His gaze lifted over her shoulder. "Leave," he commanded Weasel. "See that we're not disturbed."

When the door shut, Regan disengaged her wrist. "I'll not cry for you, Harrison."

"I don't suppose you would at that. You've come to trade the treasure for the lives of Drake's crew." He sighed when she looked shocked. "You see, sister mine, I only had to bait the hook."

"Nicholas."

"You've always had a streak of courage. I envied that. No matter what I did, I could never take that from you. I tried. God, but I tried. We're already headed to Puerto Bello," he told her. "I know the *alcalde mayores* well. We've traded often."

"One pirate to another, no doubt." Tears blurred him. "How you've shamed our family."

His gaze drifted. "Do you know why I was disinherited, Regan?"

She'd been too young to know anything but her silly adoration for him.

"When your father . . . when the *illustrious* William Welles gave the order to bring in Brendan Drake, it seemed such an easy task. One I welcomed. After all, I'm the one who found out about the treasure first. The whole thing was my idea from the beginning. The Drakes in all their uppity finesse thought they were too good for the rest of us. But they had a daughter . . ." His expression turned vacant. "She possessed the most angelic face and pale blond curls, like fine silk. I've never forgotten the way it felt in my hands."

Regan moved away from him on leaden feet. Her hand

groped for the corner of Talon's desk. Sarah. He was talking about Sarah.

"She was so fragile," he murmured distantly. "I never meant to hurt her in that way."

Aghast, Regan swallowed. "Talon has known this?"

"He's always known."

Yet, he never told her. Never once betrayed her loyalty and love for a brother who didn't deserve her spit. Even then, he'd protected her by sparing her the horrible truth.

"I tried to forget," Harrison rambled on. "But the opium never made the pain go away. Nothing did, until I saw her again. At the convent." His eyes narrowed. "Mother did that to me. She took little Sarah away. But I know where she is now."

Hackles rose on her neck. "Why are you telling me this?"

His glazed eyes lifted to Regan's appalled face. "I won. Don't you see? I got even with them all. It was so easy blaming Drake for our parents' deaths. And now the treasure is within my grasp. Your father never found it. I beat him. I beat the bloody bastard. I beat Robert. And when this is over I'm going back for Sarah."

Regan backed into the shadows of Talon's room.

"Where's the gold, Regan?"

She'd put together the clues: the date on the bottom of Robert's map was the wedding anniversary of Talon's parents. The Spanish mission on Harrison's map surely signified where Brendan Drake had married, and where the bells that had been depicted on Robert's map still tolled. They were probably painted or coated in lead.

Would they be there after all these years?

She willed herself to calm. "I'll tell you as long as Talon's crew remains unharmed. I'll tell you when we get to Puerto Bello."

"Regan." He stopped her before she could flee the room. In a completely sane voice, he said, "You were the only one who ever loved me despite everything I was."

The shocking sentiment tore into her. The horror of the past had become her reality. Struggling not to cry, Regan turned and fled the room. Nicholas was leaning against the bulkhead in the corridor.

She ran into his arms. "Keep me with you, please."

"We must go someplace . . . to rest, *chéri*."

Regan took Nicholas to the hold. But despite her effort to nurse his injuries, it was Nicholas who cared for her. Regan could not have endured without him. He forced her to eat and sleep, when all she wanted to do was curl up and die. Harrison's men stayed away. Even Weasel begrudged them distance.

"I should have known you on the beach that day in Port Royal," she said, when he took her on deck a few days later away from the smell of animals. She'd wanted to see the sunset, a piece of Talon's life. It was like touching his heart-beat.

"Ah, little monkey. You have the look of your beautiful *mére*. I would have known you anywhere."

"I was so frightened."

"You are frightened only by what your heart cannot see, *chéri*."

And her heart could no longer see hope. Talon was gone.

"Somehow we're going to get out of this, Nicholas. I'm going to England to face King William with the truth."

"You risk your life to do so. It will not be easy, *chéri*."

"Was it easy for Talon? My family stole everything."

By the third week, the blue-green smudge on the horizon grew into Puerto Bello. As the *Fury* neared the coast, a Spanish escort joined them. Flanked on both sides where a broad-side could bring Talon's *Dark Fury* to heel, they sailed into the turquoise waters of the bay. The very idea of Talon's ship in Spanish domain choked her.

Harrison summoned Regan to the cabin to change into something presentable from the chest where her clothes were stored. Desperate to get out of the filthy woolen robe she'd been wearing, she chose the elegant blue velvet gown and matching slippers Talon had bought her in Tortuga. The night before, a rainstorm had cleaned her hair. She weaved it into a coronet around her head. It was her ambition to make a presentable case to the Spanish *alcalde* to secure her freedom and that of Talon's crew.

•   •   •

Regan never got a chance to speak. The alcalde was a prune-faced man who commanded the garrisons that stood sentinel over the town. Bedecked in a crisp white uniform with shiny gold buttons that looked obscene next to the glaring poverty of the townsfolk of Puerto Bello, the infamous *alcalde* presented a dandified figure, arrogant in stature, rude in character. He and Harrison got along admirably. This was one of the men who had condemned Talon to die on a slave galleon. And he was in league with her brother.

The wind ruffled her gown as she stood on the quarterdeck beside her brother. The crews' lives were at stake. If they didn't find the treasure, Harrison would accuse her of cheating him.

Regan told him about the mission church, then waited until a runner brought back news. Somehow, she'd hoped the task would take longer. But it didn't. Brendan Drake, an English privateer, had married a Spanish noblewoman. Although it had been thirty-five years ago, the marriage had been so scandalous it rocked two countries and formed a blood feud between two powerful families that still lasted today.

As the Spanish entourage made its way through town, winding along a maze of streets, Regan eyed her pallid brother, who wallowed in the carriage seat across from her, his once proud bearing quashed beneath an opium daze. So little of him remained that Regan ached for the death of the man her brother once was.

The Spanish mission proved bigger than she imagined. Four bell towers anchored each corner of the white stucco and mortar walls. The tiny chapel was nearly hidden within the sprawling canopy of a thick banyon. Beneath the azure sky, with the golden light of the sun shining over the courtyard, Regan had never seen anything so beautiful. Talon's parents once stood on these grounds. Peace touched her briefly before Weasel gripped her arm and dragged her inside the whitewashed chapel. A tiny stained-glass window over the main entrance opened the quaint interior to scarlet and amber light.

The smell of tallow burned her senses. A long ago memory filled her. The same scent had been in the hallway that night before she entered Arabella's room. Before she opened the door and her life had been forever changed.

Harrison divided the small group and sent all but a few to each bell tower in search of the elusive promise of riches.

"You and me got unfinished business, missy," Weasel slobbered in her ear. He'd cornered her against the back wall.

"You befoul yourself in God's house, Weasel," she hissed.

"Aye." He chuckled, blocking her escape. "And the ways I see it, we got a good hour before anyone comes back."

Movement stirred. Four monks, clothed in brown woolen robes kneeled before the pulpit. The distraction was enough to discourage even the randiest pig. Regan jerked away from Weasal.

Trembling, she walked to the bench nearest the pulpit. A beautiful golden cross gleamed against the length of the front wall. The chapel smelled old. The sudden quiet alerted her to Weasel's absence. Head bowed, hands folded tightly in her lap near her babe, she sent a verbal prayer to God to cast her enemies to hell.

A brown-robed monk filled her vision. Horrified that he should have heard her blasphemy she intoned a hasty, "God forgive me," before her eyes focused on the woolen hem. Black jackboots and a sword protruded beneath.

"I'm sure he understands, Regan."

The familiar voice froze her with such intensity time stopped, vanishing into a swirling vortex that sucked the breath from her lungs. Regan's chin shot up. Silver eyes burned into hers.

Talon was here! How could that be?

His face seemed thinner, his jaw shadowed with a beard. He looked like he hadn't slept in a month.

How did he find her? The Bible.

Sarah must have given him the Bible. Then he knew everything.

A sob escaped her throat as he slid his hands into her hair and brought her up against him. "Christ, Regan. I'm not a ghost."

Her fingers knotted in his robe testing the man beneath. "My God—"

His mouth covered hers.

She didn't think to question the danger of his actions in full view of the chapel. She only knew that he was alive. Lord, he was alive! Yielding to his strength, she raised on her toes to embrace the kiss, opening her lips to his possession.

He tasted so good. She rasped his name against his mouth, kissing his chiseled jaw, his cheek. His scent filled her. The black stubble on his face scratched her tender skin. He was alive. Her hands touched his cheek and tangled in his hair, nudging the hood from his head. "I didn't know . . . I didn't know what happened."

Movement behind her stole into her consciousness and at once she remembered where they were. Frantically, she whirled. Her eyes scanned the dim light in the chapel, shocked that Harrison's men were no longer inside. Brown robed monks stood casually in their stead. Her breath caught. Clothed in the same woolen robe as the others, Captain Roth leaned against the main door of the chapel. She met his shadowed gaze beneath the cowl.

She gripped a fist to her chest and looked up into Talon's beloved face. "I don't know how you got here—"

"The *Viper* has always out-sailed the *Fury* in a good wind."

"Oh, Talon. It's so dangerous for you. You must be mad."

"With worry for you, sweet." His fingers curled into her hair then gently brushed the fading bruise on her jaw. "Weasel will never hurt you again."

His meaning rife, she tried not to feel relief but failed. She traced the width of his shoulders, down his arms, absorbing him through her fingertips. "How long have you been here?"

"Two days."

"Then you found the—"

"The bells in the mission left here years ago."

"Then everything was for naught?"

His eyes softened. "The map led me to you, Regan. And whoever has those bells probably doesn't even know the riches they hold."

An absurd panic quickened her pulse. "Please. Let's leave—"

"I can't, Regan."

Her gaze flew to the arched doorway where Harrison had ascended to the belfry. "Oh, but you must before it's too late."

He motioned to the robed figure behind her near the pulpit. "Jaime, take her to Roth."

She clutched his arm. "Please, don't kill Harrison."

An angry shadow seemed to drop over his eyes. Fear for him stripped her of logic and sense. Heedless of the danger, caring naught for herself, she tore away from Jaime.

"Please, Talon. Let this hate go. We can leave here."

"Regan . . ." With a furious sweep of the chapel, he pulled her behind the pulpit deeper into the shadows. "You're still defending the bastard?"

"He's a high government official. If you kill him, nothing will absolve you of murder."

"Murder?" He scorned the word.

"He'll die soon enough. Gangrene is eating his leg."

Talon held her gaze, his expression unfathomable as he discerned the truth of her words. With bittersweet horror, she knew now that Harrison Kendrick would always be the enemy between them.

"We have much to settle between us, milady wife. Unfortunately, this isn't the time or the place. You must leave with Roth."

Regan didn't have the energy to fight anymore. She'd been fighting everyone so long. Talon found her a world away because he was a man who never lost. Never ceded victory to anyone. Harrison was the enemy. And to his mind, she'd sided with the enemy.

Regan wanted to tell him that she would never dishonor him. That she loved him more than life. But it wouldn't matter. Not after what she'd done to him in Martinique. After what her family had done ten years before. Her character was forever blighted by the past.

Except, unlike her family, she possessed some shred of honor and decency to fight. She'd make Roth take her to England. Set to rights the injustice. Give Talon what he wanted most. His honor back.

Regan swallowed the tears burning in her throat. "Nicholas—" She wiped her face. "—your crew is still in the harbor."

"I know." Talon smoothed a lock of hair off her brow. "So, you understand why I can't leave with you."

Her eyes encompassed his face. "You're going after your ship?"

"I owe those men my life a hundred times over."

Pride for his courage caught her voice. She swiped impatiently at the tears. "How will you do it? There's two Spanish forts guarding the bay?"

He yanked the monk's cowl over his head. His expression disappeared in the shadow leaving her heart floundering in her throat. "You know me? Right through the front door."

Regan clutched Talon to her. "This is all my fault. I'm so sorry, Talon." The broken words formed into a tearful jumble as she buried her face against his chest. "I'm so sorry."

"No, Regan—"

"For ever believing in Harrison."

"Regan. Listen to me." Talon forced her chin up. His shining eyes stole the words and breath she tried to form into coherent thoughts. "It took courage to do what you did in Martinique."

Tremors shook her. "I would rather die than hurt you."

"I know, sweet. I know," he whispered repeatedly into her hair, against her tear-stained cheek, smoothing the wetness from her face. "Now go with Captain Roth. Please, Regan," he said in a voice she hardly recognized. "Get back to Sarah. Do this . . . for me."

Fighting for composure, she stepped out of Talon's arms. She already knew what she had to do for him. And for Sarah.

Before Talon could read her anguish, she whirled on silent slippers and ran across the chapel to Captain Roth's waiting arms.

Talon almost called her back.

Suddenly, Kendrick's angry voice snapped him back to reality. His expression sobered. Heavy-booted steps echoed in the stairwell leading from the belfry. From beneath his robe, Talon drew his saber. The scrape of metal sounded ugly in the weighted silence of the tiny chapel. He saw Roth snatch Regan's arm to keep her from running back to him. In utter misery, she clung to his gaze.

Compassion stirred his heart. He understood her pain better than she knew. Even if it had been a lie, whatever bond she'd once shared with her brother had been forged in a little girl's innocent love. That no matter Harrison's crimes, her brother's blood should not fall on his hands. Talon would move the oceans of the earth to ease her heart. If only he could.

Kendrick limped on a wooden cane from the tower. Two men from the Spanish garrison followed behind him. One was the *alcalde* who was the commanding officer of the garrison where Talon and Marcus had spent many an inhospitable night in damp dungeons. Flushed with rage, the *alcalde* was a dark contradiction to his crisp gold-laced uniform.

Talon felt a slow grin form. Surely, an angel watched over him. This dark contradiction was his key out of Puerto Bello.

Kendrick threw his emaciated body onto a bench. "Gone! Devil rot them all." He gazed vengefully at the ceiling. "The treasure is lost to us."

"Not lost. But found in a way you couldn't begin to understand."

Harrison's expression froze when he saw Talon. The two soldiers went for the hilt of their fancy sabers.

"*Parar!*" Talon warned in Spanish. "He is not worth your lives."

"You!" the *alcalde* snapped in furious Spanish. "*Basta ya*! You are a thief! Like your father."

Talon's grin was reckless. The man would never appreciate that the treasure he'd found was more valuable than any gold. "Sí, that I am. A very rich thief now."

"You will never get out of here. None of you."

"I'll wager your life on that, *alcalde*." He motioned for two of his men to bind them.

"You're a hard man to kill, Captain Drake." Kendrick searched out and found Regan standing with Roth at the door. "It seems your efforts to save his life worked after all, sister mine."

"Aye, Kendrick," Talon said without taking his careful eye

from the three. "More than you'll know. Keep her safe, Roth."

"Regan." Harrison came to his feet. "You can't leave me—"

Jaime cut his words off with a gag.

"That's exactly what she's going to do, Kendrick," Talon said, looking at Regan framed in the doorway of the chapel. In an hour, he could be dead and all he could think about was the brilliant shine of her tears in velvet eyes that would stop the sunset.

After they'd left, Talon approached Harrison. Planting his booted foot on the bench, he casually braced his elbow across his knee and contemplated Regan's brother over the point of his sword. "Consider yourself fortunate I love her, Kendrick. She just bought you your life, short as it will be."

Chapter Twenty-seven

Muffled by the azure sky and sea, cannon fire rumbled against the horizon. Despite Captain Roth's order to go below, Regan remained at the rail of the *Viper. Dark Fury* was engaged in battle. She'd been listening to the hideous thunder of cannon fire for over an hour. It was unbearable.

She swung around, searching for Roth among the flurry of activity on deck. His voice boomed over the crack of canvas. The wind catching in the white sleeves of his shirt, he stood near the helm on the quarterdeck, glass in hand, thumping his thigh as he stared toward Puerto Bello.

As if sensing her desperation, his obsidian gaze met hers. "You have to help him," she cried.

"Go below, Lady Regan."

Undaunted by his curt command, Regan hiked her skirts and ran up the stairs to face him. "He needs your help. You can't just leave him to die."

"By the time we reach the *Fury*, she'll either be safe out of the bay or sunk."

But Regan knew he lied. It was because of her—her presence that he would not risk the *Viper* in battle.

"I'm taking you back to Martinique, Lady Regan."

Frustrated, she spun away. "You're taking me to England. I demand it, Captain Roth."

"And I told you already once today, I'll not risk it."

Regan admitted fear of going before King William. It

would not bode well for her at court. No matter. Talon's name would be cleared if she hanged to see it done. "You know as much as I, Talon needs me in England. He needs you. He deserves this much from both of us."

"He *deserves* to have you waiting for him in Martinique."

"So help me, Captain Roth—" She gripped the front of his shirt. "—you're setting course for London."

In the distance, the cannon fire suddenly stopped.

"What?" She whirled to the rail. Terror raced through her veins. "What is it?" That God could take Talon from her life again was inconceivable. It couldn't be. "Tell me!"

"I'm not sure."

She thought her knees would buckle. "You're saying he's dead?"

He chuckled, sobering swiftly when she swung around. "I'd say your husband just slipped beneath the guns of those Spanish garrisons."

"Then . . . he made it?"

"The *alcalde's* presence no doubt encouraged cooperation, but yes. I'd say that Drake is—" his stoic gaze met hers "—free."

"Free?" she cried half-hysterical with panic. "You mock the word, Captain Roth."

"I mock nothing but this foolish endeavor of yours," he said quietly.

"He'll never be free if someone doesn't speak for him. Take me to King William. You must." This last was a whisper.

"Are you always this much trouble, milady?"

"Worse," she sniffed. "Talon always said so."

"You're as mad as that husband of yours, Lady Regan." A gloved hand lifted to tilt her chin. "And I'm sorry I didn't act sooner to claim you for myself. Though admittedly Drake never did abide by convention when it came to anything."

"Then you'll do it? You'll take me to England?"

"Aye." His mouth twisted into a grim smile. Soothing arms wrapped her to him as she finally succumbed to tears. "Because I'm the greatest idiot that ever lived," he whispered into her hair.

"No sir. You're not." Regan drew away and looked into

his bemused face. "I received that distinction long ago."

She ran below deck where Roth had put her in the cabin beside his. "Let Talon be safe," she prayed again.

The Bible she'd given Sarah lay on the bunk, stopping her. Talon must have slept in this room. The sight crushed her panic and fueled hope as nothing else could. Pressing the Bible to her heart, she dropped to the mattress. Talon's essence filled her.

He'd slept here. Regan opened the Bible to the page where she'd seen the names of Talon's family listed and her breath caught.

Someone had penned her name beneath Talon's. Beside the entry in his handwriting was their wedding date.

Talon had given her a place in his family Bible.

"We should have caught them by now," Talon yelled over the racing wind, eyeing the distance to nightfall. He turned and looked at Piers with worry. "Roth is too good to get snagged by the Spanish. Where the hell is he?"

Piers shaded his eyes. "A storm is brewing, I think."

Talon looked in the direction of Martinique. "More than that if I don't find Roth."

"Perhaps, we are not looking in the right place."

Talon hated Piers's know-it-all serenity when he was near to going mad with impatience. He'd worked for days cleaning the stink and filth of Kendrick from his ship—a ship with only half a crew intact—thinking of nothing but reaching Regan.

"She loves you, *mon ami*. What would you do in her place?"

Talon's gaze shot northward. His gut clenched. "Tell me I'm reading this all wrong."

"They are not here, *mon ami*. Where would she go?"

"Roth is taking her to England?" He looked at Piers. "How in the name of God could she talk him into that kind of insanity?"

Roth knew what awaited Regan if she went back. There was no proof she wasn't everything Harrison Kendrick had made her out to be. Treason wasn't a crime to skip around.

Even he wasn't willing to chance it anymore.

"I imagine she feels it's a small matter of saving your life. She is doing the only thing she can, *mon ami*."

With an ache in his chest, Talon looked across the sea bathed now in twilight. Stars glittered on the horizon. For all the horror in his life, he saw only beauty. The image of Regan's face filled the heavens. She was his future. The only thing that mattered. Not his name. Not victory or justice. Only her.

He was finished chasing memories. Finished with the past. All he searched for was in his heart. He needed nothing more.

Except to find her. And he had an idea that Roth wouldn't be taking any shortcut to England.

"Heave around, Piers. It's time I bring my wife home."

Regan surfaced on deck before dawn. After spending five days below in her cabin, the heat had worn her down. By now, Talon would know she hadn't gone to Martinique. Worry for him drained her.

Captain Roth stood on the quarterdeck, his legs braced against the choppy movement of the ship. She followed his gaze, but could see nothing between the dawn and the sea. Roth had moved the ship out of Spanish waters as fast as the breeze would allow, until a storm seized them, and he drew in sail.

Roth may have agreed to take her to England, but by the look of the nearly naked masts, their passage would take years. Convinced he was sabotaging her efforts to reach England at all, Regan heaved a frustrated sigh. Beside the rail, Parrot was watching the fading stars. Out of place in a dress, she looked like a stranger.

"Oi ain't never prayed in me life," Parrot said quietly, sensing Regan's presence. "Ain't never had a use for the church."

Regan took Parrot into her arms. "I imagine we all must approach ourselves in ways that best suit us."

"Oi think it's a fine thing ya be doin', milady. Goin' before the king. Oi'd not be alive, but for the cap."

A lump lodged in Regan's throat. Talon had more than saved her life. He'd given her a reason to live. And she'd never forget that.

Regan joined Roth on the quarterdeck a few moments later. The wind slashed her hair and she pulled the length tight in her fist. "A turtle can walk faster than we're sailing, Captain."

"Aye," he agreed making a grand pretense to study the sky. "The storm is very dangerous."

"The storm passed two days ago."

"Are you questioning my judgment again, Lady Regan?"

Regan's eyes narrowed. "Should I?" She was aware of feet running on the deck around her. The sound of excited voices.

Merriment sparkled in his dark eyes. "Now that all depends on one's point of view, milady?"

"Sail ho!"

The words seemed to come from a dream. Regan turned. The sun was just starting to rise and cast a burnt orange pall over the wind-roughened sea.

And then she saw it. On the horizon, the obscure shape of a ship, its dark pyramid sails barely visible against the dazzling brilliance of the sky. Her breath caught in pain and disbelief.

"No," she cried out. "It can't be."

"Milady!" Parrot called. "Milady. Come."

Regan didn't move. *Dark Fury*'s beautiful profile, now in full view of the *Viper*, was unmistakable. Regan felt a rush of joy. And panic.

"Can't we go any faster?" she called.

Roth laughed. "I already have enough explaining to do. Would you see me shot at as well?" He handed her the glass, which Regan snatched from his hand and raised immediately to her eye.

She searched the deck of the *Fury*. What if he wasn't there? What if he'd been injured? A million questions fogged her head.

Suddenly, she found him. And the world faded to a tiny pinpoint of light so bright it stopped her breath. Talon was watching her back through his glass.

Braced on powerful thighs he stood on the forecastle deck, the scarlet sash around his waist a splash of glorious color against the backdrop of an azure sea. Her heart swelled and drummed a chaotic beat in her chest. Wind whipped his hair and caught the black sleeves of his shirt. She watched him leap onto the taffrail, gripping a hand into the ratlines as he continued to watch her through the scope. Regan didn't breathe. The air in her lungs had turned to molasses.

"It won't be long now, Lady Regan," Roth said from beside her.

The thought of all her noble plans vanquished to Talon's sacrifice tore through her. She spun on her heel. "I don't want to see him. Do you understand? He'll ruin everything."

Regan ran below and bolted her door. If Talon Drake wanted in, he'd break his shoulder to do it.

For the next hour, Regan paced. Her idle flight took her to the port window more than once where she watched *Dark Fury*'s approach with horrible dread. Like a shadow looming over her, it grew ominously on the horizon.

Damn him! He'd not sway her from her purpose. He'd not!

The sound of grappling hooks tore into her thoughts. The ships scraped hulls, a thunderous racket that shivered over her. The *Viper* rose and fell in the swell, lending sound to the monstrous creaking around her.

A moment later the latch wriggled, and Regan flew to the door.

"Regan?"

Talon's voice assaulted her. She squeezed her eyes shut. "Go away," she yelled through the door. "Leave me alone."

"I'm not letting you go to England," he said.

Bending her palms over her ears, she slid down the length of the door. "What can I ever give you that could equal your life, or your lands? I'll not let you abandon the quest to see your family's name cleared. You can't stop me from doing this, Talon."

"If I don't it will never end for us."

But Regan couldn't answer. Not on this. He had Sarah to think about. His life. His whole future.

"Let me do this, Talon. It's the only way."

"Ah, Regan. You've already done more than you know. Sarah's been safe for all these years. I owe you a debt I can never repay."

"Don't you see? It won't work. It will never work. Not

with this always between us. And not with Harrison . . . Harrison will always be there reminding me that he won. That you . . . Oh, Talon I can't bear it. Just go away. Leave me alone."

There was a dark hesitation. Regan didn't hate Talon for what he did to Harrison. How could she? Her brother deserved his fate.

"I didn't kill Kendrick, Regan. I couldn't. In the end, I couldn't do it."

"What?" She wiped her eyes.

"Who's to say what insanity looms in my background after all." He was trying to sound light, but Regan knew Harrison's life weighed like granite on his shoulders. "I left him in Puerto Bello. I set the *alcalde* off in a rowboat about a mile from shore. I'm sure once he got back, he sent men to untie him."

"Oh, Talon." She felt she might go out of her mind. She was glad Harrison's murder wasn't on his hands. But it didn't change anything.

"Let me in, Regan."

"I'm begging you to go away, Talon. Please, just leave."

Talon stepped away from the solid portal. He scraped a hand through his hair, turning a frustrated glare at the ceiling.

Regan was crying. He could hear her tears. "Regan," he whispered through the door again. Agony laced his words. "I don't want to be alone anymore. I need you. I need you by my side. In my arms. I want to dance with you, make love to you, laugh and cry. All the things you gave to me. Nothing else matters. It hasn't for a long time. I have Sarah again. I have our baby." He touched the door. "You've given me more than you'll ever know. More than I deserve," he whispered. "Come back with me. To Martinique. You asked me once before to stay with you."

Silence met his plea.

"I want you to marry me, Regan."

He heard her breath catch on a sob. "But . . . we're already married."

"You, Regan. I want to marry *you* this time. Will you be my wife? To have and to hold, forever."

"But your dreams? Your family honor. Your life? I couldn't bear living with your sacrifice."

"What is honor without life, sweet," he said quietly voicing the same words she once spoke to him. Words that blared at him ever since. "You're my life, Regan." He leaned his head into the door. He could hear her breathing, feel her touch against the solid wood of the portal. "I love you."

A faltering moment passed. He heard the rustle of clothing. Movement. The door swung open.

Regan stood in the doorway, her hand clenched to the latch. Her wet face lifted to his. God, she was beautiful. The heavy shadow lifted from his life. Regan had awakened his tenderness, slain his dragons, put to rest his soul. He loved her simply and completely.

He grinned at his absurd flip-flopping heart. "I love you, Regan." He said the words again, cupping her smooth cheek. He closed his mouth over hers, kissing her, tasting the salt of her tears on lips that melded to his. The softness of her breasts pressed against him. He could feel the strength of her heartbeat beating in rhythm to his quickened pace. This felt good. Christ, it felt right.

"Come with me, Regan."

"You ask that I live with your sacrifice. When you've lost—"

A hand on her lovely mouth silenced the words. He'd had enough of her bullheadedness to last through a generation of grandchildren. "Come here." He led her into the cabin to the bunk and sat her down. "I have something to show you."

Looking around the room, he sighted the corner of the Bible sticking from beneath her pillow.

"If you'd given me a chance, I would have shown you this already." Opening the thick cover of the aged Bible, he slid his hand carefully beneath the thin cloth binding the book. Mold assailed his senses. Then he watched Regan's eyes light as he pulled out two sheets of folded vellum. Aged and cracked, they both bore the royal seal of Charles II.

Talon knelt beside Regan on the bunk. "My Letter of Marque, Regan. And my father's." He laid them in her lap. A wedding gift from her precious mama. Their future. "It's not everything, but at least it will be a start."

Her eyes lifted to encompass his. Love shone brightly in their jeweled depths.

"Roth can take these back. He's taking the *Dark Fury* as sign of my surrender. He already told me he's going before King William with the truth of Kendrick's deception."

"I . . . I don't know what to say."

"Say you'll marry me."

Huge eyes watched him back.

"Captain Roth can marry us before we leave."

She wiped the lone tear from her cheek. "That traitor?" She sniffed and suddenly smiled. "You would trust him?"

"With my life."

"I love you, Talon Drake. You've given me back the light. I thought never to see it again."

"Captain Roth is waiting." He gallantly offered his hand. "May I have this dance, Regan?"

She fell into his arms. "Aye," he heard her say before his lips found hers. "For the rest of your life, my lord pirate.